Don Quixote

de la Mancha

The Ingenious Gentleman

Don Quixote
de la Mancha

MIGUEL DE CERVANTES

With the illustrations of
José and Luis Jiminez y Aranda

THE FRANKLIN LIBRARY
Franklin Center, Pennsylvania

✧

⟨ Contents ⟩

❧ The Author's Dedication ❧

To the Duke of Bejar

Marquis of Gibraleon, Count of Benalcazar and Bañares,
Viscount of the Town of Alcocer,
and Lord of the Towns of Capilla, Curiel and Burguillos

*T*rusting *in the favourable reception and honour your Excellency accords to all kinds of books, as a Prince so well disposed to welcome the liberal arts, more especially those which, out of nobility, are not abased to the service and profit of the vulgar, I have decided to publish the* Ingenious Gentleman Don Quixote de la Mancha *under the shelter of your Excellency's most illustrious name, begging you with the respect I owe to such greatness to receive him graciously under your protection; so that, although naked of that precious adornment of elegance and erudition in which works composed in the houses of the learned usually go clothed, in your shadow he may safely venture to appear before the judgment of some who, undeterred by their own ignorance, are in the habit of condemning the works of others with more rigour than justice. For when your excellency's wisdom takes account of my good intentions, I trust that you will not disdain the poverty of so humble an offering.*

MIGUEL DE CERVANTES

Prologue

Idle reader, you can believe without any oath of mine that I would wish this book, as the child of my brain, to be the most beautiful, the liveliest and the cleverest imaginable. But I have been unable to transgress the order of nature, by which like gives birth to like. And so, what could my sterile and ill-cultivated genius beget but the story of a lean, shrivelled, whimsical child, full of varied fancies that no one else has ever imagined—much like one engendered in prison, where every discomfort has its seat and every dismal sound its habitation? Calm, a quiet place, the pleasantness of the fields, the serenity of the skies, the murmuring of streams and the tranquility of the spirit, play a great part in making the most barren muses bear fruit and offer to the world a progeny to fill it with wonder and delight. It may happen that a father has an ugly and ill-favoured child, and that his love for it so blinds his eyes that he cannot see its faults, but takes them rather for talents and beauties, and describes them to his friends as wit and elegance. But I, though in appearance Don Quixote's father, am really his step-father, and so will not drift with the current of

1

custom, nor implore you, almost with tears in my eyes, as others do, dearest reader, to pardon or ignore the faults you see in this child of mine. For you are no relation or friend of his. Your soul is in your own body, and you have free will with the best of them, and are as much a lord in your own house as the King is over his taxes. For you know the old saying: under my cloak a fig for the king—all of which exempts and frees you from every respect and obligation; and so you can say anything you think fit about this story, without fear of being abused for a bad opinion, or rewarded for a good one.

I would have wished to present it to you naked and unadorned, without the ornament of a prologue or the countless train of customary sonnets, epigrams and eulogies it is the fashion to place at the beginnings of books. For I can tell you that, much toil though it cost me to compose, I found none greater than the making of this preface you are reading. Many times I took up my pen to write it, and many times I put it down, not knowing what to say. And once when I was in this quandary, with the paper before me, my pen in my ear, my elbow on the desk and my hand on my cheek, thinking what to write, a lively and very intelligent friend of mine came in unexpectedly and, seeing me so deep in thought, asked me the reason. I did not conceal it, but said that I was thinking about the prologue I had to make for the history of Don Quixote, and that it so troubled me that I was inclined not to write one, and even not to publish the exploits of that noble knight; "For how could you expect me not to be worried," I went on, "at what that ancient lawgiver they call the public will say when it sees me now, after all these years I have been sleeping in the silence of oblivion, come out with all my years on my back, with a tale as dry as a rush, barren of invention, devoid of style, poor in wit and lacking in all learning and instruction, without quotations in the margins or notes at the end of the book; whereas I see other works, never mind how fabulous and profane, so full of sentences from Aristotle, Plato and the whole herd of philosophers, as to impress their readers and get their authors a reputation for wide reading, erudition and eloquence? And when they quote Holy

2

Scripture! You will be bound to say that they are so many St. Thomases or other doctors of the church, observing such an ingenious solemnity in it all that in one line they will depict a distracted lover and in the next preach a little Christian homily, that is a treat and a pleasure to hear or read. My book will lack all this; for I have nothing to quote in the margin or to note at the end. Nor do I even know what authors I am following in it; and so I cannot set their names at the beginning in alphabetical order, as they all do, starting with Aristotle and ending with Xenophon—and Zoilus or Zeuxis, although one of them was a libeller and the other a painter. My book must go without introductory sonnets as well—or at least sonnets, by dukes, marquises, counts, bishops, great ladies or famous poets; although were I to ask two or three friends in the trade, I know that they would give me them; and such good ones as would be unequalled by the productions of the most highly renowned poets in this Spain of ours. In fact, my dear friend," I continued, "I have decided that Don Quixote shall stay buried in the archives of La Mancha till Heaven provides someone to adorn him with all the jewels he lacks; for I find myself incapable of supplying them because of my inadequacy and scanty learning, and because I am too spiritless and lazy by nature to go about looking for authors to say for me what I can say myself without them. That is the cause of the perplexity and abstraction you found me in, for there is reason enough for my mood in what I have just told you."

When my friend had heard me to the end he slapped his forehead and broke into a loud laugh, saying, "Good Lord, brother, you have just relieved my mind of an error I have been in ever since I have known you, for I have always thought you were sensible and judicious in all your actions. But I see now that you are as far from being so as the sky is from the earth. How is it possible for matters of so little importance and so easily put right to have the power to perplex and preoccupy as ripe an intelligence as yours, so fitted to break down even greater difficulties and trample them underfoot? This does not spring from any lack of ability, I promise you, but

3

from excess of laziness and poverty of resource. Would you like to be convinced that what I say is true? Then listen to me and you will see me confute all your difficulties in the twinkling of an eye, and set right all the defects which, you say, perplex and frighten you into giving up the publication of the history of your famous Don Quixote, light and mirror of all knight errantry."

"Tell me," I replied. "By what means do you propose to fill the void of my fear and reduce the chaos of my confusion to clarity?"

"Your first stumbling block," he replied, "the sonnets, epigrams and eulogies which you lack for your introduction, and which should be by important and titled persons, can be got over by your taking a little trouble and writing them yourself. Afterwards you can baptise them and give them any names you like, fathering them on Prester John of the Indies or the Emperor of Trebizond, who, I have heard it rumoured, were famous poets; and even if they were not, and some pedants and graduates turned up to snap and growl at you behind your back in the name of truth, you need not bother about them a bit, for even if they convict you of a falsehood, they cannot cut off the hand you wrote it with.

"As to quoting in the margins the books and authors from whom you gathered the sentences and sayings you have put in your history, all you have to do is to work in some pat phrases or bits of Latin that you know by heart, or at least that cost you small pains to look up. For example, on the subject of liberty and captivity you might bring in:

" 'Non bene pro toto libertas venditur auro.'

"And in the margin cite Horace, or whoever said it. Then if you are writing of the power of death, you might make use of:

" 'Pallida mors aequo pulsat pede pauperum tabernas
Regumque turres.'

"If you are dealing with friendship and the love God bids you bear to your enemy, come to the point at once with Holy Scripture, which you can do with a little bit of research by quoting the words of no less an authority than God himself: 'Ego autem dico vobis:

4

diligite inimicos vestros.' If you are on the subject of evil thoughts, make use of the Gospel: 'De corde exeunt cogitationes malae.'

"On the instability of friendship there is Cato, who will give you his couplet:

" 'Donec eris felix, multos numerabis amicos,

Tempora si fuerint nubila, solus eris.'

"With these little bits of Latin and such like, they may even take you for a scholar; and it is no small honour and profit to be one nowadays. As to putting notes at the end of the book, you may safely follow this method: if you mention a giant in the text, see that it is the giant Goliath. And by that alone, which will cost you almost nothing, you have a grand note, since you can write, 'The giant Goliath or Golias was a Philistine, whom the shepherd David killed with a sling-shot in the Vale of Terebinth, as is recounted in the Book of Kings'—in whatever chapter you find it is. After that, to show that you are learned in the humanities and in cosmography, contrive to work some mention of the river Tagus into your story, and you will find yourself at once with another famous note, 'The river Tagus was so called by a king of Spain; it has its source in such a place and flows into the Ocean, kissing the walls of the famous city of Lisbon. It is reported to have sands of gold, etc.' If you are writing of thieves I will give you the story of Cacus, which I know by heart; if of prostitutes, there is the Bishop of Mondoñedo, who will assist you with Lamia, Laïs and Flora, and that note will gain you great credit; if of cruel women, Ovid will produce Medea for you; if of witches and sorceresses, Homer has Calypso and Virgil Circe; if of brave commanders, Julius Caesar will lend himself to you in his *Commentaries,* and Plutarch will give you a thousand Alexanders. If you are on the subject of love and have two pennyworth of Italian, you will come across Leon Hebreo, who will give you full measure. But if you do not want to travel into foreign parts, at home you have Fonseca *On the love of God,* which contains everything that you or the cleverest of them could want on the subject. In fact you have nothing more to do but to cite these names in your tale, or touch on the stories I have mentioned, and leave the task of putting in the notes and quotations to me; for I swear I will fill your margins and use up four pages at the end of the book.

"Let us come now to references to authors, which other books contain and yours lacks. The remedy for that is very simple; for you have nothing else to do but look for a book which quotes them all from A to Z, as you say. Then you put this same alphabet into yours. For, granted that the very small need you have to employ them will make your deception transparent, it does not matter a bit; and perhaps there will even be someone silly enough to believe that you have made use of them all in your simple and straightforward story. And if it serves for no other purpose, at least that long catalogue of authors will be useful to lend authority to your book at the outset. Besides, nobody will take the trouble to examine whether you follow your authorities or not, having nothing to gain by it. What is more, if I understand you rightly, this book has no need of any of the things that you say it lacks, for the whole of it is an invective against books of chivalry, which Aristotle never dreamed of, Saint Basil never mentioned, and Cicero never ran across. Nor do the niceties of truth or the calculations of astrology come within the scope of its fabulous narrative; nor is it concerned with geometrical measurements; nor with arguments which can be confuted by rhetoric; nor does it set out to preach to anyone, mingling the human with the divine; which is a kind of motley in which no Christian understanding should be dressed. In what you are writing you have only to make use of imitation, and the more perfect the imitation the better your writing will be. And since this book of yours aims at no more than destroying the authority and influence which books of chivalry have in the world and among the common people, you have no reason to go begging sentences from philosophers, counsel from Holy Writ, fables from poets, speeches from orators, or miracles from saints. You have only to see that your sentences shall come out plain, in expressive, sober and well-ordered language, harmonious and gay, expressing your purpose to the best of your ability, and setting out your ideas without intricacies and obscurities. Be careful

6

too that the reading of your story makes the melancholy laugh and the merry laugh louder; that the simpleton is not confused; that the intelligent admire your invention, the serious do not despise it, nor the prudent withhold their praise. In short, keep your aim steadily fixed on overthrowing the ill-based fabric of these books of chivalry, abhorred by so many yet praised by so many more; for if you achieve that, you will have achieved no small thing."

I listened in complete silence to my friend's words, and his arguments so impressed themselves on my mind that I accepted them as good without question, and out of them set about framing my prologue. By which, kind reader, you will see his wisdom, and my own good fortune in finding such a counsellor in a time of such need; and yourself be relieved at the straightforward and uncomplicated nature of the history of the famous Don Quixote de la Mancha; who, in the opinion of all the inhabitants of the district around the plain of Montiel, was the chastest lover and the most valiant knight seen in those parts for many a year. I do not want to exaggerate the service I am doing you by introducing to you so notable and honoured a knight. But I do want your thanks for making you acquainted with the famous Sancho Panza, his squire, in whom I think I present to you an epitome of all those squirely humours scattered through the swarm of vain books of chivalry.

And so, God give you health, and may He not forget me.

Farewell.

❧ *1* ❧

Which treats of the Quality
and Way of Life of the Famous Knight,
Don Quixote de la Mancha

*I*n a certain village in La Mancha, which I do not wish to name, there lived not long ago a gentleman—one of those who have always a lance in the rack, an ancient shield, a lean hack and a greyhound for coursing. His habitual diet consisted of a stew, more beef than mutton, of hash most nights, boiled bones on Saturdays, lentils on Friday, and a young pigeon as a Sunday treat; and on this he spent three-quarters of his income. The rest of it went on a fine cloth doublet, velvet breeches and slippers for holidays, and a homespun suit of the best in which he decked himself on weekdays. His household consisted of a housekeeper of rather more than forty, a niece not yet twenty, and a lad for the field and market, who saddled his horse and wielded the pruning-hook.

Our gentleman was verging on fifty, of tough constitution, lean-bodied, thin-faced, a great early riser and a lover of hunting. They say that his surname was Quixada or Quesada—for there is some difference of opinion amongst authors on this point. However, by very reasonable conjecture we may take it that he was called

Quexana. But this does not much concern our story; enough that we do not depart by so much as an inch from the truth in the telling of it.

The reader must know, then, that this gentleman, in the times when he had nothing to do—as was the case for most of the year—gave himself up to the reading of books of knight errantry, which he loved and enjoyed so much that he almost entirely forgot his hunting, and even the care of his estate. So odd and foolish, indeed, did he grow on this subject that he sold many acres of cornland to buy these books on chivalry to read, and in this way brought home every one he could get. And of them all he considered none so good as the works of the famous Feliciano de Silva. For his brilliant style and those complicated sentences seemed to him very pearls, especially when he came upon those love-passages and challenges frequently written in the manner of "The reason for the unreason with which you treat my reason, so weakens my reason that with reason I complain of your beauty"; and also when he read, "The high heavens that with their stars divinely fortify you in your divinity and make you deserving of the desert that your greatness deserves."

These writings drove the poor knight out of his wits; and he passed sleepless nights trying to understand them and disentangle their meaning, though Aristotle himself would never have unravelled or understood them, even if he had been resurrected for that sole purpose. He did not much like the wounds that Sir Belianis gave and received, for he imagined that his face and his whole body must have been covered with scars and marks, however skilful the surgeons who tended him. But, for all that, he admired the author for ending his book with the promise to continue with that interminable adventure, and often the desire seized him to take up the pen himself, and write the promised sequel for him. No doubt he would have done so, and perhaps successfully, if other greater and more persistent preoccupations had not prevented him.

Often he had arguments with the priest of his village, who was a scholar and a graduate of Siguenza, as to which was the better knight, Palmerin of England or Amadis of Gaul. But Master Nich-

In fact, now that he had utterly wrecked his reason, he fell into the strangest fancy that ever a madman had in the whole world. He thought it fit and proper, both in order to increase his renown and to serve the state, to turn knight errant and travel through the world with horse and armour in search of adventures. (page 13) olas, the barber of that village, said that no one could compare with the Knight of the Sun. Though if anyone could, it was Sir Galaor, brother of Amadis of Gaul. For he had a very accommodating nature, and was not so affected nor such a sniveller as his brother, though he was not a bit behind him in the matter of bravery.

In short, he so buried himself in his books that he spent the nights reading from twilight till daybreak and the days from dawn till dark; and so from little sleep and much reading, his brain dried up and he lost his wits. He filled his mind with all that he read in them, with enchantments, quarrels, battles, challenges, wounds, wooings, loves, torments and other impossible nonsense; and so deeply did he steep his imagination in the belief that all the fanciful stuff he read was true, that to his mind no history in the world was more authentic. He used to say that the Cid Ruy Diaz must have been a very good knight, but that he could not be compared to the Knight of the Burning Sword, who with a single backstroke had cleft a pair of fierce and monstrous giants in two. And he had an even better opinion of Bernardo del Carpio for slaying the enchanted Roland at Roncesvalles, by making use of Hercules' trick when he throttled the Titan Antaeus in his arms.

He spoke very well of the giant Morgante, for, though one of that giant brood who are all proud and insolent, he alone was affable and well-mannered. But he admired most of all Reynald of Montalban, particularly when he saw him sally forth from his castle and rob everyone he met, and when in heathen lands overseas he stole that idol of Mahomet, which history says was of pure gold. But he would have given his housekeeper and his niece into the bargain, to deal the traitor Galaon a good kicking.

In fact, now that he had utterly wrecked his reason he fell into the strangest fancy that ever a madman had in the whole world. He thought it fit and proper, both in order to increase his renown and to serve the state, to turn knight errant and travel through the world with horse and armour in search of adventures, following in every way the practice of the knights errant he had read of, redressing all manner of wrongs, and exposing himself to chances and dangers, by the overcoming of which he might win eternal honour and renown. Already the poor man fancied himself crowned by the valour of his arm, at least with the empire of Trebizond; and so, carried away by the strange pleasure he derived from these agreeable thoughts, he hastened to translate his desires into action.

The first thing that he did was to clean some armour which had belonged to his ancestors, and had lain for ages forgotten in a corner, eaten with rust and covered with mould. But when he had cleaned and repaired it as best he could, he found that there was one great defect: the helmet was a simple head-piece without a visor. So he ingeniously made good this deficiency by fashioning out of pieces of pasteboard a kind of half-visor which, fitted to the helmet, gave the appearance of a complete head-piece. However, to see if it was strong enough to stand up to the risk of a sword-cut, he took out his sword and gave it two strokes, the first of which demolished in a moment what had taken him a week to make. He was not too pleased at the ease with which he had destroyed it, and to safeguard himself against this danger, reconstructed the visor, putting some strips of iron inside, in such a way as to satisfy himself of his protection; and, not caring to make another trial of it, he accepted it as a fine jointed head-piece and put it into commission.

Next he went to inspect his hack, but though, through leanness, he had more quarters than there are pence in a groat, and more blemishes than Gonella's horse, which was nothing but skin and bone, he appeared to our knight more than the equal of Alexander's Bucephalus and the Cid's Babieca. He spent four days pondering what name to give him; for, he reflected, it would be wrong for the horse of so famous a knight, a horse so good in himself, to be without a famous name. Therefore he tried to fit him with one that would signify what he had been before his master turned knight errant, and what he now was; for it was only right that as his master changed his profession, the horse should change his name for a sublime and high-sounding one, befitting the new order and the new calling he professed. So, after many names invented, struck out and rejected, amended, cancelled and remade in his fanciful mind, he finally decided to call him Rocinante, a name which seemed to him grand and sonorous, and to express the common horse he had been before arriving at his present state, the first and foremost of all hacks in the world.

Having found so pleasing a name for his horse, he next decided to do the same for himself, and spent another eight days thinking about it. Finally he resolved to call himself Don Quixote. And that is no doubt why the authors of this true history, as we have said, assumed that his name must have been Quixada and not Quesada, as other authorities would have it. Yet he remembered that the valorous Amadis had not been content with his bare name, but had added the name of his kingdom and native country in order to make it famous, and styled himself Amadis of Gaul. So, like a good knight, he decided to add the name of his country to his own and call himself Don Quixote de la Mancha. Thus, he thought, he very clearly proclaimed his parentage and native land and honoured it by taking his surname from it.

Now that his armour was clean, his helmet made into a complete head-piece, a name found for his horse, and he confirmed in his new title, it struck him that there was only one more thing to do: to find a lady to be enamoured of. For a knight errant without a lady is like a tree without leaves or fruit and a body without a soul. He said to himself again and again, "If I for my sins or by good luck were to meet with some giant hereabouts, as generally happens to knights errant, and if I were to overthrow him in the encounter, or cut him down the middle or, in short, conquer him and make him surrender, would it not be well to have someone to whom I could send him as a present, so that he could enter and kneel down before my sweet lady and say in tones of humble submission, 'Lady, I am the giant Caraculiambro, lord of the island of Malindrania, whom the never-sufficiently-to-be-praised knight, Don Quixote de la Mancha, conquered in single combat and ordered to appear before your Grace, so that your Highness might dispose of me according to your will'?" Oh, how pleased our knight was when he had made up this

15

speech, and even gladder when he found someone whom he could call his lady. It happened, it is believed, in this way: in a village near his there was a very good-looking farm girl, whom he had been taken with at one time, although she is supposed not to have known it or had proof of it. Her name was Aldonza Lorenzo, and she it was he thought fit to call the lady of his fancies; and, casting around for a name which should not be too far away from her own, yet suggest and imply a princess and great lady, he resolved to call her Dulcinea del Toboso—for she was a native of El Toboso—a name which seemed to him as musical, strange and significant as those others that he had devised for himself and his possessions.

⁍ 2 ⁌

Which treats of the First Expedition
which the Ingenious Don Quixote
made from His Village

*O*nce these preparations were
completed, he was anxious to wait no longer before putting his ideas
into effect, impelled to this by the thought of the loss the world
suffered by his delay, seeing the grievances there were to redress,
the wrongs to right, the injuries to amend, the abuses to correct, and
the debts to discharge. So, telling nobody of his intention, and quite
unobserved, one morning before dawn—it was on one of those
sweltering July days—he armed himself completely, mounted
Rocinante, put on his badly mended head-piece, slung on his shield,
seized his lance and went out into the plain through the back gate of
his yard, pleased and delighted to see with what ease he had started
on his fair design. But scarcely was he in open country when he was
assailed by a thought so terrible that it almost made him abandon the
enterprise he had just begun. For he suddenly remembered that he
had never received the honour of knighthood, and so, according to
the laws of chivalry, he neither could nor should take arms against
any knight, and even if he had been knighted he was bound, as a
novice, to wear plain armour without a device on his shield until he
should gain one by his prowess. These reflections made him waver

in his resolve, but as his madness outweighed any other argument, he made up his mind to have himself knighted by the first man he met, in imitation of many who had done the same, as he had read in the books which had so influenced him. As to plain armour, he decided to clean his own, when he had time, till it was whiter than ermine. With this he quieted his mind and went on his way, taking whatever road his horse chose, in the belief that in this lay the essence of adventure.

As our brand-new adventurer journeyed along, he talked to himself, saying, "Who can doubt that in ages to come, when the authentic story of my famous deeds comes to light, the sage who writes of them will say, when he comes to tell of my first expedition so early in the morning: 'Scarce had the ruddy Apollo spread the golden threads of his lovely hair over the broad and spacious face of the earth, and scarcely had the forked tongues of the little painted birds greeted with mellifluous harmony the coming of the rosy Aurora who, leaving the soft bed of her jealous husband, showed herself at the doors and balconies of the Manchegan horizon, when the famous knight, Don Quixote de la Mancha, quitting the slothful down, mounted his famous steed Rocinante and began to journey across the ancient and celebrated plain of Montiel'?" That was, in fact, the road that our knight actually took, as he went on, "Fortunate the age and fortunate the times in which my famous deeds shall come to light, deeds worthy to be engraved in bronze, carved in marble and painted on wood, as a memorial for posterity. And you, sage enchanter, whoever you may be, to whose lot it falls to be the chronicler of this strange history, I beg you not to forget my good Rocinante, my constant companion on all my rides and journeys!" And presently he cried again, as if he had really been in love, "O Princess Dulcinea, mistress of this captive heart! You did me great injury in dismissing me and inflicting on me the cruel rigour of your command not to appear in your beauteous presence. Deign, lady, to be mindful of your captive heart, which suffers such griefs for love of you."

He went on stringing other nonsense on to this, all after the fashion he had learnt in his reading, and imitating the language of his books as best he could. And all the while he rode so slowly and the sun's heat increased so fast that it would have been enough to turn his brain, if he had had any. Almost all that day he rode without encountering anything of note, which reduced him to despair, for he longed to meet straightway someone against whom he could try the strength of his strong arm.

There are authors who say that the first adventure he met was that of the pass of Lapice. Others say it was the windmills. But what I have been able to discover of the matter and what I have found written in the annals of La Mancha, is that he rode all that day, and that at nightfall his horse and he were weary and dying of hunger. Looking in all directions to see if he could discover any castle or shepherd's hut where he could take shelter and supply his urgent needs, he saw, not far from the road he was travelling on, an inn, which seemed to him like a star to guide him to the gates, if not to the palace, of his redemption. So he hurried on, and reached it just as night was falling. Now there chanced to be standing at the inn door two young women *of easy virtue,* as they are called, who were on the way to Seville with some carriers who happened to have taken up their quarters at the inn that evening. As everything that our adventurer thought, saw, or imagined seemed to follow the fashion of his reading, as soon as he saw the inn he convinced himself that it was a fortress with its four towers and pinnacles of shining silver, complete with a drawbridge, a deep moat and all those appurtenances with which such castles are painted. So he approached the inn, which to his mind was a castle, and when still a short distance away reined Rocinante in, expecting some dwarf to mount the battlements and sound a trumpet to announce that a knight was approaching the fortress. But when he saw that there was some delay, and that Rocinante was in a hurry to get to the stable, he went up to the inn door and, seeing the two young women standing there, took them for two beauteous maidens or graceful ladies taking the air at the castle gate. Now at that very moment, as chance would have it, a swineherd was collecting from the stubble a drove of hogs—pardon me for naming them—and blew his horn to call them together. But Don Quixote immediately interpreted this in his own way, as some dwarf giving notice of his approach. So with rare pleasure he rode up, whereupon those ladies, thoroughly frightened at seeing a man come towards them dressed in armour with lance and shield, turned to go back into the inn. But Don Quixote, gathering from their flight that they were afraid, raised his pasteboard visor, partly revealing his lean and dusty face, and addressed them with a charming expression and in a calm voice, "I beg you, ladies, not to fly, nor to fear any outrage, for it ill fits or suits the order of chivalry which I profess to injure anyone, least of all maidens of such rank as your appearance proclaims you to be."

The girls stared at him, trying to get a look at his face, which was almost covered by the badly made visor. But when they heard themselves called maidens—a title ill-suited to their profession—they could not help laughing, which stung Don Quixote into replying, "Civility befits the fair; and laughter arising from trivial causes is, moreover, great folly. I do not say this to offend you nor to incur your displeasure, for I have no other wish than to serve you."

His language, which was unintelligible to them, and the uncouth figure our knight cut, made the ladies laugh the more. Whereat he flew into a rage, and things would have gone much farther, had not the innkeeper, a very fat man and therefore very peaceable, emerged at this moment. Now when he saw this grotesque figure in his equipment of lance, shield and coat of armour, which sorted so ill with his manner of riding, he was on the point of joining the young women in their demonstrations of amusement. But, fearing such a collection of armaments, he decided to speak politely, and addressed him thus: "If your worship is looking for lodging, Sir Knight, except for a bed—we have none in this inn—you will find plenty of everything."

And Don Quixote replied, seeing the humility of the warden of the fortress—for such he took the innkeeper to be, "For me, Sir Castellan, whatever you have is enough. My ornaments are arms, my rest the bloody fray."

The host thought that he had called him castellan because he took him for a safe man from Castile, though he was an Andalusian from the Strand of San Lucar, as thievish as Cacus and as tricky as a student or a page. So he replied, "At that rate, your bed shall be the cruel rock, your sleep to watch till day, and that being so, you can safely dismount here in the certainty that you will find in this house ample reason for lying awake not only for one night but for a whole year."

As he spoke he went to take Don Quixote's stirrup, and our knight dismounted with great labour and difficulty, as he had fasted all day. He then bade the host take good care of his steed, saying that no better piece of horseflesh munched oats in all the world. The innkeeper stared at the beast, which did not seem as good as Don Quixote said, not by a half. However, he put him up in the stable and, when he came back for his guest's orders, he found that the maidens had made it up with him and were taking off his armour. But although they had got off his breast-plate and back-piece, they had no idea how to get him out of his gorget, nor how to take off his counterfeit head-piece, which was tied with green ribbons that would have to be cut, as they could not undo the knot. But to this he would on no account agree, and so he stayed all that night with his helmet on, cutting the strangest and most ridiculous figure imaginable. And whilst he was being disarmed, imagining that these draggled and loose creatures were illustrious ladies and the mistresses of that castle, he addressed them most gracefully:

> "Never was there knight
> By ladies so attended
> As was Don Quixote
> When he left his village.
> Maidens waited on him,
> On his horse, princesses—

or Rocinante, which, dear ladies, is the name of my horse, and Don Quixote de la Mancha is mine. For, although I did not wish to reveal myself till deeds done in your service and for your benefit do so for me, the need to adapt this old ballad of Lancelot to the present occasion has betrayed my name to you before the due season. But the time will come when your ladyships may command me and I shall obey, and the valour of my arms will then disclose the desire I have to serve you."

The girls, who were not used to hearing such high-flown language, did not say a word in reply, but only asked whether he would like anything to eat.

"I would gladly take some food," replied Don Quixote, "for I think there is nothing that would come more opportunely."

That day happened to be a Friday, and there was no food in the inn except some portions of a fish that is called pollack in Castile and cod in Andalusia, in some parts ling and in other troutlet. They asked whether his worship would like some troutlet, as there was no other fish to eat.

"So long as there are plenty of troutlet they may serve me for one trout," replied Don Quixote, "for I had just as soon be paid eight separate *reals* as an eight *real* piece. What is more, these troutlet may be like veal, which is better than beef, or kid, which is better than goats' meat. But, however that may be, let me have it now, for the toil and weight of arms cannot be borne without due care for the belly."

They set the table for him at the inn door for coolness' sake, and the host brought him a portion of badly soaked and worse cooked salt cod with some bread as black and grimy as his armour. It made them laugh a great deal to see him eat because, as he kept his helmet on and his visor up, he could get nothing into his mouth with his own hands, and required someone's assistance to put it in; and so one of those ladies performed this task for him. But to give him anything to drink would have been impossible if the innkeeper had not bored a reed, put one end into his mouth and poured the wine into the other. All this he bore with patience rather than break the ribbons of his helmet.

While they were thus occupied there happened to come to the inn a hog-gelder, and as he arrived he blew his reed whistle four or five times; which finally convinced Don Quixote that he was at some famous castle, that they were entertaining him with music, that the pollack was trout, the black bread of the whitest flour, the whores ladies and the innkeeper warden of the castle. This made him feel that his resolution and his expedition had been to good purpose, but what distressed him most deeply was that he was not yet knighted, for he believed that he could not rightfully embark on any adventure without first receiving the order of knighthood.

❧ 3 ❧

Which tells of
the Pleasant Method by which
Don Quixote chose to be knighted

So, troubled by these thoughts, he cut short his scanty pothouse supper, and when he was done called the host. Then, shutting the stable door on them both, he fell on his knees before him and said, "Never will I arise from where I am, valiant knight, till you grant me of your courtesy the boon I am going to beg of you; it is one which will redound to your praise and to the benefit of the human race."

Seeing his guest at his feet and hearing such language, the innkeeper stared in confusion, not knowing what to do or say, and pressed him to get up; but in vain, for the knight refused to rise until his host had promised to grant him the boon he begged.

"I expected no less from your great magnificence, dear sir," replied Don Quixote. "So I will tell you that the boon I begged of you, and you in your generosity granted, is that you will knight me on the morning of tomorrow. This night I will watch my arms in the chapel of this castle of yours, and tomorrow, as I said, my dearest wish will be fulfilled, and I shall have the right to ride through all quarters of the world in search of adventures, for the benefit of the distressed, according to the obligations of knighthood and of knights errant like myself, whose minds are given to such exploits."

The innkeeper, who, as we have said, was pretty crafty and had already a suspicion that his guest was wrong in the head, was confirmed in his belief when he heard this speech, and, to make some sport for that night, decided to fall in with his humour. So he told him that he was doing a very proper thing in craving the boon he did, and that such a proposal was right and natural in a knight as illustrious as he seemed and his gallant demeanour showed him to be. He added that he, too, in the day of his youth had devoted himself to that honourable profession and travelled in divers parts of the world in search of adventures, not omitting to visit the Fish Market of Malaga, the Isles of Riaran, the Compass of Seville, the Little Market Place at Segovia, the Olive Grove at Valencia, the Circle of Granada, the Strand of San Lucar, the Colt-fountain of Cordova, the Taverns of Toledo and sundry other places, where he had exercised the agility of his heels and the lightness of his fingers, doing many wrongs, wooing many widows, ruining sundry maidens and cheating a few minors—in fact, making himself well-known in almost all the police-courts and law-courts in Spain. Finally he had retired to this castle, where he lived on his own estate and other people's, welcoming all knights errant of whatever quality and condition, only for the great love he bore them—and to take a share of their possessions in payment for his kindness.

He added that there was no chapel in the castle where he could watch his arms, for it had been pulled down to be rebuilt. But he knew that a vigil might be kept in any place whatever in case of need. So that night he might watch his arms in the courtyard of the castle, and in the morning, God willing, the due ceremonies might be performed, and he emerge a full knight, as much a knight as any in the whole world. He asked him if he had any money with him, and Don Quixote replied that he had not a penny, since he had never read in histories concerning knights errant of any knight that had. At this the innkeeper said that he was wrong, for, granted that it was not mentioned in the histories, because their authors could see no need of mentioning anything so obvious and necessary to take with one as money and clean shirts, that was no reason for supposing that knights did not carry them. In fact, he might take it for an established fact that all knights errant, of whom so many histories were stuffed full, carried purses well lined against all eventualities, and also took with them clean shirts and a little box full of ointments to cure the wounds they got. For on the plains and deserts where they fought and got their wounds they had not always someone at hand to cure them, unless of course they had some magician for a friend. A sorcerer, of course, might relieve them at once by bearing through the air on a cloud some maiden or dwarf with a flask of water of such virtue that after tasting a single drop they were immediately cured of their sores and wounds, and it was as if they had never had any injuries. However, in default of this, the knights of old made certain that their squires were provided with money and other necessaries, such as lint and ointment, to dress their wounds. But when such knights chanced to have no squires—there were only a few rare instances—they carried it all themselves on the cruppers of their horses in bags so very thin that they hardly showed, as though they contained something of even more importance. For, except for such purposes, the carrying of bags was not tolerated among knights errant. So he advised Don Quixote—though as his godson, which he was so soon to be, he might even command him—not to travel in future without money and the other requisites he had mentioned, and he would see how useful they would prove when he least expected it.

Don Quixote promised to do exactly as he recommended, and promptly received his instructions as to keeping watch over his armour in a great yard which lay on one side of the inn. He gathered all the pieces together and laid them on a stone trough, which stood beside a well. Then, buckling on his shield, he seized his lance and began to pace jauntily up and down before the trough. And just as he began his watch, night began to fall.

The innkeeper told everyone staying in the inn of his guest's craziness, of the watching of the armour, and of the knighting he

He loosened his shield and, raising his lance in both hands, dealt his adversary a mighty blow on the head with it, which threw him to the ground. . . . This done, Don Quixote gathered his arms together again and paced up and down once more with the same composure as before. (page 29) was expecting; and, wondering at this strange form of madness, they came out to observe him from a distance, and watched him, sometimes pacing up and down with a peaceful look and sometimes leaning on his lance and gazing on his armour, without taking his eyes off it for a considerable time. Night had now fallen, but the moon was so bright that she might have rivalled the orb that lent her his light, so that whatever the novice knight did was clearly visible to all. Just then it occurred to one of the carriers who was staying at the inn to go and water his mules, and to do this he found it necessary to remove Don Quixote's armour, which lay on the trough. But the knight, seeing him draw near, addressed him in a loud voice, "You, whoever you are, rash knight, who come to touch the armour of the most valorous errant that ever girt on a sword, take heed what you do. Do not touch it unless you wish to lose your life in payment for your temerity."

The carrier paid no attention to this speech—it would have been better if he had regarded it, for he would have been regarding his own safety—but, laying hold of the straps, threw the armour some distance from him. At this sight Don Quixote raised his eyes to heaven, and addressing his thoughts, as it seemed, to his lady Dulcinea, cried, "Assist me, lady, in the first affront offered to this enraptured heart! Let not your favour and protection fail me in this first trial!"

And, uttering these words and others like them, he loosened his shield and, raising his lance in both hands, dealt his adversary a mighty blow on the head with it, which threw him to the ground so injured that, if it had been followed by a second, the carrier would have had no use for a surgeon to cure him. This done, Don Quixote gathered his arms together again and paced up and down once more with the same composure as before.

A little later a second carrier, not knowing what had happened since the first man still lay stunned, came out with the same intention of watering his mules. But, just as he was going to clear the armour from the trough, Don Quixote, without uttering a word or begging anyone's favour, loosened his shield again, once more raised his lance and made more than three pieces of the second carrier's head—for he opened it in four places—without damage to his weapon. At the noise all the people in the inn rushed out, among them the innkeeper. Whereupon Don Quixote buckled on his shield and, putting his hand to his sword, cried, "O beauteous lady, strength and vigour of this enfeebled heart! Now is the time to turn your illustrious eyes on this your captive knight, who is awaiting so great an adventure."

With this it seemed to him that he gained so much courage that if all the carriers in the world had attacked him he would not have yielded a foot. When the fellows of the wounded men saw them in that plight they began to shower stones on Don Quixote from some way off. He protected himself from them as best he could with his shield, but dared not leave the trough, for fear of abandoning his armour. And the innkeeper shouted to them to leave him alone, for he had already told them that he was a madman and, being mad, would go scot-free, even though he killed them all.

Don Quixote shouted also, even louder, calling them cowards and traitors, and swearing that the lord of the castle must be a despicable and base-born knight for allowing knights errant to be so treated, and that if he had received the order of knighthood he would have made him sensible of his perfidy.

"But of you, base and vile rabble, I take no account," he cried. "Throw stones! Come on, attack! Assail me as hard as you can, and you will see what penalty you have to pay for your insolent folly!"

He spoke with such spirit and boldness that he struck a lively terror into all who heard him; and for that reason, as much as for the innkeeper's persuasions, they stopped pelting him. Then Don Quixote allowed them to remove the wounded, and returned to watch his arms with the same quiet assurance as before.

Now the innkeeper had begun to dislike his guest's pranks, and decided to cut the matter short and give him his wretched order of knighthood immediately, before anything else could go wrong. So he apologized for the insolence with which those low fellows had behaved without his knowledge, adding, however, that they had been soundly punished for their audacity. And seeing, as he had said before, that there was no chapel in that castle, there was no need, he declared, for the rest of the ceremony, for, according to his knowledge of the ceremonial of the order, the whole point of conferring knighthood lay in the blow on the neck and the stroke on the shoulder, and that could be performed in the middle of a field. And Don Quixote had already more than fulfilled the duty of the watching of arms, for he had been more than four hours on vigil, whereas all that was required was a two hours' watch.

Don Quixote believed all this, and said he was ready to obey him. He begged him to conclude the matter as briefly as possible; for if he were again attacked, once knighted, he was resolved to leave no one alive in the castle, except such as he might spare at the castellan's bidding, and out of regard for him.

Forewarned and apprehensive, the castellan then brought out the book in which he used to enter the carriers' accounts for straw and barley. Then, followed by a boy carrying a candle-end and by the two maidens already mentioned, he went up to Don Quixote and ordered him to kneel. Next, reading out of his manual, as if he were reciting some devout prayer, in the middle of his reading he raised his hand and dealt the knight a sound blow on the neck, followed by a handsome stroke on the back with the Don's own sword, all the while muttering in his teeth as if in prayer. When this was over he bade one of the ladies gird on Don Quixote's sword, which she did with great agility and some discretion, no small amount of which was necessary to avoid bursting with laughter at each stage of the ceremony. But what they had already seen of the new knight's prowess kept their mirth within bounds. And as she girt on his sword the good lady said, "God make your worship a fortunate knight and give you good luck in your battles."

Don Quixote asked her to tell him her name, as he wished to know in future days to whom he owed the favour received, for he meant to confer on her some part of the honour he was to win by the strength of his arm. She replied very humbly that her name was La Tolosa, and that she was the daughter of a cobbler in Toledo who lived among the stalls of Sancho Bienaya, adding that, wherever she might be, she was at his service and he should be her master. Don Quixote begged her, in reply, as a favour to him, henceforth to take the title of lady and call herself Doña Tolosa, which she promised to do. The other lady then put on his spurs, and his conversation with her was almost the same as with the lady of the sword. He asked her her name, and she replied that she was called La Molinera, and that she was the daughter of an honest miller in Antequera. The Don requested her also to take the title of lady and call herself Doña Molinera, renewing his offers of service and favours.

Now that these unprecedented ceremonies had been hurried through post-haste and at top speed, Don Quixote was impatient to be on horseback and to ride out in search of adventures. So, saddling Rocinante at once, he mounted; then, embracing his host, he thanked him for the favour of knighting him in such extravagant terms that it is impossible to write them down faithfully. The innkeeper, once he saw him safely out of the inn, replied to his speech rather more briefly but in no less high-flown terms, and without even asking him to pay the cost of his lodging, was heartily glad to see him go.

✦ 4 ✦

What happened to Our Knight
when he left the Inn

*I*t must have been daybreak when
Don Quixote left the inn, so pleased, so gay, so enraptured at being
now a knight that his joy seemed likely to burst his horse's girths.
But, calling to mind his host's advice about the essential provisions
he must carry, especially money and clean shirts, he decided to go
home and provide himself with them all, and with a squire as well.
He reckoned to take into his service a neighbour of his, a poor
labourer who had a large family, but was very suitable for the part of
squire in chivalry. With this in mind he turned Rocinante for home,
and the horse, as if he smelled his home pastures, began to trot with
such zest that his feet seemed not to touch the ground.

He had not gone far when from a thicket on the right he heard a
faint voice, raised, so it seemed to him, in complaint; and no sooner
did he hear this than he cried, "I thank Heaven for granting this
favour and giving me so prompt an opportunity to perform the duty
I owe to my order, and whereby I may be able to gather the fruit of
my honourable desires. These cries come no doubt from some man
or woman in distress, and in need of my protection and assistance."

Then, turning his reins, he guided Rocinante towards the place from which the voice seemed to come; and, when he had ridden a little way into the wood, he saw a mare tied to an oak, and tied to another a lad of about fifteen, naked to the waist. It was he who was shouting, and with good reason, for a well-built countryman was flogging him soundly with a belt, and accompanying each blow with mingled scolding and advice, crying, "Keep your tongue still and your eyes open."

To which the boy replied, "I won't do it again, sir. I swear to God I won't do it again. I promise I'll take better care of your sheep in future."

When Don Quixote saw what was happening he exclaimed in an angry voice, "Discourteous knight, it is unseemly to attack a defenceless person. Mount your steed, and take your lance"—for the other also had a lance leaning against the oak to which his mare was tied—"and I will teach you that you are acting like a coward."

When the countryman saw this figure in full armour come at him brandishing his lance over his head, he gave himself up for dead and answered mildly, "Sir Knight, this lad I am punishing is my servant. His job is to watch a herd of sheep that I keep around here. But he is so careless that every day I lose one. And because I'm punishing him for his carelessness or his roguery he says I'm doing it through meanness, so as not to have to pay him his due wages. But I swear to God and on my life he's lying."

"Lying, you say, and in my presence, you wretched boor?" said Don Quixote. "By the sun that shines on us, I have a good mind to run you through with this lance. Pay him now and without another word. If you do not, by God who rules us, I will despatch you and annihilate you this very minute. Untie him immediately!"

The farmer bowed his head, and without replying untied his lad, whom Don Quixote asked how much his master owed him. He answered, for nine months at seven *reals* a month. Don Quixote calculated, and found that it came to sixty-three *reals*, whereupon he told the countryman to disburse them immediately, unless he wished to pay with his life. The farmer, in a fright, swore by his present plight and the oath he had taken—though he had not taken any oath—that it did not come to so much, because they must deduct from the reckoning three pairs of shoes he had given him, and a *real* paid for two blood-lettings, when he was sick.

"That is quite right," Don Quixote answered. "But set the shoes and the blood-lettings against the undeserved flogging you have given him. For, if he broke the leather of the shoes you gave him, you have broken the skin of his body and, if the barber let his blood when he was sick, you have done the same now, when he is well. So on that score he owes you nothing."

"The trouble is, Sir Knight, I have no money here. If Andrew will come home with me I will pay him every *real*."

"I go home with him?" said the lad. "Oh Lord, no, sir! Not on your life! Because if I went alone he would flay me like St. Bartholomew."

"He will do no such thing," replied Don Quixote. "I have only to lay my command on him, and he will respect it; and on condition that he gives me his oath on the order of knighthood which he has received, I shall let him go free and will guarantee the payment."

"Think what you are saying, your worship," said the lad. "This master of mine isn't a knight, and hasn't received any order of chivalry. He is the rich John Haldudo, and lives at Quintanar."

"That is no matter," replied Don Quixote, "for there may be knights in the Haldudo family. It is very probable, for every man is the child of his own works."

"That's quite right," said Andrew, "but this master of mine, what works is he the child of, when he refuses me wages for my sweat and labour?"

"I don't refuse them, Andrew my friend," replied the farmer. "Do me the favour of coming with me, and I swear by all the orders of chivalry in the world to pay you every single *real*, and perfumed into the bargain."

"The perfuming I excuse you," said Don Quixote. "Give it him in *reals* and I shall be satisfied. But take care that you do what you have sworn, or else, by the same oath, I swear I will come back and look for you and punish you; and I shall find you, even if you hide better than a lizard. And if you wish to know who lays this command on you, so that you may feel the more strictly bound to obey it, know that I am the valorous Don Quixote de la Mancha, the redresser of wrongs and injuries. God be with you, and do not be unmindful of what you have promised under oath, on pain of the penalty pronounced."

As he spoke he spurred Rocinante, and in a short while had left them. The farmer followed him with his eyes; and when he saw that he left the wood and was out of sight, returned to his servant and said, "Come here, my lad. I want to pay you what I owe you, as that redresser of wrongs ordered me to."

"I swear you will," said Andrew. "Indeed you had better comply with that good knight's commands, God bless him! For he is such a brave man and such a fair judge that, by my life, if you don't pay me, he will come back and do what he said."

"I swear I will, too," said the countryman, "but to show you how much I love you, I want to increase the debt, so that I can increase the payment."

Then, grasping him by the arm, he tied him up once more to the tree and flogged him so soundly that he left him for dead.

"Now, Master Andrew," said he, "call on that redresser of wrongs, and he won't redress this one, you'll see. Though I have not finished yet, I think, for I have a mind to flay you alive, as you feared."

But at last he untied him and gave him leave to go and look for his judge to execute the sentence he had pronounced. Andrew set off in a fury, swearing to go and find the valorous Don Quixote de la Mancha and tell him exactly what had happened. Then his master would have to pay him sevenfold. But for all that, he wept as he went, and his master remained behind laughing; and thus did the valorous Don Quixote redress that wrong.

He rode on, however, highly delighted at what had passed, for it seemed to him that he had made a most happy and glorious beginning in his knight errantry; and, very pleased with himself, he

Now, when Don Quixote found himself alone, he tried once more to see if he could rise. But if he could not do so when he was hale and well, how could he now that he was so pounded and almost destroyed? Yet, for all this, he reckoned himself fortunate. For it seemed to him that this was a disaster peculiar to knights errant, and he attributed it entirely to the fault of his horse. (page 41) repeated half aloud as he made his way towards his village, "Well may you call yourself fortunate above all women living on earth today, O Dulcinea del Toboso, more beautiful than all beauties, since it has fallen to your lot to hold as a humble subject to your least desire and pleasure so valiant and famous a knight as is and shall be Don Quixote de la Mancha, who yesterday, as all the world knows, received the order of knighthood and today has righted the greatest injury and wrong that injustice could invent or cruelty perpetrate. Today he wrested the scourge from the hand of the pitiless enemy who was so undeservedly whipping that delicate infant."

He now came to a place where the road divided into four, and there immediately leapt into his mind those crossways where knights errant used to stop to consider which of the roads they should take. So, following their example, he halted a moment, and after deep thought he let go the reins, submitting his will to Rocinante, who followed his first instinct, which was to take the road towards his stable. When he had gone about two miles Don Quixote sighted a large crowd of people who, as he afterwards learnt, were merchants from Toledo going to buy silks in Murcia. There were six of them, riding beneath their sunshades, with four servants, all on horseback, and three muleteers on foot. As soon as Don Quixote saw them in the distance he imagined this to be matter for some new adventure, and it seemed to him that here was just the right opportunity to make the closest possible imitation of the encounters he had read of in his books. So with a gallant and resolute air he steadied himself in his stirrups, grasped his lance, covered his breast with his shield and, taking up his position in the middle of the road, awaited the arrival of those knights errant; for such he had already decided they were. So when they arrived within sight and earshot Don Quixote raised his voice, and called out in an arrogant tone, "Let the whole world stand, if the whole world does not confess that there is not in the whole world a more beauteous maiden than the Empress of la Mancha, the peerless Dulcinea del Toboso."

The merchants stopped when they heard this speech, and saw the strange figure who made it; and both from his appearance and his words they divined that the speaker was mad. But wanting to know more fully what this confession that he required of them really meant, one of them, who was a bit of a joker and very sharp-witted, said, "Sir Knight, we do not know who this good lady is that you speak of. Show her to us and, if she is as beauteous as you say, we will most willingly and without any pressure acknowledge the truth demanded of us by you."

"If I were to show her to you," replied Don Quixote, "what merit would there be in your confessing so obvious a truth? The essence of the matter is that you must believe, confess, affirm, swear and maintain it without seeing her. If you will not, you must do battle with me, monstrous and proud crew. Now come on! One by one, as the law of chivalry requires, or all together, as is the custom and evil practice of men of your breed. Here I stand and await you, confident in the right which I have on my side."

"Sir Knight," replied the merchant, "I beg your worship in the name of all these princes here present that you will kindly show us a portrait of this lady, even one no bigger than a grain of wheat; because we would not burden our consciences by testifying to something that we have never seen or heard and, what is more, something so detrimental to the Empresses and Queens of Alcarria and Estremadura. For the skein can be judged by the thread, and we shall rest assured and satisfied with this, and your worship will be pleased and content. I even think that we are so far inclined to her side already that supposing your portrait shows us that she squints in one eye and drips vermilion and sulphur from the other, even then, to please you, we will say all that you ask in her favour."

"Her eyes do not drip, vile scoundrels!" replied Don Quixote in great fury. "Her eyes do not drip what you say, but ambergris and civet. She is not squinting or humpbacked, but straighter than a spindle of Guadarrama. And you shall pay for the blasphemy you have spoken against such transcendent beauty as my lady's."

With these words he couched his lance and ran at the man who had spoken with such rage and fury that, if Rocinante had not fortunately stumbled and fallen in the road, things would have gone badly for the rash merchant. Rocinante fell, and his master went rolling some distance over the plain; but when he tried to get up it was in vain, so encumbered was he by his lance, shield, spurs and helmet, together with the weight of his ancient armour. And, whilst he was struggling to get up and could not, he kept shouting, "Fly not, you coward brood! Stay, you slavish crew! It is not my fault, but my horse's, that I lie here."

One of their muleteers who was not very good-natured, hearing the arrogant language of the poor man on the ground, could not refrain from dealing him an answer in the ribs; and going up to him, snatched his lance, and broke it in pieces. Then he began to give our Don Quixote such a beating with one of the bits that, in spite of his armour, he pounded him like wheat in a mill. The lad's masters shouted to him not to beat the knight so hard and to let him alone; but he was irritated, and would not give up the game till he had completely vented his rage. So, picking up the other bits of the lance, he broke them all over the poor prostrate knight, who beneath all that storm of blows which rained on him, never once closed his mouth, but howled continuous threats to heaven and earth against those brigands, as he took them to be. At last the lad tired himself out, and the merchants went on their way with enough to talk about for the rest of the journey on the subject of that poor belaboured gentleman. Now, when Don Quixote found himself alone, he tried once more to see if he could rise. But if he could not do so when he was hale and well, how could he now that he was so pounded and almost destroyed? Yet, for all this, he reckoned himself fortunate. For it seemed to him that this was a disaster peculiar to knights errant, and he attributed it entirely to the fault of his horse. But it was impossible for him to get up, his whole body was so battered.

⊰ 5 ⊱

Continuing the Story of
Our Knight's Disaster

*S*eeing then that he was in fact
unable to stir, it occurred to him to resort to his usual remedy, which
was to think of some passage in his books. Whereupon his madness
called into his mind that part of the story of the Marquis of Mantua,
when Carloto left Baldwin wounded on the mountain, a tale familiar
to children, not unknown to youth, and enjoyed and even believed
by old men, though for all that no truer than the miracles of
Mahomet. It seemed to him to fit his present plight to a T; and so he
began to roll about on the ground with every sign of intense pain
and to repeat in a languishing voice those words which are attributed
to the wounded Knight of the Wood:

> Oh, where are you, my lady,
> That you grieve not for my plight?
> Either you know not of it,
> Or else you are faithless and light.

He went on with the ballad in this way till he came to the lines
which go:

O noble Marquis of Mantua,
My uncle and natural lord!

As chance would have it, when he came to this verse a labourer of his own village, a neighbour of his, passed on his way to take a load of wheat to the mill and, seeing a man lying on the ground, went up and asked him who he was and what it was that made him groan so sadly. Now Don Quixote firmly believed that this was the Marquis of Mantua, his uncle, and so made him no answer, but went on with his quotation, giving an account of his misfortune and of his wife's intrigue with the Emperor's son, all in the words of the ballad. The labourer was astonished at hearing this nonsense and, taking off the knight's visor, which was now battered to pieces from the beating, wiped his dust-covered face and immediately recognized him.

"Master Quixada," he cried—this must have been his name before he lost his senses and changed himself from a quiet gentleman into a knight errant—"who has put your worship in this plight?"

But he answered every question by going on with his ballad. Therefore the good man took off his back- and breast-plates, as best he could, to see if he had any wounds. But he saw no blood nor sign of any hurt. Then he tried to get him up from the ground, and with a great effort heaved him on to his own ass, which seemed to him the quieter mount. And gathering up his arms, even to the splinters of his lance, he tied them on Rocinante and, leading him by the bridle and his ass by the halter, took the road for the village, much concerned to hear the nonsense that Don Quixote was talking. Our knight was no less concerned, being too bruised and battered to stay on the ass, and from time to time he breathed groans deep enough to reach heaven, so that his neighbour was compelled to ask him again what pain he felt. Now it must have been the Devil himself who put into his mind stories applicable to his plight; for at that instant he forgot Baldwin and remembered the Moor Abindarraez, when the governor of Antequera, Rodrigo de Narvaez, captured him and held him prisoner in his castle. So that when the labourer asked him once more how he was, and how he felt, he replied in the very words and phrases in which the captive Abencerrage answered Rodrigo de Narvaez, as he had read the story of Jorge Montemayor's *Diana*, applying it so appositely that the labourer wished himself to the Devil for having to listen to such a pack of rubbish. Realizing now that his neighbour was mad, he made haste to the village, to be quit of the nuisance of listening to Don Quixote's harangue, at the close of which the knight exclaimed, "Be it known to your worship, Don Rodrigo de Narvaez, that this beauteous Xarifa I mentioned is now the fair Dulcinea del Toboso, for whom I have done, am doing and shall do the most famous deeds of chivalry that the world has ever seen, can see or will see."

To which the labourer replied, "Look you, your worship, as I am a sinner, I am not Don Rodrigo de Narvaez, nor the Marquis of Mantua, but your neighbour Pedro Alonzo. And your worship is not Baldwin or Abindarraez, but that worthy gentleman Master Quixada."

"I know who I am," replied Don Quixote, "and I know, too, that I am capable of being not only the characters I have named, but all the Twelve Peers of France and all the Nine Worthies as well, for my exploits are far greater than all the deeds they have done, all together and each by himself."

They were deep in such conversation when they reached the village at nightfall. But the labourer waited till it was rather darker, so that no one should see the battered gentleman on so shameful a mount. When he thought it was the proper time he entered the village, and went to Don Quixote's house, which he found in a great uproar. The priest was there and the village barber, great friends of Don Quixote's, and his housekeeper was addressing them at the top of her voice, "What do you think, Doctor Pero Perez"—for that was the priest's name—"of my master's misfortune? It is three days now he has not been seen, nor his horse, nor his shield, nor his lance, nor his armour either! Oh dear! Oh dear! What can I think? It is the truth, as sure as I was born to die, that these cursed books of knight errantry of his, that he is always reading, have turned his brain. For now I come to think of it, I have often heard him talking to himself about turning knight errant and going about in those worlds in search of adventures. Satan and Barabbas take all such books for ruining the finest understanding there was in all La Mancha."

The niece said much the same and something more. "You know, Master Nicholas,"—for that was the barber's name—"it has very often happened that dear uncle has gone on reading those soulless books of misadventures for two days and nights on end. Then, when he has finished, he will fling his book down, draw his sword and go slashing the walls; and when he is exhausted he will say that he has killed four giants as tall as towers, and that the sweat that is pouring from him out of exhaustion is blood from the wounds he has got in the battle. Then he will drink a great jug of cold water and lie quiet and easy, saying that the water is a most precious draught which the sage Esquife has brought him, a great magician and a friend of his. But I am to blame for all this, because I did not tell your worships of my dear uncle's follies, so that you could have cured him before he got so far, and burnt all those cursed books. For he has a great many which well deserve to be burnt, just as much as if they were heretics."

"I agree with that," said the priest, "and I swear that tomorrow shall not pass without a public inquisition being held over them. And let them be condemned to the flames, so that they shall not cause others who read them to imitate our good friend."

The labourer, who with Don Quixote overheard all this, was confirmed in his belief that his neighbour was deranged, and so began to shout, "Open, your worships, to Sir Baldwin and to the Lord Marquis of Mantua, who comes sore wounded, and to Master Moor Abindarraez, whom the valorous Rodrigo de Narvaez, governor of Antequera, brings captive."

At this noise they all went out and, recognizing their friend, master and uncle, ran to embrace him, though he had not yet dismounted from his ass, because he could not. But he cried, "Stop, all of you, for I come sorely wounded through the fault of my steed. Carry me to my bed and, if it is possible, call the wise Urganda to examine and cure my wounds."

"See, in the name of mischief," the housekeeper broke in at this point, "if my heart didn't tell me truly on which leg my master was lame! Come up, your worship. I'm right glad to see you. We'll know how to cure you here, without sending for your Urganda. Oh, confound, confound, confound those books of chivalry which have brought your worship to this pass!"

They took him straight to his bed, but on searching for his wounds could find none. He said that he was bruised all over from taking a grievous fall with his horse Rocinante in a fight with ten of the most monstrous and audacious giants to be found anywhere on earth.

"So ho!" cried the priest. "So there are giants in the dance? Well, I swear I'll burn them tomorrow before nightfall."

They asked Don Quixote a great number of questions, but the only reply he would make was to ask them to give him something to eat and let him sleep; for that was his most urgent need. They did so, and the priest inquired of the labourer at some length how he had found their friend. The peasant told him everything and repeated the nonsense the knight had talked when he discovered him, and as he brought him home. This made the priest more eager to do what he did the next day, which was to call on his friend, master Nicholas the barber, and to go with him to Don Quixote's house.

❧ 6 ❧

Of the Great and Pleasant Inquisition
held by the Priest and the Barber over
Our Ingenious Gentleman's Library

*T*he knight was still asleep when
the priest asked the niece for the keys of the room where he kept his
books, the authors of the mischief. She was delighted to give them to
him. Then they all went in, the housekeeper with them, and found
more than a hundred large volumes, very well bound, and some
small ones as well. As soon as the housekeeper saw them, she ran out
of the room in great haste, and returned presently with a bowl of
holy water and a bunch of hyssop. "Take this, your worship," she
said, "and sprinkle this room, in case there is some enchanter about,
out of all the lot there are in these books, for fear he might put a spell
on us, to punish us for the bad turn we're going to deal him by
banishing them all out of the world."

The priest laughed at the housekeeper's simplicity, and bade the
barber hand him the books one by one, so that he could see what
they were about, for he might find some of them that did not deserve
punishment by fire.

"No," said the niece, "there is no reason to pardon any of them,
for they have all of them caused the trouble. Better throw them out

47

of the windows into the courtyard, and make a pile of them, and set them on fire; or else take them out into the back-yard and have the bonfire there, where the smoke won't be a nuisance."

The housekeeper agreed, so anxious were they both for the massacre of those innocents; but the priest would not consent without at least reading the titles first. And the first that Master Nicholas handed him was *The Four Books of Amadis of Gaul.* "This is very curious," said the priest, "for, as I have heard tell, this was the first book of chivalries printed in Spain, and all the others took their origin and beginning from it. So it seems to me that, as the first preacher of so pernicious a sect, we must condemn it to the flames without any mercy."

"No, sir," said the barber, "for I have heard that it is the best of all the books of this kind ever written. So, as it is unequalled in its accomplishment, it ought to be pardoned."

"That is true," said the priest, "and therefore let its life be granted for the present. Let us have a look at that other one beside it."

"That," said the barber, "is *The Exploits of Esplandian,* the legitimate son of Amadis of Gaul."

"In truth," said the priest, "the father's goodness shall not help the son. Take him, Mistress Housekeeper. Open that window and throw him into the yard. He shall be the foundation for the bonfire we shall have to make."

The housekeeper obeyed with great pleasure, and the good Esplandian went flying out into the yard to wait in all patience for the threatened conflagration.

"Let us get on," said the priest.

"The next," said the barber, "is *Amadis of Greece.* In fact, as far as I can see, all these on this side are of the same lineage as *Amadis.*"

"Then into the yard with all of them," cried the priest, "for rather than not burn queen Pintiquinestra and the shepherd Darinel with their eclogues and their author's devilish contorted sentences, I would burn the father that begot me as well, if he went about in the shape of a knight errant."

"I am of the same opinion," said the barber.

"Take this," your worship," she said, "and sprinkle this room, in case there is some enchanter about, out of all the lot there are in these books, for fear he might put a spell on us, to punish us for the bad turn we're going to deal him by banishing them all out of the world." (page 47)

"And I too," added the niece.

"Since that is so," said the housekeeper, "come, into the yard with them!"

They handed them to her and, as there were a great number, to spare herself the stairs she flung them down out of the window.

"What is that huge thing?" asked the priest.

"It is *Don Olivante de Laura,*" answered the barber.

"The author of that book also wrote *The Flower Garden,*" said the priest, "and to be frank with you, I cannot make out which of the two is the more truthful, or rather the less mendacious. I can only say that for its arrogant nonsense it shall go into the yard."

"This next is *Florismarte of Hyrcania,*" said the barber.

"What, is Master Florismarte here?" replied the priest. "Well, he is for a quick end in the yard, I promise you, despite his extraordinary birth and his fantastic adventures. His style is so harsh and dry he deserves nothing better. Into the yard with him and with that other one too, Mistress Housekeeper."

"With the greatest of pleasure," she replied, and with much joy she did his bidding.

"Here is *The Knight Platir,*" said the barber.

"That is an old book," said the priest. "I can find nothing in it that deserves mercy. Let him join the others without more ado." And so he did. Then they opened another book, and found its title to be *The Knight of the Cross.*

"For a title as holy as this book has, its ignorance might be pardoned. But they always say 'the devil lurks behind the cross.' So, to the fire with it." Then, taking up another book, the barber observed: "This is *The Mirror of Chivalries.*"

"I know the book well," said the priest. "Therein are Lord Reynald of Montalban and his friends and companions, worse thieves than Cacus; and the Twelve Peers, and that faithful historian Turpin. But I am for condemning them to nothing worse than perpetual banishment, if only because they had a share in inspiring the famous Mateo Boiardo, from whom the Christian poet Ludovico Ariosto also spun his web. If I find him here speaking any language but his own I shall show him no respect. But if he speaks his own tongue, I will wear him next my heart."

"I have him in Italian," said the barber, "but I don't understand him."

"It would not do you any good if you did," replied the priest. "We could have done without the good captain bringing him to Spain and making him a Castilian, for he has robbed him of much of his native value. That is what happens with all authors who translate poetry into other languages. However much care they take, and however much skill they show, they can never make their translations as good as the original. In short, I say that this book and every one we find that deals with these affairs of France, shall be thrown out and deposited in a dry well till we see, after further deliberation, what is to be done with them; excepting one, *Bernardo de Carpio*, which is here somewhere, and another called *Roncesvalles*. For they shall pass straight from my hands into the housekeeper's, and from there into the flames without remission."

The barber concurred in all this, holding it very fit and proper, for he knew the priest to be too good a Christian and too great a lover of the truth to tell a lie for anything in the world. Opening another book, they saw that it was *Palmerin de Oliva*, and beside it was another called *Palmerin of England*, at the sight of which the priest exclaimed, "Let that olive be cut to splinters and burnt, so that not so much as the ash remains. But that palm of England, let it be kept and treasured as a rarity, and a casket be made for it, like the one Alexander found among the spoils of Darius and dedicated to the preservation of the works of Homer. This book, my friend, deserves respect for two reasons: one, because it is very good in itself, and the other because it is said to have been written by a wise King of Portugal. All the adventures in the castle of Miraguarda are excellent and very well contrived, and the speeches polished and clear, for they observe and bring out the character of each speaker with great truth and understanding. I say, then, subject to your judgment, Master Nicholas, that this and *Amadis of Gaul* shall be spared the fire, and all the rest perish without any further trial or enquiry."

"No, my good friend," replied the barber, "for the one I have here is the renowned *Sir Belianis.*"

"He too," said the priest, "and his second, third and fourth parts, need a little rhubarb to purge their excess of bile. We shall have to cut out all that part too about the Castle of Fame and other nonsense more serious still. So we will allow them time to put in their defence, and as they show signs of amendment, mercy or justice shall be accorded them. Meanwhile, friend, keep them in your house, but let no one read them."

"With pleasure," replied the barber. And the priest, not being inclined to tire himself by reading any more books on chivalry, bade the housekeeper take all the big ones and throw them into the yard. His request did not fall on deaf ears, for she would rather have burnt those books than woven the broadest and finest cloth in the world. So, seizing them about eight at a time, she flung them out of the window. And as she took so many together, one fell at the barber's feet; and he, curious to see what it was, found that its title was *History of the Famous Knight Tirante the White.*

"Good heavens!" exclaimed the priest in a loud voice. "Is *Tirante the White* here? Give it to me, friend, for to my mind that book is a rare treasure of delight and a mine of entertainment. Here is Lord-have-mercy-on-us of Montalban, a valiant knight, and his brother Thomas of Montalban and the knight Fonseca, and the fight the valiant Tirante had with the great mastiff, and the witticisms of the maiden Joy-of-my-life, with the amours and tricks of widow Quiet, and the lady Empress in love with her squire Hippolito. Really, my friend, for its style it is the best book in the world. Here the knights eat and sleep and die in their beds, and make their wills before they die, and other things as well that are left out of all other books of the kind. On that account, the author is a deserving fellow. For he did not commit all those follies deliberately, which might have sent him to the galleys for the rest of his life. Take him home and read him, and you will see that all I have said of him is true."

"So be it," replied the barber. "But what shall we do with these little books that are left?"

"Those," said the priest, "are probably not books of chivalry but of poetry."

He opened one, and saw that it was Jorge de Montemayor's *Diana*, and supposing that all the rest were of the same kind, said: "These do not deserve burning with the rest, because they do not and will not do the mischief those books of chivalry have done. They are books of entertainment and can do no one any harm."

"Oh, sir," cried the niece, "your worship should have them burnt like the rest. For once my uncle is cured of his disease of chivalry, he might very likely read those books and take it into his head to turn shepherd and roam about the woods and fields, singing and piping and, even worse, turn poet, for that disease is incurable and catching, so they say."

"The girl is right," said the priest. "It would be well to rid our friend of this stumbling-block and danger for the future. And since we are beginning with Montemayor's *Diana*, I am of the opinion that it should not be burnt, but all the part dealing with the witch Felicia and the enchanted water should be taken out, and almost all the longer poems too, but we will gladly leave it the prose and the honour of being the first book of its kind."

"The next one," said the barber, "is the *Diana*, called the second, by the Salmantine; and here is another of the same name by Gil Polo."

"Let the one by the Salmantine join and increase the company of those condemned to the yard. But Gil Polo's we will preserve as if it were by Apollo himself. But get on, friend; let us hurry, for it is getting late."

"This volume," said the barber, opening another, "is *The Ten Books of the Fortune of Love*, by Antonio de Lofraso, poet of Sardinia."

"As true as I am in orders," cried the priest, "there has never been such a humorous, whimsical book written since Apollo was Apollo, the Muses Muses and the poets poets. In its way it is the best and most singular book of that kind that ever saw the light of day, and anyone who has not read it can reckon he has never read anything really delightful. Give it to me, friend, for I had rather have found this than have the present of a Florentine serge cassock."

He put it aside with the greatest delight, and the barber went on, saying: "The next are *The Shepherd of Iberia, The Nymphs of Henares,* and *The Unveiling of Jealousy.*"

"Well, there is nothing else to do with them," said the priest, "but to deliver them over to the secular arm of the housekeeper. Don't ask me why, or we shall never have done."

"The next is *Filida's Shepherd.*"

"He is no shepherd," said the priest, "but a very ingenious courtier. Let him be kept as a precious jewel."

"This big one here is called *The Treasury of Divers Poems,*" said the barber.

"If there were not so many of them," said the priest, "they would have been better thought of. This book ought to be weeded and cleansed of some poor verses it has among its finest things. Take care of it, because its author is a friend of mine, and out of respect for other more heroic and exalted works he has written."

"This," the barber went on, "is Lopez Maldonado's song-book."

"The author of that book is also a great friend of mine," replied the priest. "Everyone admires his verses that hears them from his own mouth; his voice is so sweet he enchants when he chants them. His eclogues are rather long, though you can never have too much of a good thing. Let him be preserved with the elect. But what is that book beside him?"

"The *Galatea* of Miguel de Cervantes," said the barber.

"That Cervantes has been a great friend of mine for many years, and I know that he is more versed in misfortunes than in verse. His book has some clever ideas; but it sets out to do something and concludes nothing. We must wait for the second part he promises, and perhaps with amendment he will win our clemency now denied him. In the meantime, neighbour, until we see, keep him as a recluse in your room."

"With pleasure, my good friend. Now here come three together: *The Araucana* of Don Alonso de Ercilla, *The Austriada* of Juan Rufo, magistrate of Cordova, and *The Monserrat* of Christoval de Virues, the Valencian poet."

"These three books," said the priest, "are the best in heroic verse ever written in Castilian. They can compare with the most famous in Italy. Let them be preserved as the richest treasures of poetry Spain possesses."

The priest was too tired to look at any more books, and therefore proposed that the rest should be burnt, contents unknown. But the barber had already opened one called *The Tears of Angelica.*

"I would have shed them myself," said the priest on hearing the title, "if I had ordered a book like that to be consigned to the flames. For its author was one of the most famous poets not only in Spain but in the world, and was most happy in translating some of Ovid's fables."

⊰ 7 ⊱

Of the Second Expedition of
Our Good Knight Don Quixote de la Mancha

*A*t this point Don Quixote began to shout at the top of his voice, "Here, here, valorous knights! Here there is need to show the strength of your valorous arms, for the courtiers are getting the better of the tourney!"

At this frightful noise all rushed upstairs, and the examination of the remaining books proceeded no further. And that is why, so it is believed, *The Carolea* and *The Lion of Spain,* with the *Feats of the Emperor,* compiled by Don Luis de Avila, went on the flames unseen and unheard. For no doubt they must have been among the remaining books, and perhaps if the priest had seen them they would not have suffered so severe a sentence. When they got into Don Quixote's room he was already out of bed, and repeating his shouting and raving, laying about him with his sword in all directions with slashes and back-strokes, as wide awake as if he had never been asleep. They grappled with him, and put him back to bed by main force; and when he had rested quietly a little he started to address the priest, saying:

"Certainly, my Lord Archbishop Turpin, it is a great default in us, who call ourselves the Twelve Peers, to give these courtier knights the victory in this tournament without more ado, seeing that we, the Adventurers, have gained the prize on the three preceding days."

"Peace, dear comrade," replied the priest, "for God may yet grant us a change of fortune, and what is lost today may be won back tomorrow. But for the present you must mind your health; for you seem to me to be over-wearied, if not severely wounded."

"Not wounded," said Don Quixote, "but bruised and battered. There is no doubt of that, for that bastard Roland has pounded me with the trunk of an oak, and all out of envy, since he knows I am his only rival in prowess. But let me never be called Reynald of Montalban again if, when I rise from this bed, I do not pay him for it despite all his enchantments. But for the present let me be brought food, for I believe that is what I am in most need of, and leave me to to take care of my revenge."

They did as he asked, and gave him some food, after which he went to sleep again, leaving them wondering at his madness.

That same night the housekeeper set light to all the books in the yard and all those in the whole house as well, and burnt them. Some that were burnt deserved to be treasured up among the eternal archives, but fate and the laziness of the inquisitor forbade it. And so in them was fulfilled the saying that the saint sometimes pays for the sinner.

One of the remedies that the priest and the barber then resorted to for their friend's complaint was to wall up and close the room where he had kept his books, so that he should not find them when he got up. For perhaps if the cause were removed, the effect might cease, and they might say that an enchanter had carried them off, room and all.

This was quickly done, and when two days later Don Quixote got up, the first thing he did was to go and look for his books; and when he failed to find the room where he had left them he went all over the house searching for it. Finally he went to the place where the door used to be, and felt for it with his hands, and ran his eyes over everything again and again, without saying a word. Then after a good while he asked his housekeeper whereabouts his book-closet was, and she, being well primed in her answers, replied, "What room? Or rather what on earth is your worship looking for? There is no room and no books in this house now, for the Devil himself has carried everything off."

"That was no devil," put in his niece, "but an enchanter who came one night on a cloud, after you went away, and getting down from the dragon he was riding on, went into the room. I don't know what he did inside, but after a little while he went flying out through the roof, and left the house full of smoke. And when we decided to look and see what he had done, there was no room and not a book to be seen. Only we remember very well, both of us, that as he left, the wicked old man shouted out that we would see later what havoc he had wrought in the house, out of a secret grudge he bore the owner of those books. What's more, he said he was called the sage Muñaton."

"Freston he must have said," put in Don Quixote.

"I don't know," replied the housekeeper, "whether he was called Freston or Friton. I only know that his name ended in *ton*."

"That is right," said Don Quixote. "He is a learned enchanter, and a great enemy of mine. He bears me malice, for through his arts and spells he knows that in the fullness of time I shall engage a favourite knight of his in single combat, and that I shall conquer him, and he will not be able to prevent it. That is why he tries to serve me every ill turn he can. But I tell him that he cannot gainsay or avert what Heaven has decreed."

"Who doubts that?" cried his niece. "But what concern of yours are these quarrels, my dear uncle? Wouldn't it be better to stay peacefully at home, and not roam about the world seeking better bread than is made of wheat, never considering that many go for wool and come back shorn?"

"Dear niece," replied Don Quixote, "you are a long way out in your reckoning! Before they shear me I will pluck out and tear off the beards of all who think to touch so much as the tip of one hair of mine." And neither of the women cared to make further reply, for they saw that he was getting into a rage.

As it turned out, he stayed fifteen days at home very quietly, showing no sign of any desire to repeat his former strange behaviour; and during that time he had some most pleasant arguments with his two friends, the priest and the barber, on the subject of his statement that the world's greatest need was of knights errant, and that knight errantry should be revived in his person. The priest sometimes contradicted him, and sometimes gave in to him, for if he had not resorted to this trick, he would not have stood a chance of bringing him to reason.

All this while Don Quixote was plying a labourer, a neighbour of his and an honest man—if a poor man may be called honest—but without much salt in his brain-pan. In the end, he talked to him so much, persuaded him so hard and gave him such promises that the poor yokel made up his mind to go out with him and serve him as squire. Don Quixote told him, amongst other things, that he ought to feel well disposed to come with him, for some time or another an adventure might occur that would win him in the twinkling of an eye some isle, of which he would leave him governor. These promises and others like them made Sancho Panza—for this was the labourer's name—leave his wife and children and take service as his neighbour's squire. Then Don Quixote set about raising money, and by selling one thing, pawning another, and making a bad bargain each time, he raised a reasonable sum. He also fixed himself up with a shield, which he borrowed from a friend, and patching up his broken helmet as best he could, he gave his squire Sancho notice of the day and the hour on which he proposed to set out, so that he should provide himself with all that was most needful; and he particularly told his squire to bring saddle-bags. Sancho said that he would, and that he was also thinking of bringing a very fine ass he had, for he was not too good at much travelling on foot. At the mention of the ass Don Quixote hesitated a little, racking his brains to remember whether any knight errant ever had a squire mounted on ass-back, but no case came to his memory. But, for all that, he

When they got into Don Quixote's room he was already out of bed, and repeating his shouting and raving, laying about him with his sword in all directions with slashes and back-strokes, as wide awake as if he had never been asleep. (page 57) decided to let him take it, intending to provide him with a more proper mount at the earliest opportunity by unhorsing the first discourteous knight he should meet. He provided himself also with shirts and everything else he could, following the advice which the innkeeper had given him. And when all this was arranged and done, without Panza saying goodbye to his wife and children, or Don Quixote taking leave of his housekeeper and niece, they departed from the village one evening, quite unobserved, and rode so far that night that at daybreak they thought they were safe, and that even if anyone came out to search for them they would not be found.

Sancho Panza rode on his ass like a patriarch, with his saddle-bags and his leather bottle, and a great desire to see himself governor of the isle his master had promised him. It chanced that Don Quixote took the same route and struck the same track across the plain of Montiel as on his first expedition; but he travelled with less discomfort than before, as it was the hour of dawn, and the sun's rays, striking them obliquely, did not annoy them. Then presently Sancho Panza said to his master, "Mind, your worship, good Sir Knight Errant, that you don't forget about the isle you promised me; for I shall know how to govern it, never mind how big it is."

To which Don Quixote replied, "You must know, friend Sancho Panza, that it was a custom much in use among knights errant of old to make their squires governors of the isles or kingdoms they won; and I am determined that, for my part, so beneficial a custom shall not lapse. On the contrary, I intend to improve on it, for they often, perhaps most often, waited till their squires were grown old; and when they were worn out in their service, from bad days and worse nights, they gave them some title of count, or perhaps marquis, of some valley or province of more or less importance. But if you live and I live, it may well be that before six days are gone by I may win some kingdom with others depending upon it, and one of them may prove just right for you to rule. Do not think this any great matter, for adventures befall knights errant in such unheard-of and un-thought-of ways that I might easily be able to bestow on you even more than I promise."

"At that rate," said Sancho Panza, "if by any of those miracles your worship speaks of I were to become king, Juana Gutierrez, my poppet, would be a queen, no less, and my children princes."

"Well, who doubts it?" answered Don Quixote.

"I doubt it," replied Sancho Panza, "for I'm pretty sure that even if God rained kingdoms on the earth, none of them would sit well on Mary Gutierrez' head. As a queen she would not be worth a halfpenny, sir. Countess might suit her better, with God's help."

"Put the matter in God's hands, Sancho," replied Don Quixote. "He will give her what is best for her. But do not humble your heart so low as to be content with anything less than to be Captain General."

"I won't, dear sir," replied Sancho Panza, "especially with a master as grand as your worship, who will know how to give me all that will be good for me and that I can bear."

❧ 8 ❧

Of the Valorous Don Quixote's Success
in the Dreadful and Never Before Imagined
Adventure of the Windmills,
with Other Events worthy of Happy Record

*A*t that moment they caught sight of some thirty or forty windmills, which stand on that plain, and as soon as Don Quixote saw them he said to his squire, "Fortune is guiding our affairs better than we could have wished. Look over there, friend Sancho Panza, where more than thirty monstrous giants appear. I intend to do battle with them and take all their lives. With their spoils we will begin to get rich, for this is a fair war, and it is a great service to God to wipe such a wicked brood from the face of the earth."

"What giants?" asked Sancho Panza.

"Those you see there," replied his master, "with their long arms. Some giants have them about six miles long."

"Take care, your worship," said Sancho; "those things over there are not giants but windmills, and what seem to be their arms are the sails, which are whirled round in the wind and make the millstone turn."

"It is quite clear," replied Don Quixote, "that you are not experienced in this matter of adventures. They are giants, and if you are afraid, go away and say your prayers, whilst I advance and engage them in fierce and unequal battle."

As he spoke, he dug his spurs into his steed Rocinante, paying no attention to his squire's shouted warning that beyond all doubt they were windmills and no giants he was advancing to attack. But he went on, so positive that they were giants that he neither listened to Sancho's cries nor noticed what they were, even when he got near them. Instead he went on shouting in a loud voice, "Do not fly, cowards, vile creatures, for it is one knight alone who assails you."

At that moment a slight wind arose, and the great sails began to move. At the sight of which Don Quixote shouted, "Though you wield more arms than the giant Briareus, you shall pay for it!" Saying this, he commended himself with all his soul to his Lady Dulcinea, beseeching her aid in his great peril. Then, covering himself with his shield and putting his lance in the rest, he urged Rocinante forward at a full gallop and attacked the nearest windmill, thrusting his lance into the sail. But the wind turned it with such violence that it shivered his weapon in pieces, dragging the horse and his rider with it, and sent the knight rolling badly injured across the plain. Sancho Panza rushed to his assistance as fast as his ass could trot, but when he came up he found that the knight could not stir. Such a shock had Rocinante given him in their fall.

"O my goodness!" cried Sancho. "Didn't I tell your worship to look what you were doing, for they were only windmills? Nobody could mistake them, unless he had windmills on the brain."

"Silence, friend Sancho," replied Don Quixote. "Matters of war are more subject than most to continual change. What is more, I think—and that is the truth—that the same sage Friston who robbed me of my room and my books has turned those giants into wind-mills, to cheat me of the glory of conquering them. Such is the enmity he bears me, but in the very end his black arts shall avail him little against the goodness of my sword."

"God send it as He will," replied Sancho Panza, helping the knight to get up and remount Rocinante, whose shoulders were half dislocated.

As they discussed this last adventure they followed the road to the pass of Lapice where, Don Quixote said, they could not fail to find many and various adventures, as many travellers passed that way. He was much concerned, however, at the loss of his lance, and speaking of it to his squire, remarked, "I remember reading that a certain Spanish knight called Diego Perez de Vargas, having broken his sword in battle, tore a great bough or limb from an oak, and performed such deeds with it that day, and pounded so many Moors, that he earned the surname of the Pounder, and thus he and his descendants from that day onwards have been called Vargas y Machuca. I mention this because I propose to tear down just such a limb from the first oak we meet, as big and as good as his; and I intend to do such deeds with it that you may consider yourself most fortunate to have won the right to see them. For you will witness things which will scarcely be credited."

"With God's help," replied Sancho, "and I believe it all as your worship says. But sit a bit more upright, sir, for you seem to be riding lop-sided. It must be from the bruises you got when you fell."

"That is the truth," replied Don Quixote. "And if I do not complain of the pain, it is because a knight errant is not allowed to complain of any wounds, even though his entrails may be dropping out through them."

"If that's so, I have nothing more to say," said Sancho, "but God knows I should be glad if your worship would complain if anything hurt you. I must say, for my part, that I have to cry out at the slightest twinge, unless this business of not complaining extends to knights errants' squires as well."

Don Quixote could not help smiling at his squire's simplicity, and told him that he could certainly complain how and when he pleased, whether he had any cause or no, for up to that time he had never read anything to the contrary in the laws of chivalry.

Sancho reminded him that it was time for dinner, but his master replied that he had need of none, but that his squire might eat whenever he pleased. With this permission, Sancho settled himself as comfortably as he could on his ass and, taking out what he had put into the saddle-bags, jogged very leisurely along behind his master, eating all the while; and from time to time he raised the bottle with such relish that the best-fed publican in Malaga might have envied him. Now, as he went along like this, taking repeated gulps, he entirely forgot the promise his master had made him, and reckoned that going in search of adventures, however dangerous, was more like pleasure than hard work.

They passed that night under some trees, from one of which our knight tore down a dead branch to serve him as some sort of lance, and stuck into it the iron head of the one that had been broken. And all night Don Quixote did not sleep but thought about his Lady Dulcinea, to conform to what he had read in his books about knights errant spending many sleepless nights in woodland and desert dwelling on the memory of their ladies. Not so Sancho Panza; for, as his stomach was full, and not of chicory water, he slept right through till morning. And, if his master had not called him, neither the sunbeams, which struck him full on the face, nor the song of the birds, who in great number and very joyfully greeted the dawn of the new day, would have been enough to wake him. As he got up he made a trial of his bottle, and found it rather limper than the night before; whereat his heart sank, for he did not think they were taking the right road to remedy this defect very quickly. Don Quixote wanted no breakfast for, as we have said, he was determined to subsist on savoury memories. Then they turned back on to the road they had been on before, towards the pass of Lapice, which they sighted about three in the afternoon.

"Here," exclaimed Don Quixote on seeing it, "here, brother Sancho Panza, we can steep our arms to the elbows in what they call adventures. But take note that though you see me in the greatest danger in the world, you must not put your hand to your sword to defend me, unless you know that my assailants are rabble and common folk, in which case you may come to my aid. But should they be knights, on no account will it be legal or permissible, by the laws of chivalry, for you to assist me until you are yourself knighted."

"You may be sure, sir," replied Sancho, "that I shall obey your worship perfectly there. Especially as I am very peaceable by nature and all against shoving myself into brawls and quarrels. But as to defending myself, sir, I shan't take much notice of those rules, because divine law and human law allow everyone to defend himself against anyone who tries to harm him."

"I never said otherwise," replied Don Quixote, "but in the matter of aiding me against knights, you must restrain your natural impulses."

"I promise you I will," replied Sancho, "and I will observe this rule as strictly as the Sabbath."

In the middle of this conversation two monks of the order of St. Benedict appeared on the road, mounted on what looked like dromedaries; for the two mules they were riding were quite as big. They were wearing riding-masks against the dust and carrying sunshades. And behind them came a coach, with four or five horsemen escorting it, and two muleteers on foot.

In the coach, as it afterwards turned out, was a Basque lady travelling to Seville to join her husband, who was going out to take up a very important post in the Indies. The monks were not of her company, but merely journeying on the same road.

Now no sooner did Don Quixote see them in the distance than he said to his squire, "Either I am much mistaken, or this will prove the most famous adventure ever seen. For those dark shapes looming over there must, beyond all doubt, be enchanters bearing off in that coach some princess they have stolen; and it is my duty to redress this wrong with all my might."

"This will be a worse job than the windmills," said Sancho. "Look, sir, those are Benedictine monks, and the coach must belong to some travellers. Listen to me, sir. Be careful what you do, and don't let the Devil deceive you."

"I have told you," replied Don Quixote, "that you know very little of this subject of adventures. What I say is true, and now you will see it."

So saying, he rode forward and took up his position in the middle of the road along which the monks were coming; and when they got so near that he thought they could hear him, he called out in a loud voice, "Monstrous and diabolical crew! Release immediately the noble princesses whom you are forcibly carrying off in that coach, or prepare to receive instant death as the just punishment for your misdeeds."

The monks reined in their mules, and stopped in astonishment at Don Quixote's appearance and at his speech.

"Sir Knight," they replied, "we are neither monstrous nor diabolical, but two monks of St. Benedict travelling about our business, nor do we know whether there are any princesses being carried off in that coach or not."

"No fair speeches for me, for I know you, perfidious scoundrels!" cried Don Quixote. Then, without waiting for their reply, he spurred Rocinante and, with his lance lowered, charged at the foremost monk with such vigour and fury that, if he had not slid from his mule, he would have been thrown to the ground badly hurt, if not killed outright. The second monk, on seeing his companion so treated, struck his heels into his stout mule's flanks and set her galloping over the plain fleeter than the wind itself. When Sancho Panza saw the monk on the ground, he got down lightly from his ass, ran up and started to strip him of his clothes. Upon this, two servants of the monks arrived and asked him why he was stripping their master. Sancho replied that the clothes fell rightly to his share as spoils of the battle which his master, Don Quixote, had won. The lads, who did not get the joke nor understand this talk of spoils and battles, saw that Don Quixote had gone off and was talking with the ladies in the coach, and so fell upon Sancho and knocked him down. And, pulling every hair from his beard, they kicked him mercilessly, and left him stretched on the ground, breathless and stunned. Then, without a moment's hesitation, the monk remounted his mule, trembling, terrified and as white as a sheet; and as soon as he was up he spurred after his comrade, who was waiting for him some distance off, watching to see the upshot of this sudden attack. But without caring to wait for the end of the adventure, they went on

As he spoke, he dug his spurs into his steed Rocinante,
paying no attention to his squire's shouted warning that
beyond all doubt they were windmills and no giants he was
advancing to attack. (page 66)

their way, crossing themselves more often than if they had had the Devil himself at their backs.

Don Quixote, as we have said, was talking with the lady in the coach. "Your fair ladyship may now dispose of yourself as you desire, for now the pride of your ravishers lies in the dust, over-thrown by this strong arm of mine. And lest you be racked with doubt as to the name of your deliverer, know that I am Don Quixote de la Mancha, knight errant, adventurer and captive to the peerless and beautiful lady, Dulcinea del Toboso. And in requital of the benefit you have received from me, I would ask no more of you than to go to El Toboso and present yourself on my behalf before that lady, telling her what I have done for your deliverance."

All that Don Quixote said was overheard by one of the squires accompanying the coach, a Basque. And when he saw that the knight would not let them pass, but was talking of their turning back at once to El Toboso, he went up to Don Quixote and, grasping his lance, addressed him in bad Castilian and worse Basque.

"Get along, you ill-gotten knight. By God who made me, if you do not leave coach I kill you, sure as I be Basque."

Don Quixote understood him very well, and replied with great calm, "If you were a knight, as you are not, I should have punished your rash insolence by now, you slavish creature."

"I not gentleman? I swear you liar, as I am a Christian. You throw down lance and draw sword, and you will see you are carrying the water to the cat. Basque on land, gentleman at sea. A gentleman, by the Devil, and you lie if you say otherwise!"

" 'Now you shall see,' said Agrages," quoted Don Quixote, and threw his lance down on the ground. Then, drawing his sword and grasping his shield, he rushed at his antagonist, determined to take his life. When the Basque saw him coming he would have liked to get down from his mule, as it was a poor sort of hired beast and not to be trusted, but there was nothing for it but to draw his sword. He was, however, lucky enough to be near the coach, from which he was able to snatch a cushion to serve as a shield; whereupon they immediately fell to, as if they had been two mortal enemies. The rest of the party tried to pacify them, but could not, for the Basque swore in his uncouth language that if they did not let him finish the battle, he would himself kill his mistress and all who hindered him.

The lady in the coach, amazed and terrified at the sight, made the coachman drive off a little way, and sat watching the deadly struggle from a distance. In the course of the fight the Basque dealt Don Quixote a mighty blow on one shoulder, thrusting above his shield, and had our knight been without defence he would have been cleft to the waist. When Don Quixote felt the weight of that tremendous stroke he cried out aloud, "O lady of my soul, Dulcinea, flower of beauty, come to the aid of this your knight, who for the sake of your great goodness is now in this dire peril!"

To speak, to raise his sword, to cover himself with his shield and attack the Basque: all this was the work of a moment. For he had resolved to risk everything upon a single stroke. The Basque, seeing him come on, judged Don Quixote's courage by his daring, and decided to do the same as he. So he covered himself well with his cushion and waited, unable to turn his mule in either direction, for the beast was now dead weary, and not being made for such games, could not budge a step.

Don Quixote, as we have said, rushed at the wary Basque with sword aloft, determined to cleave him to the waist; and the Basque watched, with his sword also raised and well guarded by his cushion; while all the by-standers trembled in terrified suspense, hanging upon the issue of the dreadful blows with which they threatened one another. And the lady of the coach and her waiting-women offered a thousand vows and prayers to all the images and places of devotion in Spain, that God might deliver their squire and them from the great peril they were in.

But the unfortunate thing is that the author of this history left the battle in suspense at this critical point, with the excuse that he could find no more records of Don Quixote's exploits than those related here. It is true that the second author of this work would not believe that such a curious history could have been consigned to oblivion, or that the learned of La Mancha could have been so incurious as not to have in their archives or in their registries some documents relating to this famoius knight. So, strong in this opinion, he did not despair of finding the conclusion of this delightful story and, by the favour of Heaven, found it, as shall be told in our second part.

❧ 9 ❧

Of the Conclusion of
the Stupendous Battle between
the Gallant Basque
and the Valiant Manchegan

*I*n the first part of this history we
left the valiant Basque and the famous Don Quixote with naked
swords aloft, on the point of dealing two such furious downward
strokes as, had they struck true, would have cleft both knights
asunder from head to foot, and split them like pomegranates. At this
critical point our delightful history stopped short and remained
mutilated, our author failing to inform us where to find the missing
part. This caused me great annoyance, for my pleasure from the
little I had read turned to displeasure at the thought of the small
chance there was of finding the rest of this delightful story. For it
seemed to me that the greater part was missing. It appeared to my
mind impossible, and contrary to all sound custom, that so good a
knight should have lacked a sage to undertake the writing of his
unparalleled achievements, since there never was one of those
knights errant who—as the people say—go out on their adventures,
that ever lacked one. For every one of them had one or two sages
ready at hand, not only to record their deeds, but to describe their
minutest thoughts and most trivial actions, however much con-

cealed; and so good a knight could not have been so unfortunate as to lack what Platir and the like had in such abundance. I really could not bring myself to believe that such a gallant history could have been left maimed and mutilated, and laid the blame on the malice of time, the devourer and consumer of all things, for either concealing or destroying the sequel. On the other hand, I thought that, as there had been found among Don Quixote's books some as modern as *The Unveiling of Jealousy* and *Nymphs and Shepherds of Henares,* his history must be modern too, and that, though it might not be written down, it would be remembered by the people of his village and of the neighbourhood. This thought made me anxious and eager for real and authentic knowledge of the whole life and marvels of our famous Spaniard, Don Quixote de la Mancha, the light and mirror of Manchegan chivalry, and the first man of our times, of these calamitous times of ours, to devote himself to the toils and exercise of knight errantry; to redress wrongs, aid widows and protect maidens, such as roam up-hill and down-dale with their whips and palfreys and their whole virginities about them. For there were virgins in the olden days who, unless ravished by some rogue or by a boor with his steel cap and axe or by some monstrous giant, never slept a night under a roof all their lives, and at the age of eighty went to their graves as spotless virgins as the mothers that bore them. Now I say that for this, and for many other reasons our gallant Quixote deserves continuous and immemorial praise; and even I should have my share, for my toil and pains in searching for the end of this delightful history. Though well I know that if Heaven, chance, and good fortune had not aided me, the world would have remained without the amusement and pleasure which an attentive reader may now enjoy for as much as two hours on end.

This is how the discovery occurred. One day I was in the Alcana at Toledo, when a lad came to sell some parchments and old papers to a silk merchant. Now as I have a taste for reading even torn papers lying in the streets, I was impelled by my natural inclination to take up one of the parchment books the lad was selling, and saw in it characters which I recognized as Arabic. But though I could recognize them I could not read them, and looked around to see if there was not some Spanish-speaking Moor about, to read them to me; and it was not difficult to find such an interpreter there. For, even if I had wanted one for a better and older language, I should have found one. In short, chance offered me one, to whom I explained what I wanted, placing the book in his hands. He opened it in the middle, and after reading a little began to laugh. I asked him what he was laughing at, and he answered that it was at something written in the margin of the book by way of a note. I asked him to tell me what it was and, still laughing, he answered: "This is what is written in the margin: 'They say that Dulcinea del Toboso, so often mentioned in this history, was the best hand at salting pork of any woman in all La Mancha.' "

When I heard the name of Dulcinea del Toboso I was surprised and astonished, for I immediately surmised that these books must contain the story of Don Quixote. With this idea I pressed him to read the beginning, and when he did so, making an extempore translation from the Arabic into Castilian, he said that the heading was: History of Don Quixote de la Mancha, written by Cide Hamete Benengeli, Arabic historian. I needed great caution to conceal the joy I felt when the title of the book reached my ears. Running to the silk merchant, I bought all the lad's parchments and papers for half a *real,* but if he had had any sense and known how much I wanted them, he might very well have demanded and got more than six *reals* from the sale. I then went off with the Moor into the cloister of the cathedral, and asked him to translate for me into Castilian everything in those books that dealt with Don Quixote, adding nothing and omitting nothing; and I offered to pay him whatever he asked. He was satisfied with fifty pounds of raisins and three bushels of wheat, and promised to translate them well, faithfully, and very quickly. But, to make the business easier and not to let such a prize out of my hands, I took him to my house; and there in little more than six weeks he translated it all just as it is set down here.

On the first sheet was a very life-like picture of Don Quixote's fight with the Basque. Both were shown in the very postures the story describes, with swords aloft, the one covered by his shield, the other by his cushion, and the Basque's mule so life-like that you could tell from a mile off that it was a hired one.

At the feet of the Basque was a scroll that read, "Don Sancho de Azpeitia," which no doubt was his name: and at Rocinante's was another which read, "Don Quixote." Rocinante was marvellously painted, so long and lank, so hollow and lean, with such a sharp backbone, and so far wasted in consumption that it was quite clear at a glance how wisely and rightly he had been called Rocinante. Beside him stood Sancho Panza, holding his ass by the halter, and at his feet was another label which read, "Sancho Zancas"; and according to the picture he must have had a big belly, a short body, and long shanks; which must be what gave him the names of Panza and Zancas, for he is called by both these names at different times in the history. There were some other details to be seen, but they are none of them of great importance, and have no concern with the faithful telling of this story;—and no story is bad if it is truthful.

Now, if any objection can be made against the truth of this history, it can only be that its narrator was an Arab—men of that nation being ready liars, though as they are so much our enemies he might be thought rather to have fallen short of the truth than to have exaggerated. So it seems to me, for when he could and should have let himself go in praise of so worthy a knight he seems deliberately to have passed on in silence, an ill deed and malicious, since historians are bound by right to be exact, truthful, and absolutely un-prejudiced, so that neither interest nor fear, dislike nor affection, should make them turn from the path of truth, whose mother is history, rival of time, storehouse of great deeds, witness of the past, example and lesson to the present, warning to the future. In this history I know that you will find all the entertainment you can desire, and if any good quality is missing, I am certain that it is the fault of its dog of an author rather than any default in the subject. To conclude, the second part, according to the translator, began thus:

The trenchant swords of the two valorous and furious combatants, brandished aloft, seemed to threaten the heavens, the earth, and the pit of hell, such was their courageous aspect. The first to strike his blow was the choleric Basque; and he struck with such force and fury that if the edge of his sword had not turned in its descent, that one blow would have been enough to finish the dire conflict and all our knight's adventures. But good fortune was preserving him for greater things, and twisted his enemy's sword, so that, although it struck him on his left shoulder, it did him no other injury than to disarm all that side, taking with it a great piece of his helmet with half an ear, all of which fell to the ground in hideous ruin, leaving our knight in a very evil plight.

God help me, but who is there could worthily describe the rage which now entered the heart of our Manchegan on finding himself thus treated? All that can be said is that he rose once more in his stirrups and, grasping his sword tighter in both his hands, brought it down with such fury full on the Basque's cushion and on his head, that despite that protection he began to spout blood out of his nostrils, his mouth, and his ears, as if a mountain had fallen on him. He looked as if he was going to tumble off his mule, which he would no doubt have done if he had not clung round her neck. But even so he lost his stirrups and then let go with his arms; while the beast, terrified by the weight of the blow, began to gallop about the field, and with a plunge or two threw her master on to the ground.

Don Quixote was looking on most composedly. But, when he saw the squire fall, he jumped down from his horse and, running very nimbly up to him, put the point of his sword between his enemy's eyes, bidding him surrender or he would cut off his head. The Basque was so stunned that he could not answer a word, and things would have gone badly with him, so blind with rage was Don Quixote, if the ladies in the coach, who till then had been watching the fight in dire dismay, had not run to the spot, and begged him very earnestly to do them the great kindness and favour of sparing their squire's life.

To which request Don Quixote replied very haughtily and gravely, "Certainly, fair ladies; I am most willing to do what you ask. But there must be one condition agreed, which is that this knight shall promise me to go to the town of El Toboso, and present himself from me before the peerless Lady Dulcinea, so that she may deal with him according to her pleasure."

The terrified and distressed ladies did not consider what Don Quixote required nor ask who Dulcinea was, but promised him that the squire should carry out the knight's command.

"Then, upon your word," said Don Quixote, "I will do him no other hurt, though he richly deserves it at my hands."

⊰ 10 ⊱

Of the Pleasant Conversation
between Don Quixote
and His Squire Sancho Panza

*I*n the meantime Sancho Panza had got up again after his rough handling by the monks' servants, and had stood watching the battle Don Quixote was fighting, praying to God in his heart to be pleased to grant his master the victory, and that out of it he might gain an isle of which he could be governor, as he had been promised. Then, when he saw that the contest was over and his master about to remount Rocinante, he ran up to hold his stirrup, and, before Don Quixote was up, fell down on his knees before him, seized his hand, kissed it, and said, "Be so kind, my dear lord Don Quixote, as to make me governor of the isle you have won in this dreadful fight; for however big it is, I feel strong enough to govern it as well as any man who ever governed isles in all the world."

To this Don Quixote replied, "Observe, brother Sancho, that this adventure and others of this kind are not adventures of isles but of cross-roads, from which nothing is to be gained but a broken head and the loss of an ear. Be patient, for adventures will occur whereby I shall not only be able to make you governor, but something greater still."

Sancho thanked him warmly and, once more kissing his hand and the hem of his coat, helped him to mount Rocinante. Then he got on to his ass and began to follow his master, who went off at a brisk trot without taking leave of the ladies in the coach or saying a word more to them, and rode into a near-by wood. Sancho followed him as fast as his ass could go, but Rocinante moved so swiftly that he found himself left behind, and had to shout after his master to wait for him. This Don Quixote did, reining Rocinante in until his weary squire came up, to say as he overtook him, "I think, sir, that it would be wise for us to retire to some church. For, seeing in what a bad way you left that man you fought with, I shouldn't wonder if they were to report the matter to the Holy Brotherhood and have us arrested; and, my goodness, if they do that, we shall sweat blood before we get out of gaol."

"Silence!" said Don Quixote. "Where have you ever heard or read of a knight errant being brought before a judge, however many homicides he may have committed?"

"I don't know anything about your *omecides,*" replied Sancho. "I have never tried one in my life. I only know that the Holy Brotherhood has something to say to people who fight in the fields, and the other matter's no concern of mine."

"Do not worry, my friend," said Don Quixote. "I will deliver you from the hands of the Chaldeans, let alone the Holy Brotherhood. But tell me, on your oath, have you ever seen a more valorous knight than I am on the whole face of the earth? Have you ever read in histories of one who has or had more spirit in the attack, more wind in the holding out, more art in the wounding, or more skill in the overthrowing?"

"To tell you the truth," replied Sancho, "I've never read any histories at all, because I can't read or write. But I'll stake my oath I've never served a braver master than your worship in all the days of my life. Pray God these brave deeds won't be paid for where I just said! But, I beg you, your worship, let me attend to you, for you are losing a lot of blood from that ear, and I've lint here and a little white ointment in the saddle-bag."

"All that would have been quite needless," replied Don Quixote, "if I had remembered to make a flask of the Balsam of Fierabras. One single drop of that would save us both time and medicine."

"What flask and what balsam is that?" asked Sancho Panza.

"It is a balsam," replied Don Quixote, "the recipe for which lies in my memory. With it there is no need to fear death nor so much as to think of dying of any wound. So, when I have made some and given it to you, if ever you see me cut through the middle in some battle—as very often happens—you have only to take the part of my body that has fallen to the ground and place it neatly and cunningly, before the blood congeals, on to the half that is still in the saddle, taking especial care to make them fit exactly. Then you must give me just two drops of this balsam to drink and, you will see, I shall be as sound as an apple."

"If that's so," said Panza, "from now on I renounce the governorship of the promised isle, and all I want in payment for all my good services is for your worship to give me the recipe for that marvellous liquor. For I think it would be worth more than two *reals* an ounce, and I need no more than that to spend the rest of my life in honour and comfort. But I should like to know now whether it costs much to make."

"For less than three *reals* you can make half a gallon or more," answered Don Quixote.

"Good Lord!" replied Sancho. "What's preventing you from making it, sir, and teaching me as well?"

"Hush, friend," replied Don Quixote. "I mean to teach you even greater secrets and do you even greater favours. But for the moment let us dress our wounds, for my ear hurts me more than I like."

Sancho got some lint and ointment out of the saddle-bag. But when Don Quixote saw his helmet he almost went out of his mind. Putting his hand to his sword and raising his eyes to Heaven, he cried, "I swear on oath, by the Creator of all things, and by the four Holy Gospels in which they are amply recorded, to lead the life that the great Marquis of Mantua led when he swore to avenge the death of his nephew Baldwin, vowing not to eat bread at table, nor lie with

But without caring to wait for the end of the adventure, they went on their way, crossing themselves more often than if they had had the Devil himself at their backs. (page 70) his wife—and some other things, which, though I cannot remember them, I will take as here spoken—until I have exacted entire vengeance on the man who has done me this outrage."

On hearing which Sancho exclaimed, "Consider, Don Quixote, that if the knight has complied with your orders and presented himself before my lady Dulcinea del Toboso, he will already have done his duty, and deserves no other punishment unless he commits a new crime."

"You have spoken well and justly," replied Don Quixote; "and so I annul my oath so far as it concerns wreaking fresh vengeance on him. But I swear and confirm anew, that I will lead the life I have vowed to until by force of arms I win from some knight another helmet as good. Do not imagine, Sancho, that I take this oath as a mere bubble. For I know very well what precedent I am following, since exactly similar events occurred in the case of Mambrino's helmet, which cost Sacripante so dear."

"I wish your worship would send these oaths to the Devil, dear master," replied Sancho, "for they're very bad for the health and very harmful to the conscience. Besides, tell me now—if perhaps we don't meet a man armed with a helmet for a long time, what shall we do then? Have we got to keep the vow, and put up with all the inconvenience and discomfort of lying in our clothes, and never sleeping in a village, and all those hundreds of penances in that mad old Marquis of Mantua's oath, that your worship's set on reviving? Consider carefully, sir. There aren't any men in armour travelling on any of these roads, but only carriers and carters, who not only don't wear helmets, but have probably never heard of them in all the days of their life."

"You are wrong about that," said Don Quixote, "for we shall not be two hours at these cross-roads before we see more armed men than came to the siege of Albraca to carry off the fair Angelica."

"Then I agree!" said Sancho. "And please God we come well out of it, and the time arrives when you win that isle which is costing me so dear—And then let me die!"

"I have told you already, Sancho, not to worry on that account.

For if there is no isle to be had, there is always the Kingdom of Denmark or of Sobradisa, that will fit you like a ring on your finger. What is more, you should like them better, as they are on dry land. But let us leave this to time, and see if you have anything for us to eat in those saddle-bags, because soon we are going in search of a castle where we can lodge tonight and make for ourselves the balsam I spoke of, for I swear to God this ear of mine hurts me exceedingly."

"I have an onion here and a bit of cheese," said Sancho, "and a few hunks of bread. But they are not the victuals for a valiant knight like your worship."

"How little you understand," replied Don Quixote. "I would have you know, Sancho, that it is a point of honour with knights errant not to eat once in a month, and when they do eat to take what they find nearest to hand. You would have realized this if you had read as many histories as I have. For in all the many I have read I have never found more than a passing mention of what knight errants ate, except at those sumptuous banquets they used to be given; for the rest of their days they lived on the flowers of the field. But although it is to be understood that they could not live without eating and satisfying all the other needs of nature—for of course they were men like ourselves—it must be presumed that, as they spent the greater part of their lives roaming through woods and wastes, and without a cook, their most ordinary food would be country fare, like that you are offering me now. So, Sancho, my friend, do not worry about what pleases me, nor seek to build the world anew, nor wrench knight errantry off its hinges."

"Pardon me, your worship," said Sancho, "but since, as I told you before, I can't read or write, I don't know or understand the rules of the profession of knighthood. Still from now on I will fill the saddle-bags with all kinds of dried fruit for your worship, because you are a knight. But for myself, as I am not, I'll provide something more substantial in the way of poultry."

"I do not say," replied Don Quixote, "that knights errant are obliged to eat nothing but the fruit you mention, only that it and certain herbs they used to find in the fields were their ordinary fare."

"It's a good thing," replied Sancho, "to know those herbs, for I'm inclined to think that we may need to make use of that knowledge one day."

Then he took the good things he had mentioned out of the bag, and the two of them ate their dinner peacefully and companionably. Though, as they were anxious to look for somewhere to lodge that night, they cut their poor dry meal rather short and, mounting at once, made haste to reach some inhabited place before nightfall. But both the sun and their hopes of doing so failed them together near some goatherds' huts; and so they decided to spend the night there. And if it caused Sancho distress not to reach a village, it was a source of satisfaction to his master to sleep beneath the open sky. For it seemed to him that each time he did so he was confirming his title to knighthood by a new act of possession.

⋘ *11* ⋙

What passed between
Don Quixote and Some Goatherds

*T*he knight was very warmly welcomed by the goatherds, and Sancho did what he could for Rocinante and his ass before following the odour given off by certain pieces of goat's meat, which were boiling in a pot over the fire. He would have liked at that very moment to see if they were ready to be transferred from the pot to the stomach, but refrained, as the goatherds themselves took them off the fire and, spreading some sheepskins on the ground, hurriedly set out their rustic table. Then, with a great show of goodwill, they invited knight and squire to share what they had. Six of them who belonged to the fold begged Don Quixote with rough compliments to sit on a trough which they had set upside down for him, and then seated themselves round on the skins.

The knight took this seat, but Sancho remained standing to fill his master's cup, which was a horn one. But when he saw his squire in this posture, Don Quixote said, "So that you may see, Sancho, the virtue there is in knight errantry, and how speedily those who perform any function in it may attain the honour and estimation of the world, I wish you to sit here beside me in these good people's company, and to be on terms of equality with me, who am your master and natural lord. Eat from my plate and drink from the vessel I drink from; for it can be said of knight errantry as of love: that it puts all things on the same level."

"I thank you," said Sancho, "but I must confess to your worship that so long as I have plenty to eat, I can eat it as well, and better, standing by myself, as seated beside an Emperor. And, to tell you the truth, even if it's only bread and onion that I eat in my corner without bothering about table manners and ceremonies, it tastes to me a great deal better than turkey at other tables where I have to chew slowly, drink little, and wipe my mouth often, and where I can't sneeze and cough when I want to, nor do any of those other things which solitude and freedom allow of. So, dear master, let the honours your worship means to confer on me for being a servant and follower of knight errantry—which being your squire, I am—be exchanged for something of more use and profit to me. For though I acknowledge these honours as received in full, I renounce them from now on and until the end of the world."

"You must sit down all the same, for whosoever humbleth himself, God doth exalt." And, seizing him by the arm, Don Quixote compelled Sancho to sit beside him.

The goatherds did not understand this gibberish about squires and knights errant, but just ate in silence and watched their guests, who with a good grace and appetite crammed down lumps as big as their fists. When the meat course was finished they spread a great quantity of shrivelled acorns on the skins, and set beside them half a cheese, which could not have been harder if it had been made of mortar. All this while the horn cup was not idle, for it went the rounds so often, first full and then empty like the bucket at the well, that they easily exhausted one of the wineskins which hung in sight.

After Don Quixote had sufficiently satisfied his hunger, he took up a handful of acorns and, looking at them intently, gave utterance in the following strain: "Happy the age and happy the times on which the ancients bestowed the name of golden, not because gold, which in this iron age of ours is rated so highly, was attainable without labour in those fortunate times, but rather because the people of those days did not know those two words *thine* and *mine*. In that blessed age all things were held in common. No man, to gain his common sustenance, needed to make any greater effort than to reach up his hand and pluck it from the strong oaks, which literally invited him to taste their sweet and savoury fruit. Clear springs and running rivers offered him their sweet and limpid water in glorious abundance. In clefts of the rock and hollow trees the careful and provident bees formed their commmonwealth, offering to every hand without interest the fertile produce of their fragrant toil. Spontaneously, out of sheer courtesy, the sturdy cork-trees shed their light and broad bark, with which men first covered their houses, supported on rough poles only as a defence against the inclemencies of the heavens. All was peace then, all amity, all concord. The crooked plough had not yet dared to force open and search the kindly bowels of our first mother with its heavy coulter, for without compulsion she yielded from every part of her fertile and broad bosom everything to satisfy, sustain, and delight the children who then possessed her. Then did the simple and lovely shepherdesses go from valley to valley and from hill to hill, with their tresses loose, and without more clothes than were needed to cover modestly what modesty requires, and has always required, to be concealed. Nor were there such ornaments as are in fashion today, all trumped up with Tyrian purple and silk in so many contorted shapes. Yet, with only a few green leaves of dock and ivy plaited together, they must have looked as splendid and elegant as our court ladies with the rare and outlandish inventions which idle curiosity has taught them. In those days the soul's amorous fancies were clothed simply and plainly, exactly as they were conceived, without any search for artificial elaborations to enhance them. Nor had fraud, deceit, or malice mingled with truth and sincerity. Justice pursued her own proper purposes, undisturbed and unassailed by favour and interest, which so impair, restrain, and pervert her today. The law did not then depend on the judge's nice interpretations, for there were none to judge or to be judged. Maiden modesty roamed, as I have said, wherever she would, single and solitary, without fear of harm from strangers' licence or lascivious assault, and if she was undone it was of her own will and desire.

"But now, in this detestable age of ours, no maiden is safe even though she be hidden in the centre of another Cretan labyrinth; for even there, through some chink or through the air, by dint of its accursed persistence, the plague of love gets in and brings them to ruin despite their seclusion. Therefore, as times rolled on and wickedness increased, the order of knights errant was founded for their protection, to defend maidens, relieve widows, and succour the orphans and the needy. Of this order am I, brother goatherds, whom I thank for the welcome and entertainment which you have given to me and my squire; for although by the law of nature all men are bound to befriend knights errant, yet, as you received and entertained me without knowing of this obligation, I should rightly acknowledge your goodwill with the utmost gratitude."

Our knight delivered all this harangue, which might well have been spared, only because the acorns they served him reminded him of the golden age. That is why it came into his head to deliver this purposeless discourse to the goatherds, who listened to him in fascination and bewilderment, without answering a word. Sancho was silent too, for he was busy devouring the acorns and making frequent visits to the second wineskin, which they had hung up on a cork-tree to keep the wine cool. Don Quixote devoted more time to talking than to finishing his supper, but finally the meal was over and one of the goatherds said, "So that you can truly say, Sir Knight Errant, that we have been ready and glad to entertain you, we should like to offer you the pleasure of a song by one of our mates, who will soon be here. He is a clever lad and very much in love; and, what is more, he can read and write, and plays the fiddle as beautifully as can be."

Scarcely had the goatherd finished speaking when the sound of a fiddle reached their ears, and very soon afterwards the musician came in, a very handsome lad of about twenty-two. His companions asked him if he had had supper, and on his answering yes, the goatherd who had asked the question said, "In that case, Antonio, you might do us the favour of a song or two. We want to show this gentleman, our guest, that even in the mountains and woods there are people who know something about music. We have told him of your accomplishments, and we should like you to prove to him that we spoke the truth. So sit down, please, and sing the song about your love, which your uncle the priest composed for you, the one they liked so much in our village."

"I shall be glad to," replied the lad; and without waiting to be asked twice, he sat down on the trunk of a fallen oak and tuned his fiddle. Then presently he began to sing most charmingly:

"I know, Olalla, thou dost me adore,
    Though yet to me the same thou hast not said;
Nor shown it once, by one poor glance or more,
    Since love is soonest by such tongues betrayed.

"But as I ever held thee to be wise,
    I am assured thou bearest me good will,
For he is not unfortunate who sees
    That his affections are not taken ill.

"Yet, for all this, Olalla, it is true
    I, by observance, gather to my woe
That thy mind's framed of brass, by art undue,
    And flint thy bosom is, though it seems snow.

"And yet amidst thy rigour's winter face
    And other shifts thou usest to delay me,
Sometimes hope, peeping through, doth promise grace;
    But, woe is me! I fear 'tis to betray me.

"Sweetest, once in the balance of thy mind
    Poise with just weights my faith, which never yet
Diminished, though disfavour it did find;
    Nor can increase more, though thou favouredst it.

As they were anxious to look for somewhere to lodge that night, they cut their poor dry meal rather short and, mounting at once, made haste to reach some inhabited place before nightfall. (page 89)

"If love be courtesy, as some men say
    I can expect of your humanity
That my hopes shall, howe'er thou dost delay,
    Reap their reward truly and finally.

"If many services be of esteem
    Or power to render a hard heart benign,
Such things I did for thee as make me deem
    I've gained the match and that thou shalt be mine.

"For if at any time thou'st taken heed,
    Thou more than once might'st view how I was gay
To honour thee, on Mondays, in the weed
    Which got me credit on God's holiday.

"For love and finery ever must consort
    Together, since they travel the same ways,
Which made me, when I did to thee resort,
    Come always neat and fine beneath thy gaze.

"Here I omit the dances I have done,
    And music I have at thy window given;
When at cock-crow thou listenedst alone,
    And seem'dst, hearing my voice, to be in heaven.

"Neither will I the praises here recount
    Which of thy beauty I've so often sung,
Which, though they all were true, were ever wont
    To cause the envious to judge me wrong.

"When I spoke to the maid of Berocal,
    Teresa, of thy worth and of thy shape,
'You think,' she said, 'you're in an angel's thrall,
    And yet, for idol, you adore an ape.

" 'She to her trinkets thanks may give, and chains,
    False hair and other shifts that she doth use

To mend her beauty, with a thousand pains
    And tricks, which might love's very self abuse.'

"Stung by her words, I gave her straight the lie,
    Which did her and her cousin so offend,
He challenged me to fight him presently,
    And well thou knowest how that affair did end.

"I do not seek to buy thy favours cheap,
    And when I court and woo thee to be mine
I swear thy virtue need not fear a trap,
    For purer far than that is my design.

"The church has bonds which do so surely hold
    As no silk cord for strength comes to them near;
To thrust thy neck now in the yoke be bold
    And see if I, to follow thee, will fear.

"If thou wilt not, here solemnly I vow,
    By holiest saint enwrapt in precious shrine,
Never to leave those hills where I dwell now,
    Unless it be to become a Capuchin."

Here the goatherd ended his song and, although Don Quixote asked him to give them some more, Sancho did not agree. He was more inclined for sleep than for music, and so he said to his master, "Your worship had better arrange now where you are going to rest tonight. These men work too hard all day long to be able to spend their nights in singing."

"I understand you, Sancho," replied Don Quixote. "It is indeed clear to me that your visits to the wineskin require payment in sleep rather than in music."

"God be praised, but we all enjoyed the drink," replied Sancho.

"I do not deny that," replied Don Quixote. "So settle where you will; but watching befits men of my profession better than sleep. However, it would be as well if you would dress this ear of mine again, for it is hurting me more than it need."

Sancho obeyed. But one of the goatherds looked at the wound and told him not to worry, for he would apply a remedy that would easily heal it. Then, taking some leaves of rosemary, which grew plentifully thereabouts, he chewed them and, mixing them with a little salt, applied them to the ear, which he bandaged tightly, assuring the knight that he would need no other remedy; which proved true.

⊰ *12* ⊱

Of what a Goatherd told
Don Quixote and His Companions

*M*eanwhile another lad arrived, one of those whose job it was to bring the provisions up from the village.

"Do you know what is happening in our place, fellows?" said he.

"How should we know?" answered one of them.

"Then I'll tell you," the lad went on. "The famous shepherd-student Chrysostom died this morning, and the rumour is that he died of love for that devilish Marcela, rich William's daughter, the girl who is always roaming about these parts dressed as a shepherdess."

"For Marcela, you say?" asked one.

"Yes, I do," replied the lad; "and the strange thing is that he has directed in his will that he's to be buried in the fields like a Moor, at the foot of that rock where the spring is, beside the cork-tree, because, the rumour goes—and they say they had it from his own lips—that it was at that spot he saw her for the first time. He has left some other requests as well, such odd ones that the clergy say they mustn't be carried out—and quite right too, because they have a

100

heathenish smack about them. But his great friend Ambrosio the student, who used to go about with him dressed as a shepherd too, answers that everything is to be done exactly as Chrysostom directed. The whole village is in an uproar about it. But, from all they say, they'll end up by doing just as Ambrosio and his friends the shepherds want; and tomorrow they're coming to bring him with great ceremony to the place I spoke of. It will be a sight worth seeing I can tell you, and I shan't miss it, even if it means I can't get back to the village tomorrow."

"We will all see it too," answered the goatherds, "and cast lots which of us is to stay and mind the goats."

"I agree, Peter," said one of them, "though you needn't trouble about casting lots, for I will stay behind for everybody. And don't put it down to generosity on my part or think that I don't want to see what's going on. It's only because of the splinter which stuck into my foot the other day, so that I can't walk."

"We thank you all the same," replied Peter.

Don Quixote requested Peter to tell him who the dead man was, and who was the shepherdess. Peter replied that all he knew was that the dead man was a rich gentleman from a village in those mountains, who had been studying for many years at Salamanca and had finally returned home with the reputation of being very learned and well-read. He was especially famous for knowing the science of the stars, and what the sun and moon were doing up in the skies, for he could always give accurate notice of the *clipse* of the sun and moon.

"*Eclipse* it is called, friend, not *clipse*—the obscuration of those two great luminaries," put in Don Quixote.

But Peter took no notice of this trifle, and went on with his story, saying, "Also he used to foretell whether the year would be fruitful or stale."

"*Sterile* you mean, friend," put in Don Quixote.

"*Sterile* or *stale,*" replied Peter, "it comes to the same thing. So from what he told them, his father and his friends got very rich, because they believed him and did what he advised. He used to say, This year sow barley and not wheat, or, Now you can sow chickpeas and not barley, or, Next year there will be a full crop of olive-oil, and the three years following there won't be a drop."

"That science is called Astrology," said Don Quixote.

"I don't know its name," replied Peter, "but I know that he knew all that and more too. But to come to the point: one day not many months after he came from Salamanca, he threw away the long scholar's gown he used to wear, and appeared all of a sudden dressed like a shepherd with his crook and sheepskin jacket; and at the same time his great friend Ambrosio, who had been his fellow-student, dressed himself as a shepherd too. I had forgotten to say that poor Chrysostom, the dead man, was a great one at making verses, and was so good at them that he used to write the carols for Christmas Eve and the plays for Corpus Christi, which the boys of our village used to act, and everyone said that they were first-class. When the villagers saw the two students unexpectedly dressed as shepherds they were astonished, and could not guess what had induced them to make such an extraordinary transformation. By this time Chrysostom's father had died, and he inherited considerable property, goods as well as land, and quite large flocks and herds, and a great deal of money. He was left in dissolute possession of all this, and indeed he deserved it too, for he was a very good fellow and charitable, and a friend to all good men. And he had a face like a blessing. Afterwards it came out that he had changed his dress only to wander about these wild places after that shepherdess Marcela, whom our lad spoke of a while ago, for poor dead Chrysostom had fallen in love with her. And now I must tell you, for your information, who this young baggage is, for perhaps—no, there is no perhaps about it—you won't hear anything like this in all the days of your life, even if you live longer than Sarna."

"Say *Sarah*," replied Don Quixote, who could not bear the goatherd's blunders.

"*Sarna* (the itch) lives long enough too," replied Peter. "If you make me correct my words at every turn, sir, we shan't be done in a twelvemonth."

"Pardon me, friend," said Don Quixote, "but there is such a

difference between Sarna and Sarah that I had to tell you. However, you answered very rightly, for the itch lives longer than Sarah. So go on with your story, and I will not interrupt you again."

"I was saying, then, my beloved sir," said the goatherd, "that there was a farmer in our village even richer than Chrysostom's father. His name was William and, over and above his many great riches, God gave him a daughter, whose mother, the most respected woman in all these parts, died in giving her birth. I can just see her now, with that face of hers, the sun on one side, as you might say, and the moon on the other. And what a good housewife she was, and such a friend to the poor, and I'm sure that for that alone her soul is this very moment enjoying of God in the other world. Her husband William died of grief at the death of his good wife, leaving his daughter Marcela, young and rich, in the care of one of her uncles, a priest and the parson of our village. The child grew up so beautiful that she used to put us in mind of her mother, who was a great beauty herself, though people thought that the daughter would be even lovelier. So when she was fourteen or fifteen everyone who saw her praised God for giving her such beauty, and most of them fell desperately in love with her. Her uncle kept her very carefully and seldom let her go out. But, all the same, the fame of her great loveliness spread far and wide, and for that reason as much as for her great wealth not only our villagers, but some of the best men for many miles around as well, were begging, persuading and pestering her uncle to give them her hand in marriage. However, he was a really good Christian and, though he would have liked to marry her off soon, since she was of age, would not do so without her consent. Not that he had an eye to the advantage or profit that he would get from managing the girl's estate and putting off her marriage—and that has been remarked in the good priest's favour by more than one circle of village gossips, I can promise you. For I should like you to know, Sir Errant, that in these little places they poke their noses into everything and gossip about everything. You can take my word for it, a parson has to be extraordinarily good to have his parishioners speaking well of him, especially in a village."

"That is true," said Don Quixote; "but go on. It is a very good story, and you, my good Peter, are telling it with fine grace."

"May the Lord's grace never fail me, that is the chief thing. To continue, I must tell you that, although her uncle set out and described to his niece the qualities of each one of her many suitors separately, begging her to choose and marry whom she liked, her only answer was that she didn't want to for the present, because, being so young, she did not feel able to bear the responsibilities of matrimony. And as these excuses seemed reasonable to her uncle, he ceased to press her, and waited till she should be somewhat older and know how to choose a companion to her taste. For, he said, and said rightly, parents ought not to settle their children against their will. But, lo and behold, when we least expected it, the modest Marcela suddenly appeared dressed like a shepherdess and, in spite of her uncle and everyone in the village who tried to dissuade her, off she went into the fields with the other village shepherdesses and started to tend her own flock. And once she had appeared in public and her beauty was exposed to all eyes, I couldn't truthfully tell you how many rich youths, gentlemen, and farmers put on the same dress as Chrysostom, and wandered about these fields, courting her. One of them, as I have told you, was our dead man who, they said, no longer loved her, but adored her. Now you mustn't think that because Marcela adopted this free and unconstrained way of life, with little or no privacy, her modesty or her virtue has fallen under any shadow of suspicion. Far from it; she guards her honour so well that not one of her many suitors has boasted—nor has the right to boast—that she has given him the slightest hope of obtaining his desire. For, although she does not avoid the shepherds' company and conversation, but treats them in a friendly and courteous way, if anyone comes to her to reveal his intentions even by a proper and holy proposal of marriage, she flings him off, like a stone from a catapult. And by this kind of behaviour she does more damage in these parts than if the plague had got in, for her easy manner and her beauty win the hearts of all who have to do with her. They court and love her, but her disdain and her plain speaking drive them to the verge of despair. So it is that they don't know what to say to her, but loudly call her cruel and unkind, and by other such names which clearly show her character. If you were to stay here awhile, sir, one day you would hear the hills and valleys echo with the lament of her rejected suitors. Not far from here is a place where there are about two dozen great beeches, and every one of them has Marcela's name cut on its smooth bark. Above it, too, on some of them, there is a crown carved, as if her lover meant to declare in the clearest terms that Marcela wears and deserves the crown of all human beauty. Here one shepherd sighs; there another moans; from the distance you can hear songs of love; from near at hand dirges of despair. There will be one spending all the hours of the night seated at the foot of an oak or of a crag, never closing his tear-dimmed eyes till the sun finds him there next morning, sunken and lost in his thoughts; and there will be another giving no rest or truce to his sighs, but lying stretched on the burning sand in the most sultry heat of a summer afternoon, and sending his complaints up to the merciful heavens; and over every one of them the beautiful Marcela triumphs, free and unconcerned. And all of us who know her are waiting to see how her haughtiness will end, and who will be the lucky man to come and conquer so intractable a nature and enjoy a beauty so perfect. As all that I have told you is well-known fact, I can easily understand that what our lad has said about the cause of Chrysostom's death is the truth as well. So I advise you, sir, to be sure to join us tomorrow at his burial. It will be very well worth seeing, for Chrysostom has many friends; and it's not more than a mile and a half from here to the place where he directed them to bury him."

"I will certainly be there," said Don Quixote, "and I thank you for the pleasure you have given me by telling me such a delightful story."

"Oh," replied the goatherd, "I don't know even half the things that have happened to Marcela's lovers. But maybe tomorrow we shall fall in with some shepherd on the way who may tell us more. But it would be as well for now if you were to go to sleep under

cover, for the night dew might hurt your wound, though the ointment they put on it is so good that there's no fear of trouble."

Sancho Panza also, who already wished the goatherd to the devil
with his endless story, begged his master to go and sleep in Peter's
hut. This he did and, in imitation of Marcela's lovers, he spent the
rest of the night in thoughts of his lady Dulcinea; while Sancho
Panza's sleep, as he settled down between Rocinante and his ass, was
not that of a rejected lover, but of a soundly kicked human being.

⋆ 13 ⋆

The Conclusion of
the Tale of Marcela the Shepherdess
and Other Matters

*S*carcely had day begun to show
itself on the balconies of the East when five of the six goatherds got
up, and went to wake Don Quixote and to enquire if he still intended
to go and see the famous burial of Chrysostom, for if he did they
would keep him company. Nothing delighted the knight more, and
so he got up and ordered Sancho to saddle the horse and the ass at
once. This was quickly done, and with the same despatch they all set
off on their way. They had gone less than a mile when they came to
a crossroad, where they saw approaching them along another track
some six shepherds dressed in black skins, with their heads crowned
with garlands of cypress and bitter bay. Each of them had a stout
holly-stick in his hand, and with them came also two gentlemen on
horseback, handsomely equipped for travelling, accompanied by
three servants on foot. When the two parties met they exchanged
courteous greetings, and on each one asking where the other was
going, discovered that they were all bound for the burial-place. So
they travelled together.

As they rode on, one of the horsemen observed to his companion,

"I think, Señor Vivaldo, that we can count the hours passed in attending this remarkable funeral time well spent. For, if we are to trust the strange accounts these herdsmen have given us of the dead shepherd and the merciless shepherdess, it cannot fail to be a remarkable event."

"I agree with you," replied Vivaldo, "and I would waste not one day but four rather than miss the sight."

Don Quixote asked them what they had heard about Marcela and Chrysostom. And the traveller answered that early that morning they had met the shepherds and, seeing them in such mournful attire, had asked them why they were so dressed. Then one of them had explained, and related the strange behaviour and beauty of a shepherdess called Marcela, the loves of her many suitors, and the death of that Chrysostom to whose burial they were going. In short, he had told them all that Peter had told Don Quixote. Here this conversation ceased and another began, the one called Vivaldo asking Don Quixote what made him travel thus armed in so peaceful a country. To which the knight replied, "The exercise of my profession does not allow or permit me to ride in any other fashion. Ease, luxury, and repose were invented for soft courtiers; but labour, unease, and arms alone were designed and made for those whom the world calls knights errant, of whose number, though unworthy, I am the very least."

On hearing this, they concluded that he was a madman. But, to make sure of it and to discover what kind of madness his was, Vivaldo went on to ask him what exactly he meant by knights errant.

"Have you not read, sirs," replied Don Quixote, "the annals and histories of England, treating of the famous deeds of King Arthur, whom in our Castilian tongue we commonly call King Artus. There is an ancient and widespread tradition concerning him throughout that kingdom of Great Britain, that he did not die, but by magic art was turned into a crow; and they say that in course of time he will come back to reign, and recover his kingdom and sceptre. For which reason no Englishman can be proved ever to have killed a crow,

"For he was brought to his end by a shepherdess whom he strove to render immortal in the memory of mankind, as those papers you are gazing at could well prove, if he had not ordered me to commit them to the flames as we are committing his body to the earth." (page 117)

from that day to this. Now in this good king's reign there was instituted that famous order of chivalry, the Knights of the Round Table, and there took place, exactly as they are recorded, the loves of Sir Lancelot of the Lake and Queen Guenevere, in which that honourable Lady Quintañona acted as intermediary and confidante. Whence arose that ballad so widely known and so often sung in modern Spain—

> Never was there knight
> By ladies so attended
> As was Lancelot,
> When he came from Britain—

with its sweet and charming story of his deeds of love and his bravery. Now, from that time on, this order of chivalry has been gradually growing and spreading through many and various parts of the world. Famous and renowned for their exploits in that order, were the valiant Amadis of Gaul with all his sons and grandsons to the fifth generation, the valorous Felixmarte of Hyrcania, the never sufficiently praised Tirante the White, and that knight whom we have seen and heard and spoken with almost in our own times, the invincible and valorous Sir Belianis of Greece. That, gentleman, is what it is to be a knight errant, and what I have described to you is the order of chivalry, in which, as I have already said, though a sinner, I have made my profession. What the knights I have told you of professed I profess too; and that is why I am travelling through these wastes and deserts in quest of adventures, with mind resolved to oppose my arms and my person to the greatest perils which fortune may present, in aid of the weak and those in need."

From these arguments the travellers finally decided that Don Quixote was out of his wits, and realized what form of madness it was that possessed him. And they were as astonished as everyone else had been on first making that discovery. Now Vivaldo was a shrewd and cheerful fellow and, to relieve the boredom of the short journey they had still to take before arriving at the place of burial, he tried to give Don Quixote an opportunity of continuing his wild

111

talk, and consequently observed, "It seems to me, Sir Knight Errant, that you have adopted one of the strictest professions on earth, and it is my opinion that even the Carthusian monks' is not so severe a calling."

'The monks' profession may well be as strict," replied Don Quixote, "but whether it is as necessary in the world I am within a hair's breadth of doubting. For, truly, the soldier who carries out his captain's orders does no less than the captain who gives the orders. I mean that the religious, in all peace and quiet, pray Heaven for the well-being of the world; but we soldiers and knights carry out what they pray for, defending it with the strength of our arms and the edge of our swords, beneath no roof but the open sky, exposed to the intolerable beams of the sun in summer and the biting frosts in winter. We, therefore, are God's ministers on earth, and the arms by which His justice is executed here. And whereas matters of war and things of that kind cannot be performed without sweat, toil, and labour, it follows that men whose profession is war must, unquestionably, endure more than those who in assured peace and repose are forever praying God to help the powerless. Far be it from me to say, or even to think, that the state of a knight errant is as good as a cloistered monk's. I only want to argue from my own sufferings that it is most certainly a more painful and belaboured one, hungrier and thirstier, more miserable, ragged and lousy, for there is no doubt that knights errant of old suffered much ill-usage in the course of their lives. And if some of them rose by the valour of their arms to be Emperors, they assuredly paid dearly for it in blood and sweat; and if those who did rise so high had had no enchanters or sages to help them, they would have been defrauded of their desires and cheated of their hopes."

"I agree with you," replied the traveller, "but there is one thing in particular about knights errant that seems wrong to me. That is that when they are on the point of embarking on a great and perilous adventure in which there is manifest danger to their lives, never at the moment of attack do they think of entrusting their souls to God, as every Christian in such peril is bound to do. Instead they commend themselves to their mistresses, with as much fervour and devotion as if these were their God, a practice which seems to me to smack somewhat of paganism."

"Sir," replied Don Quixote, "on no account can it be otherwise, and it would go badly with the knight errant who should act differently. For it is the use and custom of chivalry for the knight errant, in embarking on any great feat of arms, to have his lady before him, and to turn his eyes softly and lovingly upon her, as if thereby begging her favour and protection in the hazardous enterprise that faces him. And even if no one hears him, he is obliged to breathe certain words between his teeth, commending himself to her with all his heart; and of this practice we have innumerable examples in the histories. But it is not to be inferred that they neglect to commend themselves to God, for they have time and opportunity to do so in the course of their task."

"All the same," replied the traveller, "I am still uncertain on one point. I have often read of two knights beginning by bandying words. Then, little by little, their anger begins to kindle, and they turn their horses, make a wide circle in the field, and next, without more ado, charge one another at full speed, commending themselves to their ladies in the midst of the charge; and the usual result of their encounter is that one falls over the cruppers of his horse, speared right through by his opponent's lance; and his opponent too has to cling on to his horse's mane to avoid falling to the ground. Now, I cannot see how the dead man could have had the time to commend himself to God in the course of so very rapid an action. It would have been better if the words spent on commending himself to his lady as he charged had been employed in his duties and obligations as a Christian. What is more, I believe that not all knights errant have ladies to commend themselves to, for they are not all in love."

"That is impossible," replied Don Quixote. "I say that it is impossible that there could be any knight errant without a lady. For it is as right and proper for them to be in love as for the sky to have stars; and I can vouch for it that there has never been a knight errant without a lady in any history whatever. For the very fact of his having no lady would show him to be no legitimate knight, but a bastard who has entered the fortress of chivalry not through the gate but over the fence, like a thief and a robber."

"Nevertheless," said the traveller, "if I remember rightly, I have read that Sir Galaor, brother of the famous Amadis of Gaul, never had a definite lady to commend himself to, and yet was none the worse thought of for that, and was a very valiant and famous knight."

To which Don Quixote replied, "Sir, one swallow does not make a summer. Besides, I know that Sir Galaor was secretly very much in love. Indeed, his habit of paying court to any ladies who attracted him was a trait in his nature which he was unable to control. But, to be brief, it is very well authenticated that he had only one lady whom he had made mistress of his heart, and that he commended himself to her very often and secretly, for he prided himself on being a very secretive knight."

"Then, if it is essential for every knight errant to be in love," said the traveller, "it may be fairly presumed that you, your worship, being a professed knight, have also a lady. If, then, you do not pride yourself on your secrecy like Sir Galaor, I beg you most earnestly, on behalf of all this company and of my self, to inform us of the name, the country, the degree, and the beauty of your lady. For she would count herself fortunate to have all the world know that she is loved and served by such a knight as your worship appears to be."

Here Don Quixote heaved a deep sigh and said, "I cannot affirm whether my sweet enemy is pleased or not at the whole world's knowing that I serve her. I can only say, in reply to your very polite question, that her name is Dulcinea; her country El Toboso, a village in La Mancha; her degree at least that of Princess, for she is my Queen and mistress; her beauty superhuman, for in her are realized all the impossible and chimerical attributes of beauty which poets give to their ladies; that her hair is gold; her forehead the Elysian fields; her eyebrows rainbows; her eyes suns; her cheeks roses; her lips coral; her teeth pearls; her neck alabaster; her breast marble; her hands ivory; she is white as snow; and those parts which modesty has veiled from human sight are such, I think and believe, that discreet reflection can extol them, but make no comparison."

"We should like to know her lineage, race, and family," said Vivaldo.

And Don Quixote replied, "She is not of the ancient Curtii, Caii, or Scipios of Rome; nor of the modern Colonnas and Orsinis; nor of the Moncadas and Requesenes of Catalonia; nor yet of the Rebellas and Villanovas of Valencia; of the Palafoxes, Nuzas, Rocabertis, Corellas, Lunas, Alagones, Urreas, Fozes, and Gurreas of Aragon; of the Cerdas, Manriques, Mendozas, and Guzmans of Castile; nor of the Alencastres, Pallas, and Meneses of Portugal; but of El Toboso of La Mancha, a lineage which, though modern, may yet give noble birth to the most illustrious families of future ages. Let no one contradict me in this except under the conditions which Cervino put beneath the trophy of Roland's arms:

> Let no one move them
> But one who dares his prowess against Roland."

"Although I am descended from the Cachopines of Laredo," replied the traveller, "I shall not dare to compare my family with the El Tobosos of La Mancha; though, to tell you the truth, such a surname has never reached my ears till now."

"How not reached you!" exclaimed Don Quixote.

The whole party was listening most attentively to this conversation, and everyone, even the goatherds and shepherds, realized how very much out of his wits Don Quixote was. Only Sancho Panza took all that his master said for truth, knowing who he was and having known him from his birth. But where he rather hesitated was in believing all that about the fair Dulcinea del Toboso, for he had never heard of such a name or such a princess, although he lived near El Toboso. Now, as they went along deep in this talk, they saw coming down through a gap between two high mountains some twenty shepherds, all in skins of black wool and crowned with garlands which, as they made out later, were, some of them, of yew and some of cypress. Six of their number were carrying a bier

115

covered with a great variety of flowers and branches, and at this sight one of the goatherds remarked, "These men must be bearing Chrysostom's body. The foot of that mountain is the place where he directed them to bury him."

So they hurried forward, and reached the place just as the new-comers had placed the bier on the ground, and as four of them were beginning to hollow the grave beside a hard rock with their pick-axes. The parties exchanged courteous greetings, and then Don Quixote and his companions immediately went to look at the bier, on which they saw a dead body, dressed like a shepherd and apparently about thirty years old, covered with flowers; and, dead though he was, it was clear that in life he had been a handsome and courtly young man. Around him on the bier were several books and a great number of papers, some open and some sealed; and everyone there, spectators, grave-diggers and the rest, kept a strange silence, till one of the dead man's bearers said to another, "Look carefully, Ambrosio, and see if this really is the place which Chrysostom meant, since you wish all the directions in his will to be punctiliously observed."

"This is it, I know," replied Ambrosio, "for here my luckless friend often told me the tale of his misfortune. Here, he said, he first saw that mortal enemy of the human race; here it was too that he first declared to her his passion, which was as honourable as it was ardent; here it was that Marcela finally rejected and scorned him, which caused him to put an end to the tragedy of his miserable life; and here in remembrance of so much misfortune he wished to be consigned to the bowels of eternal oblivion."

Then, turning to Don Quixote and the travellers, he went on, "This body, gentlemen, which you are gazing on with eyes of pity, was the dwelling-place of a soul in which Heaven had placed an infinite portion of its riches. This is the body of Chrysostom, a man of unique genius, singular courtesy and extreme gentleness, a phoenix in friendship, magnificent beyond measure, grave without arrogance, gay without coarseness; and, in short, first in all the art of goodness, and second to none in all the ways of misfortune. He loved and was hated; adored and was disdained; he courted a savage; he strove to soften marble; he pursued the wind; he cried to the desert; he served ingratitude, whose only reward was to make him the prey of death in the midst of his life's course. For he was brought to his end by a shepherdess whom he strove to render immortal in the memory of mankind, as those papers you are gazing at could well prove, if he had not ordered me to commit them to the flames as we are committing his body to the earth."

"Then you would be more rigorous and cruel to them than their owner himself," broke in Vivaldo; "for it is neither just nor proper to carry out a man's bequests when what he orders exceeds all reason. It would not have been right in Augustus Caesar himself if he had consented to carry out all that the divine Mantuan ordered in his will. Therefore, Ambrosio, although you commit your friend's body to the earth, you should not commit his writings to oblivion; for if he was so wronged as to ask it, you should not be so unwise as to comply, but rather, by granting life to these papers, let Marcela's cruelty live forever and serve as an example to men in times to come, so that they may shun and avoid such pitfalls. For we all know the story of your enamoured and ill-fated friend; and we know of your friendship and the reason for his death, and of the instructions he left in his last hours. From this lamentable tale can be judged the greatness of Marcela's cruelty and of Chrysostom's love, and the sincerity of your friendship. We can learn from it, too, the fate of those who rush recklessly down the path which headlong love opens before their eyes. Last night we heard of Chrysostom's death, and that he was to be buried in this place; and so from curiosity and pity we have turned out of our direct way, and agreed to come and see with our own eyes what moved us to such pity when we heard of it. In return for our compassion and our desire, if it were possible to find a remedy, we pray you, wise Ambrosio—at least I do for my part—that instead of burning his papers you will let me take some of them away."

Then, without waiting for the shepherd's reply, he stretched out his hand and took some of them that lay nearest him. Seeing which,

117

Ambrosio said, "Out of courtesy, sir, I will consent to your keeping those you have taken: but it would be vain to think that I shall not burn the rest."

Vivaldo, who longed to know what was in the papers, opened one immediately, and saw that its title was *A Song of Despair*. On hearing which Ambrosio said, "That is the last piece the unhappy man wrote; and so that you may see, sir, to what a pass his misfortune brought him, read it aloud. For you will have time enough for that while they are digging his grave."

"I will do so most gladly," said Vivaldo; and, as all the bystanders were equally curious, they gathered round him in a circle, as he read in a clear voice the poem which follows.

❧ *14* ❧

The Despairing Verses of
the Dead Shepherd
and Other Unexpected Matters

Since you would have me publish, cruel maid,
From tongue to tongue, from one to the other pole,
The efficacy of thy rigour sharp
I'll constrain hell my grieving soul to aid,
And in my breast infuse a ton of dole,
Whereon my voice, as it is wont, may harp
And labour, as I wish, at once to carp
And tell my sorrows and thy murdering deed.
The dreadful voice and accents shall agree,
And, with them mixed, for greater torture, be
Lumps of my wretched bowels, which still bleed.
Then listen, and lend thy attentive ear,
Not well-consorted tunes but howling to hear,
That from my bitter bosom's depth takes flight,
And by constrainèd raving borne away
Issues forth for mine ease and thy despite.

The lion's roaring, and the dreadful cries
Of ravening wolf, and hissing terrible

Of scaly serpent; and the fearful yell
Of some grim monster; and the ominous crow's
Foreboding, sinister caw; the horrible
Sound on the tossing sea of the blustering gale;
The implacable bellow of the new-conquered bull;
The lonely widowed turtle's sobbing moan,
Most mournful, and the dreary night descant
Of the envious owl, commingled with the plaint
Of all the infernal black battalion;
Let all together cry from my aching soul
United in one sound of such sad dole
That all the senses may confounded be,
For my fierce torment needs a manner new
Wherein I may recount my misery.

The doleful echoes of such great confusion
Shall not resound o'er father Tagus' sands
Nor touch the olive-watering Betis' ears.
Of my dire pangs I'll only make effusion
'Midst these steep rocks and in the hollow lands,
With my tongue dead, yet with a living cry;
Or in some hidden vale, or on the shy
Shores that no feet of human kind defile,
Or where the sun has never shown his beam,
Or 'midst the venomous crew of beasts unclean
That draw their being from the teeming Nile.
For though amongst those lofty table-lands
The hollow echo indistinctly sounds
Thy matchless rigour and my cruel pain,
Yet, by the privilege of my niggard fates,
It will their force throughout the world proclaim.

Disdain doth kill; and, whether false or sound
Suspicions will all patience overthrow;
But jealousy with greater rigour slays;

Now whether because of Don Quixote's threats or of Ambrosio's request that they should fulfil the debt they owed to his friend, not one of the shepherds stirred or moved from the place until the grave had been dug, Chrysostom's papers burnt, and his body buried amidst the tears of the spectators. (page 129)

A lengthy absence doth our life confound;
Against fear of oblivion to ensue
Firm hope of best success gives little ease.
Inevitable death lurks in all these.
But I—amazing miracle!—still live,
Jealous, absent, disdained, and certain too
Of the suspicions that my life undo.
Drowned in oblivion, I my fire revive,
And amongst all those pains have never scope
Once to behold the shadow of a hope,
Nor, thus despairing, will I hope allow;
But rather, to exacerbate my wrong,
To live for ever hopeless here I vow.

At one same time can hope and fear exist?
Or is it reason that they should do so,
Seeing how much more cause there is for fears?
If before me dire jealousy persist,
Shall I then shut my eyes, since it will show
In my soul through a thousand bleeding scars?
Or who will not the gates unto despair
Fling open wide the moment that he spies
Murdering disdain, and notes each sad suspicion
Confirmed as truth—O bitter transformation!—
Whilst limpid truth is turned to a pack of lies?
O tyrant of love's state, fierce jealousy!
With cruel chains these hands together tie,
With twisted rope couple them, rough disdain!
But, woe is me, with bloody victory
Your memory is by my suffering slain!

And now I die; and since all hope I've lost
Ever in life or death, to prosper now,
I obstinate will rest in fantasy,
And say he does the best who loves the most,

123

And that the soul most liberty doth know
When most enslaved by Love's old tyranny.
I will swear that my constant enemy
In her fair body a fair soul contains,
That her unkindness by my fault arose,
And only by the grievous hurt he does
Can Love his empire in just peace maintain.
And in this fancy, and with this hard knot
I'll hasten my appearance in that court
Where by her bitter scorn I'm forced to come,
And offering to the winds body and soul,
Forfeit the future's laurel wreath and palm.

Thou that by multiplying wrongs dost show
The reason forcing me to violence
Against this weary life, that's now grown hateful,
Since now by signs notorious thou dost know
From my heart's deepest wound how gladly sense
Doth sacrifice me to thy scorns ungrateful,
Shouldst thou, perchance, my merits find so fruitful
As to dim the clear heaven of your eyes,
And cloud them with my death, yet weep not so.
For I'll yield you no tribute by my woe,
Nor give you my soul's booty as your prize.
But rather, laughing at my funeral sad,
Show how my end begins to make thee glad.
But 'tis a folly to advise thee this,
For I know that in hurrying on my death
Consists my glory and thy chiefest bliss.

Let Tantalus from the profoundest deeps
Come, for it is high time now, with his thirst;
And Sispyhus with his oppressive stone;
Let Tityus bring his vulture that ne'er sleeps,
Nor Ixion delay with wheel accursed;

Nor the three sisters, ever labouring on;
And let them all at once their mortal pain
Translate into my breast, and scarce aloud
(If funeral rites are granted my despair)
Chant their sad obsequies with doleful air
Over a corpse even denied a shroud.
And the three-faced infernal porter grim,
With thousand monsters and chimaeras come
And swell the mournful descant of despair;
No greater pomp than this, I fear, is due
To any constant lover on his bier.
Despairing song, I beg thee not to grieve
When my sad company thou com'st to leave;
But rather since the course whence thou didst spring
By my misfortune grows more fortunate,
Even in the grave thou must shun sorrowing.

Chrysostom's song pleased its hearers, though Vivaldo said that it did not seem to him to conform to the account he had heard of Marcela's modesty and goodness. For in it Chrysostom complained of jealousy, suspicions, and neglect, all to the prejudice of Marcela's good name and fame. But Ambrosio answered him out of the knowledge of his friend's most private thoughts, "To satisfy your doubt, sir, I must tell you that when the unfortunate man wrote this song he had voluntarily banished himself from Marcela to see if absence would have its customary effect upon him. And as there is nothing that does not vex the absent lover, and no fear that does not pursue him, so Chrysostom was tormented by imaginary jealousies and suspicions, as fearful as if they were real. Marcela's goodness, therefore, is as true as fame proclaimed it, for, except for cruelty, some haughtiness, and much scorn, there is no fault that envy itself can rightly find in her."

"That is true," replied Vivaldo. And he was going to read another of the papers which he had saved from the fire when he was prevented by a miraculous vision—for such it seemed—which suddenly appeared before their eyes. For on the top of the rock in which they were digging the grave appeared the shepherdess Marcela, looking even more beautiful than she had been described. Those of them who knew her well were just as amazed. But no sooner did Ambrosio catch sight of her than he cried with some show of anger, "Have you come here, perhaps, fiery basilisk of these mountains, to see if the wounds of this wretch, whom your cruelty killed, will bleed afresh at the sight of you? Or have you come to triumph at your nature's cruel work? Or to gaze from that height, like another pitiless Nero, upon the flames of burning Rome? Or, in your pride, to trample this miserable corpse, as Tarquin's ungrateful daughter did her father's? Tell us quickly why you have come, or what you desire. For, as I know that Chrysostom never failed to be obedient to you during his life, I will take care that even in his death all who call themselves his friends obey you."

"I have come, Ambrosio, for none of the reasons you give," replied Marcela, "but rather to defend myself, and to prove how wrong are those who blame me for their own sufferings and for Chrysostom's death. So I ask all of you here to give me your attention, for it will not take me much time or waste many words to persuade all sensible men of the truth. Heaven made me, you say, so lovely that my beauty makes you love me despite yourselves; and in return for the love you show me, you claim, and even demand, that I should be bound to love you. I know by the natural sense which God has given me that whatever is beautiful is lovable; but I do not understand why, merely because she inspires love, a woman who is loved for her beauty is obliged to love the man who loves her. Besides, it may chance that the man who loves what is beautiful is himself ugly; and, as ugliness is loathsome, it would be absurd for him to say, "I love you for your beauty; love me although I am ugly." But, even supposing that both are equally beautiful, the attraction need not therefore be equal on both sides. For not all beauties inspire love; some only please the eye, but do not subdue the heart. Now if all beauty inspired love and made conquests, the hearts of men would wander confused and astray, not knowing where to alight, for as beauties are infinite, the feelings they inspire must be infinite too. Besides, as I have heard, true love cannot be divided, but must be free and unconstrained. If this is so, as I believe it is, why do you ask me to do violence to my heart, merely because you say you love me? Tell me, if the Heavens had made me ugly instead of beautiful, should I have had the right to complain of your not loving me? What is more, you must consider that I did not choose to be beautiful. My beauty, such as it is, the Heavens gave me freely, without my choice or asking; and just as the viper deserves no blame for the poison which nature gave her, even though she kills with it, I cannot be blamed for being beautiful. For beauty in a modest woman is like distant fire or a sharp sword; the one does not burn or the other cut the man who does not come near it. Modesty and the virtues are the adornments of the soul, and without them, even if the body is beautiful, it ought not to appear so. Now if modesty is one of the virtues and the fairest adornment of the body and the soul, why must the woman who is loved for her beauty lose it to gratify the desires of a man who, for his pleasure alone, tries with all his strength and ingenuity to rob her of it? I was born free, and to live free I chose the solitude of the fields. The trees on these mountains are my companions; the clear waters of these streams my mirrors; to the trees and the waters I disclose my thoughts and my beauty. I am the distant fire and the far-off sword. Those whom I have attracted with my eyes I have undeceived with my words. If desires are nourished on hope, as I never gave any to Chrysostom or to any other, it may not justly be said that any man's end was my doing, since it was his persistence rather than my cruelties that killed him. And if it is objected that his intentions were honest, and that therefore I was obliged to reciprocate them, my answer is that when he revealed to me the honesty of his intentions on this same spot where now you are digging his grave, I told him that my will was to live in perpetual solitude, and that only the earth would enjoy the fruit of my chastity and the spoils of my beauty. If, despite all this discouragement, he chose to persist against hope and to sail against the wind, is it surprising that he should have drowned in the gulf of

127

his own folly? If I had encouraged him in hope, I should have been false; if I had gratified him, I should have acted against my better feelings and resolutions. He persisted despite discouragement, despaired although not hated. Judge then whether it is right that I should pay the penalty for his sufferings! If I have deceived anyone, let him complain; if I have broken my promise to anyone, let him despair; if I lure anyone on, let him declare it; if I encourage anyone, let him boast of it. But let me not be called cruel or murderous by those whom I have never promised, deceived, lured on, or encouraged. Heaven has not yet fated me to love; and it is folly to think that I shall love out of choice. May this general warning serve for the particular benefit of every man who woos me; and henceforth be it understood that if anyone dies on my account, he will not die out of jealousy or from rejection; for she who loves no man can make no man jealous, and discouragement must not be taken for disdain. If anyone calls me a wild beast and a basilisk, let him shun me as a mischievous and evil thing; if he calls me ungrateful, let him serve me no more; if he calls me strange, know me no more; if cruel, follow me no more; for this wild beast, this basilisk, this ungrateful, strange, and cruel creature will in no way seek, serve, know, or follow him. If Chrysostom's impatience and headstrong passion killed him, why should my modesty and reserve be blamed? If I preserve my purity in the company of the trees, why should he who would have me keep the company of men desire me to lose it? I, as you know, have riches of my own, and covet no one else's. I have a taste for freedom and no wish for subjection. I neither love nor hate any man. I do not deceive one man and encourage another. I do not trifle with one nor keep another in hope. I enjoy the modest company of the village shepherdesses and the care of my goats. My desires are bounded by these mountains, and if they extend beyond them, it is to contemplate the beauty of the sky, a step by which the soul travels to its first abode."

When she had finished, she turned round without waiting for a reply and plunged into the densest part of the nearby woods, leaving everyone as amazed at her good sense as at her beauty. Some whom the mighty arrow of her fair eyes' gaze had wounded made as if to follow her, heedless of the plain words of discouragement they had just heard. But here Don Quixote, thinking that this was an occasion to exercise his chivalry by the succouring of a maiden in distress, put his hand on his sword-hilt, and loudly and clearly exclaimed, "Let no man, of whatsoever estate or condition, dare to follow the fair Marcela, under pain of incurring my most furious indignation! She has shown with clear and sufficient argument that she bears little or no blame for Chrysostom's death, and how far she is from yielding to any of her lovers' desires. Wherefore it is right that, instead of being pursued and persecuted, she should be honoured and esteemed by all good men in the world, for she has proved that she is the only woman living with such pure intentions."

Now whether because of Don Quixote's threats or of Ambrosio's request that they should fulfil the debt they owed to his friend, not one of the shepherds stirred or moved from the place until the grave had been dug, Chrysostom's papers burnt, and his body buried amidst the tears of the spectators.

They sealed the grave with a heavy stone until such time as they should have a tombstone ready, which Ambrosio informed them he intended to have made, and inscribed with the following epitaph:

Here a poor loving swain's
Frozen corpse lies.
He was a shepherd and
Died of disdain.

Died of the cruelty
Of a coy, thankless, fair
Maid, by whom Love's empire
Widens its tyranny.

Then they spread flowers and branches in plenty over the grave, and each of the shepherds, after condoling with his friend Ambrosio, bade him good-bye. Vivaldo and his companions did the same, and Don Quixote said farewell to his hosts and to the travellers, who pressed him to come with them to Seville, which was just the place to strike adventures in, they said, for there are more to be found there, in every street and round every corner, than can be met with in any other place. Don Quixote thanked them for their advice and their evident desire to do him a service, but said that for the present he neither could nor should go to Seville until he had cleared all those mountains of the thieves and robbers who were said to infest them.

In view of this honest purpose, the travellers did not care to press him further. But once more bidding him farewell, they left him and pursued their journey, in the course of which they did not fail to discuss the story of Marcela and Chrysostom as well as the follies of Don Quixote. As for him, he decided to go in search of the shepherdess Marcela and offer her all the service in his power. But things did not turn out as he expected, as will be told in the course of this true story, of which the second part ends here.

⊰ 15 ⊱

Of the Unfortunate Adventure
which befell Don Quixote on His Encounter
with Some Merciless Yanguesans

*T*he sage Cide Hamete Benengeli relates that as soon as Don Quixote had bidden farewell to his hosts and to everyone who had been present at the shepherd Chrysostom's burial, he and his squire entered that same wood into which they had seen the shepherdess Marcela disappear. And when they had travelled through it for more than two hours, looking for her in vain in all directions, they halted in a meadow, rich in fresh grass, beside which ran a pleasant and refreshing brook, which invited them, or rather induced them, to spend the sultry hours of midday there; for the heat had already become oppressive. Don Quixote and Sancho dismounted and, leaving the ass and Rocinante at large to feed on the abundant grass, they ransacked their saddle-bags. Then, without ceremony, master and man ate the contents in peace and good fellowship. Now Sancho had not troubled to fetter Rocinante, secure in his belief that he was so mild and so little lustful a beast that all the mares in the pastures of Cordova would not provoke him to any impropriety. But as Fate, or the Devil—who is not always sleeping—would have it, there was a herd of Galician mares grazing in that valley. They belonged to some carriers from Yanguas whose habit it is to spend midday with their droves where there is grass and water; and the place where Don Quixote happened to be suited the Yanguesans very well. So it came about that Rocinante was taken with the desire to disport himself with the lady mares and, abandoning his natural pace and habits the moment he smelt them, asked no permission of his master, but set off at a brisk trot to acquaint them of his needs. But they, apparently, preferred the pastures, and gave him such a welcome with their hooves and teeth that in a very short while they had broken his girths and left him stripped of his saddle and naked. But what must have hurt him more was that the carriers, seeing the violence he was offering to their mares, ran up with pack-staves, and laid into him so hard that he was soon on the ground in a very sorry state. At this point Don Quixote and Sancho, who had witnessed Rocinante's beating, ran up panting, the knight saying to his squire, "From what I can see, friend Sancho, these are no knights, but vile and low-bred men. I say this so that you may freely help me to take due vengeance for the outrage which they have done to Rocinante before our very eyes."

"How the devil can we take revenge," replied Sancho, "when there are more than twenty of them, and we are only two—or perhaps no more than one and a half?"

"I am equal to a hundred," answered Don Quixote. Then without further discussion he drew his sword and attacked the Yanguesans, and Sancho Panza was spurred on by his master's example to do the same. At the first blow Don Quixote gave one of them a slash, which slit the leather coat he was wearing and cut a great gash in his shoulder. But the Yanguesans, seeing so many of themselves so roughly treated by a mere two men, seized their pack-staves and, surrounding the pair, began to lay into them with might and main. In fact, they stretched Sancho on the ground at their second blow, and the same fate soon befell Don Quixote, his skill and courage availing him nothing; and, as Fate would have it, he fell at the feet of the still prostrate Rocinante. All of which goes to show what hard bruises pack-staves will deal in the hands of angry rustics. Then,

Despite his pain, he harnessed his ass, who had also taken advantage of that day's excess of liberty to stray a little. He then got Rocinante up, and he, if he had had a tongue to complain with, would certainly not have been outdone by squire or master. (page 140) seeing the damage they had done, the Yanguesans loaded their beasts as fast as they could and went on their way, leaving the two adventurers in an evil plight and a worse humour.

The first to regain his senses was Sancho Panza who, finding himself beside his master, cried in a weak and piteous voice, "Don Quixote! Ah, Don Quixote!"

"What is the matter, brother Sancho?" answered Don Quixote in the same faint and plaintive tones.

"Well sir," said Sancho Panza, "I should be glad if your worship could let me have two gulps of that drink of Fair Bras's, if you've got it handy. Perhaps it might be as good for broken bones as it is for wounds."

"Why," replied Don Quixote, "if I had some here, wretch that I am, what more could I want? But I swear to you, Sancho Panza, on my word as a knight errant that, unless fortune ordains otherwise, I will have some in my possession before two days have passed, or it will be no fault of mine."

"How long does your worship suppose it will be before we shall be able to use our feet?" asked Sancho Panza.

"For myself," replied the bruised knight Don Quixote, "I must say that I can see no end to our present plight. But I take the blame for everything upon myself, for I should not have drawn my sword against men who were not dubbed knights, as I am. That is why I believe that the God of battles has permitted me to be so chastised —for breaking the laws of chivalry. So, Sancho Panza, you must be warned by what I am going to say, for it greatly concerns the welfare of us both. It is, that when you see us insulted by such rabble you must not wait for me to draw my sword on them, for I shall on no account do so. But you must draw your own and chastise them at your pleasure. Should any knights come to their aid or defence, I shall know how to protect you and shall attack them with all my strength, and you have already had a thousand signs and proofs of the height to which the valour of this strong arm of mine can reach." So arrogant was the poor gentleman at his victory over the brave Basque.

But Sancho Panza did not find his master's instructions so good that he could refrain from replying, "Sir, I am a peaceable, mild, quiet man, and I can overlook any kind of injury, for I have a wife to keep and children to bring up. So let me tell your worship by way of a hint—for it's not my place to give orders—that I shall on no account draw my sword against peasant or against knight, and that from now on, before God, I pardon whatever insults have been, or shall be, done me, whether by person high or low, rich or poor, by gentleman or by commoner, without exception of rank or quality."

On hearing this, his master replied, "I wish that I had breath enough to say a few words at my ease, and that the pain I feel in this rib would die down even slightly, so that I could convince you, Sancho Panza, of your error. Listen, wretch! Suppose that the winds of fortune, now so contrary, should turn in our favour, swelling the sails of our desires, and we should reach harbour, safely and unhurt, in one of those isles I promised you—what would become of you if I won it and made you its master? You would ruin everything by not being a knight, nor desiring to be one, having neither the courage nor the resolution to avenge insults and defend your dominions. For you must know that in newly conquered kingdoms and provinces the minds of the natives are never so quiet, or so well disposed to their new lords there, as to leave no fear of their planning some revolt, so as to reverse the state of things once more and, as they say, try their luck again. So the new master must needs have the intelligence to know how to rule, and the courage to take offensive and defensive measures in every emergency."

"I wish I had had the intelligence and courage you speak of," replied Sancho, "when this last thing happened to us, but you must take a poor man's word for it that I'm in greater need of plasters than of sermons. Try, sir, if you can't get up; and we'll see if we can help Rocinante, although he doesn't deserve it, for he was the chief cause of all the knocking about we got. I never thought it of him, for I imagined he was as chaste and peaceable a fellow as I am myself. It is a good saying, after all, that it takes a long time to get to know people, and that there's nothing certain in this life. Who would have said that after all those great sword-thrusts you dealt that wretched knight errant, this great storm of blows would have followed up so fast and burst on our shoulders?"

"Yours," replied Don Quixote, "must have been made for such a storm, but as mine were nurtured between cambrics and fine linen, clearly they are more sensitive to the pain of this mishap. If it were not that I imagine—why do I say imagine?—that I most certainly know that all these discomforts are inseparable from the profession of arms, I would be ready to die here of pure vexation."

To which the squire replied, "Sir, if these misfortunes are the fruit of chivalry, will your worship tell me if they happen very often, or if they only occur at set times? For it seems to me that after two such crops we should be useless for the third, unless God, of His infinite pity, were to come to our aid."

"You must know, friend Sancho," replied Don Quixote, "that a knight errant's life is subject to countless perils and mischances. Yet he has none the less the potentiality of rising at any moment to become King or Emperor, as experience has demonstrated in the case of many and divers knights whose histories I know in detail. If my pain would let me I could tell you now of some who have climbed, by the valour of their arms alone, to the high degree I mentioned, yet those very knights, both beforehand and afterwards, sustained various calamities and misfortunes. For the valorous Amadis of Gaul was once in the power of his mortal enemy, Arcalaus the enchanter, who, it is well attested, when he held him prisoner, tied him to a pillar in a courtyard and gave him more than two hundred lashes with the reins of his own horse. There is a little-known author too of no small reputation, who says that the Knight of the Sun, being caught in a certain castle by means of a trap-door which gave way beneath his feet, found himself after his fall bound hand and foot in a subterranean cavern; and there they administered to him what is called an enema, of snow-water and sand, which nearly killed him; and if a certain sage who was a great friend of his had not succoured him in his dreadful plight, things would have gone very badly with the poor knight. So I can well afford to suffer in such good company, since they sustained greater affronts than we are suffering now. For I would have you know, Sancho, that wounds dealt with instruments which are accidentally in the hand do not disgrace a man; that is expressly laid down in the law of the duel. So if a shoemaker strikes a man with the last he is holding, even though it is of wood, it shall not therefore be said that the man whom he stuck was cudgelled. I say this in case you may suppose that, because we have come out of this struggle soundly bruised, we are disgraced, since the arms which those men carried and pounded us with were no other than their pack-staves; and not one of them, so far as I can remember, carried a rapier, sword, or dagger."

"They did not give me a chance," replied Sancho, "to observe them so closely. For I had no sooner put my hand to my blade than they made so many crosses on my shoulders with their sticks, that they knocked the sight out of my eyes and the strength out of my feet, and laid me out where I'm lying now. I don't care a hang, down here, whether the beating was a disgrace or not, but I do mind a lot about the pain I got from it, and that's likely to stay as deeply in my memory as it bit into my back."

"For all that, brother Panza," replied Don Quixote, "let me tell you that there is no memory which time does not efface, nor any pain that death does not destroy."

"But what misfortune could be worse," replied Sancho, "than one that waits for time to efface it and death to destroy it? If ours were the sort of misfortune that could be cured with a couple of poultices it wouldn't be so bad. But I'm beginning to think that all the plasters in a hospital wouldn't be enough to give it a turn for the better."

"No more of that, Sancho," replied Don Quixote, "but make the best of a bad business, and I shall do the same. Let us see how Rocinante is, for it seems to me that the poor creature got by no means the smallest share of the disaster."

"There's nothing marvellous about that," replied Sancho, "since he's a knight errant too. What does astonish me is that my ass has got off scot-free, while we've got our ribs broken."

"Fortune always leaves one door open in disasters, to admit a remedy," said Don Quixote. "I say this because your little beast will now serve instead of Rocinante to carry me from here to some castle where my wound may be cured. What is more, I shall not consider such a mount a disgrace, for I remember reading how good old Silenus, tutor and guide to the merry god of laughter, rode most gladly on a very handsome ass when he entered the city of the hundred gates."

"It's very likely he rode as your worship says," replied Sancho; "but there's a great deal of difference between riding astride and being laid across like a sack of dung."

"Wounds received in battle," answered Don Quixote, "rather confer honour than take it away. So, friend Panza, give me no more answers, but do as I have told you. Get up as best you can and place me on your ass in any way you like. Then let us depart, before night comes and overtakes us in this wilderness."

"Yet I have heard your worship say," said Panza, "that it is quite the thing for knights errant to sleep in moorland and deserts for the greater part of the year, and to think themselves very fortunate to do so."

"That is when they cannot help it," said Don Quixote, "or when they are in love. In fact there have been knights who have stayed on a rock exposed to sun and shade and all the inclemencies of Heaven for two years, unknown to their ladies; and one of these was Amadis, when he assumed the name of Beltenebros and took up his lodging on the Bare Rock, for eight years, or perhaps eight months—for I am not sure of my reckoning. Suffice it that he was doing penance there for some displeasure the lady Oriana had caused him. But let us leave the matter, before some misfortune like Rocinante's befalls the ass."

"That would be the devil and all," observed Sancho. And then, uttering thirty groans, sixty sighs, and a hundred and twenty damns and curses on whoever it was that had got him there, he raised himself, but stopped half-way, bent like a Turkish bow, unable to straighten himself up. However, despite his pain, he harnessed his ass, who had also taken advantage of that day's excess of liberty to stray a little. He then got Rocinante up, and he, if he had had a tongue to complain with, would certainly not have been outdone by squire or master. In the end, Sancho settled Don Quixote on the ass and, tying Rocinante to his tail, led his beast by the halter, making as best he could for the direction in which he thought the highway lay.

And he had not gone more than two miles when Fortune, who was guiding their affairs from good to better, brought him to the road, on which he sighted an inn, which, to his grief and Don Quixote's pleasure, must needs be a castle. Sancho swore that it was an inn, and his master that it was no inn but a castle; and the argument lasted so long that it was not finished when they arrived there, and Sancho entered without further enquiry, followed by his string of beasts.

⇥ *16* ⇤

What happened to
the Ingenious Knight in the Inn
that he took for a Castle

*T*he innkeeper, who saw Don Quixote lying across the ass, asked Sancho what was wrong with him. Sancho replied that it was nothing, that he had fallen off a rock and bruised his ribs slightly. Now the innkeeper's wife was a woman of a different sort from the generality of hostesses, for she was kindly by nature and felt for her neighbours' misfortunes. So she immediately set about the cure of Don Quixote and made her young daughter, a very good-looking girl, help her to tend him.

There was an Asturian maid at the inn, broad-faced, flat-nosed, and with a head that seemed to have no back to it; she was blind of one eye and not too sound in the other. But she made up for her other shortcomings by her bodily allurements; she was not more than three feet high from head to toe, and her shoulders, which were rather on the heavy side, made her look down on the ground more than she liked. This charming maid, then, helped her young mistress, and the two of them made a very poor bed for Don Quixote in an attic which had evidently served once, for a long time, as a straw-loft.

There was a carrier lodging in this garret as well. His bed stood a little farther from the door than our knight's; and, although it consisted only of his mule's saddles and blankets, it was a good deal better than Don Quixote's, which was made up of four badly planed boards resting on a pair of not too even trestles; a mattress thin as a quilt and full of lumps, which were as hard as stones to the touch but appeared through various rents in the cover to be wool; two sheets, made of the leather used for shields, and a coverlet whose every thread anyone who wished could have counted without missing a single one.

On this execrable bed Don Quixote lay down, whereupon the hostess and her daughter poulticed him from head to foot, while Maritornes—for this was the Asturian maid's name—held a light.

The hostess, as she plastered him, seeing that parts of his body were covered with weals, remarked that he must have had a beating, not a fall.

"It wasn't a beating," said Sancho, "but the rock had a lot of jags and knobs, and each one must have made its mark. And, by the way, if you could be so very kind as to leave a little of that wadding, it might come in handy for someone, for my back's giving me a bit of trouble too."

"Oh, I see," replied the hostess, "you must have had a fall as well."

"I didn't fall," said Sancho, "but I got such a shock from seeing my master tumble that my body aches all over, as if I had been beaten black and blue."

"That may well be," said the innkeeper's daughter, "for very often I've dreamt I fell off a tower and never reached the ground. And when I've woken up I've found myself as bruised and bumped as if I had really tumbled."

"But here's the point, lady," replied Sancho Panza. "I wasn't dreaming. I was more wide awake than I am now, and there I was, almost as bruised as my master Don Quixote."

"What's the gentleman's name?" asked the Asturian maid.

"Don Quixote de la Mancha," replied Sancho Panza. "He's a

knight errant. One of the best and bravest the world has seen for a very long time."

"What's a knight errant?" asked the maid.

"Are you so green that you don't know that?" replied Sancho. "Then I'll tell you, my girl, that a knight errant—to cut a long story short—is beaten up one day and made Emperor the next. Today he's the most unfortunate and poverty-stricken creature in the world; tomorrow he'll have two or three kingdoms to give to his squire."

"Well, seeing that you have such a fine master," said the hostess, "how is it you aren't at least a count?"

"There's plenty of time yet," replied Sancho. "We've only been seeking adventures for a month, and up to now we haven't come across anything worth calling one; and sometimes when you're looking for one thing you find another. But I promise you that, if my master Don Quixote recovers from his wound or fall, and I'm not crippled by mine, I won't swap my chances for the noblest title in Spain."

Here Don Quixote, who had listened very attentively to all this chatter, sat up in bed as best he could and, taking the hostess's hand, addressed her, "Believe me, beauteous lady, you may count yourself fortunate to have lodging in your castle a person whom I must refrain from praising only because self-praise is said to be a practice unworthy of a gentleman. But my squire will tell you who I am. I will only say that I shall bear the services you have done me eternally inscribed in my memory, so that I may remain grateful to you all the days of my life. Had it not pleased Heaven to keep me in such abject servitude to love's laws and to the eyes of that ungrateful beauty whose name I dare hardly breathe, then the eyes of your beauteous daughter would hold my freedom captive."

The hostess, her daughter, and the worthy Maritornes were bewildered by the knight errant's words, which might have been Greek so little could they understand them, though they realized that they were all intended as thanks and compliments. But, as they were not used to such language, they stared at him in amazement; for he seemed so very different from the sort of men they were accustomed to. So, thanking him in their innkeeper's language, they left him, and the Asturian maid tended Sancho, who was in no less need of attention than his master.

Now the carrier had arranged with her that they should spend the night together in healthy sport; and she had promised that once the guests were quiet and her master and mistress asleep she would come to him and give him all the pleasure he could desire. And it is told to the credit of this good girl that she never made such promises without fulfilling them, even if she made them far away in the mountains and without any witness at all. For she prided herself on being a maiden of breeding, and did not feel degraded by serving in an inn, because only misfortune and ill-chance, as she said, had brought her to that pass.

Don Quixote's hard, narrow, miserable apology for a bed was the first in this starlit barn; and next beside him Sancho had made his, which consisted only of a rush mat and a horse-blanket, which seemed to be of threadbare canvas rather than of wool. Beyond these two came the carrier's bed, made, as we have said, of the saddles and all the trappings of the two best mules he had. He had twelve glossy, well-covered, splendid beasts, for he was one of the richest mule-teers in Arevalo, as the author of this history tells us; and he makes a special mention of this carrier, because he knew him very well, and it is even suggested that he was some relation of his. But, however that may be, Cide Hamete Benengeli was a very exact historian and very precise in all his details, as can be seen by his not passing over these various points, trivial and petty though they may be. He should be an example to those grave historians who give us so short and skimped an account of events that we scarcely taste them, and so the most substantial part of their work, out of carelessness, malice, or ignorance, remains in their ink-horns. A thousand blessings then on the author of *Tablante de Ricamonte* and the writer of that other book which tells us of the deeds of Count Tomillas, for the exhaustiveness with which they describe everything.

But to return to the story. After the carrier had visited his mules and given them their second feed, he stretched himself on his

At this point the innkeeper entered shouting, "Where are you, you whore? This is all your doing; I'm sure of it." Whereat Sancho, feeling this weight almost on top of him, thought it was a nightmare and began to strike out right and left. A good number of blows fell on Maritornes, who with the pain of them forgot her modesty and gave him as many in return. (page 149) pack-saddles and awaited his most punctual Maritornes. By now Sancho was poulticed and had lain down, but, though he tried to sleep, the pain in his sides would not allow him. Don Quixote, too, with the pain of his ribs was no more able to close his eyes than a hare. The whole inn was in silence, and there was no other light in it but that of a hanging lamp which burnt in the centre of the doorway.

This phenomenal quiet and his habitual preoccupation with the adventures that are related on every page of those books that had been his undoing wrought one of the strangest possible fancies in our knight's imagination. He thought that he had arrived at a famous castle—for, as we have said, every inn where he stayed seemed to him a castle—and that the innkeeper's daughter was really the daughter of the warden. Overwhelmed by his nobility, she had fallen in love with him and, what is more, she had promised that very night, when her parents were asleep, to come and lie with him awhile. And taking all this fantasy which he had invented for the sober truth, he began to be disturbed and to think of the critical danger to which his honour was exposed, deciding in his heart to commit no treason against the lady Dulcinea del Toboso, even though Queen Guinevere and her lady Quintañona should appear before him.

Whilst he was brooding on this nonsense, unfortunately for him the time arrived for the Asturian maid's visit. She came in her shift, with bare feet and hair done up in a fustian kerchief. With soft and noiseless steps she entered the garret in which the three men were lodged, in search of the carrier. But scarcely had she reached the door when Don Quixote heard her, and, sitting up in bed, despite his plasters and his aching ribs, he stretched out his arms to receive his beauteous maiden. She was gliding modestly and silently, groping with outstretched hands for her lover, when she stumbled into the arms of Don Quixote, who seized her tightly by one wrist and, drawing her to him, she not daring to say a word, forced her to sit on his bed.

Then he felt her shift and, although it was of sackcloth, it seemed to him of the finest, most delicate satin. The glass beads that she

147

wore on her wrist had for him the sheen of rare orient pearls. Her hair, which was coarse as a horse's mane, seemed to him strands of the most glistening gold of Arabia, whose splendour eclipsed the very sun. And her mouth, which, no doubt, reeked of the stale salad of the night before, seemed to him to breathe out a sweet and aromatic odour. In short, he bestowed on her all of the features of that famous princess who came, in the books that he had read, to visit the sore-wounded knight whom she loved so well. In every detail of dress and bearing his imagination copied her exactly. And so blind was the poor knight that neither her touch nor her breath nor anything else about the good maiden revealed his mistake to him, though she would have turned the stomach of anyone but a carrier. Far from it, he imagined that he held in his arms the goddess of beauty and, gripping her tight, in soft, amorous tones he began, "Would that I could find means, most lovely and high-born lady, with which I could repay the singular favour you have done me in displaying your great beauty. But Fortune, which is never weary of persecuting good men, has laid me on this bed, so bruised and battered that even if I wished to satisfy your desires I could not. And besides that impediment there is another and greater, the pledge of faith I have given to the peerless Dulcinea del Toboso, sole mistress of my most secret thoughts. But were I not prevented in this way, I should not be so simple a knight as to let pass the happy chance you have deigned to offer me."

Maritornes was bathed in a sweat of anguish at finding herself grasped by Don Quixote and, without understanding or paying the least attention to his protestations, tried silently to break loose. As for the good carrier, whose lusts kept him awake, he had heard his wench from the moment she came in, and had been listening attentively to the knight's every word. Suspecting that the Asturian maid had broken her promise to him in favour of another, he edged nearer and nearer to Don Quixote's bed, silently waiting to see what his incomprehensible speech might lead to. But, when he saw the maid struggling to break loose and Don Quixote trying to hold her, the jest seemed to him to have gone too far. Whereupon he raised his arm and dealt the amorous knight so terrible a blow on his lean jaws that his mouth was filled with blood; and, not content with this, he trod on his ribs and trampled him up and down at a lively rate.

The bed was rather weak and supported on no firm foundations. So, unable to bear the additional weight of the carrier, it gave way with a great crash. This woke the innkeeper, who called for Maritornes and, getting no reply, suspected that she must be the cause of the noise. With this in his mind he got up and, lighting a lamp, made his way towards the scene of the disturbance. The maid, hearing her master coming in and knowing his very bad temper, in fear and alarm climbed into the bed of the still-sleeping Sancho and huddled up in a ball.

At this point the innkeeper entered shouting, "Where are you, you whore? This is all your doing; I'm sure of it."

Whereat Sancho, feeling this weight almost on top of him, thought it was a nightmare and began to strike out right and left. A good number of his blows fell on Maritornes, who with the pain of them forgot her modesty and gave him as many in return. This dispelled his dream and, finding himself thus treated and not knowing by whom, he clinched with Maritornes, and the two of them started the most stubborn and comical scuffle in the world. Whereupon the carrier, seeing by the light of the innkeeper's lamp how ill his mistress was faring, left Don Quixote and joined in to give her all necessary help. So did the innkeeper, but with a different purpose: to beat the maid, under the impression that she was the sole cause of all that harmony. And then, as the saying goes, the cat chased the rat, the rat chased the rope, the rope chased the stick. The carrier beat Sancho, Sancho beat the maid, the maid beat him, the innkeeper beat the maid, and they all laid it on so fast that they never took a moment's rest. While, to improve the joke, the innkeeper's lamp went out and left them all in a heap in the dark, lamming out unmercifully and dealing great execution wherever they hit.

It happened that there was staying in the inn that night an officer of the Ancient and Holy Brotherhood of Toledo, who also heard the extraordinary din of the fight and, seizing his wand of office and the tin box with his warrants in it, went into the room in the dark, crying, "Stop in the name of justice! Stop in the name of the Holy Brotherhood!"

Now the first person he collided with was the poor, trampled knight, lying on his back unconscious amidst the ruins of his bed. And his hand touching the knight's beard as he groped, the officer repeated, "Help the officers of the Law!" But, seeing that the man he had seized neither struggled nor stirred, he took him for dead and the people in the garret for his murderers, which made him shout even louder, "Shut the inn door! Let no one go out. There's been a man murdered here!"

This cry alarmed them all, and as soon as they heard it they stopped the brawl. The innkeeper slipped back to his room, the carrier to his pack-saddles, the maid to her corner. Only the unfortunate Don and Sancho were unable to stir from where they lay. At this the officer let go Don Quixote's beard and went out to find a light, with the intention of seeking and arresting the criminals. But he could not find one, because the innkeeper had purposely put out the lamp when he retired to his quarters. So the officer had to go across to the hearth, where, after much time and trouble, he lit another.

⊰ *17* ⊱

Concerning Countless More Hardships
which the Brave Don Quixote
and His Good Squire Sancho Panza endured
in the Inn which he unfortunately
mistook for a Castle

*B*y this time Don Quixote had
recovered from his swoon and, in the same tones in which he had
called his squire the day before, when he was lying in the Valley of
the Stakes, began to cry, "Sancho, my friend, are you asleep? Are
you asleep, friend Sancho?"

"Sleep, confound it," replied Sancho in gloom and despair. "How
can I sleep when all the devils in hell must have been at me tonight?"

"You are right about that, for certain," replied Don Quixote.
"For, if I know anything, this castle is enchanted. You should
know—but what I am going to tell you now you must swear to keep
secret till the day of my death."

"I swear," replied Sancho.

"You must swear, because I hate to take away anyone's reputation," continued Don Quixote.

"I do swear, I tell you," repeated Sancho, "that I will keep silent
to the very last days of your honour's life. And please God I may be
free to speak tomorrow."

"Have I done you such harm, Sancho," replied Don Quixote, "that you would have me die so soon?"

"It's not that," answered Sancho, "but I hate to keep things long in case they go mouldy from over-keeping."

"Be that as it may," said Don Quixote, "I would trust even greater matters to your love and courtesy. I would have you know that tonight I have encountered one of the strangest adventures imaginable. In short, just now there came to me the daughter of the warden of this castle, the most graceful and beauteous damsel that could be found over the greater part of the world. What could I not tell you of the loveliness of her body? Of her sprightly intelligence? And of those other hidden things that, to keep the faith I owe to my lady Dulcinea del Toboso, I will let pass untouched and unspoken? I will only tell you that, whether because Heaven was envious of the great boon that this adventure had brought me, or perhaps—more probably—because, as I have said, this castle is enchanted, just as I was in sweet and amorous colloquy with her, there came a hand and an arm of some monstrous giant. Where it came from I did not see, nor could I imagine, but it gave me such a blow on the jaws that I was bathed in blood. And after that it pounded me so that I am in worse plight than yesterday, when the carriers did us the injury you know of on account of Rocinante's excess of spirits. From which I conclude that the treasure of that damsel's beauty must be guarded by some Moorish enchanter and is not for me."

"Nor for me either," replied Sancho, "for more than four hundred Moors have mauled me, so that the carriers' beating was tarts and gingerbread in comparison. But tell me, sir, what sort of a fine and rare adventure do you call it that leaves us in this plight? Indeed your worship came off best, for you had in your arms that incomparable beauty you spoke of. But what did I get but the worst beating I ever expect to get in all my life? I wish I had never been born! I am no knight errant and I don't ever expect to be one, but I get the greater share of the misfortunes for all that."

"Then you got beaten as well?" asked Don Quixote.

"Didn't I say so, devil take it?" Sancho replied.

"Do not worry about that," said Don Quixote. "For now I will make up the precious balsam, which will heal us in the twinkling of an eye."

By then the officer had lit his lamp and come in to view the supposed corpse, and Sancho, seeing an ugly-faced man in his shirt and night-cap with his lamp in his hand, asked his master, "Will this perhaps be the Moorish enchanter come to give us another hiding, in case there's anywhere he forgot to hit us last time?"

"It cannot be the Moor," replied Don Quixote, "for magicians never allow themselves to be seen by anyone."

"If you can't see them you can certainly feel them," said Sancho; "my shoulders can vouch for that."

"So might mine," replied Don Quixote; "but that is not enough to prove that that man is the Moorish enchanter."

The officer approached. But, seeing them conversing so calmly, he stopped in surprise. Don Quixote, indeed, was still lying on his back, unable to move because of his thrashing and the plasters, when the officer came up to him and said, "Well, how goes it, my man?"

"I should speak more politely if I were you," replied Don Quixote. "Is it the custom in this country to address knights errant in that way, lout?"

The officer could not suffer this treatment from a wretch of the sorry appearance of Don Quixote and, raising the lamp, which was full of oil, brought it down on the knight's head, leaving him with a fine bruise on his scalp. Then, under cover of darkness, he hurriedly left the room.

"No doubt," said Sancho Panza, "that is the Moorish enchanter. He must be keeping the treasure for someone else, and only reserving his beatings and bashings for us."

"You are right," replied Don Quixote, "but there's no point in taking any notice of matters of enchantment, nor in getting angry and enraged about them. For, as these magicians are invisible and supernatural, we shall find no one to take vengeance on, however hard we try. Get up, Sancho, if you can, and call the governor of this fortress, and try to get him to give me a little oil, some wine, some salt, and some rosemary, so that I can make the healing balsam. Indeed, I think that now I am in much need of it, for I am losing a great deal of blood from the wound that apparition gave me."

Sancho got up with sadly aching bones and went in the dark to find the innkeeper. Running, however, into the officer, who was listening to find out how things were with his enemy, he said, "Sir, whoever you are, be so very kind as to give us a little rosemary, some oil, some salt, and some wine, for they are needed to heal one of the best knights errant in the world, who is lying on that bed, sorely wounded at the hands of the Moorish enchanter who is in this inn."

When the officer heard this he thought that Sancho was out of his wits. But, as dawn was breaking by now, he opened the inn door and shouted out to the innkeeper what the poor fellow wanted. The host provided it all, and Sancho took it to Don Quixote, whom he found with his head clasped in his hands, groaning from the pain of his lamp-bashing, which, however, had done him no more harm than to raise a couple of largish bumps; what he took for blood being no more than the sweat which had poured from him in the anguish of the last storm.

In short, he took his ingredients, mixed them and cooked them for some time, till they appeared to be ready. Then he asked for a flask to put them in. But, as there was none in the inn, he decided to use a tin oil-can which the innkeeper gave him for nothing. After that he said eighty Paternosters and as many Ave Marias, Salves, and Credos over it, and at each word crossed himself by way of bene-diction. At which ceremony Sancho, the innkeeper, and the officer were present, but the carrier had by now gone peacefully off and was looking to his mules.

When this was done Don Quixote was anxious to make an immediate test of the virtue of this precious balsam, as he imagined it to be, upon himself; and so he drank off more than a pint, which would not go into the can and was still in the pot he had cooked it in. Now no sooner had he drunk it than he began to vomit, bringing up everything that was in his stomach; and with the pain and distress of his sickness he broke into so copious a sweat that he asked to be covered up and left alone. This was done, and he slept for more than three hours, at the end of which time he awoke feeling very much soothed in his body and so much better from his beating that he thought himself cured and, verily believing that he had hit upon the Balsam of Fierabras, he felt that thenceforth, with such a remedy, he could undertake without fear any assaults, battles, or fights, however perilous.

Sancho Panza, who also took his master's recovery for a miracle, begged him for what remained in the pot—and there was a good deal of it. Don Quixote granted his request; and he, taking the pot in both hands, with a strong faith and better will, gulped it down, swallowing almost as much as his master. The fact is, though, that poor Sancho's stomach was not as delicate as Don Quixote's; and so, before he was sick, he suffered so many twinges and pangs, so many sweats and swoons, that he thought his last hour had come in good earnest; and in his affliction and dismay he cursed the ointment and the scoundrel who had given it to him.

When Don Quixote saw him in such anguish, he observed, "I think, Sancho, that all this pain comes from your not being a knight; for it is my opinion that this liquor cannot be of service to any that are not."

"If your worship knew that," replied Sancho, "the devil take me and all my family, why did you let me taste it?"

At this the potion began to work and the poor man to empty himself at both ends, so violently that soon the rush mat on which he had thrown himself and the coarse blanket that covered him were of no more use. His sweats, his paroxysms, and spasms were such that he, and everyone else as well, thought that he was at the point of death. And this tornado of misery lasted almost two hours, at the end of which time, unlike his master, he was left so battered and broken that he could not stand.

But Don Quixote, as we have said, felt recovered and well, and was anxious to set out immediately in search of adventures. For it seemed to him that every moment he delayed he was depriving the world, and everyone in distress in it, of his favour and protection.

And he was encouraged in this feeling by his security and confidence in his balsam. So, urged on by this desire, he saddled Rocinante himself and bridled his squire's ass, helping Sancho to dress himself and climb on his back. Then he mounted his steed and, seeing a javelin in a corner of the inn, seized it to serve as a lance. Everyone in the inn was watching him, and there were more than twenty there. The innkeeper's daughter watched him too, and he did not take his eyes from her, but from time to time heaved a sigh which seemed to be torn from the depths of his bowels, and which everyone thought must be from the pain in his ribs; or so at least thought those who had seen him poulticed the night before.

When the two of them were on horse Don Quixote stopped at the inn door, called the host, and addressed him in very calm and grave tones, "Many and great are the favours, my lord governor, that I have received in your castle, and I shall remain deeply obliged for them all the days of my life. If I can repay you by taking vengeance for you on any proud man who may have done you wrong, know that my office is to protect the helpless, to avenge wrongs and to punish treachery. Search your memory and, if you have anything of this kind to entrust to me, you have only to say so, and I promise you, by my order of knighthood, to give you reparation and amends to your full satisfaction."

The innkeeper replied in the same grave tones, "Sir Knight, I do not need your worship to avenge any injuries, for I know how to take fitting vengeance for all wrongs done me. I only want your worship to pay the score you have run up this night in my inn, for straw and fodder for your two beasts, and for your supper and beds."

"Then this is an inn?" asked Don Quixote.

"Yes, and a very respectable one," replied the host.

"Then I have been in error till this moment," answered Don Quixote, "for I truly thought that it was a castle, and a considerable one too. But, since it is no castle but an inn, there is nothing for it now but for you to excuse my paying, for I cannot contravene the knight errant's rule. I am most certain—and I have never yet read of

Then one of them went in for the blanket from the host's bed and threw him on to it. But when they looked up they saw that the roof was rather too low for their purpose, and decided to go out into the back-yard, whose ceiling was the sky; and there, placing Sancho in the centre of the blanket, they began to toss him up and amuse themselves at his expense, as they do with dogs at Shrovetide. (page 159) any case to the contrary—that they never paid for lodging or for anything else at any inn at which they stayed. For they deserve, by privilege and right, whatever hospitality they receive, in repayment for the intolerable hardships they undergo in seeking adventures by night and day, in winter and summer, on foot and horse, in thirst and hunger, in heat and cold, subject to all the inclemencies of the skies and all the discomforts of the earth."

"That is nothing to do with me," replied the innkeeper. "Settle your reckoning, and spare us your tales and your knighthoods. I'm only concerned with getting my money."

"You are a fool and a vile hosteller," answered Don Quixote. Then, putting spur to Rocinante and brandishing his javelin, he left the inn without anyone stopping him; and without looking back to see if his squire was following, he rode for some way. When the innkeeper saw him go without paying, he ran to Sancho Panza for his money. But Sancho answered that, as his master had not been willing to pay, he would not either. For, as he was squire to a knight errant, the same rule held for him as for his master, to pay nothing in inns or hostelries. This put the host in a great temper, and he threatened, if he did not pay, to get the money out of him in a way he would not like. But Sancho persisted that by the law of knight-hood, which his master had received, he would not pay a single farthing, even if it cost him his life. For he would not be the man to break the good old custom of knights errant, nor should the squires of future knights have to complain and reproach him for violating a privilege so well deserved.

But, as ill fate would have it, among the people in the inn were four wool-combers from Segovia, three needle-makers from the Colt Square in Cordova, and a couple from the Market of Seville, cheerful, well-meaning, playful rogues who, almost of one accord, ran up to Sancho and pulled him from his ass. Then one of them went in for the blanket from the host's bed and threw him on to it. But when they looked up they saw that the roof was rather too low for their purpose, and decided to go out into the back-yard, whose ceiling was the sky; and there, placing Sancho in the centre of the blanket, they began to toss him up and amuse themselves at his expense, as they do with dogs at Shrovetide.

The poor wretch's shouts at his blanket-tossing were loud enough to reach his master's ears, and Don Quixote, stopping to listen carefully, thought that some new adventure was on the way, until he realized that it was only his squire shouting. Whereupon he turned towards the inn at a painful gallop and, finding the door shut, rode round to find somewhere to get in. But no sooner did he get to the walls of the back-yard, which were not very high, than he saw the trick they were playing on his squire. He saw him fall and rise in the air so gracefully and so nimbly that, had it not been for his rage, he would certainly have burst out laughing. He tried to get from his horse on to the thatched wall, but he was so bruised and battered that he could not even dismount. And so from his horse he began to hurl insults and abuse at Sancho's tormentors, so many that it is impossible to record them. But this did not make them stop their tossing and laughter, nor did the flying Sancho cease his lamentations, which were mixed with threats alternating with pleas, though it was all of no use, and they did not give up until they were quite exhausted. Then they brought him his ass, put him on, and threw his greatcoat over his shoulders; and the tenderhearted Maritornes, seeing that he was worn out, thought it right to restore him with a jug of water and, so that it should be really cold, went to the well to draw it. Sancho took it, but just as he was going to put it to his lips he was stopped by his master's shouts.

"My good Sancho," he cried, "don't drink it. It will kill you. Look, I have the most holy balsam here"—and he held up the can of liquor. "Drink two drops of this and you will most certainly be cured."

At these words Sancho gave his master a sidelong glance and called even louder, "Has your worship forgotten, by any chance, that I am not a knight, or would you have me bring up such guts as I've still got? Keep your liquor in the devil's name and leave me alone."

No sooner had he spoken than he began to drink. But, finding at the first draught that it was only water, he would swallow no more, and begged Maritornes to bring him wine, which out of her good nature she did, and paid for it with her own money. For it is said of her that though she was of that trade, there was some shadow and vestige of a Christian about her.

So as soon as he had finished the wine, Sancho dug his heels into his ass's sides and, the inn door being opened for him, went out, very pleased that he had had his way and not paid a penny, though it had been at the cost of his shoulders, which usually went bail for him.

The innkeeper, it is true, remained in possession of his saddlebags in payment for the reckoning, for Sancho went out in such confusion that he did not miss them. As soon as he was outside, the host wanted to bar the door after him, but the tossers would not agree, for they were the sort of men who would not have cared two straws even if Don Quixote had really been one of the Knights of the Round Table.

⊰ *18* ⊱

In which are recorded
the Conversation between Sancho Panza
and His Master Don Quixote,
and Other Noteworthy Adventures

*S*ancho was so faint and dispir-
ited when he caught his master up, that he could not drive his ass.
And, seeing him in that state, Don Quixote said, "Now I am quite
certain, my good Sancho, that that castle or inn is enchanted. For
what could those creatures who made such villainous sport with you
be but phantoms and creatures of the other world? What makes me
positive of it is that, when I was watching the acts of your sad
tragedy over the thatched wall of the yard, I could not climb on to it,
nor even dismount from Rocinante, for they must have had me
under a spell. Because I swear to you on my faith as a Christian that,
if I could have climbed on or dismounted, I would have so avenged
you that those cowardly scoundrels would have remembered the
joke as long as they lived, even if by so doing I had broken the laws
of chivalry, which, as I have often told you, do not permit of a
knight's striking one who is not a knight except in a case of urgent
and extreme necessity, in defence of his own life and person."

"I would have avenged myself, too, if I could, knight or no
knight," replied Sancho, "but I couldn't, though it's my opinion that

162

the creatures who amused themselves at my expense were not phantoms or enchanted, as your worship says, but flesh-and-blood men like ourselves. And they had all got names, for I heard them when they were tossing me; one of them was called Pedro Martinez, another Tenorio Hernandez, and I heard them call the innkeeper Juan Palomeque, the left-handed. So it was something different from enchantment that stopped your getting over the yard wall or dismounting from Rocinante. And what I gather from all this is that these adventures which we are always seeking will lead us in the long run to such misadventures that we shan't know our right foot from our left. It would be a good deal better and more proper, my little understanding tells me, for us to go home, now that it's harvest time, and look after our own affairs, and stop wandering from pillar to post, out of the frying-pan into the fire, as they say."

"How little you understand matters of chivalry, Sancho," replied Don Quixote. "Be silent and patient, for the day will come when you will see with your own eyes how honourable it is to follow this profession. Tell me now, what greater pleasure can there be in the world, what joy equal to that of winning a battle and triumphing over an enemy? There can be no doubt of it. None."

"That may well be," replied Sancho, "for all I know. But I do know that since we have been knights errant—or your worship has, for I cannot count myself of that honourable number—we have never won a battle except that one over the Basque, and even from that one your worship came off with the loss of half an ear and half a helmet. But since then it has been nothing but beatings and still more beatings, punches and still more punches,—and I got my tossing into the bargain, and that from persons enchanted, on whom I can't take revenge, and so learn for myself what pleasure there is in conquering an enemy, as your worship says."

"That is an affliction which I bear and you must bear, Sancho," replied Don Quixote. "But from now on I will try to have at hand a sword of such craftsmanship that no kind of enchantment can be worked against its bearer. It is even possible that my fortune may procure me the sword Amadis wore when he was called the *Knight of the Burning Sword.* It was one of the best ever worn by any knight in all the world. For it not only had the virtue I mentioned, but also cut like a razor, and there was no armour, however strong and enchanted, which could stand up to it."

"Such is my luck," said Sancho, "that when this comes about and your worship finds such a sword, it will only be of use and profit to knights, like that balsam. As for squires, they may sup on sorrow."

"Never fear that," said Don Quixote, "for Heaven will deal more kindly with you."

While Don Quixote and his squire rode on, deep in conversation, our knight saw a great thick cloud of dust approaching them along the road they were taking; and, on seeing it, he turned to Sancho and said, "This is the day, Sancho, on which shall be seen the good fortune which fate has in store for me. It is on this day, I say, as much as on any other, that the valour of my arm shall be displayed. Today I shall perform deeds that will remain written in the book of fame for all future ages. Do you see that dust-cloud rising over there, Sancho? It is all churned up by a prodigious army of various and innumerable nations that is marching this way."

"In that case there must be two armies," said Sancho, "for in the opposite direction there is a similar cloud of dust rising as well."

Don Quixote turned to look and, seeing that Sancho was right, rejoiced exceedingly, being quite certain that there were two armies advancing to the attack, and that they would meet in the middle of that wide plain. For every hour and every minute his mind was always full of those battles, enchantments, adventures, miracles, loves, and challenges which are related in books of chivalry; and everything that he said, thought or did was influenced by his fantasies. As for the dust-cloud he had seen, it was caused by two great flocks of sheep, which were being driven along that road in opposite directions, but owing to the dust they were not visible until they drew near. So emphatically, however, did Don Quixote affirm that they were armies, that Sancho came to believe him and asked, "Sir, what must we do now?"

"What?" cried Don Quixote. "Favour and aid those in need and distress. I must tell you, Sancho, that the army which is coming towards us is led and commanded by the great Emperor Alifanfaron, lord of the great island of Taprobana; the other which is marching behind us is the army of his enemy, the King of the Garamantas, Pentapolin of the Naked Arm, so called because he always rides into battle with his right arm bare."

"Why do these two lords hate one another, then?" asked Sancho.

"They hate one another," replied Don Quixote, "because this Alifanfaron is a furious pagan, and is in love with Pentapolin's daughter, a very lovely and, what is more, a very gracious lady, and a Christian, whose father will not give her to the pagan king unless he first foreswears the faith of his false prophet, Mahomet, and is converted to his own."

"By my beard," said Sancho, "but that Pentapolin is right, and I'll help him all I can."

"In that you will be doing your duty, Sancho," said Don Quixote, "for you do not need to be a knight to take part in battles like this."

"I can well understand that," replied Sancho. "But where shall we put this ass so as to be certain of finding him when the skirmish is over? For I don't think it has ever been the custom to ride into battle on a beast like this."

"That is true," said Don Quixote. "The only thing that you can do is to leave it to chance whether he is lost or not, for we shall have so many horses when we emerge victorious that even Rocinante will be in danger of being exchanged for another. But listen to me and look, for I want to point out the chief knights in these two armies. And so that you may see and note them better, let us retire up that slope, from which we should be able to make out both hosts."

So they did, and took up their positions on a hillock from which they would have clearly seen both the flocks which Don Quixote had transformed into armies but for the clouds of dust they raised, which obscured and blinded their vision. This, however, did not prevent Don Quixote from imagining what was neither visible nor existing and, raising his voice to say, "That knight over there in bright yellow armour, with a crowned lion couchant at a damsel's feet on his shield, is the valorous Laurcalco, Lord of the Silver Bridge. The other in the armour flowered with gold, and with three crowns argent on a field azure on his shield, is the redoubtable Micocolembo, Grand Duke of Quirocia. The other, on his right, with gigantic limbs, is the undaunted Brandabarbaran of Boliche, Lord of the three Arabias; he wears a serpent's skin for armour, and has for shield a gate which, report has it, is one of the gates of the temple that Samson pulled down when with his death he avenged himself on his enemies.

"But look in the other direction, and you will see in front, and leading the other army, the ever-victorious, never-vanquished Timonel of Carcajona, Prince of New Biscay; his armour is quartered azure, vert, argent and gold, and on his shield he bears a cat or on a field gules with a scroll inscribed 'Miau'—which is the initial of his lady, who, so they say, is the peerless Miaulina, daughter of Duke Alfeñiquen of Algarbe. The other who burdens and oppresses the back of that powerful and spirited war-horse, with armour as white as snow and a white shield without a device, is a new knight of the French nation, called Pierre Papin, Lord of the Baronies of Utrique. That other, pricking with iron heel the flanks of his piebald courser, and bearing for arms the azure cups, is the powerful Duke of Nerbia, Espartafilardo of the Wood, who bears on his shield the device of an asparagus plant, with a motto in Castilian which runs, 'Thus trails my fortune.' "

So he went on, naming many imaginary knights in each squadron, for each of whom he improvised armour, colours, devices, and mottoes, carried away by his strangely deluded imagination, and continuing without a pause, "That squadron in the front is made up of men of various nations: here are drinkers of the sweet waters of the famous Xanthus, mountaineers who tread the Massilian fields, sifters of the pure and fine gold of Arabia Felix, dwellers on the famous cool shores of clear Thermodon, men who in various ways drain golden Pactolus for its precious sand, faithless Numidians, Persians famous for their bows and arrows, Parthians, Medes who fight as they fly, Arabs with no fixed abode, Scythians as cruel as they are fair, Ethiopians with their lips bored, and countless more nations whose visages I see and recognize but whose names I do not remember.

"In that other squadron come drinkers of the crystal waters of olive-bearing Betis; men who burnish and polish their faces with the liquor of the ever-rich and golden Tagus; men who enjoy the health-giving waters of the divine Genil; dwellers in the Tartesian plains with their abundant pastures; men who enjoy the Elysian fields of Jerez; men of La Mancha, rich and crowned with golden corn; men clad in iron, survivors of the ancient Gothic race; bathers in the Pisuerga, famous for its mild current; men who graze their flocks on the broad pastures of the winding Guadiana, famous for its secret bed; men who shiver with the cold of the wooded Pyrenees and among the white snows of the lofty Apenines—in short, all whom Europe contains within its boundaries."

Good Lord! how many provinces he reeled off, how many nations he enumerated, giving to each one with marvellous readiness its proper attributes, being completely soaked and immersed in all that he had read in his lying books! Sancho Panza hung on his words and said nothing. But from time to time he turned to see if he could distinguish the knights and giants whom his master named. But, as he could not make out one of them, he said, "Sir, devil a man or a giant, or a knight your worship mentions is to be seen, for all that. At least, I can't see them. Perhaps it's all enchantment, like the apparitions last night."

"How can you say that?" replied Don Quixote. "Cannot you hear the horses neighing and the trumpets blaring and the beating of the drums?"

"The only thing that I can hear," replied Sancho, "is a great bleating of rams and ewes." And that was the truth, for the two flocks were getting near.

"It is your fear," said Don Quixote, "which prevents your seeing or hearing aright, for one of the effects of fright is to disturb the senses and make things appear as they are not. If you are so afraid, go aside a little and leave me alone, for I am sufficient on my own to ensure victory to the party to which I lend my aid."

And so saying, he spurred Rocinante, put his lance in its rest and rushed down the little slope like a thunderbolt, with Sancho shouting after him, "Turn back, Don Quixote, for I swear to God, sir, they are rams and ewes you are going to attack. Turn back! Oh, I wish I had never been born! What madness is it this time? Look, there is not a giant or a knight at all, nor cats, nor arms, nor shields quartered or entire, nor cups azure or bedevilled. What are you doing? Poor sinner that I am!"

But this did not make Don Quixote turn. Instead he went on, shouting loudly, "Ho, knights who follow and fight beneath the banner of the valorous Emperor Pentapolin of the Naked Arm, follow me, all of you, and you shall see how easily I will give him his revenge on his enemy Alifanfaron of Taprobana!" With which words he charged into the middle of the squadron of ewes and began to spear them with as much courage and daring as if he were in very truth spearing his mortal enemies. The shepherds and herdsmen who were with the flock shouted to him to stop. But, seeing that this had no effect, they unbuckled their slings and began to salute his ears with stones the size of fists.

Don Quixote took no heed of stones, but galloped all over the place, shouting, "Where are you, proud Alifanfaron? Come to me. I am a single knight, and desire to prove your valour hand to hand, and to take your life for the wrong you have done the valorous Pentapolin the Garamantan."

At that moment came a pebble from the brook and, hitting him on the side, buried two of his ribs in his body. Finding himself so battered, he thought that he was certainly killed or badly wounded. So, remembering his balsam, he took out his can, and, putting it to his mouth, began to toss the liquor into his stomach. But before he had managed to swallow what seemed to him sufficient, another sugared almond hit him on the hand and struck the can so fairly that it smashed it in pieces, taking three or four of his teeth out of his mouth on the way and badly bruising two fingers of his hand. So

He went on, shouting loudly, "Ho, knights who follow and fight beneath the banner of the valorous Emperor Pentapolin of the Naked Arm, follow me, all of you, and you shall see how easily I will give him his revenge on his enemy Alifanfaron of Taprobana!" With which words he charged into the middle of the squadron of ewes and began to spear them with as much courage and daring as if he were in very truth spearing his mortal enemies. (page 168) hard was the first blow and so hard the second that the poor knight was knocked from his horse on to the ground. The shepherds then came up to him and, concluding that they had killed him, hurriedly rounded up their flocks, took up the dead sheep, which were about seven in number, and made off without further enquiry.

All this time Sancho stood on the hill and watched his master's strange performance, tearing his beard and cursing the hour and the moment that Fortune had brought them together. But when he saw him lying on the ground and the shepherds gone, he went down the hill to him and found him not stunned but in a very bad way.

"Didn't I tell you, Don Quixote, sir," he said, "to turn back, for they were not armies you were going to attack, but flocks of sheep?"

"What a way that scoundrel of an enchanter, my enemy, has of transforming things and making them invisible! You must know, Sancho, that it is a very easy thing for enchanters to give things whatever appearance they please. For this wicked sorcerer, my persecutor, being envious of the glory he saw I was sure to gain from this battle, has turned the hostile squadrons into flocks of sheep. If you do not believe me, Sancho, do one thing, I beg of you, and you will discover that you are mistaken and that I am speaking the truth. Get on your ass, and follow them stealthily. Then you will see that as soon as they get a little way from here they will turn back to their original shapes, and will not be sheep any more but well-built proper men, as I first described them to you. But do not go now, for I have need of your help and service. Come near to me and look how many of my teeth are missing, for I do not think they have left me any in my head."

Sancho came so near as almost to thrust his eyes into his master's mouth; and that was the very moment when the balsam began to work in Don Quixote's stomach; so that just as Sancho drew close to peer into his mouth the knight threw up what was in him more violently than a shot from a gun, and sent it all over the beard of his compassionate squire.

"Holy Mary!" cried Sancho. "What has happened to me? Sure, this poor sinner is mortally wounded, since he is vomiting blood."

But on examining things a little more closely, he realized, from its colour, taste, and smell, that it was not blood but the balsam from the can, which he had seen him drinking; and this so turned his stomach that he threw up his very guts over his master; and the pair of them were then in the same pickle. Sancho ran to his ass to get out of his saddle-bags something with which to clean himself and cure his master, and when he found the bags missing almost went out of his mind. He cursed himself once more, and decided in his heart to leave Don Quixote and return home, even if he were to lose the payment for his services and his hopes of the governorship of the promised isle.

At this the knight got up and, with his left hand to his mouth to prevent the rest of his teeth from falling out, took in the other the reins of the faithful Rocinante, whose disposition was so good and loyal that he had never stirred from his master's side. Then he went over to his squire, who was leaning against his ass with his hand on his cheek, a position expressing great dejection and, seeing his melancholy mood, said to him, "I tell you, Sancho, that no man is worthier than another unless he does more than another. All these squalls which greet us are signs that the weather will soon clear and things go well with us; for neither good nor evil can last for ever; and so it follows that as evil has lasted a long time, good must now be close at hand. You must not grieve, therefore, at the disasters which befall me, for surely no share of them fell to you."

"How not?" replied Sancho. "Wasn't it my father's son who got tossed in the blanket yesterday? And the saddle-bags that I've lost today with all my valuables in them, whose were they but mine?"

"What, are your saddle-bags missing, Sancho?" asked Don Quixote.

"Yes, they are," replied Sancho.

"In that case we have nothing to eat today," said Don Quixote.

"That would be so," replied Sancho, "if there were not any of those herbs in the fields, which your worship says you know, and which unfortunate knights errant like yourself use to supply their needs in cases like this."

"All the same," replied Don Quixote, "I would rather have a hunk of bread or a loaf, and a couple of pilchards' heads, than all the herbs in Dioscorides' herbal with all Doctor Laguna's illustrations thrown in. But, anyhow, get on your ass, good Sancho, and follow me. For God, the provider of all things, cannot let us want, especially as we are engaged in His service, since He does not fail the gnats of the air, the worms in the ground, nor the tadpoles in the water, and He is so merciful that He makes the sun rise on the good and the bad, and rains on the just and the unjust."

"Your worship," said Sancho, "would make a better preacher than a knight errant."

"Knights errant, Sancho, knew—and have to know—about everything," said Don Quixote; "for in the olden times a knight errant would be as ready to deliver a sermon or make a speech in the middle of the royal camp as if he were a graduate of the university of Paris, whence it can be inferred that the lance has never blunted the pen, nor the pen the lance."

"Well, I'll take your worship's word for it," replied Sancho. "Let's go on now and try to find somewhere to lodge tonight, and pray God it may be a place where there are no blankets or blanket-tossers, or apparitions, or Moorish enchanters; for if there are, I'll fling meat and hook to the Devil."

"Ask that of God, son," said Don Quixote, "and lead me where you like, for this time I am going to leave the choice of lodging to you. But lend me your hand, and feel with your finger how many teeth are missing from the top jaw on my right side, for that is where I feel the pain."

Sancho put his fingers in and, as he felt around, asked: "How many molars used your worship to have on that side?"

"Four," replied Don Quixote, "and a wisdom tooth, all sound and whole."

"Think well what you say, sir," replied Sancho.

"I say four, or perhaps five," replied Don Quixote, "for in all my days I have never had a tooth drawn, nor one fall out, nor destroyed by decay."

"Well, in this lower jaw," said Sancho, "your worship has only two teeth and a half, and on the top not so much as a half, for it is all as smooth as the palm of my hand."

"Oh, what a misfortune!" exclaimed Don Quixote on hearing his squire's sad news. "I had rather have lost an arm, provided it were not my sword arm. For I would have you know, Sancho, that a mouth without molars is like a mill without a stone, and a tooth is more precious than a diamond. But we who profess the strict order of chivalry are subject to all such misfortunes. Mount, my friend, and lead on. I will follow at your pace."

Sancho obeyed, and took the direction in which he thought he might be likely to find lodging, keeping to the highway, which was well beaten in those parts. And as they went along slowly, because the pain in Don Quixote's jaws gave him no rest nor any disposition to hurry, Sancho tried to entertain him and divert his mind by talk. And some of the things he said will be found in the next chapter.

⊰ *19* ⊱

Of the Sensible Conversation
between Sancho Panza and His Master,
of the Adventure with a Corpse,
and Other Famous Happenings

*I*n my opinion, sir, there isn't a shadow of doubt that all these misfortunes which have happened to us lately have been a punishment for your worship's sinning against the law of chivalry by not fulfiling the oath you took, not to eat bread off a table-cloth nor lie with the queen, and all the rest of the things you swore, until you had got that helmet from Malandrino, or whatever they call the Moor—I can't remember."

"You are quite right, Sancho," said Don Quixote, "but, to tell you the truth, it had slipped my memory. And you can be just as certain that it was for not reminding me of it in time that the affair of the blanket happened to you. But I will make amends, for in the law of chivalry there are ways of compounding for everything."

"Did I swear something then, by any chance?" asked Sancho.

"It is no matter that you did not swear," said Don Quixote; "it is enough that I consider you not very clear of complicity. But whichever way it is, there will be no harm in providing a remedy."

"If that's so then," said Sancho, "take good care, your worship, not to forget that too, like the oath; or perhaps the phantoms may take it into their heads to have their fun with me again, and even with your worship, if they find you so wilful."

When darkness fell they were still on the high road deep in their conversation, and had not found any place to shelter that night; what was worse, they were dying of hunger, for with their saddle-bags they had lost their whole larder and store. And, to complete their misfortunes, there followed an adventure that did not require any contrivance actually to look like one.

The night set in dark, but still they rode on, Sancho thinking that, as they were on the highway, they should by rights find a good inn within six or eight miles. As they continued, then, on their way, the night being dark, the squire hungry and his master more than a little disposed to eat, they saw coming towards them on their road a great number of lights, which looked more like stars in motion than anything else.

Sancho was alarmed at the sight of them, and his master did not altogether like them either. The squire checked his ass, and Don Quixote his horse, and they stopped still, peering attentively to make out what it could be. They saw that the lights were coming near, and the nearer they got the bigger they seemed. At this Sancho began to tremble as if he had taken quicksilver, and the hair of Don Quixote's head stood on end. But the knight gained a little courage and said, "This, Sancho, beyond a doubt, must be a very great and most perilous adventure, and I shall need to show all my valour and courage."

"Oh dear me!" replied Sancho. "If this is an adventure with phantoms, as it seems, where shall I find ribs to endure it?"

"Never mind if they are phantoms," said Don Quixote. "I will not let them touch a thread of your garment. If they played the fool with you last time it was because I could not get over the yard wall. But now we are on open ground where I can wield my sword as I please."

"What if they put a spell on you and cramp you as they did before?" cried Sancho. "What will it matter if you are on the open ground or not?"

"Nevertheless," replied Don Quixote, "I beg you, Sancho, to have courage, for experience will give you proof of mine."

"I will, if it please God," replied Sancho. And the pair of them stood a little back from the road, and once more watched carefully to see what those travelling lights might be. Then after a while they made out a number of forms in white surplices, at which frightful vision Sancho Panza's courage absolutely vanished, and his teeth began to chatter as if he had the quartan ague. And his trembling and chattering grew even worse when they distinctly made out what it was; for they saw some twenty horsemen with blazing torches in their hands, and behind them a litter covered in black, followed by six more horsemen swathed in mourning down to their mules' feet—it was evident from their slow pace that they were not horses. The figures in white were muttering to themselves as they came, in low and mournful tones.

This extraordinary spectacle at such an hour and in such a lonely place was quite enough to strike terror into Sancho's heart and even into his master's. The squire's courage was long since exhausted, but it was otherwise with Don Quixote, for by this time his vivid imagination had suggested that this was one of the adventures out of his books. It seemed to him that the litter was a bier on which they were carrying some dead or badly wounded knight, and that the task of avenging him was reserved for himself. So without more ado he couched his lance, steadied himself in the saddle, and with exquisite bearing and courage took up his position in the middle of the road along which the white figures would have to pass. Then, when he saw them approaching, he cried, "Stop, knights, or whoever you may be, and inform me who you are, where you come from, where you are going, and what it is you are carrying on that bier. For, by all appearances, either you have done or suffered some injustice, and it is proper and needful that I should know it, either to punish you for the wrong you have done, or to avenge the outrage done upon you."

"We are in a hurry," replied one of the men in white, "for the inn is some distance away. We can't stop to answer all your questions."

Then he spurred his mule and pressed on. But Don Quixote, very indignant at this reply, laid hold of his bridle and said, "Stop, and be rather more civil. Give me the information that I asked for, or else do battle with me, all of you."

The mule was timid, and was so frightened at being seized by the bridle that she rose on her hind legs and threw her rider to the ground. A servant who was on foot saw the white-robed figure fall and began to abuse the now furious Don Quixote, who without more ado couched his lance and attacked one of the mourners, throwing him to the ground too, with a severe wound. He then turned on the others, and the speed with which he attacked and routed them was a wonder to see, for Rocinante seemed in that moment to have sprouted wings, so swiftly and proudly did he move. The men in white, a cowardly and unarmed crew, fled from the battle most promptly, and were off in one moment, running across the plain with their flaming torches, looking like nothing so much as masked figures flitting about on a carnival or festival night. As for the mourners, they were so swathed and muffled in their long skirts and gowns that they could not stir, and Don Quixote thrashed them all without the least danger to himself, forcing them to quit the field, much against their will; for they all thought that he was no man, but a devil from Hell come to bear off the corpse which they were carrying on the litter. Sancho looked on at all this, admiring his master's dauntless courage and saying to himself, "There's no doubt that my master is as valiant and mighty as he says."

There was a torch burning on the ground beside the first man who had been thrown by his mule, and as soon as Don Quixote saw him by its light he went up to him and poked his lance-point in his face, calling on him to surrender on pain of death. To which the fallen man replied, "I am surrendered enough already, since I can't move. One of my legs is broken. I beg your worship, if you are a Christian gentleman, not to kill me. You would be committing a great sacrilege, for I am a Master of Arts and have taken my first orders."

"Then, what the devil brought you here?" cried Don Quixote, "if you are a churchman?"

"What, sir?" replied the fallen man. "My bad luck."

"A still worse fate threatens you," said Don Quixote, "if you do not answer satisfactorily all the questions I asked of you in the first place."

"Your worship shall soon be satisfied," replied the Master of Arts; "and I must tell you that although I said before that I was a Master of Arts, I am only a Bachelor. My name is Alonso Lopez, native of Alcobendas. I am on my way from Baeza with eleven other priests—the men with the torches who have run away. We are going to the city of Segovia, escorting a corpse which is lying on that litter. The dead man was a gentleman who died at Baeza, where he was laid, and now, as I say, we are taking his bones to his tomb, which is in Segovia, his native town."

"And who killed him?" asked Don Quixote.

"God, by means of a pestilent fever which took him," replied the Bachelor.

"In that case," said Don Quixote, "our Lord has relieved me of the task of avenging his death, which I should have taken upon myself, had he fallen by any other hand. But seeing Who it was that killed him, there is nothing for it but to be silent and shrug my shoulders. For I should do the same were He to slay me. But I would have your Reverence know that I am a knight of La Mancha, Don Quixote by name, and that it is my office and profession to roam about the world, righting wrongs and relieving injuries."

"I don't know what this righting of wrongs may be about," said the Bachelor; "for I was all right, and by leaving me with a broken leg which will not be right for all the days of my life you have made me all wrong. The injury you have relieved in me has left me so injured that I shall remain injured for life, and it has been sufficient misadventure to have met you on your quest for adventure."

"You can never tell how things will turn out," replied Don Quixote. "The trouble, Sir Bachelor Alonso Lopez, arose from your coming in the night as you did, dressed in those surplices, with your flaming torches, muttering your prayers and swathed in mourning, for you truly looked like some evil things from the other world. I could not therefore refrain from fulfilling my duty by attacking you, and I should have attacked you even if I had known for certain that you were the very devils from Hell which I judged and took you to be."

"Since my fate would have it so," said the Bachelor, "I entreat your worship, Sir Knight Errant, who have done me such arrant mischief, to help me from under this mule, which has caught one of my legs between the stirrup and the saddle."

"I might have gone on talking till tomorrow," said Don Quixote. "How long would you have waited to tell me of your plight?"

Then he shouted for Sancho Panza. But his squire did not choose to come, because he was busy unloading one of the good gentlemen's mules, which carried the stores and was well laden with good things. Sancho made a bag from his overcoat and, cramming all that he could into it, loaded his ass. Which done, he turned to his master's call and helped to get the Bachelor from under the weight of his mule. Then he helped him on and gave him his torch, while Don Quixote bade the poor fellow follow his companions and beg their pardon on his behalf for the injury which he had been unable to avoid doing them. And said Sancho as he departed, "If by chance, these gentlemen wish to know who the valorous knight was that did them such mischief, tell them, your worship, that it was the famous Don Quixote de la Mancha, who also bears the name of The Knight of the Sad Countenance."

With that the Bachelor rode off, and Don Quixote asked Sancho what had made him call him the Knight of the Sad Countenance at that particular moment.

"I'll tell you," answered Sancho. "It's because I was watching you for a while by the light of the torch that poor wretch was carrying, and really your worship has lately got the most dismal face I've ever seen. It must be either from weariness after the battle or from your worship's losing his teeth."

*He went over to his squire, who was leaning against his ass
with his hand on his cheek, a position expressing great
dejection and, seeing his melancholy mood, said to him, "I
tell you, Sancho, that no man is worthier than another
unless he does more than another. All these squalls which
greet us are signs that the weather will soon clear and things
go well with us; for neither good nor evil can last forever."
(page 172)*

"It is from neither," replied Don Quixote, "but because the sage whose task it is to write the history of my deeds must have thought it right for me to take some title, as all knights did in the olden days. One called himself The Knight of the Burning Sword; another, of the Unicorn; one, of the Damsels; another, of the Phoenix; another, The Knight of the Griffin; and yet another, of Death; and by these' names and devices were they known all round the world. That is why I say that the sage I mentioned has put it into your thoughts and into your mouth to call me now The Knight of the Sad Countenance, a name which I intend to use from this day on; and to make it fit me better, I intend to have a very sad countenance painted on my shield when I have an opportunity."

"There's no need to waste time and money on painting a face," said Sancho. "Your worship has only to uncover your own and show it to anyone who looks at you, and they'll call you The Knight of the Sad Countenance all right, without any picture or shield, and that's the truth. Believe me, sir—though I'm speaking in fun—hunger and loss of teeth have given you such a dismal face that you can easily do without the sad painting."

Don Quixote laughed at Sancho's joke; nevertheless he decided to take that name as soon as he could have it painted on his shield or buckler, as he had proposed.

"I fear, Sancho," he said, "that I have incurred excommunication for laying violent hands on holy things—*Juxta illud, si quis suadente diabolo*, etc., although I know that I did not lay my hands on them, but this lance; and, what is more, I did not suspect that I was injuring priests or Church property, which, good Catholic and faithful Christian that I am, I respect and adore, for I thought that they were phantoms and spectres from the other world. But if it comes to the worst I remember what happened to the Cid Ruy Diaz, when he broke the chair of the King's Ambassador in the presence of his Holiness the Pope, who excommunicated him for it, notwithstanding which the good Rodrigo de Vivar bore himself like a very honourable and valiant knight that day."

By this time the Bachelor had gone, as has been said, without making Don Quixote any reply, and the knight was anxious to see if the body on the litter was a skeleton or not; but Sancho would not agree, saying, "Sir, your worship has concluded this perilous adventure at less cost to yourself than any that I have seen. But although these people are conquered and defeated, it may occur to them that they were beaten by one man alone; and that may so abash them and shame them that they will pluck up some courage and come back after us; and then we shall have work enough on our hands. The ass is all right; the mountain's near; hunger presses; and we have nothing to do but to beat a graceful retreat and, as the saying is, to the grave with the dead and the living to their bread." So, driving his ass before him, he begged his master to follow; and Don Quixote, feeling that Sancho was right, did so without another word.

They took their way between two hills, and had not gone far when they found themselves in a wide, secluded valley, where they alighted and Sancho unloaded the ass; and, stretched on the green grass, with hunger for sauce, they took their breakfast, lunch, dinner, and supper all in one, appeasing their hunger from more than one hamper which the dead man's noble clerics—who seldom fail to look after themselves—had brought on their baggage-mule. But another misfortune befell them, and to Sancho this was the worst of all: they had no wine, nor even water, to drink, and were parched with thirst. Sancho, however, saw that the meadow they were in was thick with fresh green grass, and said—what shall be recorded in the following chapter.

◅ 20 ▻

Of the Unparalleled Adventure achieved
by the Valorous Don Quixote de la Mancha
with Less Peril than
any ever achieved by Any Famous Knight
in the Whole World

*T*o judge from this grass, sir, there must certainly be a spring or a brook about here to keep it moist. So it would be a good idea if we were to go on a little farther, for we might find somewhere to quench this terribly annoying thirst, which is a great deal more distressing than hunger itself."

This suggestion seemed reasonable to Don Quixote. So he took Rocinante by the rein, and Sancho took his ass by the halter, though not till he had loaded him with what remained from their supper. Then they began to move forward through the meadow, feeling their way, for the night was so dark that they could not see anything. But before they had gone two hundred yards a great noise came to their ears, like the roar of a waterfall tumbling from some huge, high cliff. This sound cheered them enormously. But as they stopped to listen from what direction it came, they heard another loud noise, which drowned the pleasure they got from the sound of the water, especially Sancho's, for he was timid by nature and not at all courageous. What they heard was the sound of regular blows and a sort of clanking of iron and chains which, combined with the furious

185

roaring of the water, would have struck terror into any other heart but Don Quixote's. The night, as has been said, was dark, and they had happened to stray beneath some tall trees, the movements of whose leaves in the soft wind made a gentle but alarming sound; so that, taken all together, the solitude, the locality, the darkness, the roaring of the water and the rustling of the leaves produced a horror and dread, which increased when they found that the blows did not cease, nor the wind die down, nor morning dawn. And to make matters worse, they had no idea where they were. Don Quixote, however, his courage never failing, leapt upon Rocinante, braced his shield, brandished his lance, and cried, "Sancho, my friend, you must know that, by the will of Heaven, I was born in this iron age of ours to revive the age of gold or, as it is generally called, the golden age. It is for me that are reserved perils, mighty feats, and valorous exploits. It is I, I say once more, who must revive the order of the Round Table, the Twelve Peers of France, and the Nine Worthies, and consign to oblivion the Platirs, Tablantes, Olivantes and Tirantes, the Knights of the Sun and the Belianises, and all that herd of famous knights errant of olden times, by performing in this age in which I live such prodigies, such wonders, and such feats of arms as to eclipse the most famous deeds they ever performed. Observe, loyal and faithful squire, the darkness of this night, its strange silence, the dull, confused sound of these trees, the fearful noise of the water which we came to seek, and which seems to be hurled headlong from the high mountains of the moon, and that ceaseless thumping which wounds and afflicts our ears, which things, taken all together and each by itself, are sufficient to infuse fear, terror, and dread into the breast of Mars himself, and how much more so into one who is unaccustomed to such events and adventures. Yet all that I am describing to you serves only to spur and rouse my courage, and makes my heart bound in my breast with desire to embark on this adventure, however arduous it may prove. Therefore tighten Rocinante's girths a little, and God be with you! Wait for me here three days and no more; at the end of which time, if I should not come back, you may return to our village, and from there, as a favour and service to me, you will go to El Toboso and tell my incomparable lady Dulcinea that her captive knight died attempting deeds which might make him worthy to call himself hers."

When Sancho heard this speech of his master's, he began to weep most piteously, saying, "I don't know why your worship wants to start on this frightful adventure. It is night now, and no one can see us here. We can easily turn off the road and get out of danger, even if it means not drinking for three days. And, as there's nobody to see us, no one can call us cowards. What is more, I have heard the priest of our village, whom your worship knows very well, preach that the man who seeks danger perishes in it. So it isn't right to tempt Providence by taking on such a tremendous feat, from which we could only escape by a miracle. Be satisfied with the miracles Heaven has worked for your worship in saving you from the blanket-tossing I got, and bringing you off victorious, safe and sound, from all those enemies there were with that dead man. And, if all this isn't enough to soften that hard heart of yours, perhaps it will be moved by the thought that the very moment your worship has gone from here I'll be sure to give up my soul out of pure fear to anyone who may wish to bear it off. I left my country and forsook my wife and children to come and serve your worship, believing that I should do better and not worse; but as greed burst the bag, so it has rent my hopes; for just as I was most hopefully expecting to get that accursed and unlucky isle your worship has so often promised me, I see that instead you mean to leave me now in this place, far from all human company. In God's name, sir, do me not this wrong. Even if your worship will not altogether give up this exploit, put it off at least till morning. For by the science I learned when I was a shepherd, it can't be more than three hours till dawn, since the muzzle of the Bear is at the top of his head, and at midnight it is in line with the left paw."

"How can you see, Sancho, where the line is, or the muzzle, or the top of the head you speak of? The night is so dark that there is not a star to be seen in the whole sky."

"That's true," said Sancho, "but fear has many eyes, and can see things underground. So it'll easily see things up above in the sky. Besides, it's reasonable to suppose that it won't be long till dawn."

"Long or not," replied Don Quixote, "it shall never be said of me, now or at any time, that tears and prayers deflected me from my duty as a knight. Therefore, Sancho, pray be silent. For God, who has put it into my heart to embark on this unparalleled adventure, will take care to watch over my safety and to console your grief. All that you have to do is to tighten Rocinante's girths well and wait here, for I will return soon, alive or dead."

Sancho saw that his master was finally resolved, and that his tears, advice, and prayers had little effect on him. So he decided to use his ingenuity and, if he could, compel his master to wait till day. So, while he was tightening the horse's girths, slyly and unnoticed he tied Rocinante's fore-legs together with the halter of his ass, so that when Don Quixote wanted to start he could not, for his horse could move only by leaps. And when Sancho saw that his trick was successful he exclaimed, "See, sir, the Heavens are moved by my tears and prayers. They have ordained that Rocinante shall be unable to stir. If you persist in urging, spurring, and striking him, it will be provoking Fortune and, as the saying goes, kicking against the pricks."

At this Don Quixote grew exceedingly vexed, for the more he spurred his horse the less could he make him go. Therefore, without suspecting the reason, he thought it best to be calm and wait till dawn, or till Rocinante could move, no doubt ascribing the trouble to some cause other than Sancho's ingenuity. And so he said to him, "Since it is a fact, Sancho, that Rocinante cannot move, I am content to wait here until dawn smiles, although I weep at her delay."

"There's no need to weep," replied Sancho, "for I will entertain your worship and tell you stories from now till daylight, unless you would like to dismount and snatch a little sleep on this green grass, as knights errant do, so that you may be less weary when day comes and it's time to embark on this incomparable adventure that awaits you."

"Who is it you ask to dismount or to sleep?" asked Don Quixote.

"Am I by chance one of those knights who take their rest amidst dangers? Sleep yourself, for you were born to sleep, or do what you will. I will do what best suits my profession."

"Don't be annoyed, good master," replied Sancho. "I didn't mean to make you angry." Then he went closer to Don Quixote and put one hand on the pommel of his saddle and the other on the cantle, so that he stood clasping his master's left thigh without daring to stir an inch from him, so frightened was he of the blows which still continued to sound in regular succession. Don Quixote then bade him tell a tale for his entertainment, as he had promised; and Sancho replied that he would, if his dread of the noise would allow him. "But, for all that," he said, "I will endeavour to tell you a story, and if I manage to tell it without interruption, it'll be the best story in the world. Pay good attention, your worship, for I'm going to begin. Once upon a time; may good befall us all and evil strike the man who seeks it. Notice, your worship, that the ancients didn't begin their stories just as they pleased, but with a sentence by Cato, the Roman censor, who says, 'Evil strike the man who seeks it'; and that fits in here like a ring on a finger, meaning that your worship must stay quiet and not go anywhere seeking harm, but that we must turn up some other road, since nobody is making us follow this one, where there are so many terrors to frighten us."

"Go on with your story, Sancho," said Don Quixote, "and leave the road we are to follow to me."

"I tell you, then," Sancho resumed, "that in a village in Estremadura there was once a shepherd—a goatherd I should say, for he kept goats—and this shepherd or goatherd, as my story tells, was called Lope Ruiz. Now this Lope Ruiz fell in love with a shepherdess called Torralba, which shepherdess called Torralba was the daughter of a rich herdsman; and this rich herdsman—"

"If you tell your story that way, Sancho," said Don Quixote, "and repeat everything you have to say twice over, you will not be done in two days. Tell it consequentially, like an intelligent man, or else be quiet."

"The way I'm telling it," replied Sancho, "is the way all stories are told in my country, and I don't know any other way of telling it. It isn't fair for your worship to ask me to get new habits."

"Tell it as you like," replied Don Quixote, "and since it is the will of Fate that I cannot help listening, go on."

"And so, my dear master," Sancho went on, "as I said, this shepherd fell in love with the shepherdess Torralba, who was a plump, high-spirited girl, and rather mannish, for she had a slight moustache—I can almost see her now."

"Really, did you know her, then?" asked Don Quixote.

"I didn't know her," replied Sancho, "but the man who told me this story said that it was so true and authentic that when I told it to anyone else I could swear on my oath that I had seen it all. So, as the days came and the days went, the Devil, who never sleeps and tangles everything up, brought it about that the love which the shepherd had for the shepherdess turned to hatred and ill-will; and the reason was, as evil tongues told, that she caused him a number of little jealousies, such as exceeded the bounds and trespassed on the forbidden; and thenceforth the shepherd loathed her so much that, to avoid her, he decided to leave that country and go where his eyes should never see her again. But when Torralba found that Lope scorned her, she immediately fell to loving him more than she had ever loved him before."

"That is natural in women," said Don Quixote, "to scorn those who love them, and love those who loathe them. Go on, Sancho."

"It came about that the shepherd put his resolution into effect," said Sancho, "and set out driving his goats across the plains of Estremadura to cross into the kingdom of Portugal. Torralba heard of his plan, and followed him at a distance, on foot and bare-legged, with a pilgrim's staff in her hand and a satchel round her neck, which contained, the story goes, a bit of mirror and a broken comb, and some little bottle or other of washes for her face. But whatever it was she carried, I don't mean to set about inquiring now. I'll only say that the story tells how the shepherd came with his flock to cross the Guadiana river, which at that season was swollen and almost over-flowing; and at the place he struck it there wasn't a boat of any kind, nor anyone to ferry him or his flock to the other side. This put him very much out, because he saw Torralba coming near, and she was sure to bother him a great deal with her entreaties and tears. He went on looking about him, however, until he saw a fisherman close beside a boat, which was so small that it could only hold one man and one goat. But, all the same, he hailed him and arranged for him to take himself and this three hundred goats across. The fisherman got into the boat and took one goat over, came back and fetched another, and came back once more and took another. Keep an account of the goats which the fisherman is taking over, your worship, for if you lose count of one the story will end, and it won't be possible for me to tell you another word of it. I'll continue now and mention that the landing-place on the other side was very muddy and slippery, which delayed the fisherman a good deal in his journeys backwards and forwards. But, all the same, he came back for another goat, and another, and another."

"Take it that they are all across," said Don Quixote, "and do not go on coming and going like that, or you will never get them all over in a year."

"How many have got over so far?" asked Sancho.

"How the devil should I know?" replied Don Quixote.

"There now, didn't I tell you to keep a good count? Well, there's an end of the story. God knows there's no going on with it now."

"How can that be?" replied Don Quixote. "Is it so essential to the tale to know exactly how many goats have crossed that if you are one out in the number you cannot go on?"

"No, sir, not at all," answered Sancho. "But, when I asked your worship to tell me how many goats had got across and you replied that you didn't know, at that very moment everything I had left to say went clean out of my head, though there were some good and amusing things coming, I promise you."

"So," said Don Quixote, "the story is finished, then?"

"As sure as my mother is," said Sancho.

"Really," replied Don Quixote, "you have told me one of the strangest tales—true or false—that anyone could imagine in the whole world; and never in a lifetime was there such a way of telling it or stopping it, although I expected no less from your excellent intelligence. But I am not surprised, for this ceaseless thumping must have disturbed your brains."

"That may well be," replied Sancho, "but I know that so far as my story goes there is nothing more to say, for it just ends where the error begins in counting the goats that cross over."

"All right, let it end where it will," said Don Quixote. "And now let us see if Rocinante can move." He dug in his spurs once more, and the horse gave a few more leaps. Then he stood stock still, so fast was he tied.

At this point, it seems either the cold of morning, which was just breaking, or something laxative he had eaten for supper or, as seems more likely, the natural course of things, gave Sancho the inclination and desire to do what no one else could do for him; but so much fear had entered into his heart that he dared not stir a hair's breadth from his master. Yet it was quite impossible even to think of not fulfilling his needs. So what he did was to take a middle course. Very gently he moved his right hand from the crupper of the saddle, and with it neatly and noiselessly loosened the running knot, which was all that kept his breeches up, so that when it was undone they fell down and held him like fetters. After which he hitched up his shirt as best he could, and bared a pair of ample buttocks to the air. This done, which he thought was all he needed to relieve himself of his terrible griping pains, another greater problem confronted him: he was afraid that he could not relieve himself without making some report or noise. So he began to grind his teeth and contract his shoulders, holding his breath as much as he could. But despite all these precautions he was so unfortunate as in the end to make a little noise very different from the din which was causing him so much terror. And when Don Quixote heard it he asked: "What is that noise, Sancho?"

"I don't know, sir," he replied. "It must be something fresh, for these adventures and misadventures never begin for nothing."

He tried his luck again, and with such success that he relieved

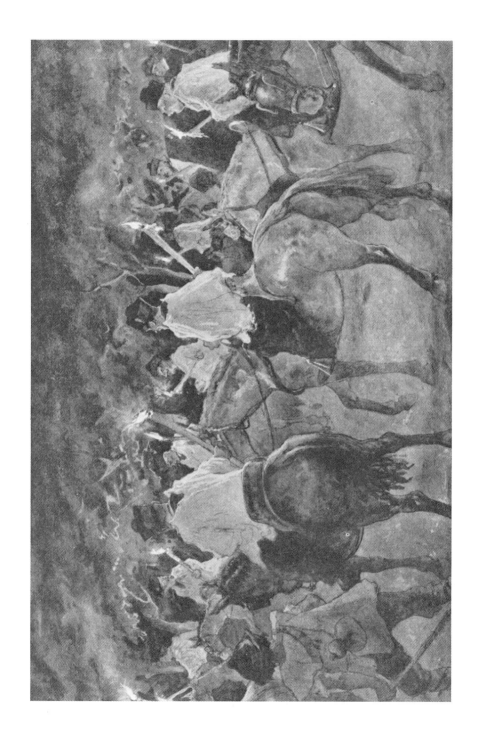

They saw some twenty horsemen with blazing torches in their hands, and behind them a litter covered in black, followed by six more horsemen swathed in mourning down to their mules' feet. (page 177) himself, without any more noise or disturbance, of the burden which had caused him such discomfort. As Don Quixote's sense of smell, however, was as keen as his hearing, and as Sancho was clinging so closely to him, it was impossible for some of the odour, which ascended almost perpendicularly, not to reach his nose; and no sooner did it get there than he went to the rescue and, holding his nostrils between two fingers, observed in rather snuffling tones: "You seem to be very frightened, Sancho."

"Yes, I am," replied Sancho, "but how is it that your worship particularly notices it now?"

"Because you smell more now, and not of ambergris," replied Don Quixote.

"That may be," said Sancho, "though it isn't my fault, but your worship's for dragging me out at such unearthly hours into such extraordinary places."

"Go two or three paces off, friend," said Don Quixote, without taking his fingers from his nose, "and pay more attention in future to your person and to the respect that you owe me; for it is my great familiarity with you that has engendered this contempt."

"I'll bet," replied Sancho, "you worship thinks that I have done —something that I shouldn't with my person."

"The less said about it the better, friend Sancho," replied Don Quixote.

Master and servant spent the night in conversation of this sort, and when Sancho saw that morning was fast approaching, he very cautiously unfettered Rocinante and tied up his breeches. And as soon as the horse found himself free, although never very mettlesome by nature, he seemed to revive, and began to paw the ground, for prancing—begging his pardon—was beyond him. Don Quixote took Rocinante's movements as a good omen and a sign for him to attempt that perilous adventure.

Dawn having broken by now and made objects distinctly visible, the knight saw that they were standing beneath some tall chestnut trees, which cast a very deep shadow. He also noticed that the blows had not ceased, though he could not see what the cause of them was.

So without more delay he put spur to Rocinante and, turning to take leave of Sancho, told him to wait for him there for three days at most, as he had already bidden him, and if he had not returned by that time, to take it as certain that, by God's will, he had ended his days on that perilous adventure. He once more spoke of Sancho's errand and of the message which he was to take on his behalf to his lady Dulcinea. As for payment for his services, said the knight, his squire need not worry. For, by the will which he had made before leaving home, Sancho would find himself completely satisfied in the matter of his wages, which would be duly proportionate to the time he had served. Should God, however, bring him through this peril safe, sound, and unharmed, his squire might reckon himself more than certain, he said, of the promised isle. Sancho burst into fresh tears at again hearing his good master's pitiful words, and determined not to leave him until the final issue and end of the business.

From these tears and this very honourable resolution the author of this history concludes that Sancho Panza must have been well born and at least an *Old Christian*. His master was rather touched by his feelings, but not sufficiently to show any weakness. On the contrary, concealing it as best he could, he began to ride in the direction from which the sounds of the water and the blows seemed to come. Sancho followed him on foot, as usual, leading by the bridle his ass, his constant companion in good and evil fortune; and when they had gone some way under those shady chestnut trees, they came out into a little meadow at the foot of a high cliff, from which fell a great head of water. Beneath the cliff were a few tumble-down houses, which looked more like ruins than dwellings, and from them, they discovered, came the hideous and still unceasing din of the hammering. Rocinante started at the noise of the water and of the thumping, but Don Quixote pacified him, and gradually advanced towards the houses, commending himself to his lady meanwhile with all his heart and imploring her to favour him in his formidable task and enterprise, and on his way he also commended himself to God that He might not forget him. Sancho did not leave his side, but craned his neck as far as he could to peer between Rocinante's legs and to make out the cause of his fears and alarms. They must have gone another hundred paces when, on their turning a corner, there appeared, clear and visible, the indubitable cause of that horrific and, to them, most dreadful sound, which had kept them all that night in such a state of terror and suspense. It was—do not take it amiss, good reader!—six fulling-hammers whose regular strokes made all that din.

Don Quixote was dumbfounded and utterly abashed at this sight and, when Sancho looked at him, his head hung down on his breast in confusion. But when Don Quixote looked at Sancho and clearly saw from his swollen cheeks and his laughing mouth that he was on the point of exploding, despite his own gloom he could not help laughing at the look of him. And as soon as Sancho saw that his master had begun, he let himself go with such violence that he had to hold his sides for fear of bursting. Four times he calmed down, and four times he broke into fresh laughter as violently as before. At this Don Quixote wished him to the devil, especially when he heard him say in mockery, "You must know, friend Sancho, that I was born by the will of Heaven in this our iron age to revive the age of gold, or the golden age. It is for me that are reserved perils, great exploits, and valorous deeds." And so he went on, repeating all or most of what his master had said when they first heard that frightful hammering.

When Don Quixote realized that Sancho was making fun of him, he got so furiously angry that he lifted his lance and dealt him two blows which would have relieved the master of the duty of paying his squire's wages, unless perhaps to his heirs, had they caught him on the head instead of on the shoulders. But when Sancho found himself so poorly rewarded for his joke, he was afraid that his master might carry the matter farther, and said to him with great humility, "Gently, your worship; I was only joking, I swear."

"You may be joking, but I am not," replied Don Quixote. "Come here, master joker. Do you think that if these fulling-hammers had

197

really been some perilous adventure I should not have shown the courage necessary to undertake it and carry it through? Am I, by chance, obliged, being as I am a knight, to recognize and distinguish sounds, and know whether they are fulling-hammers or not? For the case might be—as indeed it is—that I have never seen such things in my life, though you have seen them, wretched peasant that you are, and were born and brought up among them. But turn those six hammers into six giants, and let them beard me one by one or all together, and if I do not lay them all on their backs, make as much fun of me as you will."

"No more, dear master," replied Sancho. "I confess I laughed a little too much. But tell me, your worship, now that we are at peace—and may God bring you as safe and sound through all adventures that befall you as through this one—isn't the awful fright we were in rather a joke, and doesn't it make a good story? At least the fright that I was in, for your worship, I know very well, doesn't so much as know what fear or fright is."

"I do not deny," replied Don Quixote, "that what happened to us is a thing worth laughing at. But it is not worth telling, for not everyone is sufficiently intelligent to be able to see things from the right point of view."

"At least your worship knew how to point your lance all right when you pointed it at my head but hit my shoulders, thanks to Providence and my prompt ducking. But let that pass. It will all come out in the wash, and I have heard it said, if he makes you weep it is a sure sign he loves you. Besides, when men of quality scold their servants they generally give them a pair of breeches afterwards, though I don't know what they generally give them after a beating, unless perhaps in the case of knights errant it's isles, or kingdoms on dry land."

"The dice may so fall," said Don Quixote, "that every word you say will prove true. Forgive what is past, for you are sensible enough to know that first impulses are outside man's control. But take heed of one thing: you must abstain and refrain from overmuch speech

198

with me in future, for never in any of the countless books of chivalry which I have read have I found a squire who talked to his master as much as you do to yours. In fact I look upon it as a great fault in you and in me—in you for showing me so little respect, and in me for not making myself more respected. We read of Gandalin, the squire of Amadis of Gaul, that though he was Count of the Firm Isle he always spoke to his lord cap in hand, with bowed head and body bent in the Turkish fashion. Then what shall we say of Gasabal, Sir Galaor's squire, who was so quiet that, to inform us of the perfection of his marvellous silence, once only is his name mentioned in the whole of that great and authentic history? From all that I have said, Sancho, you must infer that a distinction must be kept between master and man, between lord and servant, and between knight and squire. So from today we must behave with more respect, and not give ourselves rope, since, for whatever reason I may be annoyed with you, it will always be the pitcher that comes off worst. The favours and benefits which I promised you will arrive in due course; and if they do not arrive, your wages at least will not be lost, as I have told you already."

"What your worship says is all very well," said Sancho, "but I should like to know, in case the time for favours never comes and we have to fall back on wages, how much a knight errant's squire earned in those days, and if they contracted by the month, or by the day like builders' labourers."

"I do not believe that squires ever worked for wages," replied Don Quixote, "only for favours; and I have assigned you some now in the sealed will which I have left at home, to provide against accidents; since I do not yet know how chivalry will fare in these calamitous times of ours, and I should not wish my soul to suffer for trifles in the other world. For I would have you know, Sancho, that there is no state more perilous than a knight errant's."

"That is true," said Sancho, "since the mere sound of the hammers of a fulling-mill was enough to alarm and disturb the heart of so valiant a knight errant as your worship. But you may rest assured that henceforth I shall not open my lips to make fun of your worship's business, but shall honour you as my master and natural lord."

"In that case," replied Don Quixote, "your days will be long on the face of the earth, for next to our parents we are bound to honour our masters as we would our fathers."

✠ *21* ✠

Of the High Adventure
and Rich Prize of Mambrino's Helmet
with Other Things which befell
Our Invincible Knight

*A*bout this time it began to rain
a little, and Sancho wanted to go into the fulling-mills, but Don
Quixote had conceived such a loathing of them, on account of the
wretched joke, that he would on no account agree. So, turning to the
right, they struck another road, like the one they had ridden on the
day before, and had not gone far before Don Quixote caught sight of
a man on a horse carrying something on his head which shone like
gold, on seeing which he turned to Sancho and said, "It seems to me,
Sancho, that there is no proverb which is not true, for they are all
drawn from experience itself, which is the mother of all sciences.
This is especially true of the saying: When one door shuts another
opens. This I say because if last night Fortune shut the door which
we were looking for, and deceived us with the fulling-mills, it is now
opening wide to us another, better, and more certain adventure.
And if I do not succeed in passing through this one, the fault will be
mine, and cannot be attributed to my scanty knowledge of
fulling-mills or to the darkness of the night. This I say because, if I
am not mistaken, there is someone approaching us bearing on his

head that helmet of Mambrino, about which I swore the oath you know of."

"Take good care what you say, your worship," said Sancho, "and even greater care what you do, for I shouldn't like some other fulling-mills to end up by milling and mashing your brains out."

"The devil take you, fellow," replied Don Quixote. "What has a helmet to do with fulling-mills?"

"I've no idea," replied Sancho, "but I swear that if I might talk as I used to, I could probably give you some reasons that would make your worship see that you are mistaken."

"How can I be mistaken, unbelieving traitor?" asked Don Quixote. "Tell me, can you not see that knight coming towards us on a dapple-grey steed with a gold helmet on his head?"

"What I see and perceive," replied Sancho, "is nothing but a man on a grey ass like mine with something glittering on his head."

"Why, that is Mambrino's helmet," said Don Quixote. "Stand aside and leave me to deal with him. You will see how, so as to save time, I shall complete this adventure without uttering a word, and the helmet I have so much desired will be mine."

"I shall take good care to stand aside," replied Sancho, "but pray God it is sweet marjoram, and not fulling-mills."

"I have told you already, brother, not to remind me again, even by so much as a thought, of those fulling-mills," said Don Quixote, "or I swear—and I will say no more—that I will mill your very soul."

Sancho fell silent, fearing that his master would fulfil the oath he had flung at him so roundly.

Now the truth of this matter of the helmet, the horse, and the horseman that Don Quixote saw is this. There were in that district two villages, one so small that it had neither an apothecary's shop nor a barber, while the other, near-by, had both. So the barber of the bigger place served the smaller, in which there was a sick man who needed bleeding and another fellow who wanted to be shaved; which was why the barber was now on the road carrying a brass basin. Now fate would have it that, as he came along, it began to rain. So, fearing that his hat, which was no doubt a new one, might get spoiled, he put the basin on his head, and, as it was clean, it shone from more than a mile away. He rode, as Sancho said, on a grey ass, and that is the reason why Don Quixote took them for a dapple-grey steed, a knight, and a golden helmet. For everything which he saw he adapted with great facility to his wild chivalrous and errant fancies. So, when he saw the luckless horseman draw near, without entering into any parley with him, he urged Rocinante into a canter and attacked him with lance couched, intending to run him through and through; and as he got up to him without checking the fury of his career, he cried out, "Defend yourself, base caitiff creature, or surrender of your own free will what is so rightfully mine."

The barber, seeing this apparition descending on him so unexpectedly and without warning, had no other means of avoiding his lance but by sliding down from his ass. But, once on the ground, he leapt up lighter than a deer, and began to run across the plain faster than the wind. The basin he left on the ground, and the delighted Don Quixote observed that the pagan had acted most prudently in imitation of the beaver, who, when hard pressed by the hunters, with his own teeth bites off what he knows by his natural instinct to be the object of the chase. So he bade Sancho pick up the helmet. And when he had it in his hands, the squire exclaimed, "By God, it's a good basin, and worth a *real* if it's worth a farthing."

He then gave it to his master, who placed it on his head, turning it round and round to find the vizor. But, unable to discover it, he remarked, "Certainly the pagan to whose measure this famous head-piece was first shaped must have had an enormous head, and the worst of it is that one half of it is missing."

When Sancho heard the basin called a head-piece he could not restrain his laughter, but suddenly he remembered his master's anger, and stopped short.

"What are you laughing at?" asked Don Quixote.

"It makes me laugh," he replied, "to think what a big head that pagan must have had, who owned that head-piece. It's like nothing so much as a barber's basin. Just like it, it is."

"Do you know what I think, Sancho? This famous piece, this

enchanted helmet, must have fallen by some strange accident into the hands of someone who did not esteem it at its true value. So, not knowing what he was doing, and seeing that it was pure gold, he must have melted down the other half for the sake of the metal, and made from this half what looks like a barber's basin, as you say. But, however that may be, its metamorphosis is of no consequence to me, who know what it really is. For I will have it set right in the first village where there is a smith, and so well that it will not be surpassed or even equalled by the helmet which the god of smithies forged and made for the god of battles. In the meantime, however, I will wear it as best I can, for something is better than nothing; and, besides, it will do very well to defend me from a stoning."

"So long as they don't shoot with slings," said Sancho, "the way they did in that battle between the two armies, when they knocked out your worship's teeth and broke the can which held that most blessed liquor that made me vomit up my guts."

"Its loss does not trouble me much," said Don Quixote, "for, as you know, I have the recipe by heart."

"So have I," replied Sancho, "but if I ever make it up or try it again in all my life, may this be my last hour. What's more, I don't mean to put myself in the way of requiring it, for I intend to use all my five senses to avoid being wounded or wounding anyone. I say nothing about another blanket-tossing, for such misfortunes are difficult to prevent, and if they come there's nothing for it but to hunch your shoulders, hold your breath, close your eyes, and let yourself go where fate and the blanket send you."

"You are a bad Christian, Sancho," said Don Quixote; "you never forget an injury once done you, though you should know that a noble and generous heart sets no store by such trifles. Did you come out with a lame foot or a broken rib or a cracked skull, that you cannot forget that jest? For, when you look at it carefully, it was only a jest and a sport; and if I had not taken it as such, I should long ago have returned there and done more execution to avenge you than the Greeks did for the rape of Helen who, if she had lived in our times, or my Dulcinea in hers, would most certainly not have had

Gino Pasamonte answered for them all, and said, "What your worship commands, lord and liberator, is of all impossibilities the most impossible for us to perform, since we cannot appear on the roads together, but must go singly and separately, each one on his own." (page 226) such a reputation for beauty as she had." And here he heaved a sigh that echoed to the clouds.

"Let it pass for a jest, then," said Sancho, "since it can't be avenged in earnest. But I know the quality of those jests and earnests, and I know, too, that they won't slip from my memory any more than the feel of them will from my shoulders. But to leave the subject, tell me, your worship, what shall we do with this dapple-grey steed that looks like a grey ass, which that fellow your worship knocked down has left abandoned? For to judge by the dust he kicked up and the way he skipped off he doesn't look as if he will ever come back for it. And I'll be blowed if the dapple is not a good ass."

"It is not my custom," said Don Quixote, "to plunder those whom I conquer, nor is it the usage of chivalry to take their horses and leave them to go on foot, unless the victor has lost his own mount in the fight, in which case it is lawful for him to take the beaten knight's as won in fair combat. Therefore, Sancho, leave the horse, or ass, or whatever you would have it be, for as soon as its master sees that we have gone away he will come back for it."

"God knows I should like to take it," replied Sancho, "or at least to swap it for my own, for it seems a better beast. Really the laws of chivalry are very strict, if they don't even stretch to letting one ass be swapped for another. But I should like to know if I couldn't at least swap the trappings."

"I am not very certain on that point," replied Don Quixote; "but, as it is a doubtful case, until I am better informed I should say that you might make the exchange, if you are in extreme need."

"So extreme," replied Sancho, "that if it were for my own person I couldn't need them more." So, with this permission, he made an immediate *mutatio capparum*, and put all the finery on his ass, which came off very much the better for the exchange. When this was done they breakfasted off the remains of the provender which they had plundered from the baggage-mule, and drank from the stream which turned the fulling-mills, though without once glancing in their direction, so heartily did they loathe them for the fright they had put them in.

Then, with their anger and even their gloom abated, they mounted, and without deciding what road to take—the custom of knights errant being to leave this matter to chance—they set out in the direction chosen by Rocinante. For his will acted as guide to his masters and to the ass as well, who always followed him in love and good fellowship, wherever he led. But all the same they came back to the highway and followed it at random without any definite plan.

As they were going along Sancho said to his master, "Sir, will your worship give me permission to say a few words? For since you laid that harsh command of silence upon me several things have been rotting in my stomach, and there's one that I have on the tip of my tongue at the moment and that I shouldn't like to go bad."

"Tell me," said Don Quixote, "and be brief in your arguments, for nothing long is ever pleasing."

"Well, sir," replied Sancho, "for several days lately I've been thinking how little profit is gained from wandering after the adventures which your worship seeks in these wastes and at these cross-roads. For even when the most perilous of them are victoriously concluded, there's no one to see or hear of them; and so they must remain in perpetual oblivion despite your worship's good intentions and their own deserts. So it seems to me that it would be better—with due deference to your worship's better judgment—for us to go and serve an Emperor or some other great Prince who is engaged in some war. In his service your worship might show the valour of your person, your great strength and greater wisdom. Then, when this lord whom we should serve came to see your worship's qualities, he would be bound to reward us, each according to our deserts; and in that case there couldn't fail to be someone to set down your worship's exploits in writing for everlasting remembrance. About my own I say nothing, because they must not be greater than a squire's should be, although I can say that, if it is customary in chivalry to record the deeds of squires, I don't think that mine will be left out."

"There is something in what you say, Sancho," replied Don Quixote, "but before he gets to that stage a knight must wander through the world, on probation as it were, in pursuit of adventures, so as to gain such a name and reputation, by achieving a few, that, if he goes to the court of some great monarch, he will already be well known by his deeds. Then as soon as the boys see him ride through the city gates, they will all follow him and surround him and shout, 'Here is the Knight of the Sun!'—or of the Serpent, or of any other device under which he may have performed his great deeds. 'Here,' they will cry, 'is that knight who in single battle conquered the great giant Brocabruno of mighty strength, the knight who freed the Great Mameluke of Persia from the long enchantment which had held him for almost nine hundred years.' Thus from mouth to mouth they will go on proclaiming his deeds, till suddenly, hearing the cries of the boys and the rest of the people, the King of that kingdom will appear at the windows of his royal palace. As soon as he sees the knight, he will recognize him by his armour or by the device on his shield, and then of course he will cry, 'Ho, there, let all the knights of my court ride out to receive the flower of chivalry, who is approaching.' All will ride out at his command, and the King himself will come half-way down his staircase, embrace him most warmly, greet him, kiss him on the cheek, and lead him to the chamber of his lady Queen. There the knight will find her with the Princess, her daughter, who is sure to be one of the loveliest and most perfect damsels to be found anywhere, however hard you may search the greater part of the known world. Then immediately afterwards, she will gaze into the knight's eyes, and he into hers, and each will seem to the other rather divine than human; and without knowing how or why, they will be enmeshed and captured in the intricate net of love, and be in great anguish of heart, not knowing in what words to reveal their feelings and desires. From there he will no doubt be taken to some richly furnished room in the palace, where they will strip off his armour and bring him a rich scarlet cloak to wear; and if he is handsome in his armour, he will look still better in the quilted jacket he wears under it. When night falls he will sup with the King, the Queen and the Princess, never taking his eyes from her, but gazing on her stealthily; and she will do the same with the same caution. For, as I have said, she is a very discreet damsel. The tables will be removed, and suddenly there will enter through the hall door an ugly little dwarf with a beautiful lady following behind him, escorted by two giants, to introduce a certain adventure, so contrived by a most ancient sage that the knight who brings it to a successful conclusion shall be accounted the best in the world.

"Then the King will immediately order all the knights present to attempt it, but none of them will bring it to a victorious conclusion except the stranger knight, to the great enhancement of his fame. At this the Princess will be much delighted, and think herself well rewarded into the bargain, in having firmly set her desires in so exalted a quarter.

"Now it happens, most fortunately, that this King, or Prince, or whatever he is, is engaged in a most stubborn war with another as powerful as himself, and the stranger knight, after some days spent at court, begs for permission to go and serve him in the said war. The King will grant his request with great pleasure, and the knight will kiss his hands most courteously for the favour. Then that night he will take leave of his lady the Princess through the railings of a garden which adjoins her sleeping-chamber, where he has spoken with her many times before by the help of a damsel much trusted by the Princess and privy to the whole matter. He will sigh; she will swoon; the damsel will bring water and be much distressed. For it will be nearly morning, and she will fear for her lady's honour that they may be discovered. Finally the Princess will come to herself and put her white hands through the railings for the knight, who will kiss them a thousand, thousand times and bathe them in tears. They will agree how to let one another know their news, good or bad, and the Princess will implore the knight to stay away as short a time as possible, which he will promise with many oaths. Once more he kisses her hands, and bids her farewell with such grief as will come near to ending his life. From there he goes to his chamber, throws himself on the bed, but cannot sleep for the grief of parting. He gets

210

up early in the morning, and goes to take his leave of the King, the Queen and the Princess. When he has bidden farewell to the royal pair they tell him that the lady Princess is indisposed and cannot receive a visit; the knight concludes that it is from grief at his departure; his heart is pierced and he very nearly betrays his sorrow. The Princess's confidante is present; must observe everything; goes to inform her lady, who receives her with tears, and tells her that one of her greatest griefs is her ignorance of her knight's name, and of whether he is of royal descent or no. The damsel assures her that such courtesy, gentleness and valour as he displays cannot exist in any but a royal and illustrious person. This consoles the Princess; she endeavours to be calm, so as not to call her parents' attention to herself; and at the end of two days appears in public.

"The knight has already gone off; he fights in the war; conquers the King's enemies; captures many cities; triumphs in many battles; comes back to court, and sees his lady in the place where he had seen her before. They agree that in reward for his services he shall ask her father for her hand in marriage, but the King will not consent, since he does not know who the knight is. Yet, however that may be, either by carrying her off or in some other way, he marries the Princess, and her father in the end considers it a most fortunate affair, for it is revealed that the said knight is the son of a valorous king—of what kingdom I do not know, for I do not think it can be on the map. The father dies; the Princess succeeds him; in fact the knight becomes king. Now comes the time for bestowing favours on his squire, and on all who have helped him to climb to his high estate. He marries his squire to one of the Princess's damsels, no doubt the one who was privy to his love, the daughter of a very important duke."

"That's what I want, a fair field and no favour," said Sancho, "and that is what I expect, for it's all literally bound to turn out like that, since your worship has taken the name of The Knight of the Sad Countenance."

"Most certainly, Sancho," replied Don Quixote, "for in that very way, and by the very steps I have described to you, knights errant rise and have risen to be Kings and Emperors. All that we need now is to look out and find some king, Christian or pagan, who is at war and has a beautiful daughter. Though there will be plenty of time to think about that. For, as I have said, we have first to win fame elsewhere before we go to court. And there is something else lacking besides, for even supposing that I find a king at war and with a beautiful daughter, and that I have won incredible fame through-out the whole universe, I do not know how it can be proved that I am of royal blood, or even second cousin to an Emperor; and the King will not want to give me his daughter for a wife until he is perfectly assured on this point, whatever the merits of my famous deeds. So I am afraid that without this proof I shall lose the rich reward of my valour. True it is that I am a gentleman of known family, of possessions and property, and that my life is worth five hundred pounds fine by the old law; and it may be that the sage who comes to write my history will so establish my parentage and descent that I shall find I am fifth or sixth in descent from a King. For I would have you know, Sancho, that there are two kinds of lineages in the world: those which trace their descent from princes and monarchs, and which little by little time has diminished and reduced to a point, like a pyramid upside down; and others which derive their origin from common folk, and climb step by step till they achieve the dignity of great lords. So that the difference is between those who were and are no longer, and those who are but once were not. It is possible that I may prove to be one of the former, and that, on enquiry, my descent may prove great and noble, which should content the King, my father-in-law to be; but if it does not, the Princess will have to love me so much that, despite her father, she will take me for her lord and husband, even though she clearly knows that I am the son of a water-carrier. And, if she does not, it is a case of stealing her and carrying her off wherever I wish, for time or death must put an end to her parents' displeasure."

"Yes," said Sancho, "it is a case too of 'Never ask as a favour for what you can take by force,' as some good-for-nothings say; al-though it would suit the situation better to say, 'A leap over the hedge is better than good men's prayers.' This I say because, if the lord King, your worship's father-in-law, shouldn't deign to yield you my lady the Princess, there's nothing for it, as your worship says, but to steal her and hide her. But the trouble is that until peace is made and you can enjoy the kingdom quietly, the poor squire may go whistle for this reward of his, unless the go-between maiden, who is to be his wife, comes away with the Princess, and he shares his misfortunes with her until Heaven ordains otherwise. For it would be quite possible, I think, for his master to give her to him straight off in lawful marriage."

"There is no one to stop that," said Don Quixote.

"Well, since that's the case," replied Sancho, "we have only to commend ourselves to God and let fortune take what course it will."

"May God grant it," replied Don Quixote, "as I desire and you require and let the man who thinks he is be wretched."

"So be it, in God's name," said Sancho, "for I'm an old Christian, and that is enough ancestry for a count."

"And more than enough," said Don Quixote. "But even if you were not it would not matter, for if I am King I can easily make you noble without either purchase or service on your part; and, if I make you a count, there you are, a gentleman, let them say what they will; for they will have to call you your Lordship, whether they want to or no."

"You can take it from me that I shall know how to bear my indignity," said Sancho.

"*Dignity* you should say, not indignity," put in his master.

"As you will," replied Sancho Panza, "I say that I shall know how to carry it off well. For I was once beadle to a brotherhood, and the beadle's gown suited me so nicely that they all said I looked important enough to be the steward of the brotherhood. So what will it be like when I wear a duke's robe on my shoulders, or dress all in gold and pearls, after the fashion of a foreign count? They'll come from hundreds of miles off to see me, I'll be bound."

"You will look fine," said Don Quixote, "but you will need to trim your beard rather often, for you wear it so thick and matted and bushy, that unless you take a razor to it every day at least they will see what you are a gun-shot away."

"Why," said Sancho, "what more have I to do than to get a barber and keep him in the house on wages? And I'll even make him follow me round at a pinch like a grandee's groom."

"But how do you know," asked Don Quixote, "that grandees have their grooms following them?"

"I'll tell you," replied Sancho. "Some years ago I spent a month about the court, and there I saw a very little gentleman taking a walk, and they said he was a great grandee. Now wherever he went he had a man following him on horseback, turning everywhere he turned, more like his tail than anything else. I asked why that fellow never caught the other man up but always rode behind him. They told me that he was his groom, and that it was the fashion for grandees to have men like that riding after them. And I've known it ever since, and it's so stuck in my head that I've never forgotten it."

"You are quite right, I admit," said Don Quixote, "and you can take your barber round like that. For customs did not all arise together, nor were they all invented at once, and you may well be the first count to carry your barber round after you. Indeed, trimming a beard is a more intimate duty than saddling a horse."

"Leave this matter of the barber to me," said Sancho, "and let your worship's job be to try and become a King and make me a count."

"So it shall be," replied Don Quixote. And, raising his eyes, he saw what shall be told in the next chapter.

◀ 22 ▶

How Don Quixote set at liberty
Many Unfortunate Creatures who were being borne,
much against Their Will,
where they had no wish to go

*C*ide Hamete Benengeli, the
Arabian and Manchegan author, relates in his most grave, eloquent,
meticulous, delightful, and ingenious history that after that conversation between the famous Don Quixote de la Mancha and Sancho
Panza, his squire, which is set down at the end of the twenty-first
chapter, Don Quixote raised his eyes and saw on the road which he
was taking some dozen men on foot, strung by the neck like beads
on a great iron chain, and all manacled. With them were two
horsemen and two men on foot, the horsemen carrying firelocks,*
the footmen javelins and swords. And as soon as Sancho Panza saw
them he said, "Here's a chain of galley-slaves, men forced by the
King, going to serve in the galleys."

"What! Men forced?" asked Don Quixote. "It it possible that the
King uses force on anyone?"

---

* Only one firelock is accounted for in the subsequent events. Cervantes seems to have
forgotten the second.

"I don't say that," answered Sancho; "but they are men condemned for their crimes to serve the King in the galleys, and they go perforce."

"In fact," replied Don Quixote, "however you put it, these men are taken, and go by force and not of their own free will."

"That is so," said Sancho.

"Then," said his master, "this is a case for the exercise of my profession, for the redressing of outrages and the succouring and relieving of the wretched."

"Consider, your worship," said Sancho, "that justice—that is the King himself—is doing no wrong or outrage to such people, but only punishing them for their crimes."

At this moment the chain of galley-slaves came up, and in most courteous terms Don Quixote begged the guards to be so kind as to inform him of the cause or causes why they were bearing those people off in that fashion. One of the horsemen replied that they were galley-slaves belonging to His Majesty on the way to the galleys, such was the truth of the matter and there was no more to say.

"Nevertheless," replied Don Quixote, "I should like to learn from each one of them separately the cause of his misfortune." He went on in such very polite language to persuade them to give him the information he desired, that the other mounted guard replied, "Although we have with us here the copies and certificates of the sentences on each of these wretches, there is no time to take them out and read them. But your worship may come and ask them themselves, and they may tell you, if they please—and they will, for they are the sort who not only enjoy acting the villain but boasting of it afterwards too."

With this permission, which Don Quixote would have taken if it had not been granted, the knight went up to the chain, and asked the first man for what sins he was in that evil plight. He replied that it was for falling in love.

"For no more than that?" cried Don Quixote. "But if they send men to the galleys for falling in love, I should long since have been rowing there myself."

"It isn't the kind of love your worship imagines," said the galley-slave. "Mine was an over-great affection for a basketful of white linen, which I clasped to me so tight that if the law hadn't wrested it from me by force I shouldn't have let it go of my own free will even to this day. I was taken red-handed; there was no need of the torture; the trial was short; they accommodated my shoulders with a hundred lashes, and three years in the *gurapas* thrown in, and the job was done."

"What are the *gurapas?*" asked Don Quixote.

"*Gurapas* are galleys," replied the galley-slave, who was a lad of about twenty-four, and came, as he said, from Piedrahita.

Don Quixote asked the same question of the second man, who was too melancholy and dejected to answer a word. But the first man replied for him, "This man is here for being a canary—I mean a musician and singer."

"How is that?" asked Don Quixote. "Do men go to the galleys for being musicians and singers?"

"Yes, sir," replied the galley-slave, "for there is nothing worse than singing in anguish."

"I have always heard the opposite," said Don Quixote. "Sing away sorrow, cast away care."

"Here it's the reverse," said the galley-slave. "If you sing once you weep for a lifetime."

"I do not understand," said Don Quixote. But one of the guards put in, "Sir, singing in anguish with these ungodly people means confessing on the rack. They put this sinner to the torture, and he confessed his crime, which was cattle-thieving; and on his confession they sentenced him to six years in the galleys, besides two hundred lashes on the back; and the reason why he is dejected and melancholy is that the rest of the thieves back there, and these marching here, abuse him and bully him, and mock him and despise him, because he confessed and hadn't the courage to say no. For, as they say, no takes no longer to say than yes, and a crook is in luck if his life depends on his own tongue and not on witnesses and proofs; and I think that they are not far wrong."

"I agree," replied Don Quixote. Then, passing to the third man, he asked him the same question as the others, and the man answered very readily and calmly:

"I am going to their ladyships the *gurapas* for five years because I was short of ten ducats."

"I will give you twenty with pleasure," said Don Quixote, "to free you from this distress."

"That," replied the galley-slave, "looks to me like having money when you're in mid-ocean and dying of hunger, and there's nowhere to buy what you need. Because if I had had those twenty ducats your worship now offers me at the right time, I should have greased the clerk's pen with them and livened up my lawyer's wits to such effect that I should have been in the Zocodover square in Toledo today, and not dragging along this road like a greyhound on a leash. But God is great. Patience—that's enough."

Don Quixote went on to the fourth, a man of venerable appearance with a white beard reaching below his chest who, when asked why he was there, began to weep and answered not a word. But the fifth convict lent him a tongue and said, "This honest fellow is going to the galleys for four years after parading the town in state and on horseback."

"I suppose you mean that he was exposed to public shame," said Sancho Panza.

"That's right," replied the galley-slave, "and the offence for which he got his sentence was trafficking in ears, in fact in whole bodies. What I mean is that this gentleman is here for procuring, and also for having a touch of the wizard about him."

"If it had not been for that touch," said Don Quixote, "and if it were merely for procuring, he would not deserve to go and row in the galleys, but to be their general and command them. For the office of procurer is no easy one. It requires persons of discretion and is a most essential office in a well-ordered state. Only men of good

All that remained were the ass and Rocinante, Sancho and Don Quixote; the ass pensively hanging his head and shaking his ears now and then, imagining that the storm of stones which had whizzed by his head had not yet ceased; Rocinante prostrate beside his master, for he had also been brought down by a stone; Sancho in his shirt and terrified of the Holy Brotherhood; and Don Quixote much distressed at finding himself so vilely treated by the very men for whom he had done so much. (page 228) birth should exercise it. Indeed, there ought to be an overseer and controller of these procurers, as there are of other professions, and only a certain number should be appointed and recognized, like brokers on the Exchange. In that way a great many troubles would be avoided, which are caused through this office getting into the hands of idiots and people of little intelligence, such as half-witted servant-maids and little pages and buffoons, raw and inexperienced folk. Then, at the critical moment, when they have a really important affair to manage, they let the morsel freeze between their fingers and their mouth, and do not know their right hand from their left. I should like to go on and explain why it is necessary to select those who are to hold so necessary a position in the State; but this is no proper place. But some day I will put the matter before those who can furnish a remedy. Now I can only say that the grief caused me by the sight of these white hairs and this venerable countenance in such distress for procuring has been entirely removed by the mention of witchcraft, though I know very well that there are no wizards in the world capable of affecting or compelling the affections, as some simple people believe; for our will is free and there is no drug or spell that can control it. What such simple servant-maids and lying rogues generally do is to make up mixtures and poisons which drive a man crazy, under the pretence that they have the power to excite love, whereas, as I have said, it is impossible to compel the affections."

"That is so," said the old fellow, "and really, sir, as to being a wizard, I was not guilty, though I can't deny the procuring. But I never thought that I was doing any harm. All I wanted was for everyone to have a good time and live in peace and quiet, without quarrels or troubles. But the best intentions didn't serve to keep me from going to a place I don't expect to come back from, being stricken in years and having a bladder complaint which never gives me a moment's rest." Here he burst into tears once more, and Sancho was so sorry for him that he took a *real* from under his shirt and gave it to him out of charity.

Don Quixote passed on and asked another his crime, and this one replied with rather more freedom than the last, "I am here for having a bit too much fun with two girl cousins of mine, and two other cousins who were not mine. In fact, I had such fun with them all that the result of the joke was an intricate tangle of relationships that is more than any devil of a clerk can make out. It was all proved against me; I had no friends; I had no money; I was within an inch of having my gullet squeezed; they sentenced me to six years on the galleys; I submitted; it's the punishment for my crime. I'm young; if only my life holds out, all may yet come right. But, sir, should your worship have anything about you to give us poor wretches, God will repay you in Heaven, and here on earth we'll be sure to beseech him in our prayers that your worship's life and health may be as long and as prosperous as your good looks deserve."

The fellow who spoke wore the dress of a student, and one of the guards said that he was a great talker and a very good Latin scholar. Behind the rest came a man of about thirty, of very good appearance except that he squinted when he looked at you. He was fettered in a different way from the others. For he had a chain on his leg so long that it was wound right round his body, and two collars about his neck, one secured to the chain and the other of the kind called a *keep friend* or *friend's foot*. From this two iron bars reached down to his waist, with two manacles attached in which his wrists were secured by a heavy padlock, so that he could neither lift his hands to his mouth nor bend his head down to his hands. Don Quixote asked why this man had so many more fetters than the rest, and the guard replied that it was because he had committed more crimes than all the others put together, and that he was so bold and desperate a criminal that even though he was chained in that way they were not sure of him, but feared he might escape.

"What crimes, then, can he have committed?" asked Don Quixote, "if they have not earned him a heavier penalty than the galleys?"

"He is going for ten years," replied the guard, "which is a sort of civil death. I need tell you no more than that this fellow is the famous Gines de Pasamonte, alias Ginesillo de Parapilla."

"Not so rough, sergeant," put in the galley-slave. "Don't let us be settling names and surnames now. I am called Gines, not Ginesillo, and Pasamonte is my surname, not Parapilla as you say. Let everyone have a good look in his own cupboard, and he'll not be doing too badly."

"A little less insolence," replied the sergeant, "you double-dyed thief, or I may have to shut you up, and then you'll be sorry."

"You may see," replied the galley-slave, "that man proposes and God disposes; but one day somebody may learn whether my name is Ginesillo de Parapilla or not."

"Isn't that what they call you, then, rogue?" asked the guard.

"Yes, they do," replied Gines, "but I'll stop them calling me that or I'll pluck them—but no matter where. If, sir, you have anything to give us, give it us now, and go in God's name, for you weary me with your prying into other men's lives. But if you want to know about mine, I am Gines de Pasamonte, and I have written my life with these very fingers."

"He is speaking the truth," put in the sergeant. "He has written his own story, as fine as you please, and left the book behind at the prison pawned for two hundred *reals.*"

"And I mean to redeem it," said Gines, "even if it were pledged for two hundred ducats."

"Is it as good as that?" said Don Quixote.

"It's so good," replied Gines, "that Lazarillo de Tormes will have to look out, and so will everything in that style that has ever been written or ever will·be. One thing I can promise you, is that it is all the truth, and such well-written, entertaining truth that there is no fiction that can compare with it."

"And what is the title of the book?" asked Don Quixote.

"The Life of Gines de Pasamonte," replied that hero.

"Is it finished?" asked Don Quixote.

"How can it be finished," replied the other, "if my life isn't? What is written begins with my birth and goes down to the point when I was sent to the galleys this last time."

"Then you have been there before?" said Don Quixote.

223

"Four years I was there before," replied Gines, "in the service of God and the King, and I know the taste of the biscuit and the lash already. I am not greatly grieved at going, for I shall have a chance there to finish my book. I have a lot more to say, and in the Spanish galleys there is more leisure than I shall require, though I shan't need much for what I have to write, because I know it by heart."

"You seem a clever fellow," said Don Quixote.

"And an unfortunate one," replied Gines, "for misfortunes always pursue men of talent."

"They pursue rogues," replied the sergeant.

"I have already requested you to use better language, sergeant," replied Pasamonte, "for your superiors did not give you that staff to maltreat us poor devils, but to guide and lead us where his Majesty commands. If you do not, by God—but enough!—perhaps one day the stains that were made at the inn will come out in the wash. And let everyone hold his tongue, live virtuously and speak better. Now let us get along, for this is a bit too much of a joke."

The sergeant raised his staff to strike Pasamonte in return for his threats. But Don Quixote interposed and begged him not to ill-treat him, for it was no great matter if a man who had his hands tied let his tongue free a little. Then, addressing the whole chain-gang, the knight said, "From all that you have told me, dearest brethren, I clearly gather that, although it is for your faults they have punished you, the penalties which you are to suffer give you little pleasure. You are going to them, it seems, very reluctantly and much against your wills; and possibly it is only lack of courage under torture in one, shortage of money in another, lack of friends in another—in short, the unfair decisions of the judge—that have been the cause of your undoing and of your failure to receive the justice which was your due. All of which is now so clear in my mind that it bids me, persuades me, and even compels me, to demonstrate on you the purpose for which Heaven has sent me into the world and made me profess therein the order of chivalry which I follow, and the vow I made to succour the needy and those who are oppressed by the strong. Conscious, however, that it is the part of prudence not to do

by foul means what can be done by fair, I would beg the gentlemen
of the guard and the sergeant to be so good as to release you and let
you go in peace, since there will be no lack of men to serve the King
out of better motives; for it seems to me a hard case to make slaves of
those whom God and nature made free. Furthermore, gentlemen of
the guard," added Don Quixote, "these poor men have committed
no wrong against you. Let everyone answer for his sins in the other
world. There is a God in Heaven, who does not neglect to punish
the wicked nor to reward the good, and it is not right that honourable men should be executioners of others, having themselves no
concern in the matter. I make this request in a calm and gentle
manner, so that I may have cause to thank you if you comply; but if
you do not do so willingly, then this lance and this sword, together
with the valour of my arm, will force you to do so under
compulsion."

"This is fine foolishness," replied the sergeant. "It is a good joke
he has taken all this time hatching! He would like us to let the King's
convicts go, as if we had authority to free them, or he had it to order
us to! Get along with you, sir, and good luck to you! Put that basin
straight on your head, and don't go about looking for a cat with three
legs."

"You are the cat, the rat, and the rascal!" replied Don Quixote.
Then, matching deeds to his words, he attacked him so swiftly that
he had dealt him a serious wound with his lance and brought him to
the ground before he had a chance to defend himself; and, luckily for
Don Quixote, this was the man with the firelock. The rest of the
guards were dumbfounded by this unexpected turn of events. They
recovered themselves, however, and the horsemen drew their
swords, while the men on foot seized their javelins and rushed at Don
Quixote, who awaited them in complete calm. And no doubt things
would have gone badly for him if the galley-slaves had not seen their
chance of gaining their liberty and taken advantage of it to break the
chain which linked them together. Such was the confusion, in fact,
that the guards ran fast to the galley-slaves, who were struggling
loose, and then to deal with Don Quixote, who was attacking, and so

achieved no good purpose. Sancho, for his part, helped in releasing Gines de Pasamonte, who was the first to leap free and unfettered into the open, where he attacked the fallen sergeant and seized his sword and his firelock. Then, first levelling the gun at one man and then picking on another, without ever firing it he cleared the field of all the guards, who fled from Pasamonte's gun and from the showers of stones, as well, flung by the now liberated galley-slaves.

Sancho was much grieved at this business, for he guessed that the guards who had fled would report the matter to the Holy Brotherhood, who would sound the alarm and come out in pursuit of the criminals. This thought he communicated to his master, begging him that they might clear out immediately and hide in the nearby mountains.

"That is all very well," said Don Quixote, "but I know what is right for us to do now." Then he called all the galley-slaves, who were running about excitedly and had stripped the sergeant to the skin; and when they had gathered around him to hear what his orders might be, he addressed them thus, "It is a mark of well-born men to show gratitude for benefits received, and ingratitude is one of the sins which most offend God. I say this, gentlemen, because you have already had good experience of benefits received at my hands, as payment for which it is my will that you bear this chain which I have taken from your necks and immediately take the road to the city of El Toboso, there to present yourselves before the Lady Dulcinea del Toboso and tell her that her knight, the Knight of the Sad Countenance, presents his service to her. Then you are to tell her, point by point, every detail of this famous adventure up to the restoration of your long-coveted liberty; and when you have done so you may go wherever you will, and good luck go with you."

Gino de Pasamonte answered for them all, and said, "What your worship commands, lord and liberator, is of all impossibilities the most impossible for us to perform, since we cannot appear on the roads together, but must go singly and separately, each one on his own. And we must try to hide in the bowels of the earth for fear of being found by the Holy Brotherhood, for there is no doubt that they will come out in search of us. What your worship can do, and what you should do, is to substitute for this service and tribute to the lady Dulcinea del Toboso some number of Ave Marias and Credos, which we will say for your worship's benefit, this being a thing which can be performed by night and by day, on the run or resting, in peace or in war. But to think of our returning now to the flesh-pots of Egypt, I mean of our taking up our chain and setting out on the road for El Toboso, is to imagine that it is already night when it is not yet ten in the morning, and you can no more ask us for that than you can ask pears from an elm-tree."

"Then I swear by Heaven," cried Don Quixote in fury, "sir son of a whore, Don Ginesillo de Parapillo, or whatever you are called,—that you shall go yourself alone, with your tail between your legs and the whole chain on your back!"

Pasamonte was quite certain from Don Quixote's crazy action in giving them their liberty that he was not right in the head; and being far from long-suffering, when he found himself treated in this way he tipped his companions the wink. They then drew back and began to rain such a shower of stones upon Don Quixote that he could not contrive to cover himself with his shield, and poor Rocinante took no more notice of the spur than if he had been made of brass. Sancho got behind his ass and used him as a defence against the cloud and hailstorm of stones which descended on the pair of them. But Don Quixote could not shield himself well enough, and was hurt by some of the pebbles, which struck him on the body with such force that they knocked him to the ground. The moment he was down the student leapt on him, and seizing the basin from his head, brought it down three or four times on his shoulders, and as many more on the ground, till it was almost smashed to pieces. They also stripped him of a jacket which he wore over his armour, and would have taken off his stockings too if his leg armour had not prevented them. While from Sancho they took his overcoat, and left him in his shirt. Then, dividing the rest of the spoils of battle, they fled, each in a separate

227

direction, more intent on escaping from the dreaded Brotherhood than on loading themselves with the chain and going to present themselves to the lady Dulcinea del Toboso.

All that remained were the ass and Rocinante, Sancho and Don Quixote; the ass pensively hanging his head and shaking his ears now and then, imagining that the storm of stones which had whizzed by his head had not yet ceased; Rocinante prostrate beside his master, for he had also been brought down by a stone; Sancho in his shirt and terrified of the Holy Brotherhood; and Don Quixote much distressed at finding himself so vilely treated by the very men for whom he had done so much.

⊰ 23 ⊱

Of what happened to
the Famous Don Quixote in the Sierra Morena,
One of the Rarest Adventures
in the Course of This True History

*F*inding himself in so bad a way,
Don Quixote said to his squire, "I have always heard, Sancho, that
doing good to base fellows is like throwing water into the sea. If I
had believed what you said to me I should have avoided this trouble.
But now that it is done, patience, and let this be a warning for the
future."

"Your worship will take as much warning," replied Sancho, "as
I'm a Turk. But, as you say that you would have avoided this disaster
if you had trusted me, trust me now and you'll avoid even worse.
For there's no trying chivalry on the Holy Brotherhood, let me tell
you. They don't care a row of pins for all the knights errant in the
world, and, believe me, I can hear their arrows whizzing past my
ears already."

"You are a coward by nature, Sancho," said Don Quixote, "but I
do not want you to say that I am obstinate and never do what you
suggest. So this time I am going to take your advice, and retire
before the fury which you so much dread. But on one condition:
never, in life or death, are you to tell anyone that I retreated and

withdrew from this peril out of fear. I do it only to humour your entreaties, and if you say otherwise it will be a lie. Yes, from now till then and from then till now I give you the lie, and say that you lie and will lie every time that you either say it or think it. Do not answer me with another word; for at the mere thought that I am retreating and withdrawing from any peril, particularly from this, which seems to have some faint shadow of danger about it, I am inclined to stay here and await alone, not only the Holy Brotherhood, whose name you speak in terror, but the Brethren of the twelve tribes of Israel, and the seven Maccabees, and Castor and Pollux, and all the brothers and brotherhoods in the world as well."

"Sir," replied Sancho, "withdrawing is not flight, nor is it prudent to stay when danger outweighs hope. It is a wise man's duty to save himself for tomorrow, and not risk everything on one day. Let me tell you that I've still got some idea of what they call good conduct, although I may be an ignorant peasant. So don't be sorry that you've taken my advice, but climb upon Rocinante if you can—or if you can't I'll help you—and follow me, for my thinking-cap tells me that we've more need of our feet just now than of our hands."

Don Quixote mounted without another word; and with Sancho leading the way on his ass, they rode into a nearby part of the Sierra Morena, it being Sancho's intention to cross the whole range and come out at Viso or Almodovar del Campo, and to hide for a few days in that rough country, so as not to be found if the Holy Brotherhood came after them. He was encouraged in this plan by finding that the provisions he carried on the ass's back had escaped from the skirmish with the galley-slaves, which he took as a miracle, considering how much they had taken and how closely they had searched everything.

Now by nightfall they had got into the heart of the Sierra Morena, where Sancho thought it would be well to spend that night, if not some days, or at least as long as the provisions they had with them should last. And so they camped between two crags among a number of cork-trees. But fatal destiny which, according to those

Sancho went through the bag, not leaving a corner of it, or of the saddle-cushion, that he did not search, pry into and explore, not a seam which he did not rip, nor a tuft of wood that he did not pick, in case anything might be lost out of carelessness or want of diligence, such was the greed aroused in him by the discovery of the money, which amounted to more than a hundred crowns. (page 237) who lack the light of true faith, guides, shapes, and disposes everything in its own way, decreed that Gines de Pasamonte, the famous cheat and robber, whom by his valour and madness Don Quixote had delivered from the chain, had decided to hide in those mountains, out of fear of the Holy Brotherhood, which he had good reason to dread. And his luck and fear took him to the spot to which the same motives had brought Don Quixote and Sancho Panza, while it was still light enough for him to recognize them and just as they were falling asleep. Now as the wicked are always ungrateful and necessity drives them to evil deeds, and as present needs outweigh any thought for the future, Gines, who was neither grateful nor well-disposed, decided to steal Sancho Panza's ass, not caring for Rocinante, a security neither pawnable nor saleable. Sancho Panza slept; Gines stole his ass;* and before morning he was too far off to be found.

Dawn came forth, bringing joy to the earth but grief to Sancho Panza, who missed his Dapple and, when he found himself without him, burst into the saddest and most doleful lament in all the world. So loud was his grief that Don Quixote woke up to hear him cry, "O child of my bowels, born in my very house, my children's playmate, my wife's delight, envy of my neighbours, ease of my burdens, and half my means of livelihood besides, for the sixpence halfpenny a day you earned me was the half of my living!"

On seeing his tears and learning the cause Don Quixote consoled his squire with the best reasoning he could, begging him to be patient and promising to give him a bill of exchange entitling him to three of the five ass-foals he had left at home. This comforted Sancho, who dried his tears, controlled his sobs and thanked Don Quixote for this favour. As for the knight, his heart grew glad as they cut into the mountains, for they seemed to him a most suitable scene for the adventures he was seeking. They recalled to his

---

* The loss of the ass is another of Cervantes' oversights. A few pages later Sancho is riding him again, and shortly after is once more without him.

memory the marvellous things which had happened to knights errant in similar wastes and fastnesses; and he rode on with his mind dwelling on such things, and so absorbed and rapt by them that he remembered nothing else. And Sancho's only thought, now that he supposed them out of danger, was of satisfying his stomach with the relics of the clerical booty; so he walked on behind his master, loaded with all that the ass should have carried, taking morsels out of the bag and cramming them into his belly; and while thus employed he would not have given a halfpenny for any other adventure.

While thus engaged, however, he looked up and saw that his master had stopped and with the point of his lance was trying to lift up some bundle lying on the ground. So he hurried on, to catch him up, and help him if necessary; and overtook his master just as he was raising on his lance-point a saddle-cushion with a leather bag attached, partly rotten, or rather entirely so and falling to pieces. But it was so heavy that Sancho had to get down and pick it up for him. His master then bade him look what was in the bag. And this he very quickly did. For, although it was secured by a chain and padlock, he could see what was inside through the rents and rotten places. There were four shirts of fine cambric, some other fine and fashionable linen, and a considerable pile of gold coins in a handkerchief, at the sight of which Sancho cried out, "Blessed be Heaven for affording us one profitable adventure!" And on a further search he found a little note-book, richly decorated. This Don Quixote asked for, but he told Sancho to take the money for himself and keep it. The squire acknowledged this favour by kissing his master's hands and, rifling the linen, stowed it in their provision bag.

Now when Don Quixote had taken all this in, he observed, "There seems to me, Sancho, to be no doubt whatever that some traveller must have lost his way in these mountains, and have been attacked by robbers, who must have killed him and brought him to this remote spot to bury him."

"That can't be so," replied Sancho, "for if they had been thieves they wouldn't have left this money here."

"You are right," said Don Quixote. "So I cannot divine or guess what it can be. But wait; let us see if there is not something written in this note-book which will give us a clue."

He opened it, and the first thing that he saw in it was a beautifully written copy of a sonnet, which he read aloud for Sancho to hear. It ran like this:

Know'st thou, O love, the pangs which I sustain,
Or, cruel, dost thou view those pangs unmoved?
Or has some hidden cause its influence proved,
By all this sad variety of pain?

If Love's a god, then surely he must know,
And knowing, pity wretchedness like mine.
From other hands proceeds the fatal blow.
Is then the deed, unpitying Chloe, thine?

Ah no, a body formed so perfectly
A soul so merciless can ne'er enclose.
Nor can it be from Heaven my ruin flows.
But it's most certain that I soon shall die,
For when the cause of the complaint's unsure
'Twould be a miracle to find a cure.

"We can learn nothing from that poem," said Sancho, "unless from that clue we can come to the thread of the matter."

"What clue do you mean?" asked Don Quixote.

"I thought your worship mentioned a clue?"

"I did not say clue, but Chloe," replied Don Quixote, "and that, no doubt, is the name of the lady the author of this sonnet is complaining about. He is a pretty good poet, I am sure, or I am a poor judge of the art!"

"Your worship knows about poetry-writing too, then?" observed Sancho.

"Yes, and better than you think," replied Don Quixote, "as you will know when you take a letter written in verse from beginning to end to my lady Dulcinea del Toboso. For I would inform you, Sancho, that all or most knights errant in the olden times were great

troubadours and great musicians as well. For these two accomplishments, or rather graces as I should say, belong with love errantry; though it is true that the poems of the knights of old have
more spirit than elegance about them."

"Read some more, your worship," said Sancho, "for we may yet
find something to satisfy our curiosity."

Don Quixote turned the page and said, "This is prose, and looks
like a letter."

"An ordinary letter, sir?" asked Sancho.

"From its opening it looks more like a love-letter," replied Don
Quixote.

"Then read it aloud, your worship," said Sancho. "I very much
enjoy this love business."

"With pleasure," said Don Quixote and, reading it aloud as
Sancho had asked him, he found what follows:

> Your false promise and my certain misfortune bear me
> to a place from which you will sooner hear the news of my
> death than the sound of my complaining. You have cast me
> off, ungrateful that you are, for one with more possessions
> but no more worth than I have. Yet if virtue were esteemed
> as wealth is, I should envy no man his fortune, nor bewail
> my own misfortune. What your beauty raised up your
> deeds have destroyed; from your form I thought you were
> an angel; from your acts I know you are a woman. Peace be
> with you, though you cause war in me; and may Heaven
> grant that your husband's deceptions remain concealed for
> ever, so that you may not eternally regret what you have
> done, nor I take a vengeance which I do not desire.

When he had finished reading the letter Don Quixote observed,
"We can gather less about the writer from this than from the verses,
except that he was some scorned lover." And fingering through the
greater part of the little book, he found more verses and letters, some
of which he could read and others not. But the contents of all alike

were complaints, laments, misgivings, longings and pains, favours and slights—celebrated or deplored. While Don Quixote examined the book, Sancho went through the bag, not leaving a corner of it, or of the saddle-cushion, that he did not search, pry into and explore, not a seam which he did not rip, nor a tuft of wool that he did not pick, in case anything might be lost out of carelessness or want of diligence, such was the greed aroused in him by the discovery of the money, which amounted to more than a hundred crowns. And although he found no more, still he thought himself well compensated for the blanket-tossing, the vomiting of the balsam, the benedictions of the pack-staves, the blows of the carrier, the loss of the saddle-bags, the stealing of his coat, and all the hunger, thirst and weariness which he had undergone in his worthy master's service. In fact he counted himself amply repaid for everything by Don Quixote's favour in handing over to him the treasure trove.

Now the Knight of the Sad Countenance had a great desire to know who was the possessor of the bag, guessing from the sonnet and the letter, from the gold coins and the fine quality of the shirts, that he must be a lover of some consequence, whom his lady's scorn and ill-treatment had brought to some desperate end. But as there was likely to be no one in this uninhabited and rugged country who could inform him, he found nothing for it but to ride on, leaving the choice of road to Rocinante—who chose the most passable—labouring under the perpetual illusion that he could not fail to find some extraordinary adventure among those thickets. As he rode on then, with this idea in mind, he saw on the top of a knoll, which showed up straight ahead, a man leaping from rock to rock and from bush to bush with extraordinary agility. He made out that the man was half-naked, with a matted black beard, his hair long and tangled, and his legs and feet bare; while his thighs were clad in a pair of breeches, which seemed to be of brown velvet but were so tattered that in many places his skin showed through. His head too was bare; and although he moved swiftly, as has been said, still the Knight of the Sad Countenance saw and noted all these details. But try as he might, he could not follow him, for it was not given to Rocinante in his weakness to travel over such rough places, he being, besides, slow and sluggish by nature. Then, presently, Don Quixote came to the conclusion that this was the owner of the saddle-cushion and the bag, and he made up his mind to seek him, even though it might mean spending a year among those mountains before he found him. And so he ordered Sancho to dismount from his ass and to cut over one side of the mountains, while he went across the other; as by such measures they might come upon the man who had run away from them so fast.

"I couldn't do that," replied Sancho, "for when I leave your worship's side fear springs upon me at once and visits me with all kinds of alarms and visions; and let these words of mine serve as a warning that I won't stir a finger's breadth from your worship's presence from now on."

"Very well," said he of the Sad Countenance. "I am glad that you rely on my courage, which shall never fail you though your soul shall desert your body. Follow me, therefore, slowly or however you can, and use your eyes for lanterns. We will go round this spur, and then perhaps we shall meet the man whom we saw. There can be no doubt that he is none other than the owner of the things we have found."

To which Sancho replied, "It would be much better not to look for him. Because if we find him and he happens to be the owner of the money, it is plain that I must give it back; and so it would be better not to take this unnecessary trouble, but for us to keep it faithfully until its real owner turns up in some less strange and laborious way. Perhaps by then I shall have spent it, and then the King's law will acquit me of responsibility."

"You are wrong on that score," replied Don Quixote, "for now that we have a suspicion of who the owner is, and have him almost before our eyes, we are obliged to seek him and restore these things to him; and if we do not seek him, the strong presumption we have of his identity makes us as guilty as if he were really the owner. So, Sancho, my friend, you must not let this search grieve you, seeing how much it will relieve my mind to find him."

Then he pricked Rocinante on, and Sancho followed on foot and loaded, thanks to Ginesillo de Pasamonte. And when they had gone round part of the mountain, they found in a stream bed a dead mule saddled and bridled, half eaten by dogs and picked by crows, all of which confirmed their suspicion that the man who had run away from them was the owner of the mule and of the saddle-cushion.

As they were gazing at it they heard a whistle like that of a shepherd guarding his flock. Then suddenly on their left appeared a great number of goats, and behind them on the mountain top their goatherd, a very old man. Don Quixote shouted to him to come down to them. And he called back to ask who had brought them into that place, which was hardly ever visited except by goats or wolves and other wild beasts which haunted the neighbourhood. Sancho replied that they would explain everything if he would come down, and so he descended, and coming to where Don Quixote was standing, said, "I'll bet that you are looking at the hired mule, lying dead in that hollow. It has been in that place a good six months, I can tell you. But tell me, have you come across its owner about here?"

"We have met nobody," replied Don Quixote, "and seen nothing except a saddle-cushion and a little leather bag, which we found lying not far from here."

"I found it too," replied the goatherd, "but I never liked to pick it up or come near it, for fear of some mishap, or of being charged with stealing it. For the devil's a sly one, and things start up under a man's feet which make him trip and fall, without his knowing how or why."

"That's just what I say," replied Sancho. "I found it too, but wouldn't go within a stone's throw of it. There I left it, and there it is just as it was, for I don't want a dog with a bell."

"Tell me, my good fellow," said Don Quixote, "do you know who is the owner of these articles?"

"All that I can say," replied the goatherd, "is that six months ago, more or less, there arrived at a certain shepherd's hut, which will be about nine miles from this spot, a good-looking, well-mannered youth on that same mule that is lying there dead, and with that same saddle-cushion and bag which you say you found and didn't touch. He asked us what part of this range was the roughest and most remote, and we told him that it was where we are now—and that's the truth. For if you were to go on a mile or two more you would possibly never find your way out again; and I am wondering how you were able to reach here, because there's no road or track leading to this place. Well, I tell you, when the youth heard our reply he turned and rode towards the spot we pointed out to him, leaving us all delighted at his handsome appearance, and astonished at his questions and at seeing him ride off so fast in the direction of the mountains. From that time on we did not see him again, until some days ago he appeared on the path in front of one of our goatherds, went up to him without a word and dealt him several punches and kicks. Then he went to our baggage-donkey and took all the bread and the cheese he carried, after which he ran back again into the mountains at an amazing speed. When we heard about this, several of our herdsmen spent almost two days looking for him in the roughest part of this mountain, and finally found him hiding in the hollow of a huge cork-tree. He came out to us, very mild, with his clothes torn and his face disfigured and scorched by the sun, so that we scarcely knew him again. But his clothes, torn as they were, were sufficiently recognizable to convince us that he was the man we were looking for. He greeted us courteously, and in a few polite words begged us not to be surprised to see him wandering about in that state, for he had to do so to fulfil a certain penance which had been laid on him for his many sins. We asked him to tell us who he was, but could not get that out of him. We also begged him to tell us where we could find him, so that we could bring him food when he stood in need of it, for without it he could not exist; and if this was not to his liking, we asked him at least to come and ask for it, and not take it from the herdsmen by force. He thanked us for our offer, asked our pardon for past assaults, and promised for the future to beg for food in God's name, and not do violence to anyone. As to his dwelling-place, he said that he had none but such as chance offered when night overtook him; and he ended his speech with such

The other, whom we may call the Ragged Knight of the Sorry—as Don Quixote was of the Sad—Countenance, after allowing himself to be embraced drew back a little and, placing his hands on Don Quixote's shoulders stood gazing at him, as if to see whether he knew him, being no less surprised, perhaps, to see Don Quixote's face, figure and armour than Don Quixote was to see him. (page 244) touching tears that we must have been made of stone if we had not wept too to hear him, considering the change in his appearance since the first time we had seen him. For, as I have said, he was a very charming and handsome young man and, to judge from his courteous and nicely chosen speech, obviously a well-born and very gentlemanly person. For though we that listened to him were country men, even our simple minds could tell from his good manners what sort of man he was. But he suddenly fell silent in the middle of his speech and fixed his eyes on the ground for quite a while. We waited quietly and expectantly, though in some alarm to see how this fit would end. He opened his eyes wide and stared fixedly at the ground for a long while without so much as stirring an eyelid. Then he closed his eyes, pressed his lips together, and scowled. From all this we could easily tell that some fit of madness had come upon him. And he quickly showed us that we were right. For in a great fury he got up from the ground, where he had thrown himself, and attacked the man nearest to him with such reckless rage that he would have punched and bitten him to death, if we hadn't pulled him off. And all the while he shouted, "Ferdinand, you traitor! You shall pay here, here, for the wrong you have done me! These hands shall tear out your heart, which harbours every crime at once, and the greatest of them all, fraud and deceit!" He went on to abuse that Ferdinand a great deal more and accused him of treachery and perjury.

"Well, we got our fellow away from him at last with no little trouble, and he left us without a word and ran off to hide in those briars and thickets, so that it was impossible for us to follow him.

"So we suppose that he gets fits of madness at times, and that someone called Ferdinand must have injured him very grievously, to reduce him to the wretched condition he is in. All this has been confirmed since, for he will very often come out on to the path, sometimes to beg the herdsmen for some of their food, and sometimes to take it by force. For when the fit of madness is on him he will not accept it, even though they offer it gladly, but prefers to attack them and snatch it from them. Yet when he is in his senses he

asks for it courteously and politely for the love of God, and accepts it
with thanks and sometimes with tears. And, to tell you the truth,
sirs," the goatherd went on, "yesterday we decided, I and four
herdsmen—two of our fellows and two friends of mine—to search
for him till we find him, and then to take him, willy-nilly, to the
town of Almodovar, which is about twenty-four miles away. There
we'll get him cured, if his disease is curable, or find out who he is
when he is in his senses, and whether he has any relations whom we
can inform of his misfortune. That, gentlemen, is all the answer that
I can give to your questions; and you may be sure that the owner of
the articles which you found is that same man whom you saw run by
so naked and so nimble"—for Don Quixote had already told him that
they had seen a man leaping among the rocks.

Our knight was amazed at the goatherd's tale, and more anxious
than ever to know who the unfortunate madman was. So he decided
to carry out a plan which he had already been considering, and to
search the whole range for him, leaving no cranny or cave unex-
plored till he found him. But chance contrived for him better than he
hoped or expected. For at that very instant there appeared from a
cleft in the mountains, which opened on the place where they were
standing, the very youth he was seeking, muttering to himself some
words that were unintelligible near-to, let alone at a distance. His
clothes were as the goatherd had described them, only when he
drew near Don Quixote noticed that the torn leather coat which he
wore still smelt of ambergris, from which he concluded that the
wearer of such clothes could not be of a very low class. When the
youth came up he greeted them in a rough and toneless voice, but
very courteously. Don Quixote returned his greetings no less politely and, charmingly and graciously dismounting from Rocinante,
advanced to embrace him, and held him for some time clasped in his
arms, as if he had known him for a long while. The other, whom we
may call the Ragged Knight of the Sorry—as Don Quixote was of
the Sad—Countenance, after allowing himself to be embraced drew
back a little and, placing his hands on Don Quixote's shoulders,

stood gazing at him, as if to see whether he knew him, being no less surprised, perhaps, to see Don Quixote's face, figure and armour than Don Quixote was to see him. In the end, the first to speak after the embrace was the Ragged Knight, and what he said will be told in the next chapter.

⊰ 24 ⊱

The Adventure in
the Sierra Morena continued

*T*he history tells that Don Quixote listened with the very greatest attention to the ill-starred Knight of the Mountains, who made him the following address, "Most certainly, sir, whoever you may be—for I do not know you—I thank you for the demonstrations of courtesy you have shown me, and I wish I were in the position to repay you for your gracious reception with more than my good-will. But my luck gives me nothing to offer in return for the kindness you have done me except the desire to respond."

"My only wish," replied Don Quixote, "is to serve you; so much so that I was determined not to leave these mountains till I had discovered you, and learnt from you if there is any sort of remedy to be found for the affliction which your strange way of life shows you to suffer under; and if so, to make every possible effort to find it. But should your misfortune be such as to close all doors to every kind of consolation, it was my intention to join you, as best I could, in your grief and lamentations, for it is still some consolation in sorrows to find someone to grieve for them. If my good intentions, then, deserve to be met by any kind of courtesy, I entreat you, sir, by the great courtesy that is clearly in your nature, and by the person whom in this life you have loved or love best, to tell me who you are, and the cause which has brought you to live and die in these wastes like a brute beast, for your dress and your person show that this is far from being your proper abode. I swear," added Don Quixote, "by the order of knighthood which I have received, although an unworthy sinner, and by the profession of knight errant, that if you will oblige me, sir, in this, I will serve you with all the endeavour which it is my duty to exert, either by relieving your misfortune, if any relief is possible, or by joining you in bewailing it, as I have promised."

When the Knight of the Wood heard the Knight of the Sad Countenance speak in this style, he stared at him in silence, gazing at him again and again, and viewing him from head to foot. Then, when he had gazed his fill, he said, "If you have anything to give me to eat, for the love of God give it to me, and when I have had some food I will do all that you ask to acknowledge the kind offer you have just made me."

Then Sancho took from his saddle-bag, and the goatherd from his pouch, enough to satisfy the Ragged Knight's hunger; and he ate what they gave him like a man in a daze, so hurriedly that he did not leave a moment between one mouthful and the next, rather gobbling his meal than eating it; and all the while he ate neither he nor the bystanders said a word. When he had finished he made signs to them to follow him, which they did; and he led them to a little green meadow that lay behind some crags a short way away. When he got there he lay down on the grass, and the others did the same, all in utter silence until the Ragged Knight had made himself comfortable, and began, "If you wish me to explain to you, gentlemen, the immensity of my misfortunes in a few words, you must promise not to interrupt the thread of my sad tale with any question or remark; for the moment you do so, my narrative will end."

These words recalled to Don Quixote's mind that tale of his squire's which had been broken off because he had not kept count of the number of goats which had crossed the river. But to return to the Ragged Knight, he went on, "This warning I give you because I should like to pass briefly over the story of my misfortunes. For to recall them to mind is only to add to them, and the less questions you ask me the quicker I shall come to the end of my tale. Yet I will not leave out anything of importance, as it is my wish to satisfy your curiosity completely."

Don Quixote promised in the name of the rest not to interrupt him, and with this assurance the Ragged One began, "My name is Cardenio; my birthplace one of the finest cities here in Andalusia; my family noble; my parents rich; my misfortunes so great that my parents were forced to weep and my relations to grieve for them, being unable to relieve them for all their wealth. For fortune's goods can do little to remedy misfortunes willed by Heaven. There dwelt in this same land a heaven in which Love had placed all the glory I could desire, such is the beauty of Lucinda, a maiden as noble and rich as I but more fortunate, and less firm in her faith than love so honest as mine deserved. This Lucinda I loved, desired and adored from my tenderest and earliest years, and she loved me with the innocence and seriousness of her youth. Our parents knew of our feelings, and were not disturbed by them, for they clearly saw that their development could lead only to marriage, which the equality of our blood and fortune seemed almost to demand. As we grew older our love grew also, till Lucinda's father thought himself obliged, for prudence's sake, to deny me the house, in this closely imitating the parents of that Thisbe so much sung of by poets. Now this denial added flame to fire and love to love; for although they silenced our tongues, they could not stop our pens, which are more freely used than tongues to express the heart's secrets to the beloved; since often the presence of the loved one confuses and silences the most resolute heart and the boldest tongue. Heavens, how many letters I wrote her! What delicate and modest replies I received! How many songs and love-poems I penned, in which my soul declared and revealed its feelings, painted its warm desires, went over its memories and refreshed its passion! In the end, my patience exhausted and my heart consumed with desire to see her, I determined to put into effect what seemed to me the most suitable plan for gaining my desired and deserved prize. This was to ask her father for her hand in lawful marriage, which I did.

"He replied by thanking me for the honour I intended him, and for wishing to honour myself with his beloved treasure; but that as my father was alive, it was properly his duty to make this request, for Lucinda was no woman to be taken or given in an underhand way without his wish and approval. I thanked him for his kindness, thinking that he was right in what he said, and that my father would consent to my proposal as soon as I told him of it. Therefore I immediately went to inform him of my desires. But when I entered the room where he was, I found him with an open letter in his hand, which he passed to me before I had uttered a word, saying, 'You will see from this letter, Cardenio, that Duke Richard wishes to do you a service.'

"This Duke Richard, you must know, gentlemen, is a grandee of Spain, whose estate lies in the richest part of Andalusia. I took and read the letter, which was so complimentary that even I thought my father would be wrong not to accept his request that I should be sent to him immediately. He wanted me as a companion—not as a servant—for his eldest son, and promised to put me in a position corresponding to his high opinion of me. I read the letter and was dumbfounded as I read. But I was even more astonished to hear my father say, 'You will set out the day after tomorrow, Cardenio, and do as the Duke wishes. Give thanks to God for opening you a way to the fortune I know you deserve.' And he added some fatherly advice.

"The day came for my departure. I talked one night with Lucinda; I told her all that had happened, and told her father too. I begged him to wait for a few days and postpone the settling of her marriage until I saw what Duke Richard wanted of me. He made me a promise, and she confirmed it with innumerable vows, made between fits of fainting. Then at last I reached Duke Richard's, and was so well received and treated that envy soon began to do its work. His old servants considered every sign of favour the Duke made me as prejudicial to themselves. But one person was most delighted at my coming, the Duke's second son Ferdinand, a gay lad with a charming, liberal and amorous disposition. In a very short time he was so eager for my friendship that everyone noticed it; but although his elder brother liked me and was kind to me, he did not show me the same extreme affection and attention as did Ferdinand.

"Now as there are no secrets between friends, and the favour which Ferdinand showed me soon ceased to be favour and turned to friendship, he told me all that was in his mind, and particularly of a love affair which was causing him some little anxiety. He was in love with the daughter of a farmer, a tenant of his father's. Her parents were rich, and she was so beautiful, so modest, discreet and virtuous that no one of her acquaintance could decide in which of these qualities she was richest. The charms of the fair farmer's daughter reduced Ferdinand to such straits that he decided to gratify his desires and overcome her virtue by a promise of marriage, knowing that it would be impossible to succeed by any other means. Prompted by friendship, I employed the best arguments I knew and warned him as strongly as I could in an endeavour to dissuade him from his purpose. But, finding it was all in vain, I decided to inform his father, the Duke, of the matter. Now Ferdinand was astute and intelligent enough to suspect and fear that; for it was obvious to him that, as a faithful servant, I could not conceal from my Lord the Duke a matter so prejudicial to his honour. So, to put me off the scent, he told me that the only means he could find of getting the beauty who so enthralled him out of his mind was to go away for a few months; and he proposed that we should spend this time together at my father's, and that he should tell the Duke by way of excuse that his journey to my city was to purchase horses, for the best in the world are bred there.

"No sooner had he made this suggestion than my own love prompted me to welcome it as the best imaginable solution, though I should have done so if it had been less good, for I saw what a rare opportunity it gave me of seeing my Lucinda again. So in this frame of mind I approved his scheme and encouraged his plan, advising him to put it into execution at the very earliest opportunity, for absence would certainly have its effect, however strong his affections.

"Now, at the time when he told me this plan, as it came out afterwards, he had already enjoyed the farmer's daughter under promise of marriage, and was waiting for an opportunity of safely divulging the matter. For he was afraid of what the Duke, his father, might do when he came to know of his infatuation. Now, as a lad's love is for the most part not love but lust and, aiming only at gratification, dies when it attains its purpose, what appears to be love then weakening, since it cannot persist beyond its natural limits, which limits do not exist in true love—I mean to say that as soon as Don Ferdinand had enjoyed the farmer's daughter his desires grew calm and his ardour cooled, so that if at first he had pretended that he wanted to go away in order to relieve his passion, now he was really anxious to go to avoid fulfilling his promise.

"The Duke gave him permission and bade me go with him. We came to my city, and my father gave him the reception due to his rank. Presently I visited Lucinda; my passion came to life, although in fact it had been neither dead nor dull and, to my undoing, I spoke of it to Don Ferdinand, for I thought that his great friendship for me forbade my keeping any secrets from him. I praised Lucinda's beauty, her grace and wit, so much so that my praise roused a desire in him to see a maiden endowed with such virtues. To my own misfortune I yielded to him, and let him see her one night by the light of a candle at a window through which it was our habit to talk.

"She was dressed in a loose wrap, looking so beautiful that he forgot all the beauties he had ever seen. He was struck dumb; he lost his senses; he was spellbound; and, in short, fell deeply in love, as you will see in the course of the tale of my misfortunes. And the more to inflame his passions, which he concealed from me but revealed to God in solitude, he chanced one day upon a letter of hers, begging me to ask her father for her hand in marriage, a letter so sensible, so modest and so full of love, that on reading it he said that in Lucinda alone were united all the charms of beauty and understanding which were the portions of all the other women in the world. It is true, as I confess now, that though I acknowledged the justice of Ferdinand's praise, it vexed me to hear this eulogy from his mouth, and I began to grow fearful and jealous of him; for there was not a moment when he did not want to talk of Lucinda, and he would start the conversation himself, even if he had to drag her in by the hair. This awoke a vague jealousy in me; not that I had any reason to fear a change in Lucinda's faith and virtue, yet, for all that, my fate made me dread the very danger against which she seemed to secure me. Don Ferdinand always tried to read the letters I sent to her and her replies. He pretended to derive great pleasure from our turns of phrase. Now Lucinda happened to ask me for a book of chivalry to read, one which she was very fond of. It was *Amadis of Gaul*—"

No sooner did Don Quixote hear mention of a book of chivalry than he exclaimed, "If you had told me, sir, at the beginning of your story that the lady Lucinda was fond of books of chivalry, you would have needed no further amplifications to convince me of the sublimity of her understanding. For it would not have been as excellent as you, sir, have described it, if she had lacked a taste for such delightful reading. So that there is no need to waste more words in declaring to me her beauty, worth and understanding; for at the mere mention of this passion of hers I pronounce her the loveliest and most intelligent woman in the world. But I could have wished, sir, that you had sent her with *Amadis of Gaul* the good *Sir Rugel of Greece,* for I know that the lady Lucinda would be delighted with Daraida and Garaya, and with the wit of the shepherd Darinel, and with those admirable lines in his bucolics, sung and performed by him with such charm, wit and freedom. But a time may come for remedying this omission. It can be amended whenever you care to come with me to my village, sir. For there I can show you more than three hundred books, which are the treasure of my heart and the delight of my life—though now it occurs to me that I have none, thanks to the malice of evil and envious enchanters. Pardon me, sir,

When Sancho Panza saw his master thus treated, he attacked the madman with clenched fists. But the Ragged Knight gave him such a reception that he had him stretched at his feet at the first blow, after which he got on top of him and trampled his ribs to his heart's content. (page 255) for having broken our promise not to interrupt your story; but when I hear of matters of chivalry and of knights errant, I can no more prevent myself from talking of them than the sun's rays can help giving heat, or the moon's moisture. So excuse me, and go on, for that is the important thing now."

Whilst Don Quixote was saying all this, Cardenio let his head fall on his breast, seemingly plunged in deep thought; and although the knight twice asked him to go on with his story, he neither raised his head nor answered a word. But at the end of a good while he looked up and said, "One thing I cannot get out of my mind, and no one in the world can persuade me or convince me otherwise—indeed, anyone holding the contrary opinion would be an idiot. That arch-scoundrel Master Elisabat was Queen Madasima's lover."

"That is false, I swear," replied Don Quixote in great wrath, bursting out in his usual fashion, "and a most malicious, or rather villainous calumny. Queen Madasima was a very noble lady, and it is not to be supposed that so great a princess would take a quack for a lover. Whoever says otherwise lies like an arrant scoundrel, and I will make him acknowledge it, on foot or horse, armed or unarmed, by night or day, or however he will."

Cardenio sat staring at him very attentively. For a fit of madness had come on him and he was in no state to continue his tale; nor would Don Quixote have listened if he had, so disgusted was he by what he had heard concerning Madasima. It was extraordinary to see him take her part as though she were in fact his real and natural mistress, such was the power his unholy books had over him.

But, as I said, Cardenio was now mad, and when he heard himself called a liar and a scoundrel and other such names, he took the joke in bad part. In fact he picked up a stone from beside him, and hit Don Quixote so hard on the chest that he knocked him backwards. When Sancho Panza saw his master thus treated, he attacked the madman with clenched fists. But the Ragged Knight gave him such a reception that he had him stretched at his feet at the first blow, after which he got on top of him and trampled his ribs to his heart's content. The goatherd, who tried to defend him, met with the same fate, and after Cardenio had threshed and bruised them all, he left them and retired quietly to his mountain ambush.

Sancho got up and, furious at his undeserved beating, ran to take vengeance on the goatherd, saying that it was all his fault for not having advised them that the man was subject to fits of madness; for had they known it, they would have been prepared to defend themselves. The goatherd replied that he had told them, and it was not his fault if Sancho had not heard. Sancho argued; the goatherd replied; and the dispute ended in their grasping each other's beards and punching each other so hard that they would have thrashed one another to pulp if Don Quixote had not interposed. But Sancho still kept a tight hold on the goatherd as he exclaimed, "Leave me alone, Sir Knight of the Sad Countenance, for he's a peasant like me and no knight, and I can safely avenge the injury he has done me by fighting him hand to hand, like a man of honour."

"That is true," said Don Quixote. "But I know that he is not to blame for what happened."

With this he pacified them, and again asked the goatherd if it would be possible to find Cardenio, for he was most anxious to hear the end of his story. The herdsman repeated, as he had done before, that there was no knowing for certain where Cardenio had his lair; but if Don Quixote were to wander much about the district he would not fail to find him, sane or mad.

⋠ 25 ⋡

Of the Strange Things which happened
to the Valorous Knight of La Mancha
in the Sierra Morena, and of His Imitation
of the Penance of Beltenebros

*D*on Quixote took leave of the
goatherd and, remounting Rocinante, bade Sancho follow him,
which he did on his ass,* most unwillingly. They then went slowly
on into the most desolate part of the mountains. Sancho all the while
was dying to talk to his master, but not wishing to disobey his
orders, waited for him to start the conversation. At last, however,
unable to bear the long silence, he said, "Don Quixote, please give
me your blessing and my liberty, for I want to go back home now to
my wife and my children. I shall at least be able to talk to them as
much as I like. For your worship's wanting me to ride through these
lonely parts day and night and never to speak to you when I've a
mind to, is like burying me alive. If nature allowed animals to talk, as
they did in Aesop's days, it wouldn't be so bad. Then I could talk to
my ass about anything I like, and forget my bad luck that way. For
it's hard, and more than patience can bear, to spend all one's life
looking for adventures and finding nothing but kicks and blanket-

* The ass is now Sancho's again, and Cervantes has forgotten its theft by Gines.

tossings, brick-battings and beatings, and still to have to keep one's mouth tight shut and not dare to say what's in one's heart, just as if one were dumb."

"I understand you, Sancho," replied Don Quixote. "You are dying for me to raise the prohibition I have imposed on your tongue. Consider it raised and say what you will, on condition this licence lasts only so long as we are travelling in these mountains."

"Very well," said Sancho. "Let me talk now, for God knows what will come afterwards; and now, to begin to take advantage of your permission, I should like to ask what made your worship stand up so warmly for that Queen Magimasa, or whatever she's called. What did it matter if that abbot was her friend or not? For if your worship had let it pass, since you were not her judge, I really think that the madman would have gone on with his story, and we should have been spared the stone and the kicks, and more than half a dozen back-handers in the face."

"I swear, Sancho," replied Don Quixote, "that if you knew, as I know, what a great and honourable lady Queen Madasima was, you would certainly say that I showed great patience in not smashing the face that mouthed such blasphemies. For it is great blasphemy to say or to think that a Queen could take a barber-surgeon for a lover. The truth of the story is that this Master Elisabat the madman spoke of was a very wise man and a very good counsellor, and served the Queen as tutor and physician, but to think that she was his lover is a folly deserving the severest punishment. Yet you must see that Cardenio did not know what he was saying, for you must remember that he was already out of his mind when he said it."

"That's what I say," answered Sancho, "and you oughtn't to have taken any notice of what a madman said. What's more, if good luck had not come to your worship's aid, and the stone had struck your head instead of your chest, we should have been in a fine way for standing up for that great lady, God damn her. And just think, Cardenio would have got off scot-free as a madman."

"Against all men, sane or mad," said Don Quixote, "it is every knight errant's duty to defend the honour of all women of whatever rank; particularly of queens as exalted and virtuous as Queen Madasima was. I have a particular regard for her on account of her good qualities; for not only was she very beautiful but prudent too, and very patient in her countless misfortunes; and the advice and company of Master Elisabat were of great advantage and comfort to her, and enabled her to bear her trials with prudence and patience. That is what made the ignorant and malicious rabble say and think that she was his mistress; and they lie, I say again, and two hundred times more I repeat that every one of them who thinks so or says so lies."

"I don't say so, nor think so," replied Sancho. "There let it rest. Let them eat the lie and swallow it with their bread. Whether the two were lovers or no, they'll have accounted to God for it by now. I have my own fish to fry. I know nothing. I'm not one to pry into other people's lives. It's no good lying about the price; your purse always knows better. What's more, I was born naked and naked I am now; I neither lose nor win. Suppose they were lovers, what's that to me? Plenty of people expect to find bacon where there's not so much as a hook to hang it on. Who can hedge in the cuckoo? Especially as God Himself is not spared."

"Good Lord!" cried Don Quixote, "what a string of nonsense, Sancho! What have all these proverbs to do with the matter we were discussing? For Heaven's sake be quiet, and in future see you spur your ass and do not interfere with what does not concern you. And get it into your five senses that all my actions, past, present and future, are very well based in reason and conform in every way to the rules of chivalry. For I know these rules better than any knights who have ever professed them in the world."

"Sir," replied Sancho, "is it a good rule of chivalry for us to get lost looking for a madman in these mountains, where there isn't a road or a track? And when we find him, perhaps he'll choose to finish the job he has begun—not his story, but breaking your head and my ribs till there isn't a whole bone left in our bodies."

"Once more, Sancho, be quiet," exclaimed Don Quixote, "for I would have you know that it is not only my wish to find the madman that draws me to these parts, but my intention of performing a deed here which will gain me perpetual renown and glory throughout all the known world. It shall be such a deed that by it I shall attain the utmost perfection and renown of which a knight errant is capable."

"And is this deed very perilous?" asked Sancho Panza.

"No," replied the Knight of the Sad Countenance, "although the dice may so fall that we throw a blank instead of a double. But everything depends on your diligence."

"On my diligence?" repeated Sancho.

"Yes," said Don Quixote, "because if you come back quickly from the place I mean to send you to, my penance will be soon over and my glory will speedily begin. But it is not right to keep you longer in suspense, hanging on the purport of my words. So I would have you know, Sancho, that the famous Amadis of Gaul was one of the most perfect of knights errant. I was wrong to say *one;* he was the sole, the first, the unique, the prince of all there were in the world in his day. A fig for Sir Belianis and for all who claimed to be in any respect his equal! For I swear they are mistaken. What is more I say that when any painter wishes to win fame in his art, he endeavours to copy the pictures of the most excellent painters he knows, and the same rule obtains for all professions and pursuits of importance that serve to adorn the commonwealth. So what any man who wants a reputation for prudence and patience must do, and does, is to imitate Ulysses, in whose person and labours Homer paints for us a lively picture of prudence and patience, just as Virgil shows us in the person of Aeneas the virtue of a dutiful son and the sagacity of a brave and skilful captain. They do not paint them or describe them as they were, but as they should have been, to serve as examples of their virtues for future generations. In the same way Amadis was the pole-star, the morning star, the sun of all valiant knights and lovers, and all of us who ride beneath the banner of love and chivalry should imitate him. This being the case, Sancho my friend, I conclude that the knight errant who best copies him will attain most nearly to the perfection of chivalry. Now one of the ways in which this knight most clearly showed his wisdom, virtue, valour, patience, steadfastness and love was when, scorned by his lady Oriana, he retired to do penance on the Bare Rock, changing his name to Beltenebros, a name most certainly significant and suitable to the life which he had voluntarily chosen. Therefore, as it is easier for me to imitate him in this way than in cleaving giants, beheading serpents, killing dragons, routing armies, shattering fleets, and breaking spells; and since this place is so fitting for such a purpose, there is no reason for me to let this opportunity pass now that it so conveniently offers me the forelock."

"What is it then that your worship really means to do in this out-of-the-way place?" asked Sancho.

"Have I not told you," replied Don Quixote, "that I intend to imitate Amadis, and to act here the desperate, raving, furious lover, at the same time following the example of the valiant Sir Roland when he found by a spring evidence that the fair Angelica had dishonoured herself with Medoro, for grief at which he turned mad, tore up trees, muddied the waters of the clear springs, killed shepherds, destroyed flocks, fired cottages, pulled down houses, dragged off mares, and performed a hundred thousand extravagant feats, which deserve eternal fame and remembrance? Now although I do not intend to imitate Roland, or Orlando, or Rotolando—for he bore all those names—exactly in all the mad things he did, said and thought, I will sketch them in as best I can, in what appear to me to be their essentials. But perhaps I shall come to be content to imitate Amadis alone, for he attained unrivalled fame by a madness that lay not in wild deeds but in tears and grief."

"It seems to me," said Sancho, "that the knights who did things like that were provoked and had a reason for their follies and penances. But what reason has your worship for going mad? What lady has scorned you, or what evidence have you found that the lady Dulcinea del Toboso has done anything she shouldn't with Moor or Christian?"

"That is the point," replied Don Quixote, "and in that lies the beauty of my plan. A knight errant who turns mad for a reason deserves neither merit not thanks. The thing is to do it without cause, and then my lady can guess what I would do in the wet if I do all this in the dry. What is more, I have sufficient reason in my long absence from my ever supreme mistress Dulcinea del Toboso. For, as you heard that shepherd Ambrosio say the other day, the absent feel and fear every ill. So, friend Sancho, do not waste time advising me to give up so rare, so happy, and so unprecedented an imitation. I am mad, and mad I must be till you come back with the reply to a letter which I intend to send by you to my lady Dulcinea. If it proves such as my fidelity deserves, my raving and my penance will be ended; but if it be unfavourable I shall be mad in earnest, and when I am I shall feel nothing. So, whichever way she replies, I shall be done with the conflict and distress in which you will leave me. For if it is good tidings you bring me, I shall enjoy them in my right mind, and if it is evil, I shall not feel them, being mad. But tell me, Sancho, have you taken good care of Mambrino's helmet? For I saw you pick it up from the ground when that ungrateful wretch tried to destroy it, though he could not do so—and that shows how finely it was tempered."

To which Sancho replied, "In God's name, Sir Knight of the Sad Countenance, I cannot endure or bear with patience some of the things your worship says. They make me think that all you tell me about chivalries and winning kingdoms and empires, and giving isles and doing other favours and mighty deeds, as knights errant do, must be just wind and lies, and all friction or fiction or whatever you call it. For to hear your worship say that a barber's basin is Mambrino's helmet, and persist in that error for more than four days, what can one think? Only that a man who persists in saying a thing like that must be cracked in the brain. I have the basin in the bag, all dented, and I'm taking it home to mend it and to use it for shaving, if God is so gracious as to let me live with my wife and children one day."

"Look you, Sancho, by the same oath as you swore just now, I swear," said Don Quixote, "that you have less brains than any squire has or ever had in the whole world. Is it possible that all this while you have been with me you have not discovered that everything to do with knights errant appears to be chimaera, folly and nonsense, and to go all contrariwise? This is not really the case, but there is a crew of enchanters always amongst us who change and alter all our deeds, and transform them according to their pleasure and their desire either to favour us or to injure us. So what seems to you to be a barber's basin appears to me to be Mambrino's helmet, and to another as something else. It shows a rare foresight in the sage who is on my side to make what is really and truly Mambrino's helmet seem to everyone a basin. For, as it is of such great value, the whole world would persecute me in order to get it from me. However, as they see that it is nothing more than a barber's basin, they do not trouble about it, as was evident in the case of the wretch who tried to destroy it and left it behind him on the ground; for I promise you that if he had recognized it he would never have left it there. Take care of it, my friend. I do not need it for the present. On the contrary, I must strip off all my armour and be naked as I was born; that is, if I decide to imitate Roland in my penance rather than Amadis."

Deep in this conversation they came to the foot of a high mountain which stood alone, almost as though it had been cut off from the many which surrounded it. At its foot ran a gentle stream, encircling a meadow so green and luxuriant that it pleased the eyes of all who saw it. There were many woodland trees there, and some shrubs and flowers that made the place pleasant. This site the Knight of the Sad Countenance chose for the performance of his penance, and at the sight of it he began to speak aloud, as if he were out of his wits, "This is the place, Heavens, where I select and choose to bewail the misfortune into which you yourselves have plunged me. This is the spot where the moisture from my eyes will swell the waters of this little stream, and my deep and incessant sighs perpetually stir the leaves of these mountain trees, in testimony and sign of the grief my tortured heart endures. On you, whoever you may be, rustic deities who have your abode in this inhospitable spot, hear the plaints of this ill-starred lover, whom long absence and some fancied jealousy have brought to mourn among these rugged wastes, and to complain of the cruel nature of that ungrateful beauty, the sum and perfection of all human loveliness! O you, wood-nymphs and dryads, whose custom it is to haunt the mountain thickets, may the swift and sensual satyrs, who love you in vain, never disturb your sweet quiet, that you may aid me to lament my ill fortune, or at least not grow weary of hearing it! O Dulcinea del Toboso, day of my night, glory of my grief, pole-star of my journeys, star of my fate, may Heaven grant you all that you pray for in full measure. Consider now the place and the condition to which your absence has brought me, and grant me in return such reward as my fidelity deserves! O solitary trees, which henceforth must be the companions of my solitude, give me some sign, by the gentle stirring of your branches, that my presence does not offend you! And you, my squire, pleasing companion of my prosperous and adverse fortunes, impress on your memory what you will see me do here, so that you may tell and recite it to the sole cause of it all!"

As he spoke, he dismounted from Rocinante and, stripping him in an instant of bridle and saddle, gave him a slap on the haunches, saying, "He who lacks liberty bestows it on you, O steed as excellent in your performance as you are unfortunate in your fate! Go where you will, for on your forehead it is written that not Astolfo's Hippogriff, nor yet the famous Frontino which cost Bradamante so dear, was your equal in speed."

At this Sancho put in, "God bless the man who has saved us the trouble of unharnessing Dapple.* He wouldn't have gone short of smacks or speeches in his praise. Though if he were here I would let nobody take off his harness. There would be no reason for it, seeing that the general rules about people in love and in despair were no concern of his, since his master was not one of them. For when it pleased God I was his master. Truly, Sir Knight of the Sad Countenance, if my journey and your worship's madness are going to be in real earnest, it would be a good thing to saddle Rocinante again to serve instead of the ass, for that'll save me time on my double

---

* Who is apparently lost again, and remains so until recovered.

And hurriedly stripping off his breeches, he stood in his skin and his shirt. And then, without more ado, he took two leaps into the air, and twice turned head over heels, revealing such parts of his person as caused Sancho to turn Rocinante's head for fear he might see them a second time. (page 275) journey. If I do it on foot I don't know when I shall get there or when I shall get back, for I am a very poor walker indeed."

"Very well, Sancho," replied Don Quixote, "it shall be as you wish. Yours does not seem a bad plan to me. And you shall leave in three days' time, for I want you in the interval to observe all that I do and say for her sake. Then you will be able to report everything to her."

"Well, what more have I to see than I've seen already?" asked Sancho.

"A great deal you know about the story!" replied Don Quixote. "There still remains the tearing of my garments, the scattering of my arms, the running of my head against the rocks, and other things of the kind which will astonish you."

"For God's sake," cried Sancho, "take care, your worship, how you go hitting your head, for you might strike a rock in such a place that you would put paid to the whole business of this penance with the first blow. But since your worship thinks that these knocks on the head are necessary, and this job can't be done without them, it's my opinion that you ought to be content, since this is all a pretence and a counterfeit and a joke,—you ought to be content, I say, with hitting your head on the water, or on something soft like cotton, and leave the rest to me. For I'll tell my lady that your worship dashed your dead against a pointed rock harder than a diamond."

"I thank you for your kind intentions, friend Sancho," replied Don Quixote; "but I would have you know that all these things which I am doing are not in jest, but very much in earnest. Otherwise I should be infringing the laws of chivalry, which bid us tell no lie on pain of degradation, and to do one thing instead of another is the same as a lie. Therefore the blows on the head must be real, hard and efficacious, without any sophistry or deception; and you will have to leave me some lint to heal me since, as ill-luck would have it, we have lost our balsam."

"Losing the ass was worse," replied Sancho, "for with him we lost the lint and all. But please, your worship, don't remind me of that accursed drink, for not only my stomach but my very soul turns over at the mere mention of it. As for the three days allowed me for seeing your mad pranks, please reckon them as already passed. For I take everything you've said for granted and I'll tell wonders to my lady. So write the letter and send me off immediately, for I'm dearly longing to come back and rescue your worship from this purgatory I'm leaving you in."

"Do you call it purgatory, Sancho?" asked Don Quixote. "You would do better to call it hell, or even worse, if there is anything worse."

"For him that's in hell," replied Sancho, "*nulla est retentio,* as I've heard say."

"I do not understand what you mean by *retentio,*" said Don Quixote.

"*Retentio,*" answered Sancho, "means that once a man is in hell he never gets out, and can't. But it'll be the reverse with your worship, or I'll wear out my heels—that is, if I take spurs to liven up Rocinante. Let me once get to El Toboso and into the presence of my lady Dulcinea, and I'll tell her such stories of the follies and mad pranks—for they're all the same—which you have done and are still doing that I'll make her suppler than a glove, even if I find her harder than a cork-tree. Then I'll come back with her sweet and honeyed answer, riding the air like a wizard, and get your worship out of this purgatory, which looks like hell and isn't. For you have a hope of getting out, and that, as I said, people who are in hell haven't got. I don't think your worship will contradict me."

"That is the truth," said the Knight of the Sad Countenance, "but how shall we manage to write the letter?"

"And the bills of asses as well," added Sancho.

"It will all be included," said Don Quixote; "and since there is no paper, it will be as well to write it as the ancients did, on the leaves of trees or on wax tablets; although they would be as difficult to find now as paper. But I have just thought of a good—no, of an excellent—place to write it, and that is in the little note-book which was Cardenio's. Then you can see that it is copied on to paper in a good hand, at the first village you come to in which there is a schoolmaster; or, failing that, a parish clerk will transcribe it for you. But do not give it to a lawyer's clerk to write, for they use a legal hand that Satan himself will not understand."

"But what's to be done about the signature?" asked Sancho.

"Amadis' letters were never signed," replied Don Quixote.

"That's all very well," replied Sancho, "but the order for the asses must have a signature, for if it is copied they will say that the signature is false, and I shall be left without the ass-colts."

"The order will be signed in the little note-book itself, so that when my niece sees it she will make no difficulty about complying with it. As for the love-letter, you will put by way of signature: 'Yours till death, The Knight of the Sad Countenance'. It will make no great difference that it is in a strange hand since, as far as I remember, Dulcinea cannot write or read, and she has never seen a letter or writing of mine in all her life. For our love has always been platonic, and never gone farther than a modest glance. And even that so occasionally that I can truly swear that in all the twelve years I have loved her more than the light of these eyes which the earth will one day devour, I have not seen her four times. And perhaps on those four occasions she did not even once notice that I was looking at her, such is the reserve and seclusion in which her father, Lorenzo Corchuelo, and her mother, Aldonza Nogales, have brought her up."

"Well, well!" exclaimed Sancho. "So Lorenzo Corchuelo's daughter is the lady Dulcinea del Toboso, otherwise called Aldonza Lorenzo?"

"She is," said Don Quixote, "and she it is who deserves to be mistress of all the world."

"I know her well," said Sancho, "and I can tell you that she pitches a bar as well as the strongest lad in the whole village. Praise be to God! She's a brawny girl, well built and tall and sturdy, and she will know how to keep her chin out of the mud with any knight errant who ever has her for his mistress. O the wench, what muscles she's got, and what a pair of lungs! I remember one day she went up the village belfry to call in some of their lads who were working in a fallow field of her father's, and they could hear her as plainly as if they had been at the foot of the tower, although they were nearly two miles away. And the great thing about her is that she's not a bit shy. There's a good deal of the court-lady about her too, for she has a crack with everybody, and makes a joke and a mock of them all. I tell you, Sir Knight of the Sad Countenance, that you're not only quite right to play your mad pranks for her, but you've good reason to despair and hang yourself for her as well. Indeed any one who knows will say you acted better then well, even though the Devil himself should carry you off afterwards. Oh, I wish I were on the road only for the joy of seeing her. I haven't set eyes on her for ever so long. She must be changed, too, for always trudging about the fields in sun and wind greatly spoils a woman's looks. But I must confess to you, Don Quixote, that I have been very much mistaken on one point up to now. I really and truly thought that the lady Dulcinea must be some princess your worship was in love with, or at least a person of quality, to deserve the rich presents you sent her, the Basque and the galley-slaves, for instance, and all the other things you must have won in all the victories your worship must have had before I was your squire. But when you come to think of it, what good is it to the lady Aldonza Lorenzo, I mean the lady Dulcinea del Toboso, to have all the knights you have conquered and sent to her, or all that you ever will send, going down on their knees before her? Just when they arrive she'll very likely be dressing flax or threshing in the barn. Then they'll be confused at seeing her, and she'll burst out laughing and not think much of your present."

"I have told you very often before now, Sancho," said Don Quixote, "that you are a very great babbler. Yet although your wits are blunt your remarks sometimes sting. But just to prove your foolishness and my wisdom, I want you to listen to a little story.

"Once upon a time there was a beautiful widow, young, gay, rich and not a bit prudish, who fell in love with a stout and lusty young lay-brother. His superior heard of it and addressed the good widow one day by way of brotherly reproof, 'I am astonished, madam,' he said, 'and with good reason, that a woman of your quality, beautiful and rich as you are, should have fallen in love with such a coarse, low, ignorant fellow as So-and-So, seeing that we have so many graduates, divinity students and theologians in this house, and you could pick and choose any of them like pears, and say 'I like this one, and not that one.' But she answered most gaily and impudently, 'You are much mistaken, my dear sir, and very old-fashioned in your ideas, if you think that I have made a bad choice in that fellow, idiot though he may seem, seeing that for all I want of him he knows as much philosophy as Aristotle, and more.' So, Sancho, for what I want of Dulcinea del Toboso she is as good as the greatest princess in the land. For not all those poets who praise ladies under names which they choose so freely, really have such mistresses. Do you think that the Amaryllises, the Phyllises, Sylvias, Dianas, Galateas, Phyllidas, and all the rest that books and ballads and barbers' shops and theatres are so full of, were really flesh-and-blood ladies, and the mistresses of the writers who wrote about them? Not a bit of it. Most of them were invented to serve as subjects for verses, and so that the poets might be taken for lovers, or men capable of being so. I am quite satisfied, therefore, to imagine and believe that the good Aldonza Lorenzo is lovely and virtuous; her family does not matter a bit, for no one will inquire into that for the purpose of investing her with any order and, for my part, I think of her as the greatest princess in the world. For you must know, Sancho, if you do not know it already, that two things arouse love more than all others. They are great beauty and a good name; and these two qualities are present in Dulcinea to a surpassing degree; for in beauty she has no rival, and few can equal her in good name. To make an end of the matter, I imagine all I say to be true, neither more nor less, and in my imagination I draw her as I would have her be, both as to her beauty and her rank, unequalled by Helen, unrivalled by Lucretia, or any other famous woman of antiquity, Greek, Barbarian or Roman. Let anyone say what he likes, for though the ignorant may reproach me for it, men of judgment will not condemn me."

"What I say is that your worship's always right," replied Sancho, "and I'm an ass. But I don't know how that word ass comes to my lips, for one shouldn't talk of halters in the hanged man's house. But give me the letter and good-bye, for I'm off."

Don Quixote took out the note-book and, drawing a little aside, very calmly set about writing the letter. And when he had finished it he called Sancho, saying that he wanted to read it to him so that he might commit it to memory in case he were to lose it on the way; for with his bad luck anything might happen.

To which Sancho replied: "Write it two or three times in the book, your worship, and give it to me. I will carry it very carefully. But it would be mad to think of my learning it by heart, for my memory's so bad that I often forget my own name. Yet read it to me all the same, your worship. I shall enjoy hearing it. It must be as good as a bit of print."

"Listen; it goes like this," said Don Quixote.

Don Quixote's letter to Dulcinea del Toboso

Sovereign and sublime lady,

One stabbed by the dart of absence and pierced to the heart's core wishes you, sweetest Dulcinea del Toboso, the health which he does not himself enjoy. If your beauty scorns me, if your merit acts to my disadvantage, if you disdain my anguish, although inured to suffering I shall be ill able to bear an affliction which is not only severe but of very long duration. My good squire Sancho will give you a full account, O ungrateful beauty and beloved enemy, of the state to which I am reduced for your sake. If it be your pleasure to relieve me, I am yours. If not, do as you will; for by my death I shall have satisfied your cruelty and my passion.

Yours till death,
The Knight of the Sad Countenance

"God bless my father!" cried Sancho on hearing the letter. "It's the finest thing I've ever heard! I'll be blowed if your worship doesn't say just what you want to! And how well the Knight of the

Sad Countenance fits into the signature. Your worship's the Devil himself, I swear, and there's nothing you don't know."

"You have to know everything," replied Don Quixote, "in the profession I follow."

"Well, then," said Sancho, "put the order for the three colts on the other side of the leaf, sir, and sign it very clearly so that they'll know your hand when they see it."

"So I will," answered Don Quixote. And when he had written it, he read it aloud.

"At sight of this my first bill of asses, dear niece, give order that three out of the five which I left at home in your charge be given to Sancho Panza, my squire. Which three colts I order to be delivered in payment for the like amount counted and received of him here; and this with his receipt shall be your discharge. Given in the heart of the Sierra Morena, on the twenty-second of August of the current year."

"That's right," said Sancho. "Please sign it, your worship."

"There is no need to sign it," said Don Quixote. "I need only put my flourish, for that is the same as a signature and will be good enough for three asses, or even for three hundred."

"I trust your worship," replied Sancho. "Now let me go and saddle Rocinante. And get ready, sir, to give me your blessing, for I'm going now. I shan't wait to see the pranks your worship's going to perform, but I'll tell her I saw you do so many that she'll be satisfied."

"At least I want you to see me naked, Sancho, and performing a dozen wild pranks or so. I will run through them in less than half an hour, and when you have seen them with your own eyes you can safely swear to any others that you may care to add. You will not tell her of as many as I mean to perform, I promise you."

"For God's sake, dear master, don't make me see you naked. It'll grieve me so that I shan't be able to stop crying, and my head is so

273

bad from the tears I shed last night for Dapple that I'm in no condition for fresh weeping. If your worship wants me to see some of your mad pranks, do some in your clothes—but short ones, and only the most important. Though really I've no need of anything of the sort. For, as I said before, if I go now it'll hasten my return with the news your worship desires and deserves. That I will bring. Otherwise let the lady Dulcinea look out. For if she doesn't reply as she should, I take my solemn oath that I'll kick and punch a kind answer out of her guts. Wouldn't it be a shame, indeed, for a famous knight errant like your worship to go mad without the least reason in the world, for a—the lady had better not give me cause to say it or, by God, I'll blurt it out and let her have it wholesale, even though it spoils the market. I'm pretty good at that. She doesn't know me. If she did, I swear she would treat me with proper respect."

"Really, Sancho," said Don Quixote, "as far as I can see, you are no saner than I am."

"I'm not so mad as you," replied Sancho, "but I've a worse temper. But never mind that. What is your worship going to eat till I return? Are you going out on to the road to steal your food from the shepherds like Cardenio?"

"Do not be troubled on that score," replied Don Quixote, "for I should not eat anything but the herbs and the fruit which this meadow and these trees provide, even if I had it. The point of this business of mine lies in my fasting and in enduring all such hardships. Farewell, then."

"But, your worship," replied Sancho, "do you know what I'm afraid of? Perhaps I mayn't be able to find my way back to the place I'm leaving you in. It's so out of the way."

"Observe the landmarks, and I will try to remain near this spot," said Don Quixote. "And I will even take the precaution of climbing the highest of these crags to look out for you on your return. But your surest way of not missing me, and not getting lost yourself, will be for you to cut some of the broom that is so plentiful around here. Scatter it at intervals as you go till you get out to open country. The sprigs will serve as landmarks and signs for you to find me by when you come back, just like the thread in Theseus' labyrinth."

"That's what I'll do," replied Sancho Panza; and cutting some broom, he asked for his master's blessing and, not without many tears on both sides, took his leave. Then he mounted Rocinante, after receiving an especial charge from Don Quixote to take as good care of him as of his own person, and set out for the plain, scattering the broom sprigs at intervals, as his master had advised. So he rode off, despite Don Quixote's repeated requests that he should stay and watch him perform at least a couple of his wild pranks. But he had not gone above a hundred yards before he turned round and said, "I think that you were quite right, your worship. It would be as well for me to watch, say, one of your mad pranks, so that I can swear I've seen you doing them with a safe conscience. Though I've seen you doing one very mad thing already, by staying here I mean."

"Did not I tell you so?" said Don Quixote. "Wait, Sancho, I will perform several as quickly as you can say a Credo."

And hurriedly stripping off his breeches, he stood in his skin and his shirt. And then, without more ado, he took two leaps into the air, and twice turned head over heels, revealing such parts of his person as caused Sancho to turn Rocinante's head for fear he might see them a second time. So he departed fully satisfied that he could swear to his master's madness. And so we will leave him pursuing his journey till his return, which was speedy.

⊰ *26* ⊱

A Continuation of
the Refinements practised by Don Quixote
to express His Love in
the Sierra Morena

*T*o continue the account of the
actions of the Knight of the Sad Countenance once he was alone,
our history tells that, after the falls or somersaults performed with
his upper parts clothed and his lower parts naked, and after he had
seen Sancho depart, unwilling to wait and see any more of his antics,
Don Quixote climbed to the top of a high rock, and there turned his
thoughts once more to a problem on which he had already pondered
many times without reaching any conclusion. This was to decide
which was the better and would stand him in the greater stead: to
imitate Roland's downright madness or Amadis' melancholy moods.
So, communing with himself, he argued, "If Roland was as good a
knight and as valiant as they all say, where is the wonder? since,
after all, he was enchanted, and no one could kill him except by
stabbing a long pin into the sole of his foot, which was the reason
why he always wore shoes with seven iron soles. But these con-
trivances were of no avail against Bernardo del Carpio, who understood them, and throttled him with his bare hands at Roncesvalles. But, setting his bravery on one side, let us consider his

madness, which certainly arose from the evidence he found beside the spring and the news which the shepherd gave him that Angelica had slept more than two afternoons with Medoro, a little curly-haired Moor and page to Agramante. Now if he believed that this was true, and that his lady had done him this foul wrong, it is not surprising that he went mad. But how can I imitate him in his madness without a similar cause? For I dare swear that my Dulcinea del Toboso has never seen a real Moor in his real Moorish dress in all her life, and that she is today as her mother bore her; and I should do her a grave injury were I to imagine otherwise and go mad, after the fashion of Roland the Furious.

"On the other hand, I know that Amadis of Gaul achieved an unrivalled reputation as a lover without ever losing his wits or having raving fits. For, as the history tells, on finding himself scorned by his lady Oriana, who had commanded him to appear no more in her presence until it was her pleasure, what he did was merely to retire to the Bare Rock in the company of a hermit; and there he wept his fill and commended himself to God so earnestly that Heaven succoured him in the midst of his greatest tribulation. Now if this is true—and it is—why do I now take pains to strip myself stark naked and give pain to these trees which have done me no harm, and disturb the clear water of these streams, which must give me drink when I am thirsty? All honour then to the memory of Amadis, and let him be the model, so far as it is possible, for Don Quixote de la Mancha, of whom it shall be said, as it was said of that other, that if he did not achieve great things he died attempting them. If I am not cast off and despised by Dulcinea del Toboso, let it suffice, as I have said, that I am absent from her. So now to work! Come into my mind, deeds of Amadis, and teach me where to begin to imitate you. I remember now that most of the time he prayed and commended his soul to God. But what shall I do for a rosary, for I have none?"

At this there came into his head a way of making one. He tore a great strip from the tail of his shirt, which was hanging down, and made eleven knots in it, one fatter than the rest; and this served him for a rosary all the time he was there, during which time he recited a million Ave Marias. But one thing did trouble him a great deal; there was no hermit in the district to hear his confession and administer consolation. He amused himself, however, by pacing about the little meadow, writing and carving in the bark of the trees and tracing on the fine sand a great number of verses, all suited to his sad state, and some of them in praise of Dulcinea. But the only ones which were found complete and could be deciphered afterwards were the following:

> Ye plants, ye herbs, and ye trees,
>> That flourish in this pleasant site
> In lofty and verdant degrees,
>> If my harms do you no delight,
> Hear my holy plaints, which are these.
> And let not my grief you molest,
>> Though it ever so feelingly went,
> Since here for to pay your rest,
> Don Quixote his tears hath addressed,
>> Dulcinea's lack to lament
>>> del Toboso.

> In this very place doth abide
>> The loyallest lover and true,
> Who himself from his lady did hide,
>> But yet felt him sorrows anew,
> Not knowing whence they might proceed.
> Love doth him cruelly wrest
>> With a passion of evil descent,
> Which robbed Don Quixote of his rest,
> Till a keg with his tears was full pressed,
>> Dulcinea's lack to lament
>>> del Toboso.

> In search of adventures he pined
>> Among these rough woods and rocks,

Don Quixote climbed to the top of a high rock, and there turned his thoughts once more to a problem on which he had already pondered many times without reaching any conclusion. This was to decide which was the better and would stand him in the greater stead: to imitate Roland's downright madness or Amadis' melancholy moods. (page 276)

Still cursing his pitiless mind;
> For a wretch amidst bushes and brakes
And crags will misfortunes find.
And Love's whip gave it him hot,
> Nor did his lashes relent
Till he'd touched his tenderest spot,
And drawn tears from poor Don Quixote,
> Dulcinea's lack to lament
> del Toboso.

His tacking of "del Toboso" on to Dulcinea's name made the discoverers of the poem laugh heartily. For they supposed Don Quixote must have imagined that the verse would not be understood unless he added del Toboso when he named Dulcinea; and they were right, as he afterwards confessed. He wrote a great number more. But, as has been said, only these three stanzas could be deciphered and were found complete. He passed the time in this writing, and in sighing and calling on the fauns and satyrs of those woods, on the nymphs of the streams and on mournful humid Echo, to listen, reply and console him. He also searched for herbs to serve as food till Sancho's return. But if he had been away three weeks instead of three days, the Knight of the Sad Countenance would have been so wasted away that he would have been unrecognizable even by the mother who bore him.

But here it will be well to leave him, deep in his sighs and verses, to tell what happened to Sancho Panza on his mission. When he had emerged on to the highway, he set out to find the El Toboso road, and the following day reached the inn where he had suffered his misadventure with the blanket. Now no sooner did he catch sight of it than he felt himself once more sailing through the air; and he had no desire to enter, even though he had come at an hour when he properly should have gone in. For it was dinner-time and he was longing for something hot to eat, since it was a long time since he had eaten anything but cold fare. His inclinations brought him close to the inn, but he was still doubtful whether to enter or not at the moment when two persons came out and presently recognized him.

"Tell me, Master Licentiate," one of them asked the other, "isn't that man on the horse Sancho Panza who, so our adventurer's housekeeper told us, went off with her master as his squire?"

"Yes, it is," replied the Licentiate, "and that is our Don Quixote's horse."

They knew him very well, for they were the priest and the barber of his own village, the same men who had performed the trial and general holocaust of the books. And once they were quite certain of Sancho Panza and Rocinante, being anxious for news of Don Quixote, the pair of them went up to him, and the priest called him by name and asked, "Friend Sancho Panza, where did you leave your master?"

Sancho Panza recognized them at once, and decided not to tell them where his master was, nor to describe the state he had left him in. So he replied that Don Quixote was occupied in a certain place with a certain matter of great importance to him, which he could not reveal for all the eyes in his head.

"No, no, Sancho Panza," said the barber; "if you don't tell us where he is, we shall imagine—in fact we already do—that you've killed and robbed him, for here you come riding on his horse. Yes, you'll certainly have to produce the owner of that mount, or it'll be the worse for you."

"You have no cause to use threats on me. I'm not the man to rob or murder anyone. Let every man die when fate decrees, or when God his Maker calls him. My master's in the heart of these mountains, doing penance and very much in his element."

Then he told them right off without stopping of the state he had left his master in, of the adventures which had befallen him, and all about the letter he was taking to the lady Dulcinea del Toboso, the daughter of Lorenzo Corchuelo, and how the knight was up to his ears in love with her. The pair of them were amazed at Sancho's tale. For, although they already knew the nature of Don Quixote's madness, they were astonished afresh every time they had news of him. They then asked Sancho Panza to show them the letter he was taking to the lady Dulcinea del Toboso. He replied that it was written in a note-book, and that his master's orders were that he must have it copied down on paper in the first village he came to. Here the priest asked to see it, and promised to write it out himself in a very good hand. Sancho Panza then felt beneath his shirt for the little book, but could not find it; and he would not have found it if he had searched till this day, because it was still in Don Quixote's possession and had never been given to him. In fact he had not remembered to ask for it.

When Sancho saw that the book was not to be found, he turned pale as death, and felt once more very hurriedly all over his body, only to realize afresh that he could not find it. Without more ado he plunged both hands into his beard and tore half of it out. Then he rapidly dealt himself a dozen blows without stopping, on the face and on the nose, until both were bathed in blood. At this sight the priest and the barber asked him what had happened to make him treat himself so roughly.

"What do you think?" replied Sancho. "Only that in a single instant I've let three ass-colts slip through my fingers, three ass-colts, each one of them as strong as a castle."

"How is that?" asked the barber.

"I've lost the note-book," answered Sancho, "which had the letter for Dulcinea in it, and a bill signed by my master, ordering his niece to give me three of the four or five ass-colts he has at home."

Then he told them about the loss of Dapple, and the priest consoled him by promising that when he found his master he would make him renew the order and draw up the bill of exchange in the usual and customary form, for orders drawn in note-books were never honoured or accepted. Sancho was comforted by this, saying that in that case he did not much care about the loss of Dulcinea's letter, for he knew it almost by heart, and so they could take it down where and when they pleased.

"Repeat it to us, then, Sancho," said the barber, "and we'll write it down afterwards."

Sancho Panza stopped and scratched his head to drag the letter up into his memory, standing first on one foot and then on the other. Sometimes he looked down at the ground and sometimes up at the sky. Then, when he had gnawed away half the top of one finger, keeping everyone who was waiting for him to speak in suspense, he burst out after a very long pause, "God's Truth, Master Licentiate, the devil take all I remember of the letter; though at the beginning it said, 'Sublime and suppressed lady.' "

"It wouldn't be suppressed," said the barber, "but superhuman or sovereign."

"That's right," said Sancho. "Then, if I remember rightly, it went on, 'He that is oppressed with sleep and wakeful and wounded kisses your hands, ungrateful and most thankless beauty.' Then it said something about the health and sickness which he sent her, and so he went running on till he ended, 'Yours till death, the Knight of the Sad Countenance.' "

The pair of them were not a little amused at Sancho's excellent memory and congratulated him warmly upon it. They asked him to recite the letter twice more so that they too might learn it by heart, and write it down when the time came. Sancho said it through three times more, and three times he repeated three thousand comical mistakes. After that he told them more about his master, but he did not say a word about the blanket-tossing he had got at the inn, and still refused to enter. He also told them that once he had brought him a favourable despatch from the lady Dulcinea del Toboso his master was going to set out and try to become Emperor, or at least Monarch, for so they had agreed between them. It was a thing that could be managed very easily, considering the valour of the knight's person and the strength of his arm. And once he had done this, his master was going to find a wife for his squire. For by that time he could not possibly fail to be a widower, and would marry one of the Empress's waiting-women, the heiress to a rich and large estate on dry land—and none of your isles or wiles, for he had no use for them.

Sancho brought all this out with such gravity, wiping his nose from time to time, and so crazily, that the pair of them were

284

astonished afresh at the strength of Don Quixote's madness, since it had carried this poor man's wits along after it. They did not fancy the trouble of dispelling the squire's illusion. In fact it seemed to them better to leave him in it, since it did no harm to his conscience, and particularly as they found it most amusing to listen to his nonsense. So they bade him pray God for his master's health, it being both possible and feasible that he might in the course of time become an Emperor, as he had suggested, or at the least an Archbishop, or something of equal dignity. To which Sancho replied, "Gentlemen, supposing that by a stroke of fate my master should take it into his head not to be an Emperor but to be an Archbishop, I should like to know here and now what Archbishops are accustomed to give to their squires?"

"Generally," replied the priest, "they give them a benefice, or a simple parish, or a sextonship, which brings them in a good tithe besides the altar-gifts, which are usually reckoned at as much again."

"But for that," replied Sancho, "the squire would have to be unmarried, and at the very least know how to assist at the Mass. Now if that's so I'm out of luck, because I'm married and don't know the first letter of the *ABC*. What will happen to me if my master gets the idea of being an Archbishop, and not an Emperor as is the use and practice of knights errant?"

"Don't worry, friend Sancho," said the barber. "We'll entreat your master and advise him, and even put it to him as a matter of conscience, that he shall be an Emperor and not an Archbishop. It'll be much the easier for him, besides, since he is more of a soldier than a scholar."

"It has always seemed like that to me," replied Sancho, "although I must say that he's clever enough for anything. What I shall do is to pray Our Lord to put him wherever it's best for him, and where he can do me the greatest benefits."

"You speak like a wise man," said the priest, "and you will be acting like a good Christian. But what we have got to do now is to contrive a way of releasing your master from that fruitless penance you say you left him doing. And if we are to think out a means of doing so and get something to eat as well—for it is time—it would be a good idea if we were to go into this inn."

Sancho answered that they might go in, but that he would wait outside, and tell them afterwards the reason why he was unwilling to enter. But he begged them to bring him out something warm to eat, and some barley too for Rocinante. So they went in and left him outside, and a little later the barber brought him out some food. And afterwards, when they had thoroughly discussed the course to be pursued if they were to achieve their purpose, the priest struck an idea very applicable to Don Quixote's humour, and to the end they had in mind. This was, as he explained to the barber, for him to dress himself up as a damsel errant, and for the barber to make the best show he could of being her squire. Then they would go in that disguise and find Don Quixote—he pretending to be an afflicted damsel in distress—and beg a boon of him. This, as a valorous knight errant, he could not refuse to grant, and the boon which the damsel would ask of him would be to come with her wherever she might lead him, to redress an injury which a wicked knight had done her. She would also beg him not to require her to remove her mask, nor to make any enquiries about her rank, until he had wreaked vengeance for her upon the wicked knight. The priest was quite certain that Don Quixote would consent to anything they might ask him on these terms, and that they could get him away in this way, and take him home to his village, where they would try to find some cure for his strange madness.

⊰ 27 ⊱

How the Priest and the Barber
carried out Their Plan,
and Other Matters worthy of Mention
in This Great History

*T*he priest's plan did not seem a
bad one to the barber—quite the opposite, in fact—and so they set
about its immediate execution. They borrowed a dress and a
head-dress from the landlady, and left the priest's new cassock for
security. Then the barber made himself a long beard from a sorrel
and grey ox tail, which the innkeeper kept to hang his comb in. And
when the landlady asked them why they wanted all this, the priest
told her something about Don Quixote's madness, and said that they
needed this disguise to entice him away from the mountains, where
he then was. The innkeeper and his wife at once realized that the
madman was their guest of the balsam and the master of the blanket-tossed squire, and told the priest the whole story, not omitting
the part which Sancho had been so anxious to conceal. In the end the
landlady equipped the priest to perfection. She gave him a cloth
dress, stiff with black velvet stripes a good eight inches wide, all
slashed, and a bodice of green velvet bordered with white satin
trimmings, both of which must have been made in the time of King
Wamba. The priest would not agree to have his head dressed like a

woman's, but put on the little quilted linen cap he generally used for a nightcap, tied one of his black taffeta garters across his forehead, and made a mask with the other, which covered his beard and his face very well. He then put on his broad hat, large enough to serve as a sunshade and, wrapping his cloak around him, mounted his mule side-saddle like a woman, while the barber got up upon his, with his beard reaching to his waist, part sorrel and part white. For, as we have said, it was made from the tail of a pied ox.

They said good-bye to everyone, including the good Maritornes, who promised to recite a whole rosary, sinner though she was, that God might give them success in the very arduous and Christian task they had undertaken. But no sooner were they out of the inn than it struck the priest that he was doing wrong in dressing up in that fashion; for it was indecent for a churchman to appear in such a garb, however deeply he was concerned in the business. This he told the barber, and asked him to change clothes. It would be more fitting, he said, if his friend were to play the distressed maiden and himself be the squire, which part would be less prejudicial to his dignity. And if the barber would not agree he refused to go a step further, even though the devil should run away with Don Quixote. At this point Sancho joined them, and could not help laughing when he saw them in their disguise. In the end the barber gave in to the priest, and they changed their plan. The priest then began to instruct the barber how to act, and what to say to Don Quixote, so as to compel him to come away and cease haunting the place which he had chosen for his fruitless penance. The barber replied that he could carry it off to perfection, without any tuition. But he refused to put on the clothes until they should reach the place where Don Quixote was; and so he folded them up. The priest then stowed away his beard, and they went on their way under the guidance of Sancho Panza, who told them as they went along the story of the madman whom they had found in the mountains. But he kept quiet about the discovery of the leather bag and about its contents, for with all his simplicity he was rather a greedy rascal.

The next day they reached the place where Sancho had strewn

In the end the landlady equipped the priest to perfection. She gave him a cloth dress, stiff with black velvet stripes a good eight inches wide, all slashed, and a bodice of green velvet bordered with white satin trimmings, both of which must have been made in the time of King Wamba. (page 287) the sprigs to guide him to the spot where he had left his master. And when he recognized the place, he told them that this was the way in, and that they had better dress up, if that was necessary for the rescue of his master. For they had already told him that it was of the utmost importance to go thus clothed and disguised, if they were to save Don Quixote from the miserable life that he had chosen; and they had impressed on him that he must not tell his master who they were, or that he knew them. And if Don Quixote were to ask him, as he was bound to, whether he had given Dulcinea the letter, he must reply that he had, but that as she could not read, she had replied by word of mouth, commanding him to come and see her immediately on pain of her displeasure. This, they assured Sancho, was most essential; for in this way, and by means of certain things they intended to say to Don Quixote themselves, they felt certain that they could bring him to a better life, and so contrive it as to put him immediately on the road to becoming an Emperor or a Monarch, for as to his being an Archbishop there was nothing to fear.

Sancho listened to all this and treasured it up in his memory. He thanked them warmly for their intention of advising his master to be an Emperor and not an Archbishop, being certain in his own mind that, so far as bestowing favours on their squires went, Emperors could do more than Archbishops-errant. He also said that it would be better if he were to go ahead to look for his master and give him his lady's reply, for that alone might be sufficient to get him away from the place, without their putting themselves to all that trouble. They approved Sancho Panza's idea, and so decided to wait for him to return with the news that he had found his master. The squire then struck into the mountain clefts, leaving the two of them in a ravine, which was watered by a little gentle stream and pleasantly cool from the shade of the rocks and trees surrounding it. It was a hot day in August, the month when the heat is usually most intense in those parts, and the time was three o'clock in the afternoon, which made the place even more pleasing. In fact it invited them to wait there for Sancho's return, which they did. But as the two of them were lying at their ease in the shade, there came to their ears a voice singing sweetly and melodiously, though unaccompanied by any instrument. Which surprised them not a little, for this seemed a most unlikely place in which to find so good a singer. For although report has it that shepherds with excellent voices are to be found in the woods and fields, that is rather poetic exaggeration than sober truth. They were even more astonished when they heard the words of his song. For they were not rough shepherd's verses, but well-turned and courtly, as will be clear from the following lines:

What turns my happiness to pain?
   Disdain.
And greater makes my woe for me?
   Jealousy.
What sorest tries my patience?
   Absence.
If that be so, then for my wrong
No remedy may I obtain,
Since my best hopes I find are slain
By disdain, jealousy, and absence long.

Who through my breast this anguish drove?
   Love.
Who doth my happiness abate?
   Fate.

Who consents to this my pain?
   Heaven.
If that be so, I fear 'twill prove
That I must die in this sad plight,
Since for my overthrow unite
The heavens, fate, and love.

Who can better hope bequeath?
   Death.
What are the means to make me free?
   Inconstancy.

And wherein lies the cure for sadness?
Madness.
If that be so, it's merely silly
To seek my passion's cure,
For there's no remedy that's sure
But death and change and folly.

The time, the season, the solitude, the voice and skill of the singer,
all astonished and delighted the two listeners, who waited quietly in
the hope of hearing more. But when the silence had continued for
rather a long while, they decided to go out and look for this musician
with so fine a voice. Just as they were going to do so, however, the
same voice came once more to their ears, and kept them motionless
throughout the singing of this sonnet:

O sacred friendship that with nimble wing,
Thy phantom leaving here on earth below,
With blessed souls in heaven communing
Up through the empyrean halls dost go.
Thence, at thy pleasure, to us is assigned
Just peace, her features covered with a hood,
But oft, instead of her, Deceit we find
Clad in the garb of virtue and of good.
Leave heaven, friendship, and do not permit
Foul fraud thus openly thy robes to wear
And so all honest purposes defeat.
For if you leave him in your semblance fair
Dark chaos will once more engulf the world
And all to primal anarchy be hurled.

The song ended with a deep sigh, and the pair of them waited
attentively to see if he would sing again; but when they heard the
music turn to sobs and groans of sorrow, they agreed to go and find
out who the unhappy person was who had so excellent a voice and so
sorrowing a heart. And they had not gone far when, on coming
round the corner of a rock, they saw a man in form and figure

resembling Sancho Panza's description of Cardenio. The man did not start at the sight of them, but stayed still, with his head on his breast in a pensive attitude, and did not raise his eyes to look at them again after their first sudden appearance. Now the priest had recognized him from Sancho's account, and consequently knew the cause of his misfortunes; and being a man of ready speech, he went up to him and implored him most persuasively in a few well-chosen words to give up his wretched way of life, and not risk dying in that desolate place, which would be the greatest of all misfortunes. At that time Cardenio was sane, and free from the wild fits which so often drove him out of his mind. Seeing, therefore, the two of them dressed so unlike the usual frequenters of those lonely parts, he could not help being surprised, and was even more so when he heard them speak of his own affairs as if they were common knowledge —for that was the impression he got from the priest's speech. And so he replied, "I see, gentlemen, whoever you may be, that Heaven, which takes care to succour the good, and often the bad as well, has sent to me, unworthy as I am, even in this remote and desolate spot so far from the traffic of human kind, some persons to show me, by forcible and lively argument, the unreasonable nature of the life I lead, and to endeavour to tempt me away from here to a better place. But not knowing, as I do, that were I to fly from this misery I should fall into a worse, they must take me for a fool, or even worse for a madman. And that would not be surprising. For I am myself aware that the strength of my misery is so intense, and drives me to such distraction, that I am powerless to resist it and am turning to stone, void of all knowledge and feeling. This I realize when I am shown the evidence of the deeds I have done under the mastery of these terrible fits. Then I can only vainly lament and fruitlessly curse my fate, and to excuse my madness tell any who will hear it the story of its cause. For when sensible men learn its cause they will not be surprised at its effects. Though they will be unable to offer me any relief, at least they will not blame me, and their anger at my violence will turn to pity for my misfortunes. If you, sirs, have come with the same intention as the others, I beg you to listen to the story of my misfortunes before you continue with your sensible arguments. For when you have heard it, you will perhaps spare yourselves the trouble of trying to offer consolation for an inconsolable sorrow."

The pair of them wanted nothing better than to hear the cause of his grief from his own mouth, and begged him to tell them his story, promising to take no measures without his consent either for his relief or for his consolation. Then the unhappy gentleman began his piteous tale, in almost the same words and phrases as he had used in telling it to Don Quixote and the goatherd a few days before, when the story had remained unfinished on account of Master Elisabat and Don Quixote's punctiliousness in defending the dignity of knight errantry. But fortunately this time Cardenio had no fit of madness and was able to tell it to the end. So, when he reached the subject of the letter which Don Ferdinand had found between the leaves of *Amadis of Gaul,* he said that he remembered it perfectly, and that it read as follows:

> Lucinda to Cardenio:
> Each day I find in you virtues which oblige and compel me to think more highly of you; and, therefore, if you would relieve me of this debt without prejudice to my honour, you may easily do so. My father knows you and loves me; he will never force me, but he will comply with your just demands, if you value me as you say, and as I believe you do.

"This letter moved me, as I have already told you, to ask for Lucinda's hand, and proved her in Don Ferdinand's opinion one of the most discreet and sensible women of her time. And it was this letter which made him determine to ruin me before my design could be put into effect. I told Ferdinand of her father's insistence that mine should make the request, and that I dared not mention the matter to my father for fear that he would not consent. Not that he was ignorant of Lucinda's rank, goodness, virtue and beauty—for he knew that she had virtues enough to ennoble any family in Spain—but because, as I understood, he did not wish me to marry before we knew what Duke Richard might do for me. To be brief, I told him that I dared not ask my father, not only because of this obstacle, but because of other vague apprehensions which made me fear that my desires would never be realized. Ferdinand's reply was that he would speak to my father for me, and make him speak to Lucinda's. O greedy Marius! Cruel Catiline! Criminal Sulla! Crafty Galalon! Treacherous Vellido! Vindictive Julian! Covetous Judas! Cruel, vindictive, crafty traitor! What harm had this poor wretch done you, who so frankly revealed to you the secrets and joys of his heart? How had I offended you? Did I ever say a word, or give you advice, which was not intended for your benefit and honour? But why do I complain, miserable wretch that I am. For it is certain that when the stars in their courses bring disaster, rushing down with fury and violence, no power on earth can stop them, no human ingenuity avert them. Who could have thought that Don Ferdinand, a noble and intelligent gentleman, indebted to me for my services and absolutely certain of success wherever his amorous fancy led him, would be bitten—as they say—with the desire to take from me my one ewe-lamb, who was not even yet mine? But these thoughts are vain and fruitless. Let them rest, and we will take up the broken thread of my unfortunate story.

"Don Ferdinand, then, finding that my presence hindered him from putting his false, wicked plan into practice, decided to send me to his elder brother, on the pretext of borrowing some money from him to pay for six horses, which he had bought on the very day he offered to speak to my father, purposely to provide himself with an excuse for getting me out of the way, the better to carry out his wicked plan. Could I have foreseen this treachery? Could I even have imagined it? No, certainly not. On the contrary, I offered to go immediately with the greatest of pleasure, and was delighted at the good bargain he had made. That night I spoke to Lucinda, told her of my arrangement with Don Ferdinand, and said that we had good reason to hope for a favourable result. She was as unsuspecting as I of Don Ferdinand's treachery, and bade me hurry back, for she was certain that the fulfilment of our desires would be delayed no longer than it would take for my father to speak to hers. I do not know how it was, but as she spoke her eyes filled with tears, and a sudden choking in her throat prevented her speaking another word, though she seemed to have much more to say. This excess of emotion, which I had never seen in her before, surprised me, because on such occasions as my good fortune and my diligence provided, we always talked happily and merrily enough, without mingling tears, sighs, jealousies, suspicions or fears with our conversation. I would expatiate on my good fortune, thanking Heaven for giving her to me for my mistress, praising her beauty, and extolling her virtue and good sense. She in reply would praise the qualities in me that seemed to her, as my lover, worthy of praise. During these conversations we amused ourselves with a hundred thousand trifles, and gossiped about our neighbours and friends; and the greatest freedom I allowed myself was to take, almost by force, one of her lovely white hands and press it to my lips, as well as the narrowness of the bars between us would allow. But on the night before the sad day of my parting she wept, moaned, and sighed and then fled, leaving me full of confusion and dread at these new and unusual signs of sorrow and tenderness in Lucinda. But, not to destroy my hopes, I attributed all this to the strength of her love for me, and to the grief which absence always causes true lovers. In short I departed, sad and thoughtful, my mind full of fancies and suspicions, but uncertain what it was I suspected or imagined —all of which clearly presaged the miserable and dark fate which awaited me.

"I came to the town I was sent to, and delivered the letters to Don Ferdinand's brother. I was well received, but not quickly dismissed. For, to my disgust, he bade me wait eight days in a place out of sight of the Duke, his father, since his brother had asked for a certain sum of money to be sent him without his father's knowledge. But all this was a stratagem of the false Don Ferdinand. For his brother was not short of money and might have sent me back with it immediately. I felt much inclined to disobey this order, for it seemed quite impossible to live so long away from Lucinda, especially as I had left her in such a state of distress. But, for all that, like a good servant I obeyed, although I knew it to be to my own detriment. On the fourth day after my arrival, however, a man came after me with a letter which by the address I knew was from Lucinda, for the writing was hers. I opened it in fear and trembling, convinced that it must be something extraordinary which had moved her to write to me in my absence, seeing how seldom she did so when I was near. Before I read it I asked the man who had given it to him, and how long he had been on the road. He told me that as he had happened to be going down one of the city streets about midday, a very beautiful lady had called him from a window, her eyes full of tears, and had said to him very earnestly, 'Brother, if you are a Christian, as you seem to be, I beg you, for the love of God, to carry this letter quickly to the place and the person to whom it is directed—for they are well known. In this you will be performing an act of charity, and that you may not lack the means to do it, take what is wrapped in this handkerchief.' 'As she said this,' he pursued, 'she threw me a handkerchief out of the window; and in it were a hundred *reals,* this gold ring here, and the letter I have given you. Then, without waiting for my reply, she left the window; though first she had seen me take up the letter and the handkerchief, and give her a sign that I would do what she asked. So, seeing how well I was paid for my trouble, and learning from the envelope that the letter was for you, sir, whom I know very well—and moved too by that beautiful lady's tears—I decided not to trust anyone else, but to come myself to deliver it to you; and in the sixteen hours since she gave it to me I have done the journey, which as you know is fifty-four miles.' While the kind impromptu messenger was speaking I hung on his words, my legs trembling so that I could scarcely stand. At length I opened the letter and read these words:

'Don Ferdinand has fulfilled his promise to persuade your father to speak to mine, more to his own satisfaction than to your advantage. I must tell you that he has asked for my hand in marriage, and that, carried away by the advantages

he thinks Don Ferdinand has over you, my father has agreed
with such eagerness that the betrothal is to take place two
days hence, so secretly and privately that the only witnesses
will be Heaven, and some of our own household. You can
imagine how I feel. Consider whether you should not return. The outcome of the matter will show you whether I
love you or not. God grant this may reach your hands before
mine are joined to those of a man who keeps his pledged
word so ill.'

"These, then, were the contents of the letter, which caused me to
set out without waiting for the answer or the money. For now I saw
clearly that it was not the purchase of the horses, but the indulgence
of his own desires, that had caused Don Ferdinand to send me to his
brother. Rage against him and fear of losing the treasure which I had
earned by so many years of love and devotion lent wings to my feet,
and the next day I reached our town at the most favourable moment
for going to speak to Lucinda. I rode in secretly and, leaving my
mule at the house of the good man who had brought me the letter, by
good luck I found Lucinda posted at the grating which had been the
constant witness of our loves. She recognized me immediately, and I
her, yet not with our usual joy. But who in the world can boast that
he has fathomed and understood the confused mind and changeable
nature of a woman? No one, of course. For as soon as Lucinda saw
me, she said, 'Cardenio, I am dressed for the betrothal. The traitor
Don Ferdinand and my greedy father are now waiting for me with
the other witnesses in the hall, but they shall rather be witnesses of
my death than of my betrothal. Do not be disturbed, my friend, but
contrive to be present at this sacrifice. If I cannot prevent it by
words, I carry a dagger about me which can oppose the most
determined violence by putting an end to my life, and proving the
love I bear and have always borne for you.'

"I answered her hurriedly and distractedly, for I was afraid that I
might lose my opportunity of replying, 'May your actions, lady,
confirm your words. If you have a dagger to secure your honour, I

have a sword here to defend you with, or to kill myself with if fortune proves adverse.'

"I do not think that she could have listened to all that I said, since I heard them hurriedly call her away. For the bridegroom was waiting. Here the night of my sadness fell; the sun of my happiness set; the light went out of my eyes, the sense from my brain. I could not go into her house nor move in any direction. But when I thought how important my presence was, whatever events might arise, I took better heart and entered. As I knew all the ways in and out, and as the whole household was in a secret bustle, no one noticed me, and I was able to take up my position in the recess formed by a window of the hall itself. This hiding-place was masked by the edges and folds of two pieces of tapestry, between which I could observe everything that happened there without myself being seen. How can I tell you with what alarm my heart beat while I stood there, what thoughts came into my head, what reflections passed through my mind? So many were they, and of such a nature, that they cannot and should not be told. Enough that Don Ferdinand came into the hall, not dressed as a bridegroom but in his usual clothes. His groomsman was a first cousin of Lucinda's, and there was no other person in the whole hall, except the servants. Shortly afterwards Lucinda came out of a dressing-room, accompanied by her mother and two of her maids, adorned as her rank and beauty deserved, and looking the very perfection of fashion and courtly splendour. My distraction and anxiety gave me no opportunity of noting in detail what she wore. I could only mark the colours, which were crimson and white, and the flashing of the jewels and precious stones on her head-dress and all over her clothes. But most beautiful of all was her lovely golden hair, which rivalled her jewels and the light of the great torches which lit the hall, and brought her beauty even more brilliantly before my eyes. O memory, mortal enemy of my peace! To what purpose do you recall to me the incomparable beauty of my beloved enemy? Would it not be better, cruel memory, to picture to me what she did next, so that, under the stress of so flagrant an injury, I may strive, if not to avenge it, at least to lose my life? Do not grow weary, gentlemen, of hearing these digressions of mine; for my grief cannot be told succinctly and methodically, since every circumstance of it seems to me to deserve a long discourse."

To which the priest replied that not only were they not weary of his tale, but that they were glad to hear the details; since they were not of the sort to be passed over in silence, and deserved the same attention as the main thread of the story.

"Then," continued Cardenio, "when they were all in the hall the parish priest came in, and took them each by the hand to perform the ceremony. When he said, 'Will you, lady Lucinda, take the lord Don Ferdinand, here present, for your lawful husband, as Holy Mother Church commands?', I stuck my whole head and neck out between the tapestries and listened with straining ears and distracted mind for Lucinda's reply, awaiting from it sentence of death or a fresh lease of life. If only I had then dared to come out and cry, 'Lucinda, Lucinda, beware what you do! Consider what you owe me! Remember you are mine, and cannot be another's! Be warned that to say yes is instantly to end my life. O treacherous Don Ferdinand, thief of my glory, death of my life! What do you want? What claim can you make? Consider that, as a Christian, you cannot achieve your desire, because Lucinda is my wife and I am her husband!' What a madman I am! Now that I am far away from the danger I say what I should have done, but did not do. Now that I have let my dear treasure be stolen I curse the robber, on whom I might have taken vengeance if I had been as prompt to act then as I now am to complain! Then I was a coward and a fool; no wonder that I am dying now, ashamed, repentant, and mad.

"The priest stood waiting for Lucinda's reply, and she did not answer for some time. But when I thought that she was going to draw her dagger in defence of her honour, or raise her voice to utter the truth, or make a protest which might redound to my advantage, I heard her say in weak and fainting tones, 'I will'. Don Ferdinand pronounced the same words and gave her the ring, and they were tied by an indissoluble bond. But as the bridegroom turned to kiss his bride she put her hand to her heart and fell fainting into her mother's arms.

"It only remains for me to describe my state of mind when I saw in that one yes my hopes deceived, Lucinda's word and promise broken, and myself for ever powerless to recover all that I had lost in that one instant. I was resourceless. Heaven, it seemed, had abandoned me; sustaining earth had become my enemy; air denied me breath for my sighs, and water moisture for my tears; only fire grew so strong that I seemed to burn all over with rage and jealousy.

"Everyone was thrown into confusion by Lucinda's fainting, and when her mother unlaced her dress to give her air a folded paper was discovered there, which Don Ferdinand immediately snatched and started to read by the light of one of the torches. When he had finished it, he sat down on a chair and put his hand to his cheek, apparently deep in thought, and paying no attention to the attempts which were being made to bring his bride round from her swoon.

"When I saw the whole household in commotion I ventured out, not caring whether I were seen or not, and determined, if I were, to do so desperate a deed that everyone would learn from my punishment of the treacherous Don Ferdinand and from the fickleness of the swooning traitress what just indignation I harboured in my breast. My fate, however, which must be preserving me for worse disasters—if there can possibly be worse—ordained that at that moment I had full use of my reason, which since then I have lacked. So, instead of taking vengeance on my greatest enemies, which would have been easy, since they had no suspicions of my presence, I resolved to inflict on myself, and with my own hand, the punishment which they deserved—a punishment perhaps more severe than I should have inflicted on them by instant execution. For sudden death swiftly ends all pain, but death which is protracted by torture forever kills but never puts an end to life.

"At last I left the house, and returned to the place where I had left my mule. I had it saddled, and without saying good-bye to my

And they had not gone far when, on coming round the corner of a rock, they saw a man in form and figure resembling Sancho Panza's description of Cardenio. The man did not start at the sight of them, but stayed still, with his head on his breast in a pensive attitude, and did not raise his eyes to look at them again after their first sudden appearance. (page 293) host I left the city, like another Lot, not daring to look back. When I found myself alone in the fields, concealed by the darkness of the night, its silence invited me to complain without fear of being heard or recognized. I then gave vent to violent curses on Lucinda and Don Ferdinand, as if that were a means of taking vengeance for the wrong they had done me. I called her cruel, faithless, false, ungrateful, but most of all mercenary, since my enemy's riches had blinded the eyes of her love, and made her take her affections from me and transfer them to a man of greater wealth. But in the middle of this storm of reproaches and abuse I found excuses for her. It was not surprising, I cried, that a maiden immured in her parents' house, and always accustomed to obey them, should willingly submit, on their proposing so noble, so rich and so well-bred a gentleman as her husband. For if she had not accepted him, she would either have been thought senseless or have incurred the suspicion of having engaged her affections elsewhere, which would have seriously prejudiced her honour and good name. Then I thought that if she had said that I was husband, they would have realized that she had not made a bad choice and must have excused her. For before Don Ferdinand made his offer they could not themselves reasonably have desired a better match for their daughter than myself. She might easily have declared, I thought, before being finally compelled to give her hand to Don Ferdinand, that I had already given her mine; and I should then have come forward and confirmed any story she might have invented. In fact, I concluded that lack of love, foolishness, ambition and the desire for greatness had made her forget her promise, which had deceived, encouraged and sustained me in my fervent hopes and honest love.

"With these reflections and in this disquietude I travelled for the rest of the night, and at dawn struck a pass into these mountains, over which I wandered for three days, far from any road or track, until I stopped in some meadows, on which side of the range I do not know. There I asked some herdsmen where the wildest parts of the mountains lay, and they pointed in this direction. Here I came at once, intending to end my life; and when I reached these crags my mule fell dead of weariness and hunger, or as I believe, to rid herself of so useless a burden as myself. So I was left on foot, exhausted and hungry, without so much as a thought of looking for help. I do not know how long I lay on the ground in this state, but at length I got up without the feeling of hunger, and found some goatherds beside me. It must have been they who had satisfied my needs, for they told me how they had discovered me talking so wildly that I must clearly have gone out of my mind. And since then I have been conscious that I am not always well, but sometimes so weak and deranged that I behave like a madman, tearing my clothes, shouting in these wastes, cursing my fortune, and vainly repeating the dear name of my enemy. My only wish and purpose at these times is to wear out my life in lamentations. And when I recover my senses, I am so exhausted and bruised that I can hardly move.

"My usual dwelling is a hollow cork-tree large enough to shelter this wretched body. The cowherds and goatherds who frequent these parts feed me out of charity. They leave me food by the tracks and on the rocks, where they expect I may pass and find it. So, even when my senses are disordered, Nature makes me know my food, and rouses the instinct in me to take it and eat it. At other times, they tell me when they find me in my senses, I rush out on to the tracks and take the food the shepherds bring up from the village to the sheepcotes. I snatch it by force, they say, even though they would give it me willingly. So I spend what remains of my miserable life till Heaven shall please to bring it to an end, or to blot Lucinda's beauty and treachery from my memory, and obliterate Don Ferdinand's perfidy as well. If Heaven should do so and not end my life, I will turn my thoughts to some better course. If not I can only implore God's infinite mercy for my soul. For I feel no strength or virtue in myself to fetch my body out of this pass into which I have elected to bring it of my own accord.

"That, sirs, is the bitter story of my misfortunes. Tell me if it deserves to be told with less emotion than I have shown. Do not trouble to persuade me or advise me to take some remedy which your reason may suggest to you. For it will be of no more use to me than a famous doctor's prescription to a patient who will not take it. Without Lucinda I do not desire health, and since it has pleased her to be another's, when she is or should be mine, let me give myself up to misery, since I might have been given up to happiness. She elected by her fickleness to make my perdition permanent, and I choose to comply with her wishes and achieve my final destruction. And it shall be an example to future generations that I alone have lacked what other wretches have in abundance. There is comfort for them in the impossibility of consolation. But for me this is the cause of greater afflictions and evils, which I truly think will not end even with my death."

Here Cardenio concluded the long recital of his sad love story. But, just as the priest was preparing to offer him some words of consolation, he was prevented by a voice, which came to his ears, uttering in mournful tones what will be related in the fourth part of this narrative. For at this point the wise and judicious historian, Cide Hamete Benengeli, brought his third part to an end.

⊰ 28 ⊱

Of a Novel
and Pleasing Adventure which befell
the Priest and the Barber
in the Same Mountains

*H*ow happy and fortunate was that age in which the boldest of knights, Don Quixote de la Mancha, was born into the world. Since, thanks to his honourable resolution of reviving and restoring to the earth the lost and almost defunct order of knight errantry, we enjoy today in our present age, which lacks all pleasant entertainment, not only the delights of his authentic history, but also the tales and episodes set in it. For in some ways these are no less agreeable, ingenious and authentic than the history itself, the thread of which, being carded, twisted, and reeled, may now be resumed. It relates that just as the priest was about to console Cardenio, he was prevented by a voice speaking in mournful tones to this effect, "O God, is it possible that I have found a spot which will afford a secret grave to the weary burden of my body, which I so unwillingly bear? This will be the place, if the solitude these hills promise does not deceive me. Miserable creature that I am, what company can I have more welcome than these crags and thickets, which will allow me to tell my misery to Heaven, since there is no one on earth from whom I can expect counsel in my perplexities, comfort in my grief, or remedy in my troubles!"

The priest and his companions heard the words distinctly, and got up to look for the speaker, who could not be far away. They had not gone twenty yards, in fact, when from behind a rock they saw a youth dressed like a peasant, who was sitting at the foot of an ash. They could not at first see his face, because his head was bent over a running stream in which he was washing his feet. And so silently did they come up that he did not hear them. For he was busily engaged in washing his feet, which looked like nothing so much as two pieces of pure crystal, lying among the other pebbles of the brook. Their whiteness and beauty astonished the gazers. For they did not seem to be made for breaking clods, nor for following oxen and the plough, as the dress of their owner suggested. So, seeing that they were unobserved, the priest, who was ahead, signed to the other two to crouch behind some near-by fragments of rock, which they did, and watched all that youth's movements attentively.

He was dressed in a short grey double cape, tied round his waist with a white cloth. He wore breeches and leggings of grey cloth and a grey cap on his head. And he had hitched his leggings half-way up his legs, which were as white as alabaster. After washing his lovely feet, he wiped them with a kerchief, which he took from under his cap. And, as he did so, he raised his face, in which the watchers saw such peerless beauty that Cardenio whispered to the priest: "Since this is not Lucinda it is no human creature. It must be divine."

The youth took off his cap; and as he shook his head from side to side, there began to fall about his shoulders hair which the sun itself might have envied. By this they realized that here was no peasant lad but a delicate woman, and the most beautiful that two of them had ever seen till then. And Cardenio would have known none lovelier, had he not gazed on Lucinda. For, as he afterwards declared, only Lucinda's beauty could compare with hers. Her long golden hair not only covered her shoulders but fell all round her, hiding her entire body except for her feet. Then she combed it with hands which in contrast to the crystal of her feet seemed to be made of driven snow. All of which increased the astonishment of the three watchers and their desire to know who she was, and so they decided to reveal themselves. But as they moved to get up, the lovely maiden raised her head and, parting her hair from before her eyes with both hands, looked to see who had made the noise. And no sooner did she see them than she got up and, without waiting to put on her shoes or tie up her hair, hurriedly seized a bundle lying beside her, which might have contained clothes, and started to run away in surprise and alarm. But she had not gone six paces when her tender feet were so hurt by the sharp stones that she fell down. At this point the three of them came out, the priest being the first to speak, "Stop, lady, whoever you are. We only desire to serve you. You have no reason to run away. Besides, it would be of no use. Your feet would not allow it, and we should not permit it."

She was so astonished and bewildered that she could make no reply. So they went up to her, and the priest, taking her by the hand, continued, "What your dress, lady, denies, your hair reveals. Clearly you must have had no trivial reason for disguising your beauty in so unsuitable a dress, and coming to so wild a spot, where it has been our good fortune to find you. If we cannot relieve your distress, we can at least advise you. For no evil short of death can be so dire that the sufferer may absolutely refuse to listen to comfort gladly offered. So, dear lady, or dear sir—whichever you prefer—dismiss the fears which our appearance cause you, and tell us of your fortune, good or bad. For in all of us together or each of us separately you will find sympathizers in your distress."

While the priest was talking, the disguised maiden stood stupefied, gazing at them without moving her lips or saying a single word, like some peasant suddenly confronted with rare treasures never seen before. But when the priest said more to the same effect, she gave a deep sigh and broke her silence, "Since these lonely mountains cannot hide me, and my hair will not permit my tongue to lie, it would be vain to make a further pretence, which you could accept only out of politeness, and for no other reason. Therefore, gentlemen, I thank you for the offer you have made me, and feel obliged to comply with your request, though I am afraid that the tale of my misfortunes will cause you grief as well as pity. For you can find no remedy nor any consolation to allay them. Nevertheless, so that you may be in no doubt as to my honour, now that you have discovered that I am a woman and seen me, young, alone and in these clothes—circumstances which singly or all together are enough to destroy any honest reputation—I must tell you what I would rather conceal if I could."

As she said all this without hesitation, she seemed not only beautiful but eloquent and sweet-voiced as well, which made them admire her good sense no less than her beauty. They once more offered her their help, and begged her to fulfil her promise. Then, after modestly putting on her shoes and tying up her hair, she sat down on a stone without more ado; and the other three sat round her, choking back the tears which sprang to their eyes, as in a calm and clear voice she began the story of her life:

"Here in Andalusia there is a town from which a Duke takes his title, by virtue of which he is a Grandee of Spain. He has two sons, the elder the heir to his estate and, apparently, to his virtues, and the younger, heir to I do not know what, unless it be Vellido's treachery and Galalon's deceit. My parents are tenants of this lord, people of humble birth, but so rich that if their rank were equal to their fortune they could have nothing more to desire. Nor, if that had been so, need I have feared to find myself in my present misfortune, for perhaps my troubles arose only because they were not noble. Not that their rank is shamefully low, but it is not high enough to make me certain that my disaster was not caused by the humbleness of their station. In short they are farmers, simple people without any taint of ignoble blood, and what is generally called 'rusty old Christians'; people whose wealth and fine way of life are gradually earning them the name of gentlefolk, or even nobles. But their greatest wealth and nobility in their own eyes lay in having me for their daughter. And, as they had no other heir, and as they were most loving parents, I was the most pampered of children. I was the light of their eyes, the staff of their old age and, save for Heaven, the sole object of their affections—and my wishes never differed from theirs by a jot, such good parents they were. Now just as I was mistress of their affections, I was also mistress of their household. It was I who engaged and dismissed the servants, and the accounts of sowings and crops passed through my hands. The oil-mills, the wine-presses, the stock list and the beehives were under my control. In fact, I kept the complete accounts of a rich farm—for rich my father's was. I was the stewardess and controller, and fulfilled my duties to their absolute satisfaction. Such part of my day as remained after dealing with the overseers, the foremen and the day-labourers, I spent in occupations proper to young ladies, sewing, lace-making and often spinning. And if I left these tasks at times to refresh my mind, I turned to some book of devotion or to playing the harp. For experience taught me that music composes disordered thoughts and eases the troubles which are born of the spirit. This, then, is how I lived in my parents' house, and if I have described it in some detail, it has not been out of ostentation, nor to show that I am rich, but to prove how little I am to blame for falling from that happy state into my present misery.

"So it was that I spent my life, busy and in almost monastic seclusion, seen by nobody, as I supposed, but the household servants. For when I went to Mass it was so early in the morning, my mother and I were so surrounded by our servants, and I was so closely veiled and guarded, that my eyes scarcely saw more of the earth than my feet trod. But for all this the eyes of love, or more correctly of idleness, which are keener than a lynx's, discovered me, the eyes of the importunate Don Ferdinand. For that is the name of the Duke's younger son, whom I spoke of."

No sooner did she mention Don Ferdinand's name than Cardenio's face changed colour, and he began to sweat and to show so much emotion that the priest and the barber looked at him in apprehension, fearing one of those attacks of madness which they had heard he was subject to. But he merely sweated and stayed still, staring hard at the farmer's daughter and reflecting who she might

But as they moved to get up, the lovely maiden raised her head and, parting her hair from before her eyes with both hands, looked to see who had made the noise. (page 310) be. She, however, did not notice Cardenio's disturbance, but went on with her story, saying, "And he had no sooner seen me, as he afterwards declared, than he fell violently in love with me, as his actions soon showed. But, to conclude the tale of my misfortunes quickly, I will pass in silence over the devices Don Ferdinand employed to declare his passion to me. He bribed all the house servants, and offered and gave presents to my relations. Every day was a festival and a holiday in our street, and at night music kept everyone awake. The love-letters which came into my hands—I do not know how—were countless, full of declarations and protestations of passion, and containing more promises and oaths than syllables. All of which did not soften me. On the contrary, they made me harder, as if he were my mortal enemy; and every-thing that he did to bend me to his will had quite the opposite effect. This was not because I disliked Don Ferdinand's gallantry, or found his wooing excessive. Not at all. I was quite pleased to be desired and admired by so great a nobleman, and not at all displeased to read my praises in his letters; for however plain we women are I think we are always pleased to hear ourselves called beautiful.

"My modesty, however, resisted, and was backed by the repeated advice of my parents, who were well aware of Don Ferdinand's feelings by now, since he did not care if the whole world knew of them. They told me that they relied on my virtue and goodness alone, and trusted me with their honour and good name. They bade me reflect on the difference between Don Ferdinand's rank and mine, and realize that his plans were directed to his own pleasure rather than to my advantage, whatever he might say to the contrary. If I wished to put an end to his wicked suit, they were willing to marry me then and there to anyone I might choose. I could have the best man in our own town or in the whole district, for with their great wealth and my good name anything was possible. With these promises and the assurance they gave me I strengthened my resis-tance, and never gave Don Ferdinand so much as a word of reply which might offer him even a distant hope of achieving his purpose.

"All my precautions, which he no doubt took for scorn, must have whetted his lascivious appetite. For that is all I can call his passion for me, since if it had been what it should have been, you would never have heard of it; I should have had no occasion to describe it to you. At length Don Ferdinand learned that my parents were going to make a match for me, so as to put an end to his hopes of possessing me, or at least so that I should have better guards to look after me; and this intelligence, or suspicion, was the cause of his doing what I shall now tell you. One night I was sitting in my room, attended by only one serving-maid, with the doors well bolted for fear that my virtue might be carelessly exposed to any peril, when suddenly—I could not imagine how—despite all my precautions I found him standing in front of me in the solitude of my silent retreat. The sight of him so disturbed me that my eyes went blind and I was struck dumb. I had no strength to shout, nor do I believe that he would have let me do so. For he came up to me immediately and took me in his arms. I was so confused, as I said, that I had not the strength to defend myself. Then he began to make violent protestations. I do not know how it is possible for the most skilful lying to make such falseness seem true.

"The traitor reinforced his words with tears and his desires with sighs. And I, poor creature, alone in the midst of my own family, and inexperienced in these matters, began—I do not know how—to believe his falsehoods, though his sighs and tears were far from moving me beyond a virtuous compassion. And so, when I had recovered from my first surprise, I began to regain my lost spirits a little, and said with more courage than I had credited myself with, 'Sir, if I were in the grasp of a fierce lion, instead of being, as I am, in your arms, and if I could only get free from them by doing or saying something to the prejudice of my honour, it would be no more possible for me to do or say such a thing than it is to alter the past. For, though you hold my body in your arms, my soul is secured by the purity of my thoughts; and how different they are from your evil ones you will see if you violently persist in your plans. I am your tenant, not your slave. Your noble blood can have no right to dishonour and insult my humility. For, peasant and farmer's daughter though I am, I count myself as good as a gentleman and a noble like yourself. Your violence will have no effect on me, nor will your riches. Your words will not deceive me, nor your sighs and tears move me. If I were to find any of your qualities in a man chosen by my parents for my husband, I should bow to his will, and have no other wishes but his. Were it not for my honour, in fact, I would freely yield to you, sir—though without pleasure —what you are trying to gain by force. This I say so that you may not think for a moment that anyone but a lawful husband can gain anything from me.

" 'If you are reluctant only on that account, most lovely Dorothea' (for that is this unfortunate woman's name), exclaimed the treacherous gentleman, 'here I give you my hand to be yours. May the Heavens, from whom nothing is hidden, be my witness, and this image of Our Lady, that you have here.' "

When Cardenio heard her say that her name was Dorothea his agitation returned, and he was confirmed in his first suspicions. He did not choose to interrupt the story, however, being anxious to hear the ending, which he had almost guessed already. And so he only said, "Then Dorothea is your name, lady? I have heard of another Dorothea whose misfortunes are perhaps similar to yours. Go on, and later I may tell you something which will both astonish you and arouse your pity."

Struck by Cardenio's words and by his strange and ragged dress, Dorothea asked him to tell her straight away if he knew anything about her affairs. For if misfortune had left her one virtue, it was courage to suffer any possible disaster in the certainty that nothing could worsen her present lot.

"I should not omit to tell you my thoughts, dear lady," replied Cardenio, "if what I imagine were true. But so far there has been no occasion to, and it would not profit you to know what is in my mind."

"Very well," replied Dorothea. "To continue my story, Don Ferdinand then took up an image which stood in the room, and

317

called on it to witness our betrothal. He pledged himself with most binding oaths and solemn vows to marry me, even though before he had finished speaking I begged him to think what he was doing, and consider how angry his father would be at finding him married to a peasant girl, one of his own tenants. I implored him not to let my beauty, such as it was, blind him, for it was not sufficient to excuse his error. If he wished to express the love he bore me by doing me a kindness, I begged him to let my fortune take a course befitting my rank, since such unequal marriages are never happy, and do not preserve for long such joy as they begin with. All these arguments I used on him and many more which I do not remember; but they did not deflect him from his purpose. For he was like a man who finds no difficulty in concluding a bargain because he does not intend to pay.

"I thought the matter over briefly at this juncture, saying to myself, 'I shall certainly not be the first to rise from low to high estate by marriage, nor will Don Ferdinand be the first whom beauty or blind love—the second is the more likely—have impelled to take a humble bride. Since, therefore, I am doing nothing that has not been done before, it would be as well to accept this honour which fortune offers. For even though his desire may last only until he has had his way, I shall be his wife in the eyes of God all the same. But if I reject him with scorn, I see that he will wickedly force me in the end, and I shall be dishonoured and universally blamed. For who could know how innocently I have come into this predicament? What reasoning could be strong enough to persuade my parents and others that this gentleman has entered my room without my consent?'

"All these reflections I turned over in my mind in a single moment. What is more, Don Ferdinand's oaths, the witnesses he invoked, the tears he shed and, finally, his charm and good looks began to incline me forcibly to a course which proved to be my undoing. For all this together with the many signs of true love he gave me were enough to conquer my heart, even one as independent and modest as mine.

"I called my maid to add her earthly witness to Heaven's. Don

Ferdinand repeated and confirmed his oaths, calling on yet more saints, and invoking innumerable curses on himself should he break his promise. The tears came once more to his eyes, and he sighed deeply. He clasped me more firmly in his arms, which had never let me go. Whereafter, when my maid had left the room, I ceased to be a maid and he became a perfidious traitor.

"Day followed on the night of my undoing, but not so fast, I think, as Don Ferdinand desired. For once the appetite is satisfied man's greatest desire is to escape. This I say because Don Ferdinand hurriedly departed with the aid of my maid—it was she who had brought him in—even before it was light in the street. As he took his leave he promised me, though with less ardour than when he came in, that I could rely on his faith and on his oaths; and as further confirmation of his words he took a fine ring from his finger and put it on mine. Finally he left, and I remained, whether sad or glad I do not know. But of one thing I am certain: I was troubled and anxious, and almost beside myself at this strange event. And either I had not the heart, or I forgot, to scold my maid for her treachery in hiding Don Ferdinand in my room; for I had not yet made up my mind if the events of the night had been good or bad. I told Don Ferdinand, however, as he departed, that he could come to me on other nights in the same way, until such time as he wished the marriage to be made public, for I was now his. He came on the following night, but never again; and for more than a month I tried in vain to see him in the street or at church, till I grew tired of fruitless waiting; for I knew that he was in the town and on most days went hunting. He was very fond of the sport.

"Indeed, these were sad, melancholy days for me, and I began to doubt, even to deny, his fidelity. I remember that I gave my maid the scolding of her presumption which she had escaped before. I had to control my tears and compose my looks for fear my parents might ask me what was making me unhappy, and I be obliged to invent a lie. But a moment arrived when my caution and delicacy came to an end, when I lost patience and my secret thoughts escaped me. This was when I heard in the town some days later that Don Ferdinand had married in the near-by city a young lady of extreme beauty and very noble family, though not so rich that her dowry could justify so great a match. Her name was said to be Lucinda, and various astonishing details were told about the wedding."

On hearing Lucinda's name Cardenio only shrugged his shoulders, bowed his head, bit his lips and frowned. But soon a flood of tears burst from his eyes. Dorothea did not pause in her story, however, but continued, "When I heard this sad news, so far was my heart from freezing that in my burning rage I could scarcely prevent myself from rushing into the streets and proclaiming the treacherous wrong he had done me. But my fury was assuaged for a while by a plan which I put into effect that very night. I borrowed the dress I am now wearing from a shepherd in my father's service. I told him my troubles, and asked him to come with me to the city where I heard that my enemy was. He first took me to task for my rashness and decried my plan. But when he saw that I was resolved, he offered to accompany me, as he said, to the end of the world. Then I packed some of my own clothes, some jewels, and some money, in a pillow-case against any eventuality; and in the silence of the night, without telling my treacherous maid, I left my home with my servant, my mind full of anxiety, and set out for the city on foot. For, though I could not prevent what had been done, I was determined at least to demand of Don Ferdinand how his conscience had allowed him to do it.

"I was two and a half days on the way, and when I got to the city I asked for the house of Lucinda's parents. The first man whom I questioned told me more than I wanted to hear. He pointed out the house and informed me of all that had happened at their daughter's betrothal. It was such common knowledge in the city that all the gossips were discussing it. He told me that on the night of the betrothal, after the bride had given her consent, she had fallen into a deep faint, and that when the bridegroom had loosened her dress to give her air, he had found in her breast a letter written in her own hand. It declared that she could not be Don Ferdinand's wife, for she was already married to Cardenio, who, this person told me, was a noble gentleman of that city. If she had said yes to Don Ferdinand, it continued, it was only so as not to disobey her parents. And the letter concluded by saying that she intended to kill herself at the end of the ceremony, and gave her reasons for ending her life. All this, they say, was confirmed when they found a dagger somewhere in her clothing. Don Ferdinand was so enraged at finding himself deluded, mocked and slighted that he attacked her before she came out of her faint, trying to stab her with the dagger which they had just found on her; and he would have succeeded if her parents and the witnesses had not prevented him. It was said that Don Ferdinand fled instantly, and that Lucinda did not recover from her faint till the next day, when she told her parents that she was in truth the wife of that Cardenio I spoke of. I learnt too that this Cardenio was said to have been present at the ceremony, and that when he saw her married, which he had never supposed she could be, he had rushed from the city in despair, leaving a letter declaring the wrong Lucinda had done him and his resolution to fly from mankind for ever.

"All this was a matter of public discussions throughout the city. Everyone was talking about it, and they gossiped even more when they heard that Lucinda was missing from her parents' house; that she could not be discovered in the town; that her parents had almost gone out of their minds and did not know what to do to find her. This news gave me some hope. For I was gladder not to have found Don Ferdinand than to have found him married, since it seemed that all possibility to redress was not yet closed to me. I thought that Heaven might have prevented this second marriage in order to show him his duty to the first and to make him realize that, as a Christian, he was more firmly bound by his conscience than by worldly considerations. I turned all these thoughts over in my mind and got some consolation, though no comfort, from inventing wan and distant hopes to sustain my life, which is now abhorrent to me.

"I was still in the city, and did not know what to do since I could not find Don Ferdinand. Then one day I heard a public crier announcing that a large reward would be paid to anyone finding me, and describing my person and the very clothes I was wearing. I even heard a rumour that I had eloped with the shepherd who had escorted me from home. It stung me to the quick to find my reputation fallen so low. For I had not only lost it by coming away, but, even worse, by my choice of so low and unworthy a companion. The instant I heard the crier I left the city with my servant, who was already showing signs of wavering in his promised fidelity; and that night through fear of being discovered we took refuge in the remotest part of these mountains.

"But one evil calls down another, as they say, and the end of one disaster is often the beginnning of a worse. So it was in my case. For, once we were alone in these wilds, my good servant, till then faithful and reliable, tried to take advantage of the opportunity which that wild spot appeared to offer him and, prompted by brutishness rather than by my beauty, lost all respect and made shameless love to me. Then, when I answered him with just contempt, he ceased the entreaties by which he had at first thought to gain his will, and tried to use force. But just Heaven, which seldom or never fails to favour virtue, so favoured mine, that despite my feeble strength I was easily able to force him back over the edge of a precipice. Whether I left him dead or alive I do not know. Then I fled with more speed than might have been expected from my fright and exhaustion, and made my way into these mountains, with no other thought or plan than to hide from my father and anyone he might send to seek me.

"I do not know how many months I had been here when I found a herdsman who took me as his servant to a village in the heart of this range. I have worked for him as a shepherd all this time, trying always to keep out in the fields so as to conceal this hair of mine, which you have now so unexpectedly discovered. All my anxieties and precautions, however, were in vain, for my master got to know that I was not a man, and conceived the same wicked idea as my servant. But as fate does not always find an immediate remedy for every ill, I found no precipice or cliff to throw my master down, as I had my servant. And so I thought it would be less unpleasant to leave him and hide in these wilds again, than to try my strength or my protests against him. So, as I said, I took to the mountains once more, to seek a place where I can implore Heaven undisturbed with sighs and tears to take pity on my plight, and to give me grace and strength to escape from it; or else to die among these wastes and leave no memory of this miserable creature, who has so innocently given men cause to speak ill of her, in her own district and abroad."

⊰ 29 ⊱

Of the Ingenious Plan contrived
to extricate Our Enamoured Knight
from the Very Severe Penance
he had set himself

*T*his, gentleman, is the true story
of my tragedy. Judge for yourselves whether my sighs, my protests
and my tears were not more than justified. Now that you know the
nature of my misfortune you will see that all consolation is vain,
since there is no possible cure. I only beg of you one favour, which
you may easily grant: to advise me where I can live in safety, free
from my present fears and from the dread of being discovered. For
although I know that my parents love me so much that they would
give me a kind welcome, I am so overwhelmed by shame at the mere
thought of appearing in their presence, so different from the
daughter they had supposed me, that I think it would be lesser evil to
banish myself for ever from their sight. Rather that than look them
in the face, and know their thoughts. For they will consider that I
have lost the honour they had the right to expect of me."

She fell silent, her blushes clearly showing her grief and shame,
and her hearers' minds were filled with pity and wonder at her
misfortunes. Then, just as the priest was about to offer her consola-

324

tion and advice, Cardenio forestalled him by saying, "Then, lady, you are the fair Dorothea, the only daughter of the rich Clenardo?"

Dorothea was startled to hear her father's name spoken by such a miserable-looking creature—for, as we have already said, Cardenio was in rags.

"Who are you, my friend," she asked, "that you know my father's name? For I have not mentioned it till now, if I remember rightly, in the whole story of my misfortune."

"I am that unfortunate Cardenio," he answered, "whom, as you said, lady, Lucinda declared to be her husband. I am the hapless Cardenio, reduced to my present state by that same man who brought you to the condition you are in. Ragged, naked, comfortless and, what is worse, out of my mind. For I am sane only in the brief intervals that Heaven grants me. I, Dorothea, was witness of Ferdinand's crime and waited to hear that yes with which Lucinda declared herself his wife. I had not the courage to see what would come of her fainting, or what became of the letter which was found in her breast. For my heart could not bear to witness so many disasters all together. So I rushed headlong from the house, only leaving a letter with my host to be put into Lucinda's hands. Here I came to these wastes with the intention of bringing my days to an end, for from that moment I loathed life as a mortal enemy. But fate has refused to end my existence and deprived me only of reason, perhaps to preserve me for my good fortune in meeting you. If your story is true, however—as I believe it is—Heaven, perhaps, has in store for us both a better ending to our misfortunes than we suppose. For, since Lucinda is mine and therefore unable to marry Don Ferdinand, as she has so publicly declared, and as he is yours and so also unable to marry, we may yet hope that Heaven will restore to us our own partners, for nothing is irretrievably lost. Since we have this comfort, then, which springs from no very distant hopes or wild imaginings, I beg you, lady, to take fresh courage, as I intend to. Let us adapt ourselves to the expectation of better fortune. For I swear to you, as a Christian gentleman, that I will not forsake you till I see you Don Ferdinand's wife; and if argument cannot bring him to acknowledge his duty to you, I will use my gentleman's privilege and duly challenge him for the wrong he has done you. I will take no account of the injuries he has done me, but leave Heaven to avenge them, whilst I revenge yours here on earth."

Dorothea was dumbfounded by Cardenio's speech. She did not know how to thank him, and tried to kiss his feet; but Cardenio would not allow her. The priest replied for himself and for her by approving Cardenio's generous determination. But he most earnestly begged, advised and urged them to come to his village, and there provide themselves with all the things they needed. And there too, he said, they could decide on their best course of action: either to search for Don Ferdinand, or to take Dorothea to her parents, or to do anything else which might seem proper. Cardenio and Dorothea thanked him and accepted his offer.

The barber, who had listened in silent amazement to all this, then made a courteous speech, offering no less generously than the priest to do them any service he could. At the same time he told them briefly what had brought the priest and himself there, described Don Quixote's strange madness, and informed them that they were waiting for his squire, who had gone to look for him. Then, like a dream, Cardenio's quarrel with Don Quixote came back into his memory, and he described it to the others, although he could not tell them the cause of the dispute.

At that moment they heard shouts, which they recognized as Sancho Panza's. For he had not found them where he had left them, and was calling out after them at the top of his voice. They went to meet him, and asked him after Don Quixote. He answered that he had found him naked except for his shirt, lean, sallow and half dead with hunger, sighing for his lady Dulcinea. He had told him of her commands that he should leave that place and come to El Toboso, where she was waiting for him. But he had replied that he was determined not to appear in her beauteous presence until he had done deeds worthy of her favour. If that went on much longer, said Sancho, there was a danger that he might never become an Emperor, as he was in honour bound to do, nor even an Archbishop,

"I will not give you a word in answer, beauteous lady,"
replied Don Quixote, "nor hear anything more of your plight
till you rise from the ground." (page 331)

which was the least he could be. Therefore they must think out a means of getting him away. The priest replied that he had no need to worry, for they would bring him with them, willy-nilly. Then he told Cardenio and Dorothea of the plan they had thought out for curing Don Quixote, or at least for getting him home. Dorothea then observed that she could play the damsel in distress better than the barber and, what was more, she had a dress with her in which she could do it to the life. They could rely on her to act the part and do all that was necessary. For she had read many books of chivalry, and knew the style in which afflicted maidens were accustomed to beg their boons of knights errant.

"Then there is nothing more we need," said the priest. "Let us get to work at once. For there is no doubt that luck is in our favour. It has unexpectedly begun to offer you, my friends, a little hope of better things, and made this job of ours easier as well."

Then Dorothea took a handsome woollen dress and a cloak of fine green cloth out of her bundle, and out of a jewel-box a necklace and other jewels. These she put on, and was instantly transformed into a rich and grand lady. All these things and more, as has already been said, she had brought from home in case she should need them, but had had no use for them till then. Her gracefulness, her elegance and her loveliness charmed them all, and showed up Don Ferdinand's lack of taste in deserting such a beauty. But most admiring of all was Sancho Panza, who thought that he had never seen so lovely a creature in all the days of his life—and indeed he had not. He asked the priest most insistently to tell him who this beautiful lady was, and what she was looking for in those wild parts.

"This beautiful lady, brother Sancho," replied the priest, "is, to be very brief, heiress in the direct male line of the great Kingdom of Micomicon. She has come to seek your master to beg of him a boon, which is to redress a wrong or injury which a wicked giant has done her. For, thanks to your master's reputation as a brave knight throughout all the known world, this princess has come from Guinea in quest of him."

"She's been lucky to find him," exclaimed Sancho Panza. "And she'll be even luckier if my master is so fortunate as to undo that injury, and redress that wrong, and kill that son of a whore—I mean that giant you mentioned, sir. And he'll kill him if he finds him, unless he's a phantom; for my master has no power at all against phantoms. But there's one thing I particularly beg of you, Master Priest. Advise my master to marry this princess right off, sir, so that he doesn't take it into his head to be an Archbishop, as I very much fear he may. Then he'll be capable of taking Archbishop's orders, and he'll easily come to his Empire, and I shall get everything I want. For I've thought the matter over, and I've figured it out that it won't suit me for my master to be an Archbishop. For I'm no good for the Church, you see, being a married man; and going about getting dispensations to let me hold a church living, seeing that I have a wife and children, would be an endless job. So it all depends on my master marrying this lady straight away, sir—I don't know her name yet, so I can't call her by it."

"Her name," replied the priest, "is Princess Micomicona, as obviously it would be since her kingdom is called Micomicon."

"Of course," replied Sancho. "I've known plenty of men take their titles and surnames from the places they live in—people like Pedro de Alcala, Juan de Ubeda, and Diego de Valladolid. The custom must be the same over there in Guinea, and the queens there take their names from their kingdoms."

"Yes, you must be right," said the priest, "and in this matter of your master's marrying, I will do everything in my power."

Sancho was content with his assurance; and the priest was amazed at his simplicity, and at the hold these absurdities of his master's had on his imagination. For he seemed seriously to believe that Don Quixote would become an Emperor.

By this time Dorothea had mounted the priest's mule, and the barber had fixed his ox tail beard to his chin. So they told Sancho to guide them to Don Quixote, warning him not to say that he knew the priest or the barber, because the whole matter of his master's becoming an Emperor hung on their not being recognized. Neither

Cardenio nor the priest would go with them. For Cardenio was afraid that the sight of him might remind Don Quixote of their quarrel, and the priest did not consider his own presence necessary for the moment. So they let the others ride ahead, and followed slowly on foot. The priest, however, could not forbear instructing Dorothea in the part she had to play. But she said that there was no need for him to worry, for she would conform in every way to the details prescribed in books of chivalry. They had gone little more than two miles when they caught sight of Don Quixote among a maze of rocks, dressed now, but without his armour. Sancho pointed him out to Dorothea, who immediately whipped on her palfrey, followed by the well-bearded barber. When they reached the knight, the squire leapt from his mule to take Dorothea in his arms, and she dismounted with great sprightliness and fell on her knees at Don Quixote's feet. From which position, despite his efforts to raise her, she addressed him in this fashion, "I will not arise from here, valorous and courageous knight, until your goodness and courtesy grant me a boon, which will redound to the honour and glory of your person and to the advantage of the most disconsolate and wronged damsel beneath the sun. For if the valour of your mighty arm corresponds to the report of your immortal fame, you are obliged to protect this luckless wight who comes from a far country, attracted by the odour of your fame, to seek from you a remedy for her misfortunes."

"I will not give you a word in answer, beauteous lady," replied Don Quixote, "nor hear anything more of your plight till you rise from the ground."

"I will not rise, sir," replied the afflicted damsel, "ere of your courtesy you have granted me the boon I crave."

"I grant it freely," replied Don Quixote, "provided my compliance be not to the disservice or prejudice of my King, my country, or of that lady who holds the key of my heart and liberty."

"It is not the disservice or prejudice of any of these, my dear sir," replied the sorrowing damsel.

At this point Sancho Panza put his lips to his master's ear, and whispered very softly, "Your worship can easily grant her the boon she begs. It's only a trifle—just to kill a great giant. And the lady herself is the high and mighty princess Micomicona, Queen of the great Kingdom of Micomicon in Ethiopia."

"Whoever she may be," replied Don Quixote, "I shall act as my duty and my conscience dictate, and in obedience to the rules of my profession." And turning once more to the maiden, he said, "Fairest lady, arise, for I grant you whatever boon you would ask of me."

"What I ask," said the damsel, "is that, of your magnanimity, you shall come with me instantly where I shall lead you; and that you promise me to engage in no other adventure or enterprise till you have avenged me on a traitor who has usurped my kingdom in despite of all law, human or divine."

"I repeat that I grant your request," replied Don Quixote; "and so, lady, from henceforth you may cast off the melancholy which oppresses you, and allow your fainting hopes to recover new strength and courage. For, with the help of God and my right arm, you shall soon see yourself restored to your kingdom, and seated on the throne of your ancient and high estate, in despite and defiance of all rogues who would oppose it. Now, hands to the wheel! For in delay, it is said, lies danger."

The distressed damsel struggled persistently to kiss his hands, but Don Quixote, who was in every respect a civil and courteous knight, refused to allow her. On the contrary, he forced her to rise, and embraced her most civilly and courteously. Then he bade Sancho look to Rocinante's girths, and arm him with all speed. The squire took down his armour, which was hanging from a tree like a trophy, looked to the girths and speedily armed his master, who cried as soon as he saw himself in armour, "Let us go from hence, in God's name, to succour this great lady."

The barber was still on his knees, taking great care to hide his laughter and keep his beard from falling off. For their fine plan might miscarry if it fell. But seeing the boon already granted and Don Quixote diligently preparing to fulfil his promise, he got up and took his lady by the other hand, the two of them helping her on to her mule. Then Don Quixote mounted Rocinante, and the barber settled on his mount, leaving Sancho on foot, which made him grieve afresh for the loss of Dapple, whom he now missed. But he bore it all cheerfully, since now his master seemed to be on the way, and just on the very point of becoming Emperor. For Sancho had not the slightest doubt that he would marry the Princess and become at least King of Micomicon. One thought alone distressed him: that this kingdom was in Negro country, and that the people he would have for subjects would all be black. But he at once invented a good remedy for this, saying to himself, "What do I care if my vassals are black? I've only to put them on board ship and bring them to Spain, where I shall be able to sell them, and be paid in cash. Then with the money I can buy a title or a post on which I can live at my ease for all the days of my life. I've got eyes in my head, and I'm fly enough to sell ten thousand subjects in the winking of an eye—or thirty thousand even. I'll shift 'em, the little ones with big ones, or any other way I can. Never mind how black they start, I'll turn them into whites or yellows. I think I know how to lick my own fingers." With these thoughts he trudged on in such good spirits that he forgot the fatigue of going on foot.

Cardenio and the priest had watched all that passed from behind some brambles, and could think of no pretext for joining the company. But the priest, who was a great schemer, presently invented one. With a pair of scissors, which he carried in a case, he hastily cut off Cardenio's beard and dressed him in his own grey jacket and black cape, himself remaining in his breeches and doublet. This so transformed Cardenio's appearance that he would not have known himself if he had looked in a mirror. This done, although the others had gone ahead while they were changing clothes, they had no difficulty in gaining the main road before them. For the thickets and broken paths thereabouts did not allow horsemen to go as quickly as men on foot. In fact they took up their position on the plain, where the pass comes down from the mountains. When Don Quixote and his comrades emerged, the priest stared at the knight for some time, pretending that he was trying to recognize him. Then, after standing for some time gazing at him, he ran up to him with open arms, crying, "Welcome, mirror of chivalry, my good compatriot Don Quixote de la Mancha, flower and cream of gallantry, protector and aid of the needy, quintessence of knight errantry."

And as he spoke he clasped Don Quixote's left knee. The knight was alarmed at the man's appearance and at his language, and surveyed him carefully. When he finally recognized him too, he was still amazed to see him, but made a great effort to dismount. The priest, however, would not allow him to, which caused Don Quixote to exclaim, "Permit me, Master Priest. It is not right that I should be mounted, and so reverend a person as your worship should be on foot."

"On no account will I allow you," said the priest. "Remain mounted, since on horseback it was that your Mightiness performed deeds and exploits unparalleled in our age. I am but an unworthy priest, and it shall be enough for me to ride muleback behind one of those gentlemen of your company, if they are agreeable. And truly I shall count myself mounted on the steed Pegasus, or on the zebra or courser of the famous Moor Muzaraque, who lies to this day beneath a spell on the great hill Zulema, not far from the grand Compluto—"

"I did not think of that, my dear Master Priest," replied Don Quixote, "but I know that my lady the Princess will be delighted, as a favour to me, to order her squire to give you the saddle of his mule. For he can ride on the crupper if the beast will stand it."

"Yes, the beast will stand it, I think," replied the Princess, "and I am sure that there will be no need to command my squire, for he is too courteous and well-bred to suffer an ecclesiastic to go on foot when he may ride."

"That's right," replied the barber. And quickly getting down, he offered the priest the saddle, which he took without much pressing. But unfortunately as the barber was getting up behind, the mule, which was a hired one—and that is as much as to say that it was a bad beast—reared its hind quarters and gave two such kicks, that if they had caught Master Nicholas on the chest or on the head, he would have cursed the day he started rambling after Don Quixote. As it was he fell down in a fright, with so little care for his beard that it came off. Now when he found that he had lost it he could not think what to do except to clasp both hands hurriedly to his face, and cry out that his jaw was broken. Then, seeing all that mass of beard lying without jaws or blood some distance away from the fallen squire's face, Don Quixote exclaimed, "Good Heavens! This is a great miracle! His beard has been torn as clean from his face as if he had been shaved."

The priest saw the danger of his plot being discovered. So he instantly ran to the beard and to Master Nicholas, who was still moaning. He quickly clasped the barber's head to his chest, and stuck the beard on in a twinkling, mumbling some words over him, which he said were an infallible charm for refixing beards, as they should see. Then, when it was fixed, he moved away, leaving the squire as well bearded and as sound as before. Don Quixote was vastly amazed at this, and begged the priest to teach him the charm when he had the time. For he was convinced that its efficacy must extend beyond the mere refixing of beards, since clearly the flesh must have been all lacerated and bloody when the beard was torn out. So, as the spell had effected a complete cure it must be good for more than just beards.

"It is," said the priest, and promised to teach it him at the first opportunity.

They agreed that the priest should ride first, and after him the three of them take turns till they came to the inn, which must have been six miles off. So three of them being now mounted—Don Quixote, the Princess and the priest—and three on foot—Cardenio, the barber and Sancho Panza—Don Quixote addressed the damsel, "Lead on, your Highness, in whatever direction you will."

But before she could reply, the priest put in, "To what kingdom will your ladyship guide us? Is it perhaps to Micomicon? It must be so surely, or I know very little about kingdoms."

And Dorothea was quick-witted enough to know that she had to agree, which she did.

"Yes, sir, towards that land my way lies."

"If that is so," said the priest, "we have to pass through my village. From there your worship will take the route for Cartagena, where, if you are fortunate, you may find a ship. Then, if you have a favourable wind, a calm sea and no storms, in less than nine years you will be in sight of the great Meona lake, I mean the Meotis— from which it is little more than a hundred days' journey to your Highness's kingdom."

"You are mistaken, my good sir," said she. "For I left less than two years ago, and have had bad weather all the way. But for all that I am here and have seen the person I so ardently desired to see—that is my lord Don Quixote de la Mancha. His renown came to my ears the moment I set foot in Spain, and impelled me to seek him in order to commend myself to his courtesy and entrust my just cause to the strength of his invincible arm."

"No more. Cease your praises!" cried Don Quixote at this juncture. "I hate any kind of flattery and, although this may not be flattery, still such compliments offend my chaste ears. All that I can say, my lady, is that, whether I have valour or no, such as I have or have not shall be employed in your service, even to the death. But leaving this matter till its due time, I beg you to tell me, Master Priest, what has brought you into these parts, alone like this, without attendants, and so thinly clad that you alarm me?"

"I will reply briefly," answered the priest. "I must tell you, sir, that I was travelling to Seville with Master Nicholas, our barber and friend, to collect some money sent me by a relative of mine, who settled in the Indies long ago. And it was no small sum either, but more than sixty thousand silver dollars, which is a tidy bit. Now as we were travelling in these parts yesterday we were attacked by four highwaymen, who stripped us to our very beards, so that the

But unfortunately as the barber was getting up behind, the mule, which was a hired one—and that is as much as to say that it was a bad beast—reared its hind quarters and gave two such kicks, that if they had caught Master Nicholas on the chest or on the head, he would have cursed the day he started rambling after Don Quixote. (page 335) barber thought it wise to put on a false one. And as for this young man here"—pointing to Cardenio—"he was quite transformed. The strange thing is that it is well known about here that the men who robbed us were galley-slaves. They are said to have been set free almost at this very spot, by a man so very valiant that he released them despite the sergeant and the guards. He must either be out of his senses or as great a rogue as they. He can have no soul or conscience to have let the wolf out amongst the sheep, the fox amongst the hens, the fly amidst the honey. For he has deliberately defrauded justice, and rebelled against his King and natural lord, for he acted against his legal authority. He deliberately robbed the galleys of their hands, I tell you, and alarmed the Holy Brotherhood, who have been undisturbed for many years. In short, he has done a deed by which his body will gain nothing and his soul may be lost."

Sancho had told the priest and the barber the adventure of the galley-slaves, which his master had concluded with so much glory; and the priest laid it on so thick in telling his story to see what Don Quixote would do or say. The knight changed colour at every word, and dared not confess that he had been those good people's liberator.

"Well," said the priest, "those were the men who robbed us. May God, in his mercy, pardon the man who prevented their going to the punishment they deserved."

◆ 30 ◆

Of the Fair Dorothea's Cleverness
and Other Pleasant and Amusing Matters

*S*carcely had the priest finished
when Sancho cried out, "It was my master, Sir Priest, who did that deed. I swear it was. And not for want of my telling him before-hand. I warned him to look out what he was doing. I said it was a sin to set them at liberty. For they were all going to the galleys because they were very great villains."

"Blockhead!" broke in Don Quixote. "It is no concern or duty of knights errant to investigate whether the distressed, chained and oppressed persons they meet on the roads are brought to that pass, or suffer that anguish, for their crimes or for their whims. Their only task is to succour them because they are in distress, taking account of their sufferings and not of their villainies. I met some mournful, miserable wretches strung together like beads on a rosary, and did for them what my duty requires. The rest is no affair of mine. If anyone objects, saving Master Priest's holy dignity and his reverend person, I say that he knows very little of the matter of chivalry, and that he lies like the son of a whore and a bastard. And I will prove it on him with my sword, which shall answer him at greater length."

As he said this he steadied himself in his stirrups and pulled down his head-piece. For he carried the barber's basin, which was Mambrino's helmet in his estimation, hanging at his saddle-bow, till such time as the damage which the galley-slaves had done to it could be repaired.

Dorothea was too quick and intelligent not to understand Don Quixote's crazy humour. She saw that everyone except Sancho Panza was making fun of him, and was anxious not to be left out. So, seeing him in such a rage, she said to him, "Remember, Sir Knight, the boon your worship granted me, and that you are bound by it not to interpose in any other adventure, however urgent it may be. Calm your spirit, therefore. For if the worthy priest had known that it was by that unconquered arm that the galley-slaves were freed, he would have put three stitches through his lips, or even bitten his tongue three times, rather than have uttered a word which might redound to your worship's disparagement."

"I swear I would," said the priest. "I would even have pulled out one of my moustaches."

"I will be silent, my dear lady," said Don Quixote, "and restrain the just anger which has risen in my breast. I will remain quiet and peaceful till I have accomplished the promised boon for you. But, to reward this resolution of mine, I beg you to tell me—if it does not cause you too much pain—the nature of your distress, and the number, names and qualities of the persons on whom I have to take dire, satisfactory and complete revenge."

"I will do so with all my heart," replied Dorothea, "if it will not weary you to hear of griefs and misfortunes."

"It will not weary me, my lady," replied Don Quixote.

To which Dorothea replied, "Since that is so, then give me your attention, your worships."

With that Cardenio and the barber caught up with her, wishing to hear what sort of story the ingenious Dorothea would invent; and Sancho, who was as much taken in by her as was his master, did the same. Then, settling comfortably into her saddle, after a preliminary cough and other preparatory gestures, she began her story with considerable dash, "First, gentlemen, you must know that my name is—" And here she stopped a moment because she had forgotten the name the priest had given her. But he saw what had happened and rushed to her aid, saying, "It is no wonder, my lady, that your Highness is confused and embarrassed at telling your misfortunes. For affliction often impairs the memory to such an extent that miserable sufferers cannot even remember their own names, as has happened in the case of your exalted Ladyship, who has forgotten that she is the princess Micomicona, lawful heiress to the great Kingdom of Micomicon. Now with this reminder your Highness will be able to call to your distracted memory all that you wish to tell us."

"You are right," replied the damsel. "From now on I think I shall be in no need of prompting, and I shall bring my true story to its proper conclusion. To continue then, My father, King Tinacrio the Sage, was very skilled in what are called the magic arts, and foresaw by his science that my mother, Queen Jaramilla, would die before him, and that very soon afterwards he too would die, and I be left an orphan. But this, he would say, disturbed him less than the certain knowledge that a monstrous giant, ruler of a large island almost bordering on our kingdom, would attack me. This giant bears the name of Pandafilando of the Frowning Eye—for it is a well-known fact that, although his eyes are straight and set in the proper place, he always squints as if he were cross-eyed. This he does out of ill-nature and to strike fear and dread into all on whom he looks. Well, as I told you, my father knew that once this giant heard that I was left an orphan he would invade my kingdom with a powerful army, and take it all from me, not leaving me so much as a little village to retire to. And though he knew that I could avert all this ruin and misfortune by marrying the giant, my father thought it very unlikely that I should ever consent to such an ill-assorted match. He was quite right, for I have never so much as thought of marrying that giant, or any other, however huge and monstrous. My father's counsel was not to stay after his death nor put up any defence against Pandafilando's invasion of my kingdom, for that would be my ruin, but to leave the kingdom voluntarily to him, if I wished to avoid the death and total destruction of my good and loyal subjects, since I should be unable to defend myself against the giant's hellish power. He bade me instantly set out with some of my subjects for Spain, where I should find a relief for my troubles by meeting a knight errant, whose renown at that time would extend throughout the whole kingdom, and whose name, if I remember rightly, was to be Don Azote or Don Gigote."

"Don Quixote he must have said," put in Sancho Panza, "otherwise called the Knight of the Sad Countenance."

"You are right," said Dorothea. "He also said that he would be a tall, thin-faced man, and that he would have a dark brown mole with hair on it like bristles on his right side under his left shoulder, or somewhere thereabouts."

Here Don Quixote said to his squire: "Come, Sancho, help me to strip. I want to see if I am the knight this sage king spoke of in his prophecy."

"Why should your worship want to take off your clothes?" asked Dorothea.

"To see if I have that mole your father spoke of," replied Don Quixote.

"There's no reason to strip," said Sancho. "I know your worship has a mole just like that in the middle of your spine. It's a sign of strength."

"That is enough," said Dorothea; "for there is no need to look into such trifles among friends, and whether it is on your shoulder or your spine scarcely matters. Enough that you have a mole; wherever it is, it is all the same flesh. No doubt my father was right in all respects. And I am right in commending myself to Don Quixote, for he it is my father meant. That is proved by his features and by the renown he bears not only in Spain but throughout La Mancha. For as soon as we landed at Osuna I heard so many tales of his exploits that my heart told me at once he was the knight I had come to seek."

"But how, dear lady, did you come to land at Osuna," asked Don Quixote, "since it is not a seaport?"

But before Dorothea could reply, the priest put in, "The lady princess surely means that after she landed at Malaga, the first place where she had news of your worship was Osuna."

"That is what I meant," said Dorothea.

"That clears things up," said the priest. "Will your Majesty continue?"

"There is no more to say," replied Dorothea, "except that finally I have had the good fortune to find the noble Don Quixote, and reckon myself now as good as Queen and Mistress of my whole Kingdom. For, of his courtesy and generosity, he has granted me my boon, and will follow me wherever I conduct him, which shall be into the presence of that Pandafilando of the Frowning Eye, that he may slay him and restore to me what this giant has so wrongfully usurped. All this will come to pass to the letter, for that is the prophecy of my good father, Tinacrio the Sage. He left it recorded too in Chaldean or Greek writing—I cannot read it—that if after beheading the giant this knight of the prophecy should wish to marry me, I should give myself to him without demur as his lawful wife, and grant him possession of my kingdom and my person."

"What do you think, friend Sancho?" cried Don Quixote at this point. "Do you hear that? Did I not tell you? See if we have not a kingdom to rule already, and a Queen to marry."

"I swear you have," said Sancho. "Devil take the bastard who wouldn't marry as soon as Sir Pandafilando's windpipe's split! And she isn't a bad bit of goods, the Queen! I wish all the fleas in my bed were as good."

At that he leapt into the air twice in sign of extreme delight. Then he ran to seize the bridle of Dorothea's mule and, making her stop, fell on his knees before her, beseeching her to give him her hands to kiss, in token that he took her for his Queen and Mistress. And not one of the party could help laughing at the master's madness and the man's simplicity. Dorothea held out her hands to him, and promised to make him a great lord in her kingdom, as soon as she should by the grace of Heaven recover it and enjoy it again. And Sancho thanked her in such language that they all burst out laughing afresh.

"That, gentlemen," Dorothea went on, "is my story. It only remains to tell you that of the attendants I brought with me out of my kingdom none but this well-bearded squire survives. All the rest were drowned in a great storm which struck us within sight of harbour. By a miracle he and I got ashore on a couple of planks; and indeed the whole course of my life has been one long miracle and mystery, as you will have noted. And if I have exaggerated in any way, or have not been as exact as I should be, remember what the reverend gentleman said at the beginning of my story. For perpetual and extreme hardships deprive the sufferer even of memory."

"They will not rob me of mine, exalted and courageous lady," said Don Quixote, "however many I may endure in your service, and however great and unprecedented they may be. So once more I confirm the boon I have granted you, and swear to go with you to the end of the world, till I confront your fierce enemy, whose proud head, by the help of God and my strong arm, I mean to cut off with the edge of this—I will not say good sword, thanks to Gines de Pasamonte, who carried mine off." These last words he muttered under his breath, and then went on, "When I have cut off his head and restored to you the peaceful possession of your kingdom, it shall rest with your own choice to dispose of your person in whatever manner you please. For, so long as my memory is engrossed, my heart captive and my mind enthralled by that—I say no more; it is impossible that I could so much as think of marriage, even with the Phoenix."

Sancho was so taken aback at his master's last words on the subject of not wishing to marry that he exclaimed in great fury, "Good God, your worship! You must be out of your mind, I swear! How could there possibly be any doubt about marrying a grand princess like this one? Do you think fortune will offer you a stroke of luck like this round every corner? Can my lady Dulcinea possibly be more beautiful? Of course she isn't, not by half. I should say she isn't good enough to tie this lady's shoes. A poor chance I have of getting my countship if your worship goes fishing for dainties at the bottom of the sea. Marry her! Marry her at once, for the devil's sake, and lay hold of this kingdom, that's falling into your hands like a ripe cherry. And when you're a king, make me a marquis or a viceroy, and then to hell with the rest!"

When Don Quixote heard these blasphemies against his lady Dulcinea he could bear no more. So he raised his lance and, without word or warning, he dealt Sancho two such blows that he knocked him down. And if Dorothea had not called out to the knight to stop he would no doubt have taken his squire's life on the spot.

"Do you think, miserable villain," asked Don Quixote, after a while, "that I must always let you pull me by the nose, and that there is to be nothing but sinning on your side and pardoning on mine? Do not think that, excommunicate rogue! For that you certainly are, for defaming the peerless Dulcinea. Do not you know, you clod, you ignominious vagabond, that but for the power she infuses into my arm I should not have the strength to kill a flea? Tell me, you viper-tongued villain, who do you think has conquered this kingdom and cut this giant's head off, and made you a marquis—for I take all this as an accomplished fact—if it is not the might of Dulcinea, employing my arm as the instrument of her exploits? She fights and conquers through me, and I live and breathe and have my life and being in her. You villain, you son of a whore! What ingratitude you show, seeing yourself raised up out of the dust of the earth to be a titled lord, and your only thanks for such a benefit is to malign the lady that bestowed it on you!"

Sancho was not too badly hurt to hear his master's reproaches. He got up rather hurriedly, ran behind Dorothea's palfrey, and addressed his master from there, "Now think, sir, if your worship's determined not to marry this great princess, it's plain that the kingdom will not be yours. Now in that case what favours can you do me? That's what I'm complaining about. Marry this Queen, sir, once for all, now that we have her here, dropped down from heaven as it were. You can go back to my lady Dulcinea afterwards, for there have been plenty of kings in the world who have kept mistresses. As for the matter of beauty, it's no affair of mine. To tell you the truth, they both seem handsome to me, though I've never seen the lady Dulcinea."

"What! You have never seen her, blasphemous traitor?" cried Don Quixote. "But have not you just brought me a message from her?"

"I mean that I didn't have time to observe the beauty of her fair features one by one," said Sancho, "but she looked all right to me on the whole."

"Well, I pardon you now," said Don Quixote, "and you must forgive me the injury I have done you. For primary impulses are not within man's power to check."

"So I see," replied Sancho, "and in me the need to talk is a primary impulse, and I can't help saying right off what comes to my tongue."

"All the same," said Don Quixtoe, "watch what you say, Sancho, for the pitcher can go too often to the well—I say no more."

"Well, well," replied Sancho, "God's in heaven and sees all man's tricks. He'll judge which of us is wickeder, I for my bad words or your worship for your bad actions."

"No more of that," said Dorothea. "Run, Sancho, kiss your master's hand, and beg his pardon. And from now on be more careful with your praises and slanders, and say nothing against this lady Tobosa, of whom all I know is that I am her humble servant. And put your trust in God that he will not fail to bring you to an estate where you can live like a prince."

Sancho hung his head and begged his master for his hand, which Don Quixote gave him in all gravity. Then, when he had kissed it, the knight gave him his blessing, and bade him come ahead a little, for he had something to ask him and matters of great importance to discuss with him. Sancho obeyed, and once they were slightly in advance of the others Don Quixote said, "Since your return I have had neither the time nor the opportunity to ask you for many details about the message you took and the answer you brought back. But now that chance has given us both time and opportunity, do not deny me the pleasure that your good news will give me."

"Ask any questions you like, your worship," replied Sancho, "I'll get out of all of them as easily as I got in. But I beseech your worship not to be so vindictive in future."

"Why do you say that, Sancho?" asked Don Quixote.

"The beating you gave me just now, you know," replied Sancho, "was because of the quarrel the Devil raised between us the other night, and not for what I said against my lady Dulcinea, whom I reverence like a holy relic—of course she's nothing of the sort—but I love her just because she belongs to your worship."

"No more of this talk, Sancho, at your peril," said Don Quixote, "for it offends me. I pardoned you then, and you know the saying very well, 'Fresh sin, fresh penance!' "

As they were talking they saw a man on an ass coming down the road, and when he got nearer they made him out to be a gipsy. But whenever Sancho Panza saw a donkey he followed it with his eyes and with his heart, and no sooner did he catch sight of the man than he knew that he was Gines de Pasamonte. Now this clue of the gipsy led him to recognize his ass, for it was his own Dapple which Pasamonte was riding. He had put on gipsy dress so as to be able to sell the ass unrecognized, speaking, as he did, the gipsy language and many others like a native. But Sancho knew him as soon as he saw him, and instantly shouted out, "Gines, you thief! Let go my jewel! Let go my life! Don't rob me of my comfort! Let go my ass! Let go my treasure! Get out, you bastard! Get away, you thief! Give up what isn't yours!"

There was no need of all those words or curses, for Gines jumped down at the first, and took to his heels at a lively trot. In one second, in fact, he had disappeared from before their eyes. Sancho meanwhile ran up to his Dapple and embraced him, crying, "How have you been, my dear, my darling Dapple, my darling companion?"

And all the time he kissed him as if he had been a human being. The ass stayed quiet and let Sancho caress him without answering a

When Don Quixote heard these blasphemies against his lady Dulcinea he could bear no more. So he raised his lance and, without word or warning, he dealt Sancho two such blows that he knocked him down. And if Dorthea had not called out to the knight to stop he would no doubt have taken his squire's life on the spot. (page 346) word. Then the others came up and congratulated the squire on recovering his beast, most of all Don Quixote, who said that he would not annul the draft for the three colts all the same. Sancho returned him thanks for this.

Whilst the pair of them were engaged in their conversation, the priest congratulated Dorothea on her ingenuity in telling her story, on its brevity and its close resemblance to the tales of knight errantry. She owned that she had often amused herself by reading them, but that she did not know where provinces and seaports lay, and so had said at a venture that she had landed at Osuna.

"I realized that," said the priest. "That was why I interrupted as I did, and put everything right. But is it not marvellous to see how easily this poor gentleman believes all these inventions and lies, simply because they are in the same style as the nonsense in his books?"

"It is," said Cardenio. "It is so strange and rare that I do not know whether anyone trying to invent such a character in fiction would have the genius to succeed."

"There is another strange thing about it," said the priest. "If you talk to the good gentleman about anything that does not touch on his madness, far from talking nonsense, he speaks very rationally and shows a completely clear and calm understanding. In fact nobody would think him anything but a man of very sound judgment, unless he were to strike him on the subject of chivalries."

While they were engaged in this conversation Don Quixote continued with his, saying to Sancho, "Let us let bygones be bygones, friend Panza, and tell me now, forgetting all anger and rancour, where, how and when did you find Dulcinea? What was she doing? What did you say to her? What did she answer? How did she look when she read my letter? Who copied it for you? Tell me every detail you think I should wish to know about the matter. Do not add or invent anything to please me, and please do not cut the tale short, for that will spoil my pleasure."

"To tell the truth, sir," replied Sancho, "no one copied the letter for me, because I had no letter with me."

"Yes, it is just as you say," replied Don Quixote. "For I found I had the little note-book I wrote it in still in my possession two days after you had gone. It grieved me deeply, since I did not know what you would do when you found that you had not got the letter. I always thought that you would come back as soon as you missed it."

"So I should have done," replied Sancho, "if I hadn't learnt it by heart when your worship read it to me. So that I repeated it to a parish clerk, who wrote it down exactly from my memory. He said he had never read as nice a letter in all the days of his life, although he had seen and read plenty of letters of excommunication."

"Do you still remember it now, Sancho?" asked Don Quixote.

"No, sir," replied Sancho. "For as soon as I had said it to him; I saw it wouldn't be any more use, and let it out of my mind. If I remember anything at all it's that 'Suppressed'—I mean 'sovereign-lady,' and the ending, 'Yours till death, the Knight of the Sad Countenance.' And in between I put more than three hundred 'souls,' 'lives' and 'dear eyes.' "

⊰ *31* ⊱

Of the Delectable Conversation
which passed between Don Quixote
and Sancho Panza His Squire,
and Other Incidents

*A*l this does not displease me at
all. Go on," said Don Quixote. "You got there; and what was that
queen of beauty doing? I am sure that you found her stringing
pearls, or embroidering a device with thread of gold for this, her
captive knight."

"No, she wasn't doing that," replied Sancho, "but winnowing a
couple of bushels of wheat in her back yard."

"Then you can be certain," said Don Quixote, "that the grains of
that wheat turned to pearls at the touch of her hand. Did you
observe, my friend, whether it was of the white or brown sort?"

"It was neither, but red," replied Sancho.

"Then I promise you," said Don Quixote, "that, winnowed by
her hands, it made the finest white bread. There can be no doubt of
that. But go on. When you gave her my letter, did she kiss it? Did
she put it on her head? Did she perform any ceremony worthy of
such a letter? Or what did she do?"

"When I went up to give it to her," said Sancho, "she was in the
middle of the job with a good lot of wheat in her sieve, and she said,

"Put the letter down, friend, on that sack. I can't read it till I've finished sifting what I have here."

"A wise lady," said Don Quixote. "That must have been so that she could read and enjoy it at her leisure. Go on, Sancho. And whilst she was about her task, what speech did she hold with you? What questions did she ask concerning me? And what did you reply? Come, tell me everything. Do not leave a drop in the inkhorn."

"She didn't ask me anything," said Sancho. "But I told her how your worship was here doing your penance for her service, naked from the waist up, buried in all these mountains like a savage, sleeping on the ground, never eating bread off a table-cloth, nor combing your beard, and weeping and cursing your fate."

"You spoke wrong in saying that I was cursing my fate," said Don Quixote. "On the contrary, I bless it, and shall bless it all the days of my life, for making me worthy of loving so high a lady as Dulcinea del Toboso."

"So high," answered Sancho, "that I swear she's a good hand's breadth taller than I am."

"How do you know that, Sancho?" asked Don Quixote. "Did you measure yourself against her?"

"I did," replied Sancho. "Like this. I went to help her load a sack of corn on to an ass, and so we got very close together. That's how I noticed she was a good hand's breadth taller than I am."

"But is it not true," replied Don Quixote, "that her great height is accompanied and adorned by a thousand million intellectual graces? One thing you cannot deny me, Sancho. When you stood close to her, did you not smell a spicy odour, an aromatic fragrance, something unutterably sweet to which I cannot give a name? I mean an essence or aroma, as if you were in some rare glover's shop?"

"All that I can say," answered Sancho, "is that I got a sniff of something rather mannish. It must have been because she was running with sweat from the hard work."

"It would not be that," replied Don Quixote. "You must have had a cold or have smelt yourself. For well I know the scent of that rose among thorns, that lily of the field, that liquid ambergris."

"It's quite possible," replied Sancho, "for very often there's that same smell about me that seemed to be coming from the lady Dulcinea. But it's not surprising, for one devil is like another."

"Well, then," continued Don Quixote, "she has finished winnowing her corn and sent it to the mill. What did she do when she had read my letter?"

"She didn't read the letter," said Sancho, "for she said she couldn't read or write. She tore it up instead, and told me she wouldn't give it to anyone to read, so that her secrets shouldn't be known all over the village. She said it was quite enough that I had told her by word of mouth about your worship's love for her and about the extraordinary penance you had stayed behind to do for her sake. She ended up by telling me to tell your worship that she kissed your hands, and that she had far rather see you than write to you. So she begged and commanded you, at sight hereof, to leave these bushes and briars and stop doing these mad antics, and set out at once on the road for El Toboso, if more important business didn't prevent you, for she was most anxious to see your worship. She laughed a lot when I told her how you were called the Knight of the Sad Countenance. I asked her if that Basque of yours had been there. She said that he had, and that he was a very decent sort of man. I asked her about the galley-slaves too, but she said that she hadn't seen any of them yet."

"So far so good," said Don Quixote. "But tell me, what jewel did she give you on your departure, in thanks for the news you brought her of me? For it is an ancient and time-worn custom among knights errant and their ladies to reward squires, damsels or dwarfs who bring them news of their ladies or knights with some rich jewel in gratitude for their welcome news."

"That's very likely, and I think it's a good custom. But they must have done that in the olden times, for nowadays the habit seems to be just to give them a bit of bread and cheese. That's what my lady Dulcinea gave me, anyhow, over the top of the yard wall when she said good-bye to me. And what's more, it was a sheep's-milk cheese."

"She is generous in the extreme," said Don Quixote; "and, if she did not give you a gold jewel, it was no doubt only because she had not one there at hand to give you. But it is never too late. Gifts are still good after Easter. I will see her, and all shall be put right. But do you know what does astonish me, Sancho? You must have gone and returned through the air. For you have only taken three days travelling to El Toboso and back, and it is a good ninety miles. From which I conclude that the sage necromancer, who is my friend and looks after my affairs—for I certainly have such a friend, or I should not be a true knight errant—I say that this necromancer must have assisted you on your journey without your knowing it. For there are enchanters who have picked up a knight errant asleep in his bed, and next day, he will not know how or why, but he will wake up more than a thousand miles from the place where he went to sleep. If it were not for that, it would be impossible for knights errant to come to one another's aid in their perils, as they do at every turn. One of them, perhaps, is fighting in the Armenian mountains with some dragon or fierce monster, or with another knight. He is getting the worst of the battle, and is just at the point of death. Then, when you least expect it, there appears another knight, on a cloud or in a chariot of fire. This friend, who was the moment before in England, comes to his assistance, saves his life and is back that night in his own lodging, enjoying his supper. Very often the distance from the one place to the other is six or seven thousand miles. Now all this is effected by the skill and wisdom of these sage enchanters who watch over valorous knights. So, friend Sancho, I do not find it difficult to believe that you made the journey to and from El Toboso in so short a time, since, as I have said, some friendly sage must have carried you through the air without your knowing it."

"That may be so," said Sancho, "for certainly Rocinante went like a gipsy's ass with quicksilver in its ears."

"Quicksilver!" exclaimed Don Quixote. "And a legion of devils besides, for they are the sort of gentry who travel—and make others travel—tirelessly, as much as they please. But, to leave the subject, what do you think I ought to do about my lady's command to go and see her? For, although I am clearly obliged to fulfil her behests, I find myself prevented by the boon I have granted to the Princess in whose company we are, and the law of chivalry compels me to put my oath before my pleasure. On the one hand I am perplexed and harassed by the desire to see my lady, on the other incited and summoned by my pledged faith and the glory I shall gain in this enterprise. What I propose to do is to press on and get quickly to the place where this giant is. Then, when I get there, I will cut off his head, restore the Princess peacefully to her throne, and instantly return to behold the light which illumines my senses. I will offer her such excuses that she will come to approve my delay. For she will see that it all redounds to her greater glory and fame, since everything which I have achieved, am achieving and shall achieve by force of arms in this life proceeds wholly from her favour and from my being her knight."

"Oh dear!" cried Sancho. "Your worship must be downright crazy! Tell me, sir, do you mean to take the journey for nothing, and let a rich and princely marriage, with a kingdom for dowry, slip through your fingers? They say that her country's more than sixty thousand miles round, and full of everything you want to support human life. I've heard that it's bigger than Portugal and Castile put together. Don't talk any more, for Heaven's sake. You ought to be ashamed of what you've said. Take my advice, please, and marry her straight away, in the first village where there's a priest. Or else there is our own priest here, who'll do the job a treat. I'm old enough, mind you, to offer advice, and what I advise you now fits the case like a glove. For a bird in the hand is worth two in the bush, and he who had good and chose bad must not be vexed for the ill he had."

"Look you, Sancho," replied Don Quixote, "if you are advising me to marry, so that I may be king when I have killed the giant, and have the means of doing you favours and fulfilling my promise to you, I would inform you that I can very easily gratify your wishes without marrying. For I will make it a condition before I go into battle that when I come off victorious, they shall give me part of the kingdom which I can bestow on anyone I will, even though I do not marry her. And when I get it, whom do you think I shall give it to but you?"

"That's fair enough," replied Sancho. "But take good care, your worship, to choose a piece on the coast, so that if I don't like the life I can put my black subjects on board ship, and do what I said with them. Don't trouble to go and see my lady Dulcinea for the time being, but go and kill the giant, and let's settle that business. For I swear to God I think it'll bring us great honour and profit."

"Yes, Sancho," said Don Quixote, "you are in the right, and I will take your advice about going with the Princess before I visit Dulcinea. But I warn you to say nothing to anyone about what we have been discussing and arranging, not even to our companions. For since Dulcinea is so shy that she does not want her feelings known, it would not be right for me, or for anyone acting for me, to reveal them."

"But if that's the case," said Sancho, "why, your worship, do you make everyone you conquer by your mighty arm present himself to my lady Dulcinea? For that says you love her and that she's your sweetheart, as clearly as if you'd put your signature to the fact. And seeing that you force them to go down on their knees in her presence, and to say that they come from your worship to offer her their obedience, how can the feelings of the pair of you stay hidden?"

"Oh, how stupid and simple you are!" exclaimed Don Quixote. "Do you not see, Sancho, that this all redounds to her greater glory? You must know that in this our state of chivalry it is a great honour for a lady to have many knights errant serving her, with no greater ambition than of serving her for what she is, and without hope of any other reward for their zeal than that she shall be pleased to accept them as her knights."

"That's the kind of love," said Sancho, "I've heard them preach about. They say we ought to love our Lord for Himself alone,

without being moved to it by hope of glory or fear of punishment.
Though as for me, I'm inclined to love and serve Him for what He
can do for me."

"The devil take you!" said Don Quixote. "What a peasant you
are, and yet what apt things you say at times! One would almost
think you had been to school."

"But I swear I can't read," replied Sancho.

At this point Master Nicholas called out to them to wait a bit, for
the company wanted to stop and drink at a small spring by the
roadside. Don Quixote halted, much to Sancho's satisfaction, since
by this time he was tired of telling all those lies, and afraid that his
master might catch him out. For although he knew that Dulcinea
was a peasant girl from El Toboso, he had never seen her in his life.
In the meantime Cardenio had put on the clothes which Dorothea
was wearing when they met her, and although they were not very
good they were a great improvement on his own. They all dismounted at the spring, and with the provisions which the priest had
brought from the inn did something to satisfy their great hunger.

And whilst they were thus occupied a lad, who chanced to be
passing along the road, stopped and stared at the party, and then,
after a moment, rushed up to Don Quixote and clasped him round
the legs, most opportunely bursting into tears, "Oh, my lord," he
cried, "don't you know me? Take a good look at me. I'm the boy
Andrew whom your worship untied from the oak I was bound to."

Don Quixote recognized him and, taking him by the hand,
turned to say to the others: "To convince you of the importance of
having knights errant in the world to redress the outrages and
wrongs which are committed here by insolent and wicked men, I
would have your worships know that some days ago, as I was passing
by a wood, I heard most piteous shouts and cries, as of someone
afflicted and in distress. Immediately, as was my duty, I hastened in
the direction from which the sad cries seemed to come, and there I
found this lad who is now before you bound to an oak. And now my
soul rejoices at the sight of him, for he shall be my witness and will
not let me stray from the truth in any way. He was tied to a tree, I

tell you, naked to the waist; and a country fellow, who I learnt afterwards was his master, was lashing him with the reins of his horse. As soon as I saw him I demanded the reason for this atrocious flagellation, and the brute replied that he was beating him because he was his servant and for certain negligences of his which seemed to spring rather from roguery than from foolishness. At this the child cried, 'Sir, he is only whipping me because I asked him for my wages.' The master answered with some sort of talk and excuses, which I of course heard but did not admit. To be brief, I made the peasant untie the boy, and made him swear to take him and pay him *real* for *real*—and perfumed at that. Now, is not this all true, Andrew my lad? Did you not note with what authority I gave my orders, and with what humility he promised to do all that I commanded and specified and required? Answer; do not be confused or hesitant. Tell these good gentlemen what happened, so that they may see and reflect how useful it is, as I say, to have knights errant on the roads."

"All that your worship has said is quite true," replied the boy, "but the end of the business was very much the opposite of what you suppose."

"How the opposite?" demanded Don Quixote. "Did not the peasant pay you, then?"

"Not only didn't he pay me," replied the boy, "but as soon as your worship was out of the wood and we were alone, he tied me up again to the same oak and beat me again so hard that I was left flayed like St. Bartholomew. And at every stroke he gave me, he mocked and jibed at your worship. So that, if it hadn't been for the pain, I should have burst out laughing. In fact, he gave me such a welting that I've been in a hospital ever since, getting cured of the injuries the wicked wretch did me. And your worship's to blame for it all. For if you'd gone on your way and not come when you weren't called, and not interfered with other people's business, my master would have been content to give me a dozen or two lashes. Then he would have let me go and paid me what he owed me. But as your worship abused him so needlessly and called him so many names, he got into a temper, and seeing that he couldn't vent it on you he let fly

Sancho meanwhile ran up to his Dapple and embraced him, crying, "How have you been, my dear, my darling Dapple, my darling companion?" And all the time he kissed him as if he had been a human being. (page 348) such a rain of blows on me, once we were alone, that I shall never be a whole man again for the rest of my life."

"The trouble was," said Don Quixote, "that I went away. I should not have gone till I had seen you paid. For, as I ought to have known from long experience, there is never a peasant who keeps his word if he finds it does not suit him. But you remember, Andrew, that I swore I would go and look for him if he did not pay you, and find him too, even if he hid in the whale's belly."

"That's right," said Andrew, "but it wasn't any good."

"Now you will see if it is any good or not," exclaimed Don Quixote, getting up very quickly and bidding Sancho bridle Rocinante, who had been browsing during their meal.

Dorothea asked him what it was he intended to do. He answered that he was going to look for the villain, punish him for his wicked conduct, and see that Andrew was paid to the last farthing, in despite of and in the teeth of every peasant in the world. But she replied by reminding him that he could not. For by the boon he had granted her, he must not engage in any enterprise until hers was accomplished. And as he knew this better than anyone else, he must restrain his anger until his return from her kingdom.

"That is true," replied Don Quixote, "and Andrew must be patient till my return, as you say, my lady. But I swear again, and renew my promise, not to rest until I have seen him avenged and paid."

"I don't believe in these vows," said Andrew. "I'd rather have something now to get me on to Seville, than all the vengeance in the world. Give me something to eat and take with me, if you have anything here. Then God bless your worship and all knights errant, and may they be as good errants for themselves as they've been for me."

Sancho took a piece of bread and some cheese out of his bag and gave it to the lad, saying, "Take this, brother Andrew, for each of us has a share in your misfortune."

"Well, what's your share, then?" asked Andrew.

"This share of bread and cheese that I'm giving you," replied

Sancho. "God knows whether I mayn't need it myself. For I must tell you, my friend, that we squires of knights errant are subject to great hunger and bad luck, and to other things too, which are better felt than told."

Andrew seized his bread and cheese and, when he saw that no one was going to give him anything more, made his bow and took to the road; though, as he turned to go, he said to Don Quixote, "For God's sake, Sir Knight Errant, don't come to my help if you meet me again, even though you see me being cut to pieces. But leave me to my troubles, for they can't be so bad that the results of your worship's help won't be worse. And God blast you and every knight errant ever born on the face of the earth!"

Don Quixote started up to punish him, but he ran off so fast that nobody attempted to follow. Our knight was very much abashed at Andrew's story, and the others had much trouble in not completing his discomfiture by laughing outright.

⊰ 32 ⊱

Of what befell Don Quixote
and All His Company at the Inn

*A*s soon as their excellent meal was over they saddled at once, and arrived next day without any noteworthy incident at that inn which was the dread and terror of Sancho Panza. But although he would rather not have gone in, this time he could not avoid it. And when they saw Don Quixote and Sancho coming, the innkeeper, his wife, their daughter and Maritornes came out to receive them with a great show of pleasure. The knight accepted their welcome with gravity and approbation, and bade them put him up a better bed than they had given him the time before. To which the landlady replied that she would give him one fit for a prince, if he would pay them better than the last time. Don Quixote answered that he would, and so they provided him with a tolerable one in the same loft as before. And there he lay down immediately, for he was severely shaken in body and mind. But no sooner had he shut himself in than the landlady attacked the barber, seizing him by the beard and crying, "Bless my soul! You shan't use my ox tail for a beard any more. Give me back my tail, for my husband's what-d'ye-call-it's so kicked about on the floor that it's a shame. I mean his comb that he used to stick into my tail."

But the barber would not part with it for all her tugging, until the priest told him to give it to her, since they had no more need of disguise. For he could reveal himself in his own shape now, and tell Don Quixote he had fled to that inn after he had been robbed by the galley-slaves. Then, if the knight were to ask after the Princess's squire, they could tell him that she had sent him ahead to inform her subjects that she was on her way, and was bringing their common liberator with her. At this the barber cheerfully returned the landlady her tail, and they gave her back all her property too that she had lent them for Don Quixote's deliverance.

Everyone in the place was struck by Dorothea's beauty, and by the handsomeness of the shepherd Cardenio. The priest ordered them to prepare such food as the inn could provide, and the landlord, in hope of better payment, quickly served them with a tolerable meal. All this while Don Quixote slept, and they agreed not to wake him, since he was in greater need of sleep than of food. The landlord, his wife, his daughter, Maritornes and all the travellers were at the table, and they discussed Don Quixote's strange madness and the state in which they found him. The landlady told them of his adventures with the carrier. Then she looked to see if Sancho was present and, finding that he was not, told them the tale of his tossing in the blanket, which amused them quite a bit. But when the priest said that it was the books of chivalry which he had read that had turned Don Quixote's brain, the landlord remarked, "I don't know how that can be, because really I think there's no better reading in the world. I have two or three of them here and some other writings. They've truly put life into me, and not only into me but into plenty of others. For at harvest time a lot of the reapers come in here in the mid-day heat. There's always one of them who can read, and he takes up one of those books. Then as many as thirty of us sit round him, and we enjoy listening so much that it saves us countless grey hairs. At least I can say for myself that when I hear about those furious, terrible blows the knights deal one another, I get the fancy to strike a few myself. And I could go on listening night and day."

"I agree absolutely," said the landlady, "for I never get any peace in my house except when you're listening to the reading. You're so fascinated then that you forget to scold for once."

"That's right," said Maritornes. "I tell you I enjoy hearing them all too. They're very pretty, particularly the parts when some lady or other is lying in her knight's embraces under some orange trees, and there's a damsel keeping watch for them, dying of envy and frightened to death. It's all as sweet as honey, I say."

"And you, what do you think about it, young lady?" the priest asked the innkeeper's daughter.

"I don't know, sir, truly I don't," she answered. "I listen too, and really, though I don't understand it, I do enjoy it. But I don't like the fighting that pleases my father so much. I prefer the complaints the knights make when they're away from their ladies. Sometimes they actually make my cry, I pity them so much."

"Then you would give them some relief, young lady," asked Dorothea, "if they were weeping for you?"

"I don't know what I'd do," replied the girl. "Only I know that some of those ladies are so cruel that their knights call them tigers and lions and lots of other nasty names. And, Jesus, I can't imagine what sort of heartless, conscienceless folk they can be to leave a decent man to die or go mad, rather than look at him. I don't know what's the good of all their coyness—if it's for the sake of their virtue, let 'em marry them, for that's what the gentlemen are after."

"Be quiet, girl," said the landlady. "You seem to know rather much of these matters, and it's not right for young ladies to know or talk so much."

"But as this gentleman asked me," she answered, "I couldn't help answering him."

"Well, well," said the priest, "bring in those books, Master Landlord. I should like to see them."

"With pleasure," he replied; and going into his room, brought out a little old trunk, fastened with a small chain, which he undid, revealing three big books and some manuscript papers written in a very fine hand. The first book he opened was *Don Cirongilio of*

Thrace, the others *Felixmarte of Hyrcania* and *The History of the Great Captain Gonzalo Hernandez of Cordova* together with the *Life of Diego Garcia de Paredes*.

On reading the titles of the two first, the priest observed to the barber, "We need our friend's housekeeper here now, and his niece."

"No, we don't," replied the barber, "for I'm just as capable of carrying them to the yard or to the fireplace; and there's a very good fire there now."

"What," said the innkeeper, "does your worship want to burn my books?"

"Only these two," replied the priest. "This Don Cirongilio and this Felixmarte."

"Are my books heretical or phlegmatic, by any chance," asked the innkeeper, "that you want to burn them?"

"Schismatic, you mean, my friend," said the barber, "not phlegmatic."

"Yes, yes," said the innkeeper. "But if you've a mind to burn any, let it be this one about the Great Captain and Diego Garcia, for I'd rather have one of my children burnt than either of the others."

"My friend," pronounced the priest, "these two books are full of lies and foolishness and vanity. But the one about the Great Captain is true history, and relates the deeds of Gonzalo Hernandez of Cordova, whom the whole world deservedly called The Great Captain, on account of his many great exploits. It is a famous and illustrious name which was earned by none but him. And that Diego Garcia de Paredes too was a noble gentleman, born in the city of Truxillo in Estremadura, a very brave soldier, and of such natural strength that with one finger he stopped a mill-wheel turning at full speed. Once too when he was posted with a two-handed sword at the approaches of a bridge, he prevented a whole vast army from crossing. He did so many other things of that sort too that if instead of his writing them down himself with the modesty of the gentleman who is his own chronicler, a stranger had written a free and dispassionate account of them, his deeds would have cast the ex-

ploits of all your Hectors, Achilleses, and Rolands, into oblivion."
"Tell that to my father!" said the innkeeper. "So that's what
astonished you. Just stopping a millwheel! I swear you ought to see
what I've read about Felixmarte of Hyrcania. He cut five giants in
half with one back-stroke, just as if they'd been so many beans that
children make their mannikins of. And another time he attacked a
huge and most powerful army of more than one million six hundred
thousand soldiers, all in armour from head to foot, and routed them
all as if they had been flocks of sheep. I wonder what would you say
about the worthy Don Cirongilio of Thrace. He was a valiant and
courageous knight, as you may read in the book, where it tells you
how once, a fiery serpent came out of the water as he was sailing on
a river. As soon as he saw it he rushed at it, got astride its scaly
shoulders, and pressed its throat so hard with both his hands that it
had no other way of saving itself from being throttled than by diving
to the bottom of the river, dragging the knight, who would not leave
go, after it. And when they got there, he found himself among such
marvellously beautiful palaces and gardens! Then the serpent
turned into an old man, and told him such things as were never
heard before. Say no more, sir, for if you were to listen to that book
you would go mad with pleasure. A fig each for your Great Captain
and your Diego Garcia!"

At this Dorothea whispered to Cardenio, "Our host is not far
short of being a second Don Quixote."

"I agree," replied Cardenio. "To judge by what he says, he takes
everything in those books for gospel truth, and the barefoot friars
themselves wouldn't make him believe otherwise."

"See here, brother," began the priest, "there never were such
people in the world as Felixmarte of Hyrcania, or Don Cirongilio
of Thrace, or any of the other knights in those books of chivalry.
They are all fictions, invented by idle brains who composed them
for the very purpose you spoke of, to pass the time as your
reapers do in reading them. For I swear to you that really such
knights never existed in the world, and all these feats and follies
never happened."

"Try that bone on another dog!" replied the innkeeper. "As if I didn't know how many beans make five, and where my own shoe pinches! Don't try to feed me with pap, your worship, for I wasn't born yesterday! It's a nice thing for you to try and persuade me that all these fine books say is only nonsense and lies, when they're printed by licence of the Lords of the Privy Council—as if they were people who would allow a pack of lies to be published, and enough battles and enchantments to drive you out of your wits!"

"I have told you already, my friend," replied the priest, "that it is done to divert our idle moments. Just as in all well-ruled states such games as chess, tennis and billiards are permitted for the amusement of men who do not want to work, or do not have to, or cannot, so these books are allowed to be published, in the very reasonable belief that there can be no one so ignorant as to take any of them for true history. If I were permitted now, and my hearers desired it, I would say something about the qualities that books of chivalry require in order to be good. This might perhaps make them useful to some people, and enjoyable too. But I hope that a time will come when I can explain my ideas to those who can turn my criticism to account. In the meantime, Master Landlord, believe what I tell you. Take your books, and decide for yourself whether they are truth or lies, and such good may they do you! But I pray God you never limp on the same foot as your guest Don Quixote."

"I shan't do that," replied the innkeeper. "I shall never be fool enough to turn knight errant. For I see quite well that it's not the fashion now to do as they did in the olden days when they say those famous knights roamed the world."

Sancho had entered in the middle of this conversation and was much astonished and depressed to hear that knights errant were now out of fashion, and that all books of chivalry were nonsense and lies. And so he decided in his own mind to wait and see how this expedition of his master's turned out, and if the result was not up to his expectations, he resolved to leave Don Quixote and go back to his wife and children and to his usual occupation.

The innkeeper was just taking away the trunk and the books

when the priest said to him, "Wait. I should like to see what is in those papers that are written in such a good hand." The landlord took them out, and handed them to the priest who found about eight sheets of manuscript, and at the beginning a title in large letters, *The Tale of Foolish Curiosity.* He then read some three or four lines to himself, and said, "Really, the title of this tale rather takes my fancy, and I have a mind to read it through."

At which the innkeeper replied, "Your reverence might do well to read it. Let me tell you that some of my guests who've read it here have enjoyed it very much and have pressed me to give it to them. But I wouldn't let them have it, as I mean to return it to the man who left this trunk behind with all these books and papers. He must have forgotten them, but he may quite likely come this way again some time. Then I'll certainly return him the books, though I know I shall miss them. For I may be an innkeeper, but still I'm a Christian!"

"You are very right, my friend," said the priest, "but all the same, if I like the tale you must let me copy it."

"With the greatest of pleasure," replied the innkeeper.

Whilst the two of them were talking, Cardenio had picked up the tale and begun to read it. He formed the same opinion of it as the priest had done, and begged him to read it aloud so that they could all hear it.

"I would," said the priest, "if it were not better to spend our time in sleeping than in reading."

"It will be sufficient rest for me," said Dorothea, "to pass an hour listening to a story, for my mind is not yet quiet enough to let me sleep."

"Well, in that case," said the priest, "I will read it, if only out of curiosity. Perhaps there will be something pleasant in it."

Master Nicholas urged him to do so, and Sancho as well. So seeing that it would give them all pleasure, and himself as well, the priest began, "Well, well! Listen to me, all of you, for this is how the tale begins."

371

⊰ 33 ⊱

The Tale of Foolish Curiosity

*I*n Florence, a wealthy and
famous Italian city in the province called Tuscany, lived Anselmo
and Lothario, two rich and noble gentlemen, and such close friends
that everyone who knew them referred to them as *The Two Friends*.
They were bachelors, lads of the same age and the same habits,
which was sufficient reason for the affection that united them. It is
true that Anselmo was rather more inclined to affairs of the heart
than was Lothario, who was fonder of hunting. But when the
occasion arose, Anselmo would give up his pleasures to take part in
Lothario's, and Lothario his to follow Anselmo's. Their minds, in
fact, worked in such unison that no clock could keep better time.

Anselmo fell deeply in love with a noble and beautiful damsel of
that city. So good was her family and so good was she that he
decided, with the approval of his friend Lothario, without which he
did nothing, to ask her parents for her hand. And this he did.
Lothario himself was the messenger, and it was he who concluded
the business so much to his friend's satisfaction that in a short time
Anselmo gained the object of his desires. Camilla too was so pleased

to have got Anselmo for a husband that she never ceased to thank Heaven and Lothario, the joint agents of her good fortune. For the first few days—which as in all marriages, were spent in feasting—Lothario continued to visit his friend Anselmo's house as usual, striving to do him honour and to entertain and amuse him in every possible way. But once the wedding celebrations were over and the stream of visitors and congratulations had subsided, he began deliberately to visit Anselmo's less often; since it seemed to him, as it should to all reasonable men, that men should not continue to haunt the houses of their married friends as they did when they were bachelors. For though good and true friends should not be in any way suspicious, yet a married man's honour is so delicate that it can be injured even by his own brother. How much more so by his friend.

Anselmo noticed the falling off in Lothario's visits, and made it the subject of loud complaints. He said that he would never have married if he had known that his marriage was going to deprive him of his friend's company. He begged him not to let the charming title of *The Two Friends,* which they had earned by their bachelor harmony, lapse through exaggerated caution. He implored him, in fact, if such a word could rightly be used between them, to treat his house as his own again, and to come and go as before. He assured him that his wife Camilla had no pleasure or desire except such as he wished her to have, and that she was troubled to see Lothario turned so shy, knowing as she did the warmth of their friendship.

Lothario replied to this and to the many arguments Anselmo used to persuade him to come to the house again as he used to do, so prudently, discreetly and judiciously, that Anselmo was satisfied with his friend's decision, and they agreed that Lothario should dine with him twice a week and on feast-days. But although this was settled between the pair of them, Lothario decided to do no more than what seemed best to serve his friend's honour, for he prized Anselmo's good name more than his own. He used to say, and rightly, that a married man on whom Heaven has bestowed a lovely wife has to take as much care of what friends he brings to the house as of what women friends his wife consorts with. For what is not done or arranged in market-places and churches, or at public shows or church-goings—which a husband cannot always deny his wife—is often managed and facilitated at the house of that very woman friend or relative in whom he has most confidence. Lothario used to say too that every married man has need of a friend to warn him of the shortcomings of his behaviour. For it often happens that out of his great love for his wife, a husband does not warn her, for fear of annoying her, that some of her actions may redound either to his honour or to his shame. Though all this could easily be remedied if he had a friend to advise him. But where might a man find a friend as discreet, as loyal and as faithful as Lothario postulated? Indeed I do not know. Lothario alone was the man, for he guarded his friend's honour with so much care and vigilance that he tried to reduce, shorten and diminish the agreed times for his visits to the house, for fear that the idle crowd and straying malicious eyes might criticize the visits of a rich, noble and high-born young man with the attractive qualities which he considered himself to have, to the house of so lovely a woman as Camilla. For even though her goodness and worth might be sufficient to bridle malicious tongues, he did not want to have her good name or his friend's called into question. Therefore he spent most of the days agreed upon in other business and amusements, and pretended that these were unavoidable. So it was that a great part of the hours they spent together passed in complaints on one side and excuses on the other.

Now it happened one day, as the two friends were taking a walk in the fields outside the city, that Anselmo addressed the following remarks to Lothario, "You may think, friend Lothario, that I am incapable of responding with sufficient gratitude for the favours which God has bestowed on me in making me the son of such parents and in giving me with no mean hand both of nature's and of fortune's goods, and for the greatest blessing of all which He bestowed on me in giving me you for a friend and Camilla for a wife—two treasures which I value as much as I am able, if not as much as I should. Yet with all these blessings, which are commonly

Sancho took a piece of bread and some cheese out of his bag and gave it to the lad, saying, "Take this, brother Andrew, for each of us has a share in your misfortune." (page 363) the sum with which men should and do live content, I am the most fretful and discontented man in all the world, since for some time now I have been vexed and bothered by a desire so strange and peculiar that I am astonished at myself. I blame and scold myself for it when I am alone, and try to stifle it and to conceal it from my own thoughts. But all this has been of so little use that my whole intention might have been to proclaim it to the world. And since it must come out in the end, I should like it to be kept in the secret archives of your breast. For I am confident that in that way, and through the efforts which you, as my faithful friend, will take to relieve me, I shall be quickly freed from the distress it causes me. Through your sympathy I expect to become as happy as by my own foolishness I am now unhappy."

This speech of Anselmo's astonished Lothario, for he had no idea where its long preface or preamble was leading to. For although he tried to imagine what desire could possibly be tormenting his friend, he was always wide of the mark. So to rid himself quickly of the distress which this suspense caused him, he answered that Anselmo was doing a clear injustice to their great friendship by searching for round-about ways of telling him his most secret thoughts. For he could count on him either for advice or for help.

"That is true," replied Anselmo. "I am confident of that, and I will tell you, friend Lothario, what distresses me. It is the question whether my wife Camilla is as good and perfect as I think. I cannot be sure of the truth except by testing her by an ordeal which shall prove the purity of her virtue, as fire shows the purity of gold. For it is my opinion, my friend, that a woman is good only in proportion to her temptations, and that the only constant woman is one who does not yield to promises, gifts, tears or the continuous importunities of persistent lovers. What reason has one to thank a woman for being good," said he, "if no one has tempted her to be bad? What merit is there in her being reserved and modest, if she has no opportunity of going astray and knows that she has a husband who will kill her if he catches her in her first slip? That is why I do not have the same regard for the woman who is good out of fear or lack of opportunity as for the woman who is wooed and pursued, yet comes off with the crown of victory. So, for these reasons and for many others that I could give you, I want support and confirmation for the opinion I hold. I want my wife Camilla to pass through the ordeal, and be purged and refined in the fire of temptation and solicitation by someone worthy of her. Then, if she comes out, as I believe she will, with the palm of victory, I shall account myself the most fortunate of men. I shall be able to say that the cup of my desires is full. I shall say that I have been fated to possess the virtuous woman of whom the wise man says, 'Who shall find her?' And if things should turn out contrary to my expectations, with the satisfaction of having proved the truth I shall bear uncomplainingly the pain that so dearly bought an experiment will cause me. Now it being understood that nothing you say in opposition to my purpose will be of the slightest effect in dissuading me from it, I want you, my friend Lothario, to prepare to be the instrument for carrying this plan of mine into effect. I shall give you an opportunity of doing it, and I shall omit nothing that seems to me necessary, if you are to woo a woman who is chaste, honourable, reserved and in no way mercenary. What most urges me to entrust this arduous enterprise to you is the knowledge that if Camilla is conquered by you, you will not carry your victory to the ultimate extreme, but only do what is necessary by the terms of our agreement. And so I shall be wronged only in the intention, and my injury will remain buried in your virtuous silence, which, I know, will be as eternal as the silence of death, in any concern of mine. Therefore, if you want me to enjoy anything deserving the name of life you must now enter into this conflict of love, not half-heartedly or sluggishly, but with the earnestness and diligence which my plan requires, and with the loyalty our friendship assures me of."

These were Anselmo's arguments, to which Lothario listened so attentively that he did not open his lips until his friend had finished, except to say the few words here recorded. And then he stared at him for some time as if he were gazing at some dreadful and amazing object, the like of which he had never seen before.

"I cannot persuade myself, friend Anselmo," he said, "that what you have just been saying is not a joke. For, if I had thought you were in earnest, I should not have let you go so far. I should not have listened, and that would have cut short your long speech. It is my belief that either you do not know me or I do not know you. But no, I know very well that you are Anselmo, and you know that I am Lothario. The trouble is that I think you are not the Anselmo you used to be, and you seem to have imagined that I am not the Lothario I ought to be. For what you have just said to me is unworthy of my friend Anselmo, and you should not have made the demands you did of the Lothario you know. Good friends ought to use and prove their friends, as the poet says, *usque ad aras;* I mean that they must not use friendship for purposes offensive to God. And if such was the opinion of a heathen, how much more must a Christian hold to it, knowing as he does that the divine friendship must not be forfeited for a human one? When a friend goes so far as to set aside his duty to God to fulfil that of friendship, it must not be for trifles and trivialities, but for something on which his friend's life and honour depend. Now tell me, Anselmo, is it your life or your honour that is in such danger that I must risk myself to satisfy you, and do the detestable thing you are asking of me? Neither most certainly. On the contrary, as far as I understand, you are asking me to try hard to rob you, and to rob myself of life and honour. For if I take your honour it is clear that I take your life, since a man without honour is worse than dead. If I become the instrument of such an evil as you wish, should I not emerge dishonoured and, consequently, dead? Listen, Anselmo my friend, and have the patience not to answer till I have finished telling you all my thoughts on the subject of this request of yours. There will be time enough after that for you to reply and for me to listen."

"Most willingly," said Anselmo. "Say what you like."

Then Lothario went on to say, "You seem to me, Anselmo, to be in the position of the Moors, who cannot be convinced in the error of their sect by quotations from Holy Scripture, nor by arguments drawn from intellectual speculation or based on the canons of faith, but have to have examples, palpable, simple, intelligible, demonstrable and indubitable, with irrefutable mathematical proof, like, 'If equals be taken from equals the remainders are equal.' And when they do not understand this in words, as in fact they do not, then you have to show it to them with your hands and put it in front of their eyes. But even then no one can convince them of the truths of our holy faith. Now I shall have to use the same method with you. For this new desire of yours is so extravagant and so far from all shadow of sense that it seems to me it would be a waste of time to try and convince you of your foolishness—for that is the only name I can give it at present. Yes, I am even inclined to abandon you to your folly as a punishment for your wickedness. But my friendship for you will not let me treat you so cruelly as to leave you in such obvious danger of destruction. Now, to make the matter clear to you, Anselmo, tell me, did you not ask me to solicit a modest woman? To tempt a chaste one? To bribe an honest one? To woo a prudent one? Yes, that is what you asked. But if you know that you have a modest, chaste, honest, prudent wife, what are you searching to find out? If you believe that she will emerge victorious from all my attacks—as no doubt she will—what titles do you intend to give her afterwards better than those she already has? What more will she be afterwards than she is at present? Either you do not take her for what you say, or you do not know what you are asking. If you do not take her for what you say, why do you want to test her instead of treating her as a bad woman, and punishing her as you think she deserves? But if she is as good as you think, it will be an impertinence to experiment with truth itself, for when the trial is over it cannot have a higher value than it had before. So we must conclude that to attempt things which are more likely to result in harm than in good is the mark of unreasoning and rash minds. All the more so if they attempt such things voluntarily, when it is clear from a mile away that the attempt is sheer madness. Difficult works are attempted for the sake of Heaven, for the world's sake, or for both. The first are tasks undertaken by the saints, who attempt to live the lives of angels in human frames. The second are performed by men who navigate the boundless ocean, and journey through distant countries and changing climates, to acquire what are called the goods of fortune. And those who brave hazardous enterprises for the sake of both God and man are stout soldiers, who no sooner see in the enemy's rampart a breach made by a single cannon-ball than, regardless of all fear and danger, they are borne on the wings of ambition to fight for their faith, their nation and their king, and rush boldly into the midst of death which awaits them in a thousand shapes.

"Such are the hazards commonly undertaken, and it is honour, glory and gain to attempt them, however charged they may be with difficulties and danger. But the project you suggest attempting will gain you glory neither from above, nor the goods of fortune, nor renown among men. For, supposing that the result is satisfactory, you will be no happier, no richer, and no more honoured than you are at present; and if you do not succeed, you will be in the greatest imaginable misery. It will do you no good then to think that no one knows your misfortune, for it will be enough to afflict and undo you that you know it yourself. As confirmation I will quote a stanza of the famous poet Luis Tansilo from the end of the first part of his *Tears of St. Peter,* which goes like this:

> In Peter's heart the shame and anguish grew
> As the day broke, and though no man was by
> To see his sin, he knew his own offence
> And blushed deep for his guilt. A noble heart
> Needs no observer to arouse his shame,
> But is abashed at sight of his own guilt.
> Though no one but the heavens and earth can see it.

"So you will not alleviate your grief by secrecy, but will have cause for incessant tears. For even though you may not weep openly, tears of blood will flow from your heart. So wept that simple doctor of whom our poet tells, who made the trial of the cup which the cautious Rinaldo, with greatest discretion, declined. Even though that is a poetic fiction, it contains a hidden moral worth observing and following. Moreover, if you will listen to what

I am now going to say, you will be finally convinced that it is a great error you now wish to commit. Tell me, Anselmo, if the Heavens or good fortune had made you the owner and lawful possessor of a very fine diamond, and every jewel merchant who saw it was satisfied of its goodness and quality; and if, all together and with one voice, they said that it attained the utmost possible perfection in every respect, and you believed them yourself and had not a suspicion to the contrary—supposing all this, would it be reasonable for you to take it into your head to pick up this stone and put it between the anvil and the hammer, and thus by mere weight of blows and brawn prove whether it was as hard and as fine as they said? Now would it be any more reasonable to put this plan of yours into effect? For supposing that the stone resisted such a stupid trial, would it have any greater value or reputation for that? And if it broke—which well might happen—would not everything be lost? Yes, and its owner would count in the general estimation as a fool.

"Now think of Camilla, Anselmo my friend, as a rare diamond, both in your estimation and others', and consider whether there is any reason for exposing her to the risk of destruction; for even if she remains unbroken, she cannot rise to a greater value than she now has. But, if she fails and does not stand up to the trial, reflect on the state you would be in without her. Think what reason you would have for self-reproach if you were to be the cause of her destruction and your own. For there is no jewel in the world so precious as a chaste and virtuous woman, and the whole honour of women lies in their good reputation. Now, since your wife's virtue is the very highest imaginable, as you know, why should you want to call its truth into question? Look, my friend, woman is an imperfect creature, and you must not put stumbling-blocks in her path, so that she may trip and fall, but rather clear her road of every obstacle, so that she may run free and unburdened to gain the perfection she lacks, which consists in a good life.

"Naturalists tell us that the ermine is a little animal with a fur of extreme whiteness, and that when hunters wish to catch it they use this trick: they find the places it usually passes and frequents, and stop them up with mud, and then, starting their quarry, they drive it that way. Now, when the ermine reaches the mud it stands still and lets itself be seized and caught rather than pass through the dirt, and soil and lose its whiteness, which it values more than its life and liberty. The chaste and virtuous woman is an ermine, and the virtue of chastity is whiter and purer than snow. If man does not wish her to lose it, but to keep and preserve it instead, he must not treat her like the ermine. He must not put mud in front of her—that is to say the gifts and addresses of importunate lovers—for perhaps—no, certainly—she has insufficient virtue and natural strength to trample down and pass through those obstacles on her own. He must remove them from her way, therefore, and set before her the purity of virtue and the beauty which lies in a good name. For a good woman is also like a mirror of clear and shining glass, which is liable to be stained and dimmed by every breath which touches it. A chaste woman must be treated like holy relics, which are to be adored but not touched. A good woman must be guarded and prized like a beautiful garden full of flowering roses, whose owner does not allow anyone to walk in it or to touch them; enough that they enjoy its fragrance and beauty from afar off through its iron railings. Last of all I want to quote you some verses which have come into my mind, and which I heard in a modern play; they seem to me very much to our present point. A shrewd old man is advising another, the father of a young lady, to look after her, guard her and keep her in the house, and among other reasons he adduces these:

Truly woman's made of glass;
Therefore no one ought to try her
Whether she may break or no,
Seeing all may come to pass.

For the break's the likelier,
And it's very foolish
To risk a thing so brittle
And, once smashed, beyond repair.

So I would have all men dwell
In this sound opinion;
For if Danäes abound,
There are golden showers as well.

"All that I have said to you so far, Anselmo, touches yourself, but now you must hear something from my side. Forgive me if I am long-winded, for the labyrinth you are in, and which you want me to get you out of makes me so. You count me your friend, yet you wish to deprive me of that honour, which is against all friendship. And not only that, but you want me to rob you of your own honour as well. It is clear that you want to deprive me of mine. For when Camilla sees me wooing her, as you wish, she is sure to take me for a man without principles or honour, seeing me attempt something so contrary to my duty to myself and my friendship to you. There is no doubt that you wish me to rob you of your own honour. For when Camilla sees me wooing her she will think that I have detected some lightness in her, that has made me so bold as to reveal my wicked desires to her; and when she considers herself dishonoured, her disgrace will affect you as a part of her. From this arises a well-known situation: although the husband of an adulterous woman does not know her guilt, and has never given his wife an excuse for being what she should not be, or even had it in his power to prevent his misfortune, which does not arise from his carelessness or lack of precaution, he is still called by a vile and opprobrious name, and to some extent regarded with eyes of contempt rather than of pity by those who know of his wife's guilt, even though it is not by his fault, but by his guilty partner's will that misfortune has struck him. But I could tell you the reason why the guilty woman's husband is dishonoured, although he does not know of her wickedness, and is not to blame, and has had no hand in it nor ever given her an excuse for her sin. Do not grow tired of listening; it will all serve for your advantage.

"When God created our first father in the earthly paradise, Holy Scripture tells us that He caused a deep sleep to fall on him, and in

But no sooner had he shut himself in than the landlady attacked the barber, seizing him by the beard and crying, "Bless my soul! You shan't use my ox tail for a beard any more. Give me back my tail, for my husband's what-d'ye-call-it's so kicked about on the floor that it's a shame. I mean his comb that he used to stick into my tail." (page 365) his sleep took one of the ribs of his left side and created our mother Eve; and when Adam awoke and looked on her, he said, 'This is now bone of my bones and flesh of my flesh.' And God said, 'Therefore shall a man leave his father and his mother, and they shall be one flesh.' Then was instituted the divine sacrament of marriage, whose bonds are soluble only by death. This miraculous sacrament has such strength and virtue that it makes two different persons one single flesh; and with happily married couples it does more, for though they have two souls they have only a single will. Hence it arises that, as the flesh of the wife is one with the flesh of the husband, the blemishes which fall on her or the defects she incurs recoil upon the flesh of the husband, although, as I have said, he may be in no respect the cause of the trouble. For, just as the whole body feels the pain of the foot or any other limb, since they are all one flesh; and the head feels the ankle's pain, although it is not the cause of it; so the husband shares his wife's dishonour, being one with her. Now as all this world's honours and dishonours spring from flesh and blood, and the bad wife's are of this kind, part of them must inevitably fall on the husband; and he must be considered dishonoured, even though he does not know of it. Reflect, then, Anselmo, on the danger you expose yourself to in seeking to disturb your good wife's peace. Consider what vain and foolish curiosity it is that prompts you to stir the passions which now lie quiet in your chaste wife's breast. Be warned that you stand to gain little and to lose so unspeakably much that words fail me to express its value. But, if all that I have said is not enough to deflect you from your wicked plan, you must certainly look for someone else to effect your disgrace and misery. For I do not intend to play the part, even though I lose your friendship by refusing; and that is the greatest loss I can imagine."

With these words the virtuous and wise Lothario concluded, and left Anselmo so troubled and thoughtful that he could not reply with so much as a word for some time. But at length he said, "I have listened with attention to all that you have said, Lothario my friend, and your arguments, examples and comparisons prove your great wisdom and perfect friendship. I see too—and I confess it—that if I do not follow your opinion but my own, I shall be abandoning the good and pursuing the evil. Yet, though I admit this, you must consider that I am now suffering from an illness common in women, which makes them long to eat earth, chalk, coal and other worse things, loathsome to the sight and much more loathsome to the palate. It is necessary, therefore, to find some art to cure me; and this can easily be done, if you will only begin to make up to Camilla, even weakly and hypocritically; for she cannot be so frail that her virtue will fall at the first encounter. I shall be content with just a beginning, and then you will have done what our friendship requires, for not only will you be restoring me my life but convincing me that I retain my honour. This you must do for one reason alone, and that is, that as I am determined to put this plan into practice, you cannot allow me to reveal my obsession to any other person, and so endanger my honour which you are so anxious to save. Even if your own does not stand as high as it should in Camilla's estimation, while you are wooing her, that hardly matters at all; for in a very short time, when we find the integrity in her which we expect, you will be able to tell her the simple truth about our plot; and then you will stand as high in her opinion as before. So since you can give me so much happiness at so little risk to yourself, do not refuse to do as I ask, whatever difficulties it may involve for you. For, as I have said, if you will make only a beginning, I will reckon the matter concluded."

When Lothario saw Anselmo's resolution, he did not know what further instances to choose, or what fresh arguments to use, in order to dissuade him. Seeing, therefore, that he threatened to divulge his wicked plan to some one else, he resolved to give in to him, to prevent greater mischief, and to do as he wanted, with the sole object and intention of so managing the business that Anselmo should be satisfied at no cost to Camilla's peace of mind. So he replied by asking his friend not to tell anyone else of his plan, and promised to undertake the enterprise and to begin whenever he pleased. Anselmo embraced Lothario tenderly and affectionately, and thanked him for his offer, as if his friend had done him some great favour. Then the pair of them agreed that the work should begin on the very next day. Anselmo would give Lothario time and opportunity to speak to Camilla alone, and provide him too with money and jewels to offer her as presents. He advised him to serenade her and to write verses in her praise, and if he would not, offered to be at the pains of composing them himself. All this Lothario undertook, though not with the intention which Anselmo imagined; and with this understanding they went back to Anselmo's house, where they found Camilla worried and anxiously awaiting her husband, for he was later than usual in coming back that day.

Lothario went home, leaving Anselmo contented, but very puzzled himself as to what line he should take to get out of this stupid business. But that night he thought of a way of deceiving Anselmo without offending Camilla; and the next day he came to dine with his friend and was welcomed by Camilla, who always received him very cordially, knowing how fond her husband was of him. When they had finished dinner and the table-cloths were removed, Anselmo asked Lothario to stay with Camilla while he went out on some urgent business, from which he would be back within an hour and a half. Camilla begged him not to go, and Lothario offered to accompany him, but all to no purpose. For Anselmo pressed Lothario all the harder to stay till his return, as he had something of great importance to discuss with him. Also he told Camilla not to leave Lothario alone till he got back. In fact, the excuse for his absence was so well sustained that no one could tell it was false.

Anselmo departed, and Camilla remained alone at table with Lothario, for the rest of the household had gone off to dinner. So Lothario found himself engaged in the duel, as his friend desired, facing an enemy capable of conquering a squadron of armed horsemen with her beauty alone. Indeed, Lothario had reason to fear her! But all he did was to place his elbow on the arm of his chair and his hand on his cheek. Then, begging Camilla's pardon for his bad manners, he said that he wanted to take a little rest, till Anselmo's return. Camilla replied that he would rest more comfortably on cushions than in a chair, and begged him therefore to go into the withdrawing room and sleep. But Lotario refused, and stayed there dozing till Anselmo's return. When his friend came back, and found Camilla gone to her room and Lotario sleeping, he concluded that he had been out long enough to give the pair of them time to talk and to sleep as well, and could hardly wait for Lotario to wake, so anxious was he to go out with him and learn what success he had had.

Everything fell out as he wished. Lotario woke up; the pair of them left the house. Then in answer to Anselmo's questions Lotario replied that he had not thought it advisable to reveal himself entirely the first time, and so had merely praised Camilla's beauty, saying that there was no other subject of conversation in the whole city but her loveliness and intelligence. "This," he said, "seemed to me a good way of gaining her confidence and inclining her to listen to me with pleasure next time. It is the method the Devil uses when he wants to deceive the wary. Angel of darkness though he is, he transforms himself into an angel of light, and assumes a cloak of virtue before finally revealing his true character. It is a plan which usually succeeds, unless the deception is discovered at the outset." This satisfied Anselmo, who said that he would give his friend the same opportunity every day. He would not leave the house, however, but would be so busy there that Camilla would not suspect his plot.

After that came many days on which Lotario never spoke a word to Camilla, but told Anselmo that he had talked to her yet never been able to draw from her the slightest sign of encouragement, or even so much as a shadow of hope. On the contrary, he said, she threatened him that she would have to tell her husband if he did not give up his wicked designs.

"That is good," said Anselmo. "Up to now Camilla has resisted words. Now we must see how she resists deeds. Tomorrow I will give you two thousand crowns in gold to offer her—no, to give to her—and the same amount to buy jewels to tempt her. For women, particularly beautiful women, are very fond of being well dressed and looking handsome, however chaste they are. If she resists this temptation I shall be satisfied and trouble you no more."

Lothario answered that, having begun it, he would see the plot through to the end, since he believed that he would come out of it weary and vanquished. The next day he accepted the four thousand crowns in great perplexity, for he did not know what new lie to invent. But, in the end, he made up his mind to tell Anselmo that Camilla was as impervious to gifts and promises as to words, and that there was no purpose in his troubling himself further, since he was wasting his time. But fate guided matters in another way. For when Anselmo had left Lothario and Camilla alone as before, he shut himself into a room and stood at the keyhole, to watch and to listen. And when he saw that Lothario did not throw a single word to Camilla in more than half an hour, and would not have done if he had waited a century, he realized that all his friend had told him about Camilla's replies was nothing but fiction and lies. To make certain of this he came out of the room and, calling Lothario aside, asked him what news he had, and what frame of mind Camilla was in. Lothario answered that he would not budge another step in the business, for she had answered him so sharply and rudely that he had not the courage to speak to her again.

"Oh, Lothario, Lothario," cried Anselmo, "how badly you fulfil your duty to me, and my great trust in you! I was watching you just now through the keyhole of that door, and I saw you did not address a word to Camilla, from which I must infer that you have not said a word yet. If that is so,—and I have no doubt it is—why are you deceiving me? Why are you trying to deprive me, by this trick of yours, of the only means I can find of obtaining my desire?"

Anselmo said no more, but this was enough to leave Lothario abashed and confused. Being caught in a lie Lothario took almost as a blemish on his honour, and he swore to Anselmo that from that moment he would undertake to satisfy him, and tell no more lies, as his friend would see if he watched carefully. But Anselmo need not put himself to any trouble, because what he now intended to do would satisfy him entirely and free him from all suspicions. His friend believed him and, to give him an opportunity free from interruption, decided to leave his house for a week and go to a friend who lived in a village not far from the city. He arranged with this same friend to send and summon him very urgently, so that he should have an excuse for his departure that would satisfy Camilla.

Unfortunate and ill-advised Anselmo, what are you doing? What are you plotting and contriving? See, you are acting against yourself, plotting your own dishonour, and contriving your own undoing. Your wife Camilla is virtuous; in peace and security you possess her; no one interferes with your pleasures; her thoughts do not pass beyond the walls of her house; you are her Heaven upon earth, the goal of her desires, the fulfilment of her joys and the measure by which she rules her will, adapting it in every way to yours and to that of Heaven. Then, since the mine of her honour, beauty, modesty and virtue yields you without any toil all the riches it contains and that you can desire, why must you dig the earth and seek fresh veins of new and unseen treasure? You are taking the risk that everything may collapse, seeing that it is held up only by the feeble props of her frail nature. Remember that by seeking the impossible you may justly be denied the possible or, as a poet has expressed it better:

> In death I seek for life,
> Health in infirmity,
> In jail for liberty;
> I look for rest in strife,
> And faithfulness in treachery.
>
> But envious fate, which still
> Conspires to work my ill,
> With Heaven has decreed
> That easy things shall be denied,
> Since what I crave's the impossible.

Next day Anselmo went to the village, telling Camilla that Lothario would come to look after the house and dine with her while he was away, and that she was to take care to treat him as she would himself. Being a sensible and honest woman, Camilla was distressed at her husband's order, and asked him to consider how wrong it was for anyone to occupy his chair at table while he was away. If this, she said, was because he had no confidence that she could manage the house, let him try for once and learn by experience that she was capable of even greater responsibilities. Anselmo replied that such was his wish, and that she had nothing to do but to bow her head and obey. Camilla acquiesced, though against her will, and Anselmo departed. The next day Lothario came to his house and Camilla gave him an affectionate and modest welcome. She never sat in any room, however, where Lothario might find her alone, but went about surrounded by her men-servants and maids, particularly by her own maid, Leonela, of whom she was very fond. For they had been brought up together from her girlhood in Camilla's parents' house, and she had brought her to Anselmo's when she married him.

For the first three days Lothario did not say a word, though he had an opportunity when the cloth was removed and the household went off to their dinner, which, by Camilla's instructions, was a hurried one. Camilla gave her maid orders to dine before she did and never to leave her side. But the girl had no thought except for her own pleasure, and needed the time for her own affairs. So she did not always comply with her mistresses's orders, but instead left them alone together, as if by instruction. Camilla's modest behaviour and gravity of expression, however, were sufficient to curb Lothario's tongue.

But whatever advantage they gained from Camilla's virtues silencing Lothario's tongue led afterwards to harm for both of them. For, if his tongue was silent, his thoughts ran on; and he had time to contemplate, one by one, Camilla's perfections of mind and body—and they were enough to inspire love in a marble statue, let alone in a heart of flesh. Lothario gazed at her all the time he should have been speaking to her, thinking how worthy of his love she was; and this reflection began little by little to impinge on his respect for Anselmo. A thousand times he made up his mind to leave the city and go where Anselmo would never see him again, nor he Camilla; but his new-found delight in gazing at her prevented him and kept him back. He struggled and fought with himself to resist the pleasure he felt in looking at her. When he was alone he blamed himself for his madness, calling himself a bad friend, and even a bad Christian. He reasoned, and made comparisons between himself and Anselmo; but he always concluded by saying that Anselmo's folly and over-confidence were greater than his own breach of faith, and that, if he had as good an excuse before God as before men, he would fear no punishment for his crime.

In fine, Camilla's beauty and goodness, combined with the opportunity which the ignorant husband had put in his way, completely overthrew Lothario's loyalty; and when Anselmo had been away three days, during which time he had continuously battled to resist his passion, he began to woo Camillla, without thought for anything but his own gratification. He was so impetuous, in fact, and so warm in his language that Camilla got up shocked, and could think of nothing else to do but retire to her room, without answering so much as a word. But Lothario's hopes were not discouraged by her coldness, for hope is always born with love. On the contrary, he valued Camilla even more highly. She, however, seeing this unexpected side of Lothario's character, did not know what to do. But, as it seemed to her neither safe nor proper to give him an opportunity to speak to her again, she decided to send one of her servants to Anselmo that same night with a letter in which she wrote as follows:

⊰ 34 ⊱

The Tale of Foolish Curiosity
continued

*I*t is generally said that an army looks ill without its general and a castle without its warden, and I say that a young married woman looks even worse without her husband, unless he is detained by the most urgent business. I am so badly off without you, and so powerless to bear your absence, that if you do not come quickly I shall have to go and stay at my parents' house, even though I leave yours unguarded. For the guardian you have left me—if he is here in that character—is more concerned with his own pleasures than with your interest. As you are a wise man I need say no more, and it is as well that I do not."

When Anselmo received this letter, he realized that Lothario had begun the enterprise, and that Camilla must have responded as he himself would have wished. So, in extreme delight, he sent to Camilla a message in reply, telling her on no account to move from the house, for he would be back in a very short time. Camilla was astonished at this reply, which threw her into greater confusion than ever; she dared not stay at home, and was even more afraid to go to her parents. For by remaining she would endanger her honour, and in going disobey her husband's orders. Finally she resolved on what proved to be the wrong course, which was to stay, and not to avoid Lothario, for fear of giving her servants cause to talk. And now she was sorry that she had written as she had to her husband, and afraid that he might think that some frivolity in her conduct had encouraged Lothario to forget the respect he owed her. But, confident in her virtue, she trusted in God and in her own resolve to answer anything Lothario might say by silence, and to say no more to her husband about the matter, so as not to involve him in any quarrel or unpleasantness. She even thought out ways of excusing Lothario to Anselmo when he should ask her what had prompted her to write him that letter.

Firm in these resolutions, which did more credit to her honour than to her wisdom, Camilla stayed next day to listen to Lothario, and so pressing was he that her steadfastness began to waver; and her virtue had all it could do to guard her eyes, and prevent their showing signs of the compassion which Lothario's tears and arguments had stirred in her breast. All this Lothario observed, and his desire grew the warmer. In the end it seemed to him necessary to take full advantage of the opportunity which Anselmo's absence gave him, and to intensify the siege of the fortress. So he assailed her self-love with praise of her beauty, for there is nothing which reduces and levels the embattled towers of a beautiful woman's vanity so quickly as this same vanity posted upon the tongue of flattery. In fact, he most industriously mined the rock of her integrity with such charges that Camilla would have fallen even if she had been made of brass. Lothario wept, beseeched, promised, flattered and swore, with such ardour and with such signs of real feeling, that he overcame Camilla's chastity and achieved the triumph which he least expected and most desired.

Camilla gave in; she gave in. But what wonder, if Lothario's friendship could not stand its ground? A clear proof that the passion of love can only be conquered by flight, and that it is vain to struggle against so powerful an enemy. For divine force is needed to subdue the power of the flesh. Only Leonela knew of her mistress's failing,

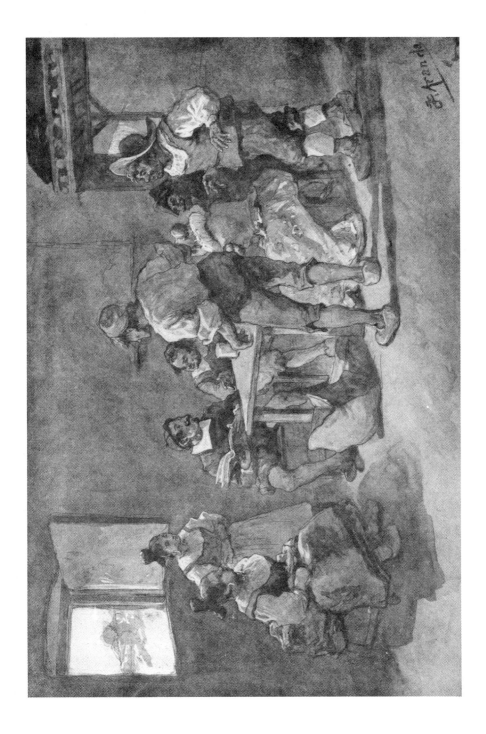

"My friend," pronounced the priest, "these two books are full of lies and foolishness and vanity. But the one about the Great Captain is true history, and relates the deeds of Gonzalo Hernandez of Cordova, whom the whole world deservedly called the Great Captain, on account of his many great exploits." (page 368)

for this pair of treacherous lovers could not conceal it from her. Lothario did not tell Camilla of Anselmo's scheme, nor of his having purposely afforded him the chance of doing what he had done. For he was afraid that she might set less store by his love, and think that it was by chance that he had wooed her, and not by premeditation.

A few days later Anselmo returned, and did not see that the treasure he had held most lightly, yet valued most, was missing. He immediately went to see Lothario, found him at home and, when they had embraced, asked him for the fateful news.

"The news I have for you, friend Anselmo," said Lothario, "is that you have a wife worthy to be called the model and crown of all good women. The words I spoke to her were wasted on the air; my promises she scorned; my gifts she refused; my pretended tears she greeted with open mockery. In fact Camilla is not only the sum of all beauty, but the treasure-house where modesty resides and where dwell gentleness, prudence and all the virtues which make an honest woman praiseworthy and happy. Take back your money, my friend. Here it is. I have had no need to touch it. For Camilla's integrity will not yield to such low things as gifts and promises. Be content, Anselmo, and make no more trials. You have passed dry-shod over a sea of difficulties and dispelled those suspicions which men are bound to have on the subject of women. Do not return to the gulf of fresh disquietudes, nor test with another pilot the good-ness and strength of the ship which Heaven has allotted to you, to bear you over the seas of this world. Consider yourself now safe in harbour, moor yourself with the anchors of happy thoughts, and stay until one comes to demand of you the debt which no privilege of nobility exempts you from paying."

Anselmo was highly delighted at Lothario's speech, and believed in it as firmly as if it had been pronounced by an oracle. But he begged him all the same not to abandon the enterprise, even if it were for nothing more than curiosity and amusement. Although in future, he said, he would not use such urgent methods as he had hitherto. All that he wanted his friend to do was to write some verses in her praise under the name of Chloris. He would give Camilla to

399

understand that his friend was in love with a lady to whom he had given that name, so that he might write to her without injuring her modesty. And, should Lothario not wish to take the trouble to write the verses, he would do so himself.

"There will be no need of that," said Lothario. "The muses are not so much my enemies that they do not visit me now and then during the year. Tell Camilla of this fictitious love affair of mine. I will write the verses, and if they are not as good as the subject deserves, at least they shall be the best I can compose."

So the foolish husband and his treacherous friend agreed. And when Anselmo returned home he asked Camilla her reason for writing him that letter she had sent him. She was surprised he had not asked before, and replied that Lothario had seemed rather freer in his glances than when her husband was at home, but that she now knew she had been mistaken. It had been merely her imagination, for Lothario had avoided seeing her and being alone with her. Anselmo said that she might well dismiss the suspicion, because he knew that Lothario was in love with a noble maiden of the city, and wrote verses to her under the name of Chloris. But, even if he were not, she had no cause to doubt Lothario's loyalty and his great friendship for them both. Now, if Camilla had not been advised by Lothario that this love of his for Chloris was an invention and that he had himself told Anselmo about it so that he could now and then write poems in Camilla's own praise, she would no doubt have fallen into the desperate snare of jealousy, but as she was forewarned she survived this assault unharmed.

The next day, when the three of them were at table, Anselmo begged Lothario to recite some of the verses he had composed for his beloved Chloris. For, as Camilla did not know her, he could safely say what he pleased.

"Even though she did know her," replied Lothario, "I should conceal nothing. For when a lover praises his lady's beauty and taxes her with cruelty he does no harm to her good name. But, however that may be, I will tell you that I wrote a sonnet yesterday on the ingratitude of this Chloris. It runs like this:

"In the dead silence of the peaceful night,
   When others' cares are hushed in soft repose,
   The sad account of my neglected woes
To conscious Heaven and Chloris I recite.
And when the sun with his returning light
   Forth from the east his radiant journey goes,
   With accents such as sorrow only knows
My griefs to tell is all my poor delight.
And when bright Phoebus from his starry throne
   Sends rays direct upon the parched soil,
Still in the mournful tale I persevere;
   Returning night renews my sorrow's toil;
And though from morn to night I weep and moan,
Nor heaven nor Chloris my complainings hear."

The sonnet pleased Camilla much, but Anselmo even more. He was loud in its praises, and said that the lady who did not respond to such patent truth was excessively cruel. And Camilla's comment was, "So everything that these love poets say is true, then?"

"They do not say it as poets," answered Lothario. "But as lovers they are both slow to complain and truthful."

"There is no doubt of that," replied Anselmo, anxious to support Lothario's opinions before Camilla, who had no suspicion of Anselmo's trick, so deeply was she in love with Lothario.

And so, delighted as she was with anything of his and, moreover, taking it that his feelings and verses were addressed to herself and that she was the real Chloris, she begged him to recite another sonnet or poem, if he had one by heart.

"I have," replied Lothario, "but I do not think that it is as good as the first or, to put it better, any less bad. But you can judge, for here it is:

"Fair and ungrateful one, I feel the blow,
   And glory in the near approach of death;
   For when thou seest my corpse devoid of breath,
My constancy and truth thou sure willst know.

401

Welcome to me Oblivion's shade obscure!
Welcome the loss of fortune, life, and fame!
But thy loved features, and thy honoured name,
Deep graven on my heart, shall still endure.
And these, as sacred relics, will I keep
   Till that sad moment when to endless night
   My long-tormented soul shall take her flight.
Alas for him who on the darkened deep
   Floats idly, sport of the tempestuous tide,
   No port to shield him and no star to guide!"

Anselmo praised this sonnet too, as he had the first, and so he went on adding link on link to the chain in which he was embroiling himself and binding up his own dishonour. For the more Lothario dishonoured him, the more he assured him of his unblemished honour. And so the lower Camilla sank into the abyss of infamy, the higher she rose, in her husband's opinion, towards the peak of virtue and renown. Now once, when Camilla was alone with her maid, she happened to say to her, "I am ashamed, Leonela, my friend, to see how cheap I have made myself by not making Lothario spend some time purchasing the full posesssion of what I gave him so quickly and so willingly. I am afraid that he must despise my easiness and lightness, and not realize that he used such violence with me that I could not resist him."

"Do not worry on that score, my lady," replied Leonela, "for it is not worth it. There is no reason why a thing should lose its value because it is easily given, if in fact the gift is a good one and valuable in itself. They even say that he who gives quickly gives twice over."

"Yes," said Camilla, "but they say too that what costs little is little prized."

"That saying does not apply to you," replied Leonela, "because love, I have heard it said, sometimes flies and sometimes walks. With one person it runs, with another creeps; some it cools and some it burns; some it wounds and others it kills; in a single instant it starts

402

on the race of passion, and in the same instant concludes and ends it; in the morning it will besiege a fortress, and by evening it has subdued it, for there is no force that can resist it. That being so, what is it that alarms you and frightens you? For the very same thing must have happened to Lothario, when love took my master's absence as the instrument of your defeat. It was unavoidable that the plan love had determined on should be carried through in that time, and leave no chance of the work's being cut short by Anselmo's return. For love has no better minister to execute its desires than opportunity; it uses opportunity in all its enterprises, but especially in their beginnings. I know all this very well, more by experience than by hearsay, and one day I will tell you, my lady, for I am flesh and blood too, and young blood at that. What is more, lady Camilla, you would never have given yourself over or spoken so soon if you had not first seen Lothario's whole soul in his eyes, in his sighs, in his declarations, his promises and his gifts, and learnt from its perfection how worthy he was of your love. So, since that is the case, do not let these scruples and prudish thoughts seize hold of your imagination, but be certain that Lothario values you as you value him. Be content and satisfied, since you have fallen into love's snare, that your captor is a worthy and honourable man, who not only possesses the four *S*'s, which they say all good lovers should have, but a whole *ABC* as well. Just listen to me, and you will see that I know it by heart. He is, as I see it, and as far as I can judge, Amiable, Bountiful, Courteous, Discreet, Enamoured, Firm, Gallant, Honourable, Illustrious, Loyal, Mild, Noble, Open, Prudent, Quiet, Rich—and the *S*'s, according to the saying—and then, True, Valorous. *X* does not fit him because it is a harsh letter; *Y*—yes, I have said it, and *Z*—he is zealous of your honour."

Camilla laughed at her maid's *ABC*, and concluded that she was more practiced in matters of love than she said. In fact, she confessed as much by telling Camilla that she was having a love affair with a young gentleman of that city, which disturbed her mistress, who feared that this might endanger her own honour. Camilla pressed to know if their affair had gone farther than mere words, and Leonela

403

quite shamelessly and brazenly replied that it had. For it is certain that the mistress's failings rob their maids of all shame. Since, when they see their ladies trip, girls think nothing of stumbling themselves, and do not care if it is known. Camilla could only beg Leonela not to say anything about her mistress's affairs to the young man she said was her lover, and to manage her own with secrecy, so that they should not come to the notice of Anselmo or Lothario. Leonela agreed, but her way of keeping her promise was enough to confirm Camilla's fears that she would lose her reputation through her maid. For the immoral and brazen Leonela, once she saw that her mistress's behaviour was not what it used to be, had the effrontery to bring her lover into the house and keep him there, confident that her mistress would not dare to expose him, even if she were to see him. This is one of the troubles that mistresses pile up for themselves by their sins. Thus they become the slaves of their own maids, and are obliged to conceal their dishonesties and vices, as happened in Camilla's case. For although she very often knew that Leonela was with her lover in one of the rooms of the house, she not only did not dare to scold her, but gave her the chance to hide him, and removed every obstacle from his path for fear that her husband might see him. But she could not prevent Lothario from observing him come out on one occasion at daybreak. At first he did not recognize him, but thought that he must be a ghost. But when he saw him walk away, carefully and cautiously wrapping and muffling himself up, he abandoned this silly notion for another, which would have been the ruin of them all if Camilla had not found a remedy. Lothario did not think that the man whom he had seen leave Anselmo's house at such a strange hour could have gone in for Leonela's sake, for he did not even remember Leonela's existence. He only thought that Camilla was being just as easy and light with someone else as she had been with him. For these are the consequences a bad woman's wickedness brings with it; she loses her reputation for honour with the very man to whose prayers and entreaties she has yielded; and he believes that she gives herself even more easily to others, and places implict credence in any suspicion that comes into his head.

All Lothario's common sense certainly failed him at this juncture, and all his wise reasonings went out of his mind. For without so much as a single sound—or even a reasonable thought—impatient and blind with the jealous rage which gnawed at his entrails, and dying to take vengeance on Camilla, who had done him no sort of wrong, he went without more ado to Anselmo, who had not yet got up, and said, "I must tell you, Anselmo, that I have been battling with myself for a long time, and doing myself violence in not telling you something that it is neither possible nor right for me to conceal any longer. You must know that Camilla's fortress has now surrendered and is at my absolute mercy. If I have delayed in revealing this fact to you, it has only been to see if it were merely a light fancy in her, or if it was to test me and see whether the love I addressed to her by your permission was seriously meant. I believed too that, if she were what she should be and what we both thought her to be she would already have informed you of my wooing. Seeing, however, that she had not yet done so, I realize that the promises which she has given me are in earnest, and that the next time you are away from home she will speak with me in the closet where you keep your valuables."—that in fact was the place where Camilla generally received him—"I do not want you to rush wildly into taking some sort of vengeance. For the sin so far has been commited only in intention, and it may be that, between now and the time for action, Camilla will change her mind and repentance will be born instead. So, since you have always followed my advice, either wholly or in part, take the advice I am going to give you now. Then you will be able to satisfy yourself, without any possibility of error, as to the best measures to take. Pretend to go away for two or three days, as you have done before, but contrive to hide in your closet instead. The tapestries there, and other possible coverings, will make this extremely easy. Then you and I will see with our own eyes what Camilla will do; and if she is guilty, which is possible but by no means certain, you may then silently, cautiously and discreetly avenge your wrongs."

Anselmo was astonished, amazed, stunned, by Lothario's statements, which caught him at a time when he least expected to hear them. For now he thought of Camilla as triumphant over Lothario's pretended assaults, and was beginning to enjoy the glory of her victory. He was silent for some time, gazing at the ground without so much as moving an eyelash. But finally he said, "Lothario you have done all that I expected of your friendship. I must follow your advice in everything. Do what you please, and keep this matter secret. That is the only course in this incredible business."

Lothario promised he would. But by the time he left he had completely repented of what he had said, and realized how stupidly he had acted, since he might have revenged himself on Camilla in a less cruel and dishonourable way. He cursed his stupidity and his feeble resolution. But he was at a loss for a means of undoing what he had done, and could think of no way out. Finally he decided to tell Camilla the whole story and, as there was no lack of opportunity, that same day he found her alone. But as soon as the chance offered it was she who spoke, "Lothario, my friend, my hearts pains me so that I think it will burst in my breast. It will be a miracle if it does not. Leonela's shamelessness has gone so far that she lets her lover into this house every night, and stays with him till morning. It will greatly harm my reputation, for any one who sees him come out of my house at such an unusual hour will be perfectly free to condemn me. What troubles me is that I cannot punish her or scold her, because her knowledge of our affairs puts a bridle on my tongue, and I must be silent about her. I am afraid that some harm will come of this."

At the beginning of this tale of Camilla's Lothario thought that it was a trick to make him believe that the young man whom he had seen come out of the house was Leonela's lover and not hers. But when he saw her tears and her distress, and when she asked for his help, he realized the truth, and in that moment was filled with confusion and remorse. But, for all that, he told Camilla not to worry, for he would contrive a means of stopping Leonela's insolence. He told her, too, what his furious rage of jealousy had driven him to say to Anselmo, and how it was agreed that her husband should hide in the closet and witness her faithlessness to him. He begged her to forgive him this folly, and to advise him how to remedy it and find a way out of the tortuous labyrinth his stupidity had put him into.

Camilla was alarmed at Lothario's story, and turned on him in a great fury with justifiable reproaches, cursing his wicked suspicions and the bad and foolish scheme he had contrived. But, as women have naturally a readier wit for good or for evil than men, although it fails them when they set about deliberate reasoning, Camilla instantly found a way of remedying this seemingly irremediable business. She told Lothario to try to get Anselmo to hide next day in the place he had spoken of, for she thought she could turn this hiding to good purpose. They might, in fact, be able to take their pleasure together in future without any fear of surprise. She did not tell him the whole of her plan, but warned him, once Anselmo was hidden, to be certain to come as soon as Leonela called him, and to answer any questions she might ask him just as he would if he did not know that Anselmo was listening. Lothario pressed her to tell him the whole of her scheme, so that he could do whatever might seem needful with more certainty and caution.

"I assure you," said Camilla, "that there are no more precautions to take. Only answer the questions I shall ask you."

Camilla did not want to tell him her intentions beforehand because she was afraid that he would not follow this plan, which seemed so excellent to her, and might think out another which might not be so good.

At this Lothario went off, and the next day Anselmo left the house, making the excuse of a visit to that friend of his in the country. He then came back to hide, which he conveniently could because Camilla and Leonela had deliberately given him the opportunity. Anselmo was now concealed, and his state of anxiety can be imagined, for he expected to see the very heart of his dishonour laid bare before his own eyes. He saw himself, in fact, on the point of losing the supreme treasure which he supposed that he possessed in his beloved Camilla. Then, once Camilla and Leonela were certain that Anselmo was hidden, they went into the closet; and Camilla was no sooner in than she heaved a deep sigh and said, "Leonela, my friend, before I carry out my intention, which I do not wish you to know for fear you may try to prevent me, would it not be better if you were to take Anselmo's dagger, which I have asked for, and plunge it into this wicked heart of mine? But do not do it; it would not be right for me to bear the burden of another's sin. First I must know what it is that Lothario's bold, licentious eyes saw in me to give him the courage to reveal his evil designs against his friend and against my honour. Stand at that window, Leonela, and call him, for he is certainly in the street, waiting to carry out his wicked purpose. But first I shall carry out mine, which shall be both cruel and honourable."

"Oh, my lady," answered the wily Leonela, who was in the plot, "what are you going to do with that dagger? Do you perhaps mean to take your own life, or Lothario's? Whichever you do will involve the loss of your honour and good name. Better hide your injury, and not give that wicked man a chance to come into the house now and find us alone. Think, my lady, how weak we women are. He is a man, and resolute. And, being bent on such a villainous purpose, in his blind passion he may possibly do something to you that will be worse than murder, before you have a chance of carrying out your plan. I blame my master Anselmo for making that shameless scoundrel so free of his house. But if you kill him, my lady, as I think you mean to, what shall we do with him when he is dead?"

"What then, my friend," replied Camilla. "We will leave him for Anselmo to bury. For he should have the agreeable task of burying his own dishonour. Call him quickly, for every moment I delay in taking due vengeance for my wrong I seem to be failing in the loyalty I owe my husband."

Anselmo was listening to all this, and at each word that Camilla spoke his mind changed. But when he heard that she was resolved to

In his right hand was his naked sword, with which he was lamming out in all directions, shouting all the time as if he were really fighting with a giant. The cream of the joke was that his eyes were not open, because he was asleep, and dreaming that he was battling with the giant. (page 419) kill Lothario he decided to emerge and reveal himself, for fear she might do so. But he was restrained by his desire to see where this spirited and virtuous resolution would end. So he decided only to come out just in time to prevent the act.

At this point Camilla fell into a deep swoon; and Leonela, laying her on a bed which was there, began to weep more bitterly, crying, "Oh, what a misfortune to have, dying here in my arms, the flower of the world's chastity, the crown of pure women, the pattern of virtue!"

And she said so much more in that style that anyone overhearing her would have thought she was the most piteous and faithful maidservant in the world, and her mistress another persecuted Penelope. Camilla was not long, however, in coming round from her faint, and as she came to, she said, "Why do you not go, Leonela, and call that most loyal of friends the sun ever saw or the night hid? Be quick, run, hurry, go, or the fire of my anger may be quenched by the delay and the rightful vengeance I desire pass off in threats and curses."

"I am going to call him now, my lady," said Leonela. "But first you must give me the dagger, for fear you may do something with it while I am away, which would leave all of us who love you weeping for the rest of our lives."

"Do not fear, friend Leonela, I shall not do it," replied Camilla. "For though in your eyes I may seem bold and rash for defending my honour, I shall not be as bold as Lucretia. They say she killed herself although she had committed no crime, and without first slaying the cause of her dishonour. I will die, if I must. But my vengeance must be satisfied on the man who has brought me to this pass, in which I weep for his insolence, though it sprang from no fault of mine."

Leonela required some further entreaties before going out to call Lothario. But at last she went and, whilst awaiting her return, Camilla spoke, as if in soliloquy, "Heaven help me! Would it not have been better to have sent Lothario away, as I have often done before, and not have allowed him, as I have done now, to think me dishonest and wicked, if only for the little time I must wait before undeceiving him. It would certainly have been better, but then I should not be revenged; nor would my husband's honour be satisfied if he were to escape so neatly and easily from the predicament his wickedness has brought him into. Let the traitor pay for his lecherous desires with his life. Let the world know—if it ever does—that Camilla not only kept faith with her husband, but avenged him on the man who dared to offend him. Yet perhaps it would be better to tell Anselmo of this. Though I have already hinted at it in the letter I sent to him in the country. Seeing that he did not hasten to remedy the trouble I wrote of, I can only imagine that pure goodness and trustfulness prevents his believing that so much as a thought of his dishonour can dwell in the breast of so staunch a friend. I did not believe it myself for a long while, and I should never have believed it if his insolence had not grown so great, and his open bribes, his grand promises and continual tears had not made it clear to me. But, why all these speeches now? Can a brave resolution have need of any arguments? No, indeed no! Away with you, then, traitors! Now for vengeance! Let the false villain enter; let him come; let him draw near; let him die and be done with, come what may! Pure I came into the possession of the husband Heaven gave me; pure I must go from him, even though I go bathed in my own chaste blood, and in the impure blood of the falsest friend that ever was in all the world."

As she talked, she paced about the room with the dagger unsheathed, taking such uneven and unsteady strides, and striking such gestures, that she seemed to be out of her wits. She was like no delicate woman, but a desperate ruffian.

All the while Anselmo looked on in utter amazement, concealed behind some tapestries. What he had seen and heard already seemed to him sufficient to refute even graver suspicions, and he would willingly have dispensed with the further proof upon Lothario's arrival, for he was afraid of some sudden disaster. But, as he was on the point of showing himself and emerging to embrace and reassure his wife, he stopped. For Leonela returned leading Lo-

412

thario by the hand. And as soon as Camilla saw him she drew with the dagger a long line on the floor before her, and said:

"Listen to me, Lothario. If you dare by any chance to pass beyond this line here, or even to approach it, I will plunge this dagger I hold in my hand into my breast, the moment I see you are going to. Now, before you reply by so much as a word, I want you to hear me speak. Afterwards you may answer as you please. Tell me first, Lothario, if you know my husband Anselmo, and what opinion you hold of him. And next, I want to know whether you know me. Answer me. Do not be confused or hesitant in your replies, for these are not riddles that I am asking you."

Lothario was not so stupid as not to have realized Camilla's plan when she told him to make Anselmo hide. So he fell in with her scheme most cleverly and aptly, and the pair of them made their imposture pass for truer than truth itself. Therefore he answered Camilla in this way, "I did not think, beauteous Camilla, that you had summoned me to ask me questions so far from the purpose for which I have come. If your intention is to put off granting the favour you promised, you might have postponed it from a greater distance. For the nearer our hopes of possession the more we are tormented by our desires. But, so that you shall not accuse me of not replying to your questions, I will answer that I know your husband Anselmo, and that we have known one another since our tenderest years. Of our friendship I will say nothing. You know all about that, and I do not want to testify against myself. But the wrong I am doing, love—which excuses the greatest of faults—compels me to do. You too I know, and I value you as highly as he does. If that were not so, for lesser charms than yours, I should not have transgressed the holy laws of friendship, which I have now broken and violated at the instigation of that mighty enemy love."

"If you confess to that," replied Camilla, "mortal enemy of all true love, how can you have the effrontery to appear before the woman whom you know to be his very mirror and reflection? If you would look at yourself in her eyes you would see how little excuse you have for wronging him. But now, poor wretch that I am, I know

413

what has made you break your faith. It must have been some lightness in me. I will not call it immodesty, for it did not spring from deliberate design. It was just one of those indiscretions into which women often carelessly fall when they think that reserve is unnecessary. But tell me, traitor, when did I answer your entreaties with so much as a word or sign that could awaken any shadow of hope in you of accomplishing your wicked desires? When were your words of love not sternly and bitterly and scornfully rejected? When did I accept your presents, or believe in your many promises? But I know that no one can persevere in his wooing unless sustained by some hope. So I will take the blame for your insolence, for no doubt it is my negligence that has made you persist in your suit so long. I will punish myself, therefore, and inflict the penalty of your guilt upon myself. I have brought you here to see that, being so cruel to myself, I could not be anything but cruel to you, and so that you may witness the sacrifice I intend to make to the wounded honour of my most honoured husband. You injured him with the greatest possible deliberation, and I by my lack of precaution in giving you an opportunity—if I did so—of furthering your wicked desires. What troubles me most, I repeat, is my suspicion that some carelessness of mine bred these rash thoughts in you. And that I most fervently desire to blot out with my own hands; for if I were to have any other executioner, my guilt would be more public.

"But before I die, I mean to satisfy my desire for vengeance, and take with me the man who has reduced me to this desperate plight. For when in that other place, wherever it may be, I see the punishment which impartial and unswerving justice will award him, I shall be completely satisfied."

As she spoke she sprang upon Lothario with incredible strength and swiftness, flourishing the naked dagger; and so determined she appeared to bury it in his heart that even he was almost uncertain whether her demonstrations were false or true. For he had to use all his dexterity to prevent her stabbing him.

So convincingly did she perform her extraordinary act of deceit and fraud that she even shed her own blood to lend it colour. Finding that she could not wound Lothario—or pretending that she could not—she said, "Though fate denies me complete satisfaction, at least it shall not be so strong as to prevent my attaining it in part."

At this she wrenched her dagger-hand free from Lothario's grasp and, pointing the knife where it could not wound her deeply, she stabbed herself, burying the weapon above her breast under her left shoulder. She then let herself fall to the ground, as if in a faint.

Leonela and Lothario were speechless with astonishment at this unexpected act, and did not know what to think when they saw Camilla stretched on the ground, and bathed in her own blood. Breathless and shaken with fright, Lothario hurriedly ran to pull out the dagger. But when he saw how small the wound was his fears vanished, and he was amazed afresh at the fair Camilla's ingenuity, coolness and ready wits. But, to play his part, he broke into a long and doleful lament over her body, just as if she were dead, calling down great curses upon himself and also on the man who had been the cause of the catastrophe. And, knowing that his friend Anselmo was listening, he spoke so that anyone hearing him would have pitied him even more than Camilla, even if he had supposed that she was dead. Leonela took her in her arms and placed her on the bed, begging Lothario to go and find someone to attend to her in secret. She asked him also to advise her what they should say to Anselmo about his mistress's wound, if he were to return before she was healed. He replied that they might say what they pleased, for he was no person to give useful advice. He only told her to try to staunch the blood, for he was going where no man should see him again. Then he left the house with a great show of grief and emotion. But, once he was alone and unobserved, he could not stop crossing himself in amazement at Camilla's ingenuity and Leonela's very apt acting. He reflected how positive Anselmo must be that his wife was a second Portia, and longed to meet him so that they might rejoice together at the most plausible imposture imaginable.

Leonela staunched her mistress's blood as she was told, though there was only just enough to make her performance convincing. Then she washed the wound with a little wine, and bound it up as

415

best she could, making such an outcry as she did so that, even if nothing had been said before, that alone would have been enough to convince Anselmo that in Camilla he possessed the image of chastity. To Leonela's protestations Camilla added others of her own. She reproached herself for cowardice, and for lacking the courage to end her own days at that moment when it was most necessary, for life was abhorrent to her. She asked her maid's advice whether she should tell her beloved husband all that had happened or not, and Leonela advised her not to. For this would compel him to take vengeance on Lothario, which would involve him in great risk to himself. It was a good wife's duty, said the maid, to give her husband no occasion for quarrels, but rather to save him as many as she could. Camilla replied that this was good advice, and that she would follow it; but they would certainly have to find some explanation of her wound, for Anselmo would not fail to see it. Leonela's only reply to this was that she could not tell a lie, even in jest.

"Then how should I, my dear?" asked Camilla. "I should not dare to invent or brazen out a lie if my whole life depended on it. If we cannot think how to get out of this fix, it would be better to tell him the naked truth than for him to catch us out in a lying tale."

"Do not worry, my lady," replied Leonela. "Between now and tomorrow I will think out something to say. Perhaps you may be able to hide the wound, it being where it is, and he will not see it. Then Heaven may smile on the justice of our case. Be calm, my lady, and try to control your feelings, so that my master shall not find you upset. Leave the rest to me and to God, who always aids good intentions."

Anselmo had stood listening and watching with rapt attention at this tragedy representing the death of his honour, and performed by the players with such strange and moving passion that they seemed transformed into the very characters they were acting. He longed for night, which would give him an opportunity of slipping out of the house and going to his friend Lothario, to rejoice with him over the pearl which he had found, in the unveiling of his wife's virtue. The pair of them took care to give him an opportunity of getting away, and he took advantage of it to go immediately in search of Lothario. It is impossible to recount how often he embraced him when he found him, what he said in his delight and how much he praised Camilla. Lothario listened to all this without being able to show any signs of joy, for he could not get out of his mind the thought of how greatly his friend was deceived and how cruelly he had wronged him. But, although Anselmo noticed that Lothario did not show any joy, he supposed that it was because Camilla had been wounded and he had been responsible. So, in the course of their conversation, he told him not to worry about Camilla's accident, for the wound must certainly be a slight one, since they had agreed to hide it from him. Lothario, in fact, had nothing to fear, he said, but should rejoice and be gay with him, since it was through his friend's means and contriving that he had been raised to the highest attainable peak of happiness. What was more, he would have no other pastime from that day on but to write verses in Camilla's praise, to render her memory eternal for future ages. Lothario commended his resolution and promised to assist him in raising so noble an edifice.

From that time on Anselmo was the most deliciously deluded man in the whole world. He himself led home by the hand the man who had completely destroyed his good name, in the firm belief that he had brought him nothing but glory. Camilla received Lothario with seemingly averted glances but with a smiling heart; and this deception lasted for some time, until after many months Fortune turned her wheel, their cunningly concealed wickedness became public and Anselmo's foolish curiosity cost him his life.

⋠ 35 ⋟

Of the Fierce
and Monstrous Battle which Don Quixote
fought with Some Skins of Red Wine,
with the Conclusion of
the Tale of Foolish Curiosity

*V*ery little more of the tale
remained to be read when Sancho Panza rushed in alarm from the
loft where Don Quixote was lying, shouting at the top of his voice,
"Come quickly, gentlemen, and help my master. I've never seen
such a fierce and stubborn battle as he's got himself into. God in
Heaven! He's dealt that giant, the lady Princess Micomicona's
enemy, such a slash that he's sliced his head clean off like a turnip."

"What's that you say, brother?" asked the priest, leaving the
rest of the tale unread. "Are you in your senses, Sancho? How the
devil can all that be true, seeing that the giant is six thousand
miles away?"

Here they heard a tremendous noise in the room and Don
Quixote shouting, "Hold, thief, scoundrel, braggart! Ah, I have you
at last. Your scimitar will not help you now."

And he seemed to be slashing at the walls.

Then Sancho said, "You shouldn't stand there listening. You
ought to go in and get between them, or go to my master's aid.

Though there'll be no need now, for the giant's certainly dead by now, and giving an account to God of the wicked life he's led. I saw his blood on the floor, and his head cut off and fallen on one side. It's as big as a great wine-skin."

"Good God!" exclaimed the innkeeper at this point. "If that Don Quixote, or Don devil, hasn't been slashing at one of the skins of red wine at the head of his bed! Full they were, and what this fellow takes for blood must be the wine spilt on the floor."

With that he ran into the room, and the others after him. They found Don Quixote in the strangest outfit in the world. He was in his shirt, which was not long enough in front to cover his thighs completely, and was six inches shorter behind. His legs were very long and thin, covered with hair, and not over-clean. On his head he wore a little greasy red cap which belonged to the innkeeper, and round his left arm he had wound the blanket of the bed—against which Sancho bore a grudge, and very well he knew why. In his right hand was his naked sword, with which he was lamming out in all directions, shouting all the time as if he were really fighting with a giant. The cream of the joke was that his eyes were not open, because he was asleep, and dreaming that he was battling with the giant. For his imagination was so bent on the adventure which he was going to achieve, that it made him dream he had got to the kingdom of Micomicon and was already at grips with his enemy.

What is more, he had slashed the wine-skins so many times, in the belief that he was getting at the giant, that the whole room was flooded with wine. At the sight of this the innkeeper flew into such a fury that he fell on Don Quixote, and began punching him repeatedly with his clenched fists. Indeed if Cardenio and the priest had not pulled him off he would soon have put an end to the war with the giant. But, despite all this, the wretched knight did not wake up until the barber brought a large pitcher of cold water from the well and threw it with a jerk all over his body. This awakened Don Quixote, but not sufficiently for him to realize the state he was in. Seeing how lightly and scantily he was dressed, Dorothea did not care to go in and see the battle between her champion and her adversary; and as for Sancho, he went about looking all over the floor for the giant's head and, not finding it, observed, "Now I know that everything about this house is enchanted. The last time, right in this very spot where I'm standing, I got a regular punching and beating, yet I never knew who gave it me and never saw anybody at all. And this time the head isn't to be found, though I saw it cut off with my own eyes, and the blood pouring from the body like a fountain."

"What blood and what fountain are you talking about, enemy of God and His saints?" cried the innkeeper. "Can't you see, you great thief, that your blood and your fountain are nothing else but these skins here, which are slashed through, and the red wine which this room is swimming in? I should like to see the soul of the man who slashed them swimming in hell."

"All I know," replied Sancho, "is that I'm going to be very unlucky. If I don't find that head, my countship will melt away like salt in water." For Sancho awake was worse than his master asleep, so obsessed was he with the promises which his master had made him.

The innkeeper was in despair at the imperturbability of the squire and the damage which his master had done, and swore that this time he should not get away without paying, as he had done the time before, and that the privileges of knighthood should not save him from settling both reckonings, down to the very cost of the patches which would have to be stuck on to the torn wine-skins.

The priest was holding Don Quixote down by the hands, when, thinking that he had finished the adventure and was now in the presence of Princess Micomicona, the knight dropped on his knees before him and said, "Exalted and most famous lady, Your Highness may henceforth live secure from any ill this low-born creature may do you; and, from today too, I also am released from the pledge which I gave you. For, by the help of God on high and through the favour of her for whom I live and breathe, I have perfectly fulfilled it."

"Wasn't that just what I said?" exclaimed Sancho, when he heard this. "So I wasn't drunk then. It looks as if my master has pickled the

The four horsemen, who had a very well-bred appearance and bearing, dismounted and helped the lady down from her side-saddle. (page 430) giant sure enough. The bulls are all right; I'm sure of my countship."

Could anyone have kept from laughing at the nonsense of these two, master and servant? Everyone did laugh except the innkeeper, who cursed his luck. At length the barber, Cardenio, and the priest managed, with no little labour, to get Don Quixote into the bed, where he dropped off to sleep in a state of great exhaustion. They left him sleeping and went out to the inn door to console Sancho Panza for not having found the giant's head, although they had more to do to pacify the innkeeper, who was in despair at the sudden death of his wine-skins. The landlady too was shouting and screaming, "It was an ill wind which blew that knight errant into my house. I wish I'd never set eyes on him, so dear he's cost me! Last time he went off he owed us for the night. Supper and bed for him and his squire, straw and barley for a horse and an ass. He said that he was a knight adventurer—God send a bad end to his adventures, and the like to all other adventurers in the world!—and that he wasn't supposed to pay anything, that it was written so in the knight errantry regulations. And now, because of him, there comes this other gentleman and takes away my tail, and gives it me back with a pretty pennyworth of damage, with the hair all off, so that it's no good any more for what my husband wants it for. And on top of all that, to burst my wine-skins for me and spill out the wine. I'll see his blood spilt, I will! He shan't get away with it. By my poor father's bones and my blessed mother's grey hairs, if they don't pay me every single penny I'm not called what I am, and I'm not my father's daughter!"

This and more like it the landlady poured out in a great fury, and her good maid Maritornes backed her up, but her daughter kept quiet and smiled from time to time. The priest quieted them down by promising to compensate them for their loss as far as he was able, both for the skins and for the wine, and especially for the damage to the tail, which they made so much of. Dorothea consoled Sancho Panza by promising that, as soon as ever it was certain that his master had cut off the giant's head and once she was in peaceful possession of her kingdom, she would give him the best countship in it. At this Sancho took comfort, vowing that she could be certain that he had seen the giant's head, and, as proof more positive, that the monster had had a beard down to his waist. But, if it did not turn up, it was because everything which happened in that house was bewitched, as he had found the last time he had stayed there. Dorothea said that she believed him, and that he had no need to worry, for all would go well and turn out to his heart's content.

When everyone was quiet the priest expressed a wish to finish reading the tale, for he saw that there was very little left. Cardenio, Dorothea, and all the others begged him to do so and, being anxious to please them all, besides wanting to read it himself, he went on with the story.

So it came to pass that through the satisfaction which Anselmo took in Camilla's virtue he led a happy and carefree life; and Camilla purposely looked sourly on Lothario, so that Anselmo should take her feelings for him to be the opposite of what they were. And to reinforce this pretence, Lothario asked leave not to come to the house, saying that he could clearly see how much Camilla disliked seeing him. But the deluded Anselmo replied that he would not agree on any account; and thus in a thousand ways Anselmo was the architect of his own dishonour, while he believed that he was making happiness for himself. At this time Leonela's pleasure in finding herself licensed in her love affair reached such a pitch that she pursued it unrestrainedly without any other thought, confident that her mistress would screen her, and even show her how to carry it on without arousing more than slight suspicion. But finally, one night, Anselmo heard steps in Leonela's room and, when he tried to go in and see who it was, found the door barred against him; which made him the more eager to force it. He pushed so hard, in fact, as to prise it open, and broke in just in time to see a man leap out of the window into the street. But when he ran quickly to catch him or see who he was, he could do neither, because Leonela clung to him, crying, "Calm yourself, my lord, and don't make a disturbance. Don't follow the man who jumped out there. It's my affair; in fact he's my husband."

Anselmo would not believe her, but blind with rage, drew his dagger and tried to wound her, commanding her to tell him the truth or he would kill her. Then, out of fear, and not knowing what she was saying, she exclaimed, "Do not kill me, sir, and I will tell something more important than you can imagine."

"Tell me, then, at once," said Anselmo. "If not, you are a dead woman."

"I can't just now," said Leonela. "I'm so upset. Give me till tomorrow, and then I'll tell you something which will amaze you. But I swear to you that the man who jumped out of this window is a young man of this city, who has given me his word that he will marry me."

Anselmo was satisfied with this, and content to wait the time she asked, for he did not expect to hear anything against Camilla, so absolutely satisfied was he of her virtue. So he went out of the room and left Leonela locked up, saying that she would not be let out till she had told him all that she had promised to reveal.

Then he went straight to Camilla and told her all that had passed between him and her maid, and of her promise to tell him something great and important. There is no need to say whether Camilla was alarmed or not. For so great was her fright, believing as she did and had good reason to, that Leonela was going to tell Anselmo all that she knew about her unfaithfulness, that she had not the courage to wait and see whether her suspicions were justified or not. That same night, when she thought that Anselmo was asleep, collecting her finest jewels and some money, she left the house unobserved and went to Lothario's. Once there, she told him what had happened, and begged him to find a hiding-place for her, or to take her away somewhere where they would both be safe from Anselmo. Lothario was thrown into such confusion that he could not answer a single word, still less make up his mind what to do. In the end he decided to take Camilla to a nunnery of which one of his sisters was prioress.

Camilla agreed to this, and with the swiftness which the situation demanded Lothario took her and left her at the nunnery, then himself immediately quitted the city, informing no one of his departure.

When the day broke, so eager was Anselmo to learn what Leonela was going to tell him that he did not notice Camilla's absence from his side, but got up and went to the room where he had left the maid locked up. He opened the door and went in, but could not see Leonela. All he found were some sheets knotted to the window-bars—evidence that she had climbed down and fled. Then he returned at once rather sorrowfully to tell Camilla, and was astounded not to find her in bed or anywhere in the house. He asked the servants where she was, but no one could answer his question. Then, by chance, as he was searching for her, he noticed that her boxes were open and most of her jewels missing. From this he began to realize his disaster, and that Leonela was not the cause of his trouble. So, just as he was, without troubling to finish dressing, he went sadly and dejectedly to tell his friend Lothario of his misfortune. But when he found him gone, and his servants told him that their master had departed that night and had taken all the money he had with him, he thought he would go out of his mind. And on top of all this, when he got back to his house he found not one of the men or maid-servants there, and the house silent and deserted.

He did not know what to think or say or do, but little by little his wits seemed to be returning to him. He reflected, and saw himself at one blow wifeless, friendless and servantless, seemingly abandoned by the Heavens above and, worst of all, robbed of his honour. For in Camilla's flight he saw his own damnation. Finally, after a long while, he resolved to go to his friend in the country, with whom he had stayed when he had given them their opportunity of contriving the whole disaster. He locked the doors of his house, mounted his horse and with failing heart set out on the road. But he had gone no more than half-way when, harassed by his thoughts, he was compelled to dismount and tie his horse to a tree, at the foot of which he lay down, heaving piteous and sorrowful sighs. There he stayed almost till nightfall, when he saw a man coming on horseback from the city, of whom, after greeting him, he asked what news there was in Florence.

"The strangest news that we've heard there for many a long day," replied the townsman. "It's publicly reported that Lothario, Anselmo's great friend, the rich man who used to live at San Giovanni, carried off Anselmo's wife Camilla last night, and that Anselmo himself is also missing. All this was revealed by a servant of Camilla's, whom the Governor found, last night also, letting herself down from the window of Anselmo's house by a sheet. I don't know, indeed, exactly what happened. I only know that the whole city is amazed at the business, for such a thing was most unexpected, considering the great and intimate friendship between these two. It was so remarkable that they're supposed to have been called *The Two Friends.*"

"Do you know by any chance," asked Anselmo, "what road Lothario and Camilla have taken?"

"I've no idea," replied the townsman, "although the Governor has been very active in looking for them."

"God be with you, sir," said Anselmo.

"And with you," replied the townsman and rode off.

At this disastrous news Anselmo was not merely on the point of going out of his mind, but on the verge of putting an end to his life. He got up as best he could, and reached the house of his friend, who had not yet heard of his misfortune. But when he saw him come in, pale, exhausted and haggard, he realized that some serious misfortune had befallen him. Anselmo begged them at once to help him to bed and give him some writing materials, which they did, and left him alone in bed with the door locked, just as he asked. Once alone, he was so overwhelmed by the thought of his disaster that he clearly saw his life was drawing to a close. So he decided to leave an account of the cause of his strange death. He began to write. But before he had finished setting down all he wished his breath failed him, and he yielded up his life into the hands of that grief which his foolish curiosity had brought upon him. The master of the house, seeing that it was late and Anselmo had not called out, decided to go in and find out if he was any worse. He discovered him lying on his face, with half of his body on the bed and the other half on the desk, and with the paper he had written unsealed and the pen still in his hand. But, seeing that he did not respond and finding him cold, he realized that he was dead. Amazed and deeply grieved, he called his household to see the disastrous end that had befallen Anselmo and, later, read the paper on which he recognized Anselmo's hand. It said:

> A foolish and ill-judged craving has cost me my life. If the news of my death should come to Camilla's ears, let her know that I pardon her. For she was not obliged to perform miracles nor did I need to ask her to. So, since I was the contriver of my own dishonour, there is no reason why—

Anselmo had written only so far, and it was clear that his life had ended before he could finish his sentence. The next day his friends advised Anselmo's relations of his death. They already knew of his misfortune and of Camilla's retreat to the nunnery, where she was almost in a state to accompany her husband on his inevitable journey, not because of the news of his death, but from what she had heard of her absent lover. It was said that, although she was now a widow, she would not leave the nunnery, nor even less take nun's vows. But not many days later news reached her that Lothario had been killed in a battle, which took place just then between Monsieur de Lautrec and the great Captain Gonzalo Hernandez de Cordoba, in the kingdom of Naples where Anselmo's friend had retired, repentant too late. When Camilla heard this news she made her profession as a nun, and not long afterwards yielded her life into the cruel hands of sorrow and melancholy. This then was the end of these three, arising from such foolish beginnings.

"I like the tale," said the priest, "but there is something unconvincing about it. If the author invented it he did it badly, for it is impossible to believe that there could be a husband so stupid as to want to make the costly experiment Anselmo did. If it were a case of a lover and his mistress it might pass, but between husband and wife there is something impossible about it. Though as for the manner of its telling, that does not displease me at all."

⊀ 36 ⊁

Of Other Strange Events at the Inn

Just then the landlord, who was standing at the inn door, called out, "Here's a fine troop of guests coming. If they stop here we can sing "Praise the Lord."

"What sort of people?" asked Cardenio.

"Four men on horseback," replied the innkeeper, "riding with short stirrups, with lances and shields, and all in black travelling-masks. There's a woman dressed in white with them riding side-saddle, with her face covered too, and two others, servants, on foot."

"Are they very near?" asked the priest.

"So near," replied the landlord, "that they are here already."

Hearing this, Dorothea veiled her face, and Cardenio went into Don Quixote's room; but they had hardly had time to do this when the whole party the host had described came into the inn. The four horsemen, who had a very well-bred appearance and bearing, dismounted and helped the lady down from her side-saddle. Then one of them took her in his arms and seated her in a chair, which stood at the entrance of the room where Cardenio had hidden. All this time neither she nor they had taken off their masks, nor said a word.

Only, as she sat down, the lady in the chair heaved a deep sigh, and let her arms fall, as if she were ill or in a faint. The servants then led the horses to the stable.

The priest looked on and, wishing to know who these people were, so strangely dressed and so silent, went over to the servants and asked one of them. His answer was, "Indeed, sir, I can't tell you who they are. All I know is that they seem to be important people, especially the man you just saw take the lady in his arms. Why I think so is because all the others pay him respect, and do nothing but obey his orders and directions."

"And who is the lady?" asked the priest.

"I couldn't say either," answered the servant, "for I haven't set eyes on her face the whole way. I have only heard her sigh very often and moan as if she were ready to give up the ghost. It's not surprising that we don't know more than we've told you, because my mate and I have only been with them for the last two days. We met them on the road, and they begged and persuaded us to come with them as far as Andalusia, and offered to pay us very well."

"Have you heard the name of any of them?" asked the priest.

"No, I haven't," answered the servant. "They all ride in perfect silence. It's very queer. The only sound we hear from any of them is the poor lady's sighs and sobs, which make us feel sorry for her. It's our firm belief that she's being forced to go wherever it is she's going and, as far as we can gather from her dress, she's a nun, or is going to become one more likely. Perhaps it's because she isn't taking the veil of her own free choice that she looks so sad."

"That is very possible," said the priest, and left them, to join Dorothea, whose natural pity was so stirred by the sighs and groans of the lady in disguise, that she went up to her and asked, "What is your trouble, dear lady? If it is anything that it is in a woman's power to relieve, I would most willingly help you."

The sorrowful lady made no reply and, although Dorothea repeated her offer, she remained silent till the masked horse-man—the one whom the servant had said the others obeyed—came up and said to Dorothea, "Do not weary yourself, lady, by showing this woman any courtesy, for she is always most ungrateful for whatever is done for her; and do not press her to reply if you do not want to hear her tell you some lie."

"I have never told one," exclaimed the lady, breaking her silence at this point. "It is because I have been so truthful and so guileless that I am in my present unhappy plight. I call you as a witness to that, since it is the pure truth in me which shows you up as a false liar."

Cardenio heard these words clearly and distinctly, as he was extremely near the speaker, only the door of Don Quixote's room being between them; and directly they came to his ears he cried out, "Good God! What is that I hear? What voice is that?"

The lady turned her head in alarm at these cries and, not seeing who it was that spoke, rose to her feet and made to go into the room. But the gentleman immediately held her back and would not let her move a step. In her disturbance and agitation, however, her mask fell off, revealing a face of marvellous and incomparable beauty, though pale and frightened. For her eyes searched every spot within sight in such distress that she seemed to be out of her mind; and Dorothea, and all who saw her, were filled with pity for her, though they did not understand the reason for her behaviour. The gentleman held her firmly by the shoulder, but was so busy keeping his grip that he could not manage to hold up his mask, which in the end fell off. So when Dorothea, who had caught the lady in her arms, looked up, she saw that the man who was also holding her was her husband, Don Ferdinand; and the moment she recognized him she fell back senseless, uttering a deep and heartfelt groan. In fact if the barber had not been close by and caught her in his arms, she would have fallen to the ground. The priest at once hastened to take off her veil and throw water in her face; and as soon as he uncovered it, Don Ferdinand—for he it was who was holding the other lady in his arms—recognized her and was almost struck dead by the sight. Nevertheless he did not let go of Lucinda—for she it was—who was struggling to get free from his arms, having recognized Cardenio by his cry, as he had recognized her. Cardenio also heard Doro-

With these words he embraced her once more, pressing his face to hers with such tender feeling that it was all he could do not to burst into tears in true sign of his love and repentence. But Lucinda, Cardenio, and almost all the rest of the company as well, showed no such restraint. (page 440) thea's moan as she fell fainting and, thinking that it was Lucinda's, rushed terrified out of his room. The first person he saw, however, was Don Ferdinand, holding Lucinda in his arms; and as Don Ferdinand also recognized Cardenio at once, all three, Lucinda, Cardenio, and Dorothea, were struck dumb with amazement, hardly knowing what had happened to them.

They all gazed at one another in silence, Dorothea at Don Ferdinand, Don Ferdinand at Cardenio, Cardenio at Lucinda, Lucinda at Cardenio. But the first to break the silence was Lucinda, who addressed Don Ferdinand, "Leave me, Don Ferdinand, out of regard for yourself if for no other reason. Let me cling to the wall of which I am the ivy, to the prop from which neither your persistence, your threats, your promises, nor your bribes have been able to part me. See how Heaven, by ways strange and mysterious to us, has brought me to my true husband; and well you know by a thousand costly proofs that only death can blot him from my memory. So let this plain declaration tell you—since you have no alternative—to turn your love to rage, your affection to hatred, and put an end to my life. Yet, as I shall die before the eyes of my dear husband, I shall account my life well lost. For it may be that he will be convinced by my death that I have kept faith with him to the last act of my life."

During this time Dorothea had come to herself, and had been listening to the whole of Lucinda's speech, from which she had realized who she was. Then, seeing that Don Ferdinand still did not let her go or reply to her words, she summoned up all the strength she could, got up, and threw herself on her knees at his feet. Then, bursting into a flood of lovely and piteous tears, she began to speak, "If, my dear lord, the rays of that sun which you are holding in eclipse within your arms have not dimmed and darkened the light of your eyes, you will have seen that she who kneels at your feet is, as long as you will have it so, the luckless and unhappy Dorothea. I am that humble country girl, whom you chose, out of your kindness or for your pleasure, to raise to the height where she could call herself yours. I lived a contented life, enclosed within the bounds of virtue

435

until, at the voice of your persistent and seemingly genuine and loving affection, I opened the gates of my modesty and entrusted the keys of my liberty to you, a gift which you appreciated very little, as is clearly shown by my being forced to hide in the place where you find me now, and by my seeing you as I do now. But, for all that, I would not have you think for one moment that I have come here along the road of dishonour; grief alone has brought me here, and sorrow at seeing myself deserted by you. It was your wish that I should be yours; and you wished it to such effect that, although now you would not have it so, it will be impossible for you ever to cease to be mine. Think, my lord, that the matchless love I have for you may be a compensation for the beauty and nobility of her for whom you are deserting me. You cannot be the fair Lucinda's, because you are mine; nor can she be yours, because she is Cardenio's. It will be easier, if you will think a moment, to make your heart love the woman who loves you, than to force into loving you a woman who loathes you. You pursued my innocence; you wore down my integrity with your prayers; you were not ignorant of my rank; well you know how completely I gave myself up to your will; you have no ground or reason to plead deception. If that is the truth, as it is, and you are a Christian and a gentleman, why do you put off, with all these evasions, making me as happy at the end as you did at the beginning? If you do not want me for what I am, your true and lawful wife, desire me at least and have me for your slave. For if I am in your possession I shall count myself happy and fortunate. Do not leave me and abandon me so that my shame becomes the subject of gossip, or cause my parents a miserable old age. For they have given your parents loyal tenant's service and do not deserve such treatment. If you think that your blood will be debased by mixing with mine, reflect that there is little or no nobility in the world which has not travelled the same road, and that descent on the woman's side is not what counts in the most distinguished lineage. Moreover true nobility lies in virtue and, if you forfeit that by denying me my just rights, I shall be left with higher claims to it than you. Finally, sir, my last word is that I am still your wife, whether you like it or not.

Your own promise is a witness which must not and cannot speak falsely, if you pride yourself on possessing what you despise me for lacking. Let your own signature testify, and Heaven, which you invoked to bear testimony to your promise. Should all these fail, your own conscience cannot but whisper in the midst of your joys, repeating the truth I have just spoken to disturb your greatest pleasures and delights."

The unhappy Dorothea said this, and more like it, with such feeling and tears that everyone present sympathized with her, including even the men who had come with Don Ferdinand. That gentleman himself listened without answering a word till she finished speaking, and broke into such sobbing and sighing that only a heart of bronze would not have been melted by signs of such distress. Lucinda stood gazing at her, pitying her grief and admiring her good sense and her beauty. But, although she wanted to go and say something to comfort Dorothea, Don Ferdinand still held her tight in his arms and prevented her. Though, after gazing fixedly at Dorothea for some time, he was overwhelmed with shame and horror, and opened his arms to let Lucinda go.

"You have conquered, fair Dorothea," he said. "You have conquered. I cannot possibly have the heart to deny a combination of so many truths."

When Don Ferdinand released her, Lucinda almost fell down from the faintness that had seized her. But Cardenio was close by, having taken up his position behind Don Ferdinand so as not to be recognized—and, setting fear aside, he defied all danger, ran up to catch her, and clasped her in his arms.

"If merciful Heaven," he cried, "be pleased to grant you some rest at last, my loyal, steadfast and lovely lady, nowhere, I believe, will you find it more securely than in these arms which clasp you now as they clasped you once before, when Fortune was pleased to let me call you mine."

At these words, Lucinda, who had first begun to recognize him by his voice, fixed her gaze on Cardenio and, assuring herself with her eyes that it was he, almost beside herself and regardless of the proprieties, threw her arms around his neck. Then, putting her face close to his, she said, "Yes, my dear lord, you are the true master of this slave of yours, however much adverse fortune may oppose us and threaten this life of mine, which depends on yours."

This was a strange spectacle for Don Ferdinand, and for all the rest, who were astonished at such unforeseen happenings. Dorothea, however, seeing Don Ferdinand change colour and move his hand in the direction of his sword, imagined that he intended to take his revenge on Cardenio, and instantly, with extraordinary quickness, clasped him round the knees, kissing them and holding them so fast he could not move. Then, without ceasing her tears, she said, "What is it you mean to do, you who are my only refuge in this unexpected crisis? Here at your feet is your wife, and the woman you desire is in her husband's arms. Reflect whether it will be right or possible for you to undo what Heaven has done; or whether it will not be better to decide to raise to your level one who stands before you, steadfast in her faith and constancy despite all obstacles, and bathing her true husband's face and breast in loving tears. For God's sake, and your own, I beg you not to let this public exposure increase your anger, but rather to allay it; so that you may be able calmly and peacefully to suffer these two lovers to live all the days that Heaven allows them, without any hindrance from you. In that way you will show the generosity of your illustrious and noble soul, and the world will see that reason has more power over you than passion."

While Dorothea was speaking Cardenio did not take his eyes from Don Ferdinand, even though he held Lucinda in his arms. For he was determined, if he saw him make any hostile movement, to defend himself, and to resist any attack to the uttermost, even at the cost of his life. But at this point Don Ferdinand's friends—with the priest and the barber, who had been present all the time, and even honest Sancho Panza—all surrounded Don Ferdinand, imploring him to be moved by Dorothea's tears and, if she was speaking the truth, as they believed she was, not to suffer her to be defrauded of her just expectations. They begged him to reflect that it was not by chance, as it appeared, but by a special providence of Heaven, that they had all come together in such an unexpected place. The priest warned him, too, that only death could part Lucinda and Cardenio, and that they would joyfully accept their death, even if they were sundered by the sword's edge. In these irremediable circumstances, he said, it would be wisdom to restrain and conquer himself, and to show a generous heart by allowing these two, of his own free will, to enjoy the good fortune which Heaven had granted them. If he would turn his gaze on Dorothea's beauty, he would see that few or none could equal her, much less excel her. And besides her beauty he should consider her humility and her very great love for him. Above all, he must remember that, if he counted himself a gentleman and a Christian, he could not fail to honour his promises, and in doing so he would be doing his duty to God and be applauded by all men of good sense. For they know and recognize that it is the prerogative of beauty, even though in a humble subject, to rise equal to any dignity. For so long as it is united with virtue, it casts no shadow of reflection on the man who raises it to his own level. For where the strong laws of passion obtain, so long as there is no sin no man can be blamed for obeying them.

In short, he added so many compelling arguments that Don Ferdinand's valorous heart—which was, after all, nurtured by generous blood—softened, and allowed itself to be conquered by the truth, which he could not deny if he would. And the sign he gave of his surrender and acceptance of the priest's good advice, was to stoop down and embrace Dorothea saying, "Rise, my lady! The woman I hold in my heart must not kneel at my feet. If I have given no proof of what I say till now, perhaps it has been by Heaven's decree, that by seeing how faithfully you love me I might know how to value you as you deserve. What I beg of you is not to upbraid me for my misconduct and my neglect, for the same compelling reason which moved me to win you for mine drove me to struggle against being yours. For proof that this is true, turn and look into the eyes of the now happy Lucinda. There you will find an excuse for all my errors. Now, since she has obtained her desires, and I have found my fulfilment in you, I wish her a long and peaceful life, safe and happy

439

with her Cardenio, and I pray Heaven to grant me the same happiness with my Dorothea."

With these words he embraced her once more, pressing his face to hers with such tender feeling that it was all he could do not to burst into tears in true sign of his love and repentance. But Lucinda, Cardenio, and almost all the rest of the company as well, showed no such restraint and began to shed so many tears, some for their own happiness and some for others', that it might have been thought some grievous disaster had befallen them all. Even Sancho Panza wept, though he said afterwards that he was only crying at finding that Dorothea was not, as he had believed, that Queen Micomicona from whom he had expected such benefits. It was some time before the general weeping and amazement calmed down; and then Cardenio and Lucinda went down on their knees before Don Ferdinand and thanked him so courteously for the kindness he had shown them that he did not know how to reply. So he raised them up and embraced them with every mark of politeness and affection.

Then he asked Dorothea to tell him how she had come to that place so far from her home. She told him, briefly and sensibly, all that she had previously told Cardenio; and Don Ferdinand and his companions were so delighted with her story that they would have liked it to last longer, so charmingly did she tell the tale of her misfortunes. As soon as she had finished, Don Ferdinand related what had happened to him in the city, after he found the paper in Lucinda's breast in which she had declared that she was Cardenio's wife and could not be his. He said that he had wanted to kill her, and would have done so if her parents had not prevented him. Then he had left the house angry and ashamed, and determined to take his revenge on a more convenient occasion. On the next day he had learnt that Lucinda had left her parents' house and that no one could say where she had gone; and finally, after some months, he had discovered that she was in a nunnery and intended to spend the rest of her life there, if she could not spend it with Cardenio. As soon as he had learnt of this he had chosen those three gentlemen for his companions and gone to the place where she was. But he would not speak with her for fear that, if they knew he was there, the convent would be better guarded. So he had waited for a day when the porter's lodge was open, and left two of his companions to secure the door, while he and the third had gone into the nunnery to look for Lucinda, whom they had found in the cloisters talking to a nun. Then they had snatched her up without giving her a chance to resist, and taken her to a place where they provided themselves with everything necessary for her abduction. All this they had been able to do in perfect safety as the nunnery was in the country, a good way outside the town. He said that when Lucinda found herself in his power she lost all consciousness, and when she came to herself did nothing but weep and moan, and never spoke a single word. So, to the accompaniment of silence and tears, they had reached the inn, which to him was like reaching Heaven, where all the ills of the earth are over and done with.

◀ *37* ▶

A Continuation of the History
of the Renowned Princess Micomicona,
and Other Pleasant Adventures

*T*o all this Sancho listened in no
small distress of mind, seeing that his hopes of a title were disappearing and going up in smoke, since the lovely Princess Micomicona had turned into Dorothea, and the giant into Don Ferdinand, while there was his master sound asleep and quite oblivious of all that had happened. Dorothea could not feel certain that her happiness was not a dream. Cardenio was in the same state, and Lucinda's thoughts ran a similar course. Don Ferdinand gave thanks to Heaven for favours received, and for extricating him from the intricate labyrinth in which he had been within an ace of losing his honour and his soul. And everyone at the inn was pleased and delighted too, at the happy turn which this difficult and desperate situation had taken. The priest, like a man of sense, set everything in its true light, and congratulated everyone on what each had gained. But the most joyful and contented person in the inn was the landlady, because of the promise which Cardenio and the priest had made her to pay her all the cost and damage she had suffered on Don Quixote's account. Only Sancho, as we have said, felt wretched, disappointed and sad; and so, with a melancholy expres-

sion, he went in to his master, who was just then waking up, and said, "You can sleep soundly for as long as you like, Sir Sad Countenance, and not trouble about killing any giant or restoring the Princess to her kingdom. For it's all done and finished already."

"I believe you," replied Don Quixote, "for I have fought the most monstrous and outrageous battle with that giant that I ever expect to fight in all the days of my life. With one back stroke— whack!—I slashed his head to the ground; and so much blood poured from him that it ran in streams along the earth, just like water."

"More like red wine, you might say," answered Sancho; "for I would have your worship know, if you don't already, that the dead giant is a slashed wine-skin, and his blood the twelve gallons of red wine it had in its belly, and the head you cut off is—my bitch of a mother—and the devil take the lot!"

"What is that you say?" retorted Don Quixote. "You must be crazy, man!"

"If your worship will get up," said Sancho, "you'll see what a fine job you've done, and what we shall have to pay. And you'll see the Queen turned into an ordinary lady called Dorothea, and the other things which will make you wonder, when you get the hang of them."

"I should marvel at nothing of that sort," replied Don Quixote. "Last time we were here, if you remember rightly, I told you that everything which happened in this place was by way of enchantment. So it would not be surprising if it were the same this time."

"I should believe it all," answered Sancho, "if my blanket-tossing had been that sort of thing. But it wasn't. It was real and true enough. I saw this innkeeper, who is here today, holding one end of the blanket, bouncing me up and down in fine trim, and laughing for all he was worth. I may be a simpleton and a sinner, yet it's my opinion that where you start recognizing people there's no enchantment about it, but plenty of bruising and bad luck."

"Well, God will remedy that," said Don Quixote. "Give me my clothes and let me go out there. I want to see these changes and transformations you speak of."

Sancho handed him his clothes, and while he was dressing, the priest told Don Ferdinand and the others of Don Quixote's madness, and of the trick they had played to get him away from the Bare Rock where, as he imagined, his lady's disdain had brought him. He told them too almost all the adventures which Sancho had described to him, at which they wondered and laughed quite a bit, thinking, like everyone else, that it was the strangest kind of madness that ever attacked a distraught mind. The priest said also that, since the lady Dorothea's good fortune would prevent their going on with their scheme, they would have to invent and work out another way of bringing him home to his village. Cardenio, however, offered to carry on with the original plan and suggested that Lucinda should take over and play the part of Dorothea.

"No," cried Don Ferdinand, "that must not be. I wish Dorothea to carry on the scheme herself. This good knight's village cannot be very far away, and I shall be very glad to see him cured."

"It is not more than two days' journey from here."

"Even if it were more I should be glad to make the journey for such a good purpose."

At this moment Don Quixote came out, armed with all his gear; with Mambrino's helmet, bashed in as it was, on his head, grasping his shield, and leaning on his tree-branch, or lance. Don Ferdinand and the others were astounded at his extraordinary appearance, and gazed upon his face, half a mile long, shrivelled and sallow, his miscellaneous weapons and his grave bearing in attentive silence until, staring very solemnly and intently on the fair Dorothea, the knight pronounced, "I am informed, beauteous lady, by this squire of mine that your greatness has been cast down and your very being destroyed, since, from the Queen and great lady that you were, you have turned into a humble maiden. If this has been by command of the necromancer King, your father, out of his fear that I shall not give you due and necessary aid, I say that he has never known, and does not know, the half of his art, and that he has very little acquaintance with histories of chivalry. For, had he read them and studied them as attentively and as much at his leisure as I have, he

"If your worship will get up," said Sancho, "you'll see what a fine job you've done, and what we shall have to pay. And you'll see the Queen turned into an ordinary lady called Dorthea, and the other things which will make you wonder, when you get the hang of them." (page 443)

would have found at every step how other knights, of less renown than I, have achieved things much more difficult. For it is no great matter to kill a paltry giant, however arrogant he may be. Not very long ago, in fact, I fought with him myself and—I prefer to be silent, in case I may be accused of falsehood. But time, which unveils all mysteries, will reveal this one when we least expect it."

"It wasn't a giant you fought, but two wine-skins," put in the innkeeper at this point. But Don Ferdinand told him to be quiet and on no account to interrupt Don Quixote's remarks. Then the knight went on, "Indeed, as I say, exalted and disinherited lady, if for the reasons I have stated your father has performed this meta-morphosis in your person, you should put no trust in him at all. For there is no peril on earth through which my sword cannot cleave a way, and in the shortest time I can cast your enemy's head to the earth and place the crown of your country upon yours."

Don Quixote said no more, but waited for the Princess's reply, and she, knowing that Don Ferdinand intended to continue the deception until they had brought Don Quixote home, answered very gracefully and gravely, "Whoever told you, valorous Knight of the Sad Countenance, that I have altered and transformed myself, did not tell the truth, for I am the same today as I was yesterday. It is true that certain strokes of good fortune have worked some change in me, by giving me the desire nearest to my heart. But, for all that, I have not ceased to be the person I was before, nor to have the same intention as I have always had, of availing myself of the might of your valorous and invincible arm. Therefore, dear sir, of your grace, restore his honour to the father who begot me and think of him as a man far-seeing and wise, in that he found by his science such an easy and certain way of remedying my misfortune. I believe, sir, that if it were not for you, I should never have succeeded in gaining the happiness I have; and in this I speak nothing but the truth, as most of these gentlemen here will bear witness. All that remains is for us to set out on our way tomorrow, for we shall not be able to travel far today. And the rest of the good fortune that I expect, I will leave to God and the valour of your heart."

So spoke the subtle Dorothea and, when he had heard her, Don Quixote turned to Sancho, and said with signs of great indignation, "Now I tell you, miserable Sancho, that you are the most despicable rogue in Spain. Tell me, you vagabond thief, did not you say just now that this Princess had turned into a damsel called Dorothea, and that the head, which, as I believe, I cut off a giant, was the bitch that bore you, and all sorts of other nonsense that put me into the greatest perplexity I have ever known in all the days of my life? I swear"—he looked up to Heaven and gritted his teeth—"that I have a mind to work such havoc on you as will put salt into the brainpans of all the lying squires of knights errant in the whole world, from now till the end of time."

"Please be calm, my dear master," replied Sancho. "It's very possible that I was mistaken in the matter of the lady Princess Micomicona's transformation. But as for the giant's head, or rather the piercing of the skins, and the blood being red wine, I swear to God I'm not mistaken. For there the skins lie slashed at the head of your worship's bed, and the red wine has turned the room into a lake. If you don't believe me, you'll see it when the eggs are fried—I mean when his honour the innkeeper here asks you to pay for all the damage. As for the rest, my heart rejoices that the lady Queen is the same as she always was, for I shall get my share and so will every neighbour's child."

"Now really, Sancho," said Don Quixote, "you are a loon, forgive the expression. And now let us drop the subject."

"Enough," said Don Ferdinand. "Let no more be said of the matter and, since the lady Princess says that we must ride on tomorrow because it is too late today, let us do so. We shall be able to spend the night in pleasant conversation till daybreak. Then we will all bear Don Quixote company, for we are anxious to witness the valorous and incredible exploits he is to perform in the course of this great enterprise which he has undertaken."

"It is I who shall serve you and bear you company," replied Don Quixote, "and I am very grateful for the favour you have done me and the high opinion you have of me, which I shall try to justify, or it shall cost me my life—and even more, if that is possible."

Many compliments and offers of service passed between Don Quixote and Don Ferdinand. But they were all cut short by a traveller who entered the inn at that moment, a man who by his dress seemed to be a Christian newly arrived from the land of the Moors. He wore a short blue cloth cape with half sleeves and no collar, his breeches were of linen and blue also, and he wore a cap of the same colour. He had long boots, date-brown, and a Moorish short sword slung on a strap across his breast. Behind him on an ass came a woman dressed in Moorish fashion, with her face covered and a veil on her head, wearing a little cap of gold brocade, and swathed in a cloak which enveloped her from her shoulders to her feet. The man was of a robust and pleasant appearance, a little more than forty, rather dark-skinned, with long moustaches and a very well-trimmed beard. It was obvious, in fact, from his appearance that if he had been well dressed he would have passed for a person of birth and quality.

On entering he asked for a room, and seemed annoyed when he heard that there was not one to be had in the inn; but going up to his companion, who seemed from her dress to be Moorish, he lifted her down. Lucinda, Dorothea, the landlady, her daughter, and Maritornes were attracted by the novelty of her dress, which was strange to them, and gathered round the Moorish lady; and Dorothea, who was always charming, courteous and sensible, seeing that both she and her escort were troubled at there being no room, said to her, "Do not be concerned, dear lady, at the lack of accommodation here, for it is the way of inns to have none. But, all the same, if you would care to lodge with us"—pointing to Lucinda—"perhaps you would find your reception better than some you may have met with in the course of your journey."

The veiled lady made no answer, but simply got up from her seat and, crossing her hands on her breast and bowing her head, inclined her body from the waist in token of thanks. From her silence they concluded that she must certainly be a Moor and not know the Christian tongue. Presently the gentleman who up to then had been busy with other things, drew near and, seeing that they were all grouped round his companion and that she did not reply to anything they said, remarked, "Ladies, this young woman can hardly understand our language, and can only speak the tongue of her own country. She has not replied to your questions because she cannot."

"The only thing we have asked her," replied Lucinda, "is whether she will accept our company for tonight and share our sleeping-room, where she shall have as much comfort as the accommodation will allow. We will do her every kindness, for we are bound to serve all strangers who are in need, and women most of all."

"On her behalf and mine," replied he, "I kiss your hands, my lady, and value your offer as highly as it deserves. For on an occasion like this, and from such people as your appearance shows me you are, it is clearly a great favour."

"Tell me, sir," said Dorothea, "is this lady a Christian or a Moor? For her dress and her silence make us think that she is what we hope she is not."

"Moorish she is in body and dress, but in her soul she is a very good Christian, for she has the greatest desire to become one."

"Then she is not baptised?" asked Lucinda.

"There has been no opportunity," replied he, "since we left Algiers, her country and her home; and up to now she has not been in such instant peril of death as to be obliged to receive baptism without first being instructed in all the ceremonies our Mother, the Holy Church, requires. But, please God, she will soon be baptised with the formalities due to her rank, which is greater than her dress or mine shows."

This answer roused the curiosity of all the party to know who the Moorish lady and the gentleman were. But no one cared to ask just then, for at that time of night it was clearly better to help them get some rest than to ask them questions about their lives. Dorothea took the Moorish lady by the hand, made her sit down beside her, and asked her to take off her veil. But the stranger looked towards her escort, as if to ask him what they were saying and what she should do. He told her in Arabic that they were asking her to take off her veil, which she did, revealing a face so lovely that Dorothea thought her more beautiful than Lucinda, and Lucinda judged her lovelier than Dorothea, while the others were of the opinion that if any woman was the equal to those two in looks it was the Moorish lady; and some of them thought that in some ways she was the loveliest of the three. Now as it is the privilege of beauty to win over all hearts and attract all minds, everyone yielded instantly to the desire of waiting on the lovely Moor.

Don Ferdinand asked her escort for her name, and he replied that it was Lela Zoraida; but when she heard his answer, understanding what the Christian had asked, she broke in hastily and charmingly, though in some dismay, "No, no, Zoraida; Maria, Maria"—giving them to understand that her name was not Zoraida but Maria.

Her words and the feeling with which she spoke drew tears from some of her hearers, especially from the women, who were naturally tender-hearted. Lucinda embraced her most warmly and said, "Yes, yes, Maria, Maria."

And the Moorish lady replied, "Yes, yes, Maria; Zoraida *macange*"—that is to say, not Zoraida at all.

Meanwhile night had fallen, and under the supervison of Don Ferdinand's companions the innkeeper had taken considerable pains to provide the best supper he could. So, when the time came, they all sat down together at a long refectory table, for there was not a round or a square one in the inn. They gave the most important seat at the head to Don Quixote, though he repeatedly declined it. And he asked the lady Micomicona to sit beside him, since he was her protector. Next Lucinda and Zoraida took their places, and opposite them Don Fernando and Cardenio, beside them the newcomer and the rest of the gentlemen, and next to the ladies the priest and the barber. So they ate their supper with great pleasure, which grew still greater when they saw Don Quixote leave off eating and, moved by the same spirit that had prompted his long speech when he supped with the goatherds, prepare to address them, "Most truly, gentlemen, if the matter be deeply considered, great and most extraordinary are the experiences of those who profess the order of knight errantry. For who is there of all men living upon earth who would judge us and know us for what we really are, if he were to come in now through the gate of this castle and see us as we appear at present? Who would be able to guess that this lady at my side is the great queen we all know her to be, and that I am that Knight of the Sad Countenance, so trumpeted by the mouth of Fame? Now there is no doubt that this art and exercise is greater than any discovered by man, and must be the more highly valued the more perils it is subject to. Away with those who say that Letters have the advantage over Arms. For I will tell them that they do not know what they are saying, whoever they are. The argument which such people generally use, and on which they most rely, is that the labours of the spirit are greater than those of the body, and that Arms is only an exercise of the body; as if the practice of it were mere labourer's work for which nothing is needed but sheer bodily strength; or as if the pursuit of what we, who follow it, call the profession of arms, did not entail acts of courage that require great intelligence to carry them through; or as if a warrior commanding an army or defending a besieged city does not labour with his mind as well as with his body. Let it be shown, then, how by mere bodily strength he can come to guess at and know the enemy's intentions, plans, stratagems and traps, and how foresee what dangers are impending; for all these are activities of the mind, in which the body plays no part. Seeing, therefore, that Arms, like Letters, require intelligence, let us consider now which of the two performs the greater mental labour, the man of letters or the man of war; for this will be decided by the end and object at which each is aiming—since the purpose which has the noblest end in view must be the more highly valued. The end and object of learning—I am not speaking now of theology, whose goal is to aid souls on the way to Heaven, for no other aim can be compared to a purpose so infinite as that—I am speaking of the humanities, whose aim is to maintain impartial justice, to give every man his rights, to make good laws, and to see that they are kept. That is certainly a lofty and generous aim, and highly praiseworthy, though not so much so as the profession of Arms, whose aim and object is peace, the greatest good which men can desire in this life. For the first good news the world and mankind received was proclaimed by the angels on that night which was our day, when they sang in the sky, 'Glory to God in the highest and peace on earth to men of good will'; and the greeting which the best Master on earth or in Heaven taught His favoured disciples to give when they entered a house was, 'Peace be to this house.' And many other times He would say, 'My peace I give unto you; my peace I leave with you; peace be with you'; which, given and bequeathed by such a hand, was a jewel and a treasure, indeed such a jewel that there can be no happiness on earth or in Heaven without it. This peace is the true aim of war, for Arms and war are all one. Admitting then this truth, that the aims of war are peace, and that thereby it excels the art of Letters, let us come now to the bodily hardships of the scholar and of the man whose profession is Arms, and see which are the greater."

Don Quixote pursued his discourse so rationally and in such well-chosen language that none of his hearers could possibly take him for a madman just then. On the contrary, as most of them were gentlemen connected with the profession of Arms, they listened with great pleasure, as he went on speaking, "I say then that the hardships of the student are, first of all, poverty (not because they are all poor, but to put the case as strongly as possible) and when I say that they suffer poverty I do not think that there is anything more to say about their misery, for the poor man lacks everything that is good. This poverty they suffer in various forms, sometimes hunger, sometimes cold, sometimes nakedness, sometimes all of them together. But, all the same, things are not so bad that they do not eat, although it may be a little later than they are used to, or from the leavings of the rich man's table; for what students call 'going on the soup', or begging for their supper, is their worst misery. And

453

moreover they do share someone's brazier or hearth, which may not warm them but at least takes the edge off the cold; and, last of all, they sleep under cover at night. I do not want to go into other details—lack of shirts, for instance, and shortage of shoes, or scanty and threadbare clothing—or to describe their way of stuffing themselves over-eagerly when Fortune sends them a feast. But by the rough and difficult path which I have indicated, stumbling at times and falling, getting up and falling once more, they do acquire the degree they desire. And when they have got it, I have seen many of them, once passed through those shoals, those Scyllas and Charybdises, as if borne on the wings of Fortune's favour—I say that we have seen them command and govern the world from an armchair, their hunger exchanged for a full stomach, their cold for a pleasant coolness, their nakedness for fine clothes and their sleep on a mat for comfortable rest on fine linen and damask, the justly merited rewards of their virtue. But if we set their hardships against those of the militant soldier and compare them, they are left far and away behind, as I shall now explain."

❧ *38* ❧

Don Quixote's Curious Discourse
on Arms and Letters

*D*on Quixote then went on,
"Since we began in the case of the student by dealing with his
poverty and its circumstances, let us consider whether the soldier is
any richer. We shall see that he is the poorest of the poor. For he is
limited to his wretched pay, which comes either late or never, or to
what he can loot with his own hands, at considerable risk to his life
and his conscience. Sometimes too he is so naked that a slashed
doublet serves him both for uniform and for shirt, and in the open
field in the depth of winter he has nothing to warm him against the
inclemencies of heaven but the breath of his mouth which, coming
out of an empty place, must certainly come out cold, against all the
laws of nature. But wait till night-fall, for then he can rest from his
discomforts in the bed which awaits him, and which, except by his
own fault, will not sin by being too narrow. For he can measure out
as many feet as he likes on the earth, and roll about to his heart's
content without fear of the sheets rumpling up. Then, at last, comes
the day and the hour for him to receive his degree in his art; the day
of battle dawns, when they will put on him a doctor's cap made of

lint, to heal some bullet wound which may have pierced his temples or left him maimed in arm or leg. And if this does not happen, but merciful Heaven preserves him and keeps him whole and alive, he will very likely remain in the same poverty as before; and there must needs be one skirmish after another and one battle after another, and he must come out victorious from every one, before he has any success at all; but such miracles rarely occur. Now tell me, gentlemen, if you have ever considered it, how many more perish by war than profit by it? Unquestionably your reply will be that there is no comparison. For there is no counting the dead, and those who have benefited by war and survived can be reckoned in three figures.

"It is quite the reverse with scholars; for by their salaries—I will not say by their perquisites—they have all enough to make do, so that although a soldier's hardships are greater, his rewards are less. But you may reply that it is easier to reward two thousand scholars than thirty thousand soldiers; because scholars are rewarded by the gift of posts given to men of their profession, but soldiers cannot be recompensed except out of the very poverty of the lord they serve. This impossibliity makes my argument even stronger.

"Leaving this on one side, however, for it is a very difficult labyrinth to find a way out of, let us come back to the pre-eminence of Arms over Letters—a question which remains still to be resolved, since each puts up so many arguments on its own behalf. Besides those which I have given, the scholars say that without them arms could not survive. For war too has its laws and is subject to them, and laws fall within the province of letters and learning. But to this Arms reply that laws could not surivive without them; because by Arms states are defended, kingdoms preserved, cities guarded, the roads kept safe, and the seas swept free of pirates. In short, if it were not for them, states, kingdoms, monarchies, cities and the highways on land and sea, would be subject to the savagery and confusion which war entails, so long as it lasts and is free to exercise its privileges and powers.

"What is more, it is a well-known truth that what costs most is,

Meanwhile night had fallen, and under the supervision of Don Ferdinand's companions the innkeeper had taken considerable pains to provide the best supper he could. So, when the time came, they all sat down together at a long refectory table, for there was not a round or a square one in the inn. They gave the most important seat to Don Quixote, though he repeatedly declined it. (page 451) and should be, the most highly valued. Now to attain eminence in the learned professions costs a man time, nights of study, hunger, nakedness, headaches, indigestion and other such things, some of which I have mentioned already. But to reach the point of being a good soldier, requires all that it requires to be a student, but to so much greater a degree that there is no comparison; for the soldier is in peril of losing his life at every step. What fear of poverty or want that can befall or afflict a student can compare with the fear a soldier knows when he is besieged in a fortress, on watch or guard in some redoubt or strongpoint, knowing that his enemies are mining towards the spot where he is, and that he may on no account leave his post, or run away from the danger which threatens him so closely? The only thing which he can do is to inform his captain of what is happening, in the hope that he will meet the situation with a counter-mine; and he must stand calmly, though in fear and expectation of suddenly rising to the clouds without wings and sinking again to the depths against his will. If this seems a small danger, let us see if it is equalled or surpassed in the head-on collision of two galleys in the midst of the high seas. For when ships are locked and grappled together, the soldier has no more space left him than two feet of plank on the beak-head. But though he sees in front of him countless pieces of artillery threatening from the enemy's side, each a minister of death, and no more than a spear's length from his body, and though he knows that at his first careless step he will go down to visit the deep bosom of Neptune, nevertheless with undaunted heart, sustained by the honour which spurs him on, he exposes himself as a mark for all their shot and endeavours to pass along that narrow causeway into the enemy's ship. And, most amazing of all, no sooner does one man fall, never to rise again this side of Doomsday, than another takes his place; and if he, in turn, falls into the sea, which lies in wait for him like an enemy, another, and yet another, takes his place, without a moment passing between their deaths, the greatest display of valour and daring to be found in all the hazards of war. Blessed were the times which lacked the dreadful fury of those diabolical engines, the artillery, whose inventor I

firmly believe is now receiving the reward for his devilish invention
in hell, an invention which allows a base and cowardly hand to take
the life of a brave knight, in such a way that, without his knowing
how or why, when his valiant heart is fullest of furious courage,
there comes some random shot—discharged perhaps by a man who
fled in terror from the flash the accursed machine made in firing
—and puts an end in a moment to the consciousness of one who
deserved to enjoy life for many an age. And when I think of that, I
am tempted to say that it grieves me to the heart to have adopted this
profession of knight errantry in such a detestable age as we now live
in. For although no danger frightens me, still it causes me misgivings
to think that powder and lead may deprive me of the chance of
winning fame and renown by the strength of my arm and the edge
of my sword, over all the known earth. But let Heaven do what it
will. If I achieve my purpose, I shall be the more highly esteemed for
having faced greater dangers than did the knights errant of past
ages."

All this long rigmarole Don Quixote spoke whilst the others
were eating their supper, forgetting to put a mouthful into his mouth
although Sancho Panza urged him several times to eat, with
the remark that he would have time to say all he wanted to afterwards. His hearers were moved once more to pity at seeing a man,
apparently of such sound intelligence and with such understanding
of everything he spoke of, lose it so entirely on the subject of his foul
and accursed chivalry. The priest said that there was much
justice in all that he had said in favour of arms, and that he was of
the very same opinion himself, although a scholar and a graduate.

Then, their supper finished, the table-cloths were removed, and
whilst the landlady, her daughter and Maritornes were clearing up
Don Quixote de la Mancha's attic, where they had decided that the
women should be lodged by themselves that night, Don Ferdinand
asked the newcomer to tell them his life's story. For, from so much
as they had gathered by his coming in Zoraida's company, it could
not fail to be strange and enjoyable. He replied that he would most
gladly comply, only he feared that his story would not give them as

much pleasure as he would like. But he would tell it all the same, rather than appear disobliging. The priest and all the others thanked him and pressed him to begin, and when he found them all so urgent he assured them that there was no need of entreaties, for their mere request was enough.

"Listen then, gentlemen, and you will hear a true story, and I doubt whether you will find its equal in the most detailed and careful fiction ever written."

At these words they all sat down in perfect silence, and when he saw them quiet and waiting for him to speak, he began in a smooth and pleasant voice.

⟦ *39* ⟧

The Captive tells the Story of
His Life and Adventures

*M*y family had its origin in a
village among the mountains of Leon; and nature was kinder and
more generous to them than fortune was, although in those very
poor villages my father had the reputation of being rich; and indeed
he would have been if he had been as good at keeping his money as
he was at spending it. This liberal and wasteful disposition of his
came from his having been a soldier in the days of his youth. The
soldier's trade is a school in which the mean man learns to be liberal
and the liberal man prodigal; for if there are sometimes soldiers who
are misers, they are, like monsters, rarely seen. My father passed the
bounds of liberality and verged on those of prodigality, a quality
which is no advantage to a married man with children to inherit his
name and station. My father had three, all sons and all of an age to
choose their professions. So, seeing that he could not, as he said,
bridle his nature, he decided to deprive himself of the cause and
means which made him a prodigal and a spendthrift, in other words,
to give up his estate, without which Alexander himself would have
been reckoned a miser. So, calling us all three one day into a room
alone, he addressed us in some such way as this, 'My sons, to assure
you that I love you, it is quite enough to say that you are my sons;

and to convince you that I do not love you, it is enough to say that I do not control myself in order to preserve your fortune. But so that you may know in future that I love you like a father and do not want to ruin you like a stepfather, I intend to do something for you, which I have been thinking over for a long time, and have decided on after mature consideration. You are of an age to take up a calling, or at least to choose some profession that will bring you honour and profit when you are older. My plan is to divide my estate into four parts. Three of them I will give you, an absolutely equal portion for each side, and I shall live on the fourth part for as long as Heaven is pleased to preserve my life. But I want each one of you, once you have received your share of the estate, to follow one of the paths which I shall indicate. There is a proverb in this Spain of ours—a very good one I think, as all of them are, for they are brief maxims collected from long and deep experience. The one I am thinking of is, "The Church, the Sea, or the King's Palace." The meaning of that is, if you want to be powerful and rich, follow the Church, or go to sea and practice the merchant's calling, or take service with kings in their palaces. For it is said, "Better the King's crumb than the lord's favour." I mean by all this that I wish one of you to pursue learning, another commerce and the third to serve the King in his wars, as it is difficult to get a place in his household; for although war does not bring much riches, it generally brings great fame and renown. Within a week I will give you each your share in money, to the last farthing, as you will see. Tell me then if you are willing to follow my counsel and take the advice I have offered you.'

"He called on me, as the eldest, to answer, and I entreated him not to part with his fortune, but to spend it as freely as he liked, for we were young enough to be able to win one ourselves. But in the end, I said that I would obey his wishes and that my choice would be to follow the profession of arms, thereby serving God and my King. My younger brother protested to the same effect, and then elected to go to the Indies and invest his portion in merchandise. The youngest, and I think the wisest of us, said that he would follow the Church and go and complete his studies at Salamanca.

"So when the agreement was made and we had each chosen our profession, our father embraced us all, and carried out his promise just as quickly as he had said he would, giving us each, as I remember, three thousand ducats in money, an uncle of ours having bought the estate so that it should not go out of the family, and paid for it in cash. We all three bade our dear father good-bye on the same day. But it seemed to me inhuman to leave so old a man with so little means, and I made him take two thousand of my three thousand ducats, the rest being sufficient to provide me with all that a soldier needs. My two brothers followed my example, and each give him a thousand ducats; so that he was left with four thousand ducats in money and three thousand more, the value of his share of the estate, which he was unwilling to sell but had kept in land. Well, as I said, we took our leave of him and of this uncle of ours, with great emotion and tears on all sides, they insisting that we should let them have news of us, good or bad, at any favourable opportunity. We promised to do so, embraced them, and received our father's blessing. Then one of us took the road for Salamanca, one for Seville and I for Alicante, where I had heard that there was a Genoese ship loading with wool for Genoa.

"It is now twenty-two years since I left my father's house, and for all that time I have heard nothing of him or of my brothers, although I have written several letters; and what I have gone through in the interval I will tell you briefly. I went aboard at Alicante, arrived after a prosperous voyage at Genoa, went from there to Milan, where I bought arms and some military clothing, and from there decided to go and enlist in Piedmont. But as I was on the road to Alessandria I got news that the great Duke of Alva was marching into Flanders. So I changed my plans, went with him, and served him in all his campaigns, being present at the deaths of Counts Egmont and Horn. I rose to be an ensign under a famous captain from Guadalajara by the name of Diego de Urbina. After some time news came to Flanders of the alliance his Holiness Pope Pius V, of happy memory, had made with Venice and Spain against the common enemy, the Turk, whose fleet had just then taken the famous island of Cyprus, which had been under the rule of the Venetians, a lamentable and disastrous loss. It was known for certain that the commander of this alliance would be Don John of Austria, the natural brother of our good King Don Philip, and news was abroad of the great preparations which were being made for the war. All this aroused in me a great desire to take part in the expected campaign. So, although I had hopes and almost certain prospects of being promoted to a captaincy as soon as occasion offered, I decided to give it all up and go to Italy, which I did. As my luck would have it, Don John of Austria had just arrived at Genoa on his way to Naples to join up with the Venetian fleet, which he afterwards did at Messina. So, to be brief, I was present at that most glorious battle, being by that time a captain of infantry, to which honourable rank I was promoted rather by luck than merit. On that day, so fortunate for Christendom, since then the world and all the nations learnt how wrong they were in supposing that the Turks were invincible on the sea—on that day I say, when the insolent pride of the Ottomans was broken for ever—among all the fortunate men there—for the Christians who died there were more fortunate than those who survived victorious—I alone was unlucky. For in place of some naval crown, which I might have expected in the days of ancient Rome, I found myself on the night following that famous day with chains on my feet and handcuffs on my hands.

"This is how it happened. Aluch Ali, King of Algiers, a bold and successful pirate, had attacked and beaten the Maltese flagship; and only three knights were left alive in her, and those three badly wounded. Then Juan Andrea's flagship, aboard which I was with my company, came to the rescue, and, doing what was my duty in the circumstances, I jumped aboard the enemy's galley; which then disengaged from our ship, that had grappled her, and thus prevented my men from following me. So I found myself alone among my enemies, unable to resist as they were so many. In fact they took me prisoner, covered with wounds. Now, as you will have heard, gentlemen, Aluch Ali escaped with his whole squadron, and I remained a prisoner in his power, being the only sad man among so many that rejoiced, the only prisoner among all those set free. For there were fifteen thousand Christians rowing that Turkish fleet who that day gained their coveted liberty.

"They took me to Constantinople, where the Grand Turk Selim made my master Commander of the Sea—for doing his duty in that battle and bearing off the standard of the Knights of Malta, as a proof of his valour. The next year—that was 'seventy-two—I was at Navarino, rowing in the admiral's flagship, and witnessed the opportunity of catching the Turkish fleet in harbour which was then lost. For every Turkish sailor and janissary aboard was quite certain that they would be attacked in the port itself, and had his clothes and his *passamaques*—which are their shoes—ready, to escape at once by land without waiting to fight; such terror had our navy inspired in them. But Heaven ordained otherwise, through no fault or neglect of our commander but for the sins of Christendom, and because God ordains that there shall always be some scourge to chastise us. In the end Aluch Ali took refuge in Modon, an island close to Navarino and, putting his men ashore, fortified the entrance to the port and stayed there quietly till Don John had retired. In this expedition the galley called 'The Prize' was taken. Her captain was a son of the famous pirate Barbarossa. The flagship of Naples, 'The She-Wolf,' took her, under the command of that thunderbolt of war and father to his soldiers, that fortunate and unbeaten captain, Don Alvaro de Bazan, Marquis of Santa Cruz.

"I do not want to leave out what happened at the capture of 'The Prize.' The son of Barbarossa was so cruel, and treated his slaves so badly, that as soon as the rowers saw 'The She-Wolf' galley nearing them and about to board, they all dropped their oars at once and seized hold of him, where he stood at his station shouting at them to row hard. Then they tossed him from bench to bench, from stern to prow, biting him again and again, so that he had hardly gone farther than the mast before his soul had passed into hell, so cruelly did he treat them, as I said, and so bitterly did they hate him.

"We returned to Constantinople, and the next year—that was 'seventy-three—the news came that Don John had conquered

"So when the agreement was made and we had each chosen our profession, our father embraced us all, and carried out his promise just as quickly as he had said he would, giving us each, as I remember, three thousand ducats in money, an uncle of ours having bought the estate so that it should not go out of the family, and paid for it in cash." (page 464)

Tunis, wresting that kingdom from the Turks and giving it to Muley Hamet, which deprived Muley Hamida, the cruellest and bravest Moor in the whole world, of his hopes of recovering the throne. The Grand Turk felt this loss very severely and, with the cunning natural to all his house, made peace with the Venetians, who wanted it much more than he. Then the following year, which was 'seventy-four, he attacked the Goletta, and the fort near Tunis which Don John had left half constructed. In all these actions I was at the oar, without any hope of liberty—at least I had no hope of getting it by ransom, for I was resolved not to send the news of my misfortunes to my father.

"In the end the Goletta was lost, and the fort as well. Attacking these places were seventy-five thousand Turkish regular soldiers, and more than four hundred thousand Moors and Arabs from all over Africa. This vast host was supplied with such a quantity of ammunition and material, and with so many sappers, that they could have buried the Goletta and the fortress deep in earth with their bare hands alone. The Goletta, which had been considered impregnable till then, was the first to fall. It was through no fault of its garrison, who defended it to the best of their power and ability, but because, as experience showed, earthworks could be thrown up very easily in that sandy desert; for though water used to be found about sixteen inches down, the Turks did not strike it now at six feet. So with a great quantity of sandbags they raised their works high enough to command the walls of the fort and fired from above, so that no one could stay there to put up a defence.

"It was generally thought that our men should not have shut themselves up in the Goletta, but should have opposed the landing in open country. But the people who say that speak from a distance and with little experience of such matters. For as there were hardly seven thousand soldiers in the Goletta and the fort together, how could so small a number, however resolute, have taken the field, as well as held the forts against the enemy's great numbers? And how is it possible not to lose a fort which is not relieved, particularly when it is besieged by such a host of determined enemies and in their own country? Many, however, were of the opinion—as I was myself—that Heaven bestowed a special grace and mercy on Spain by permitting the demolition of that breeding-place and cloak of iniquities, that glutton, sponge and sink of the infinite money which was wasted there to no advantage, to serve no other purpose than to preserve the memory of its conquest, the auspicious memory of the most invincible Charles V—as if that tract of earth were needed to make his name eternal, as it is and ever will be.

"The fort fell as well. But the Turks had to win it foot by foot. For the soldiers defending it fought so bravely and fiercely that they killed more than twenty-five thousand of the enemy in the twenty-two general assaults they made. Not one of the three hundred survivors was taken unwounded, a clear and manifest proof of their fierceness and bravery and of how well they defended and maintained their positions. A small fort or tower in the middle of the lake, under the command of Don Juan Zanoguera, a Valencian gentleman and a famous soldier, surrendered on terms. They captured Don Pedro Puertocarrero, the commander of the Goletta, who had done everything he could to defend his post, and felt its loss so much that he died of grief on the way to Constantinople, where they were taking him as a prisoner. They also captured the commander of the fort, Gabriel Cervellon by name, a Milanese gentleman, a great engineer and a most courageous soldier. In those two fortresses died many people of note, one of whom was Pagan Doria, a Knight of the Order of St. John, a man of generous character, as was shown by his very liberal treatment of his brother, the famous John Andrew Doria. What made his death even more deplorable was that he fell at the hands of some Arabs in whom he had trusted when he saw that the fortress was lost. They had offered to take him, disguised as a Moor, to Tabarca, a small seaport or station on that coast held by the Genoese, who are engaged in coral-fishing. These Arabs cut off his head and took it to the commander of the Turkish fleet, who proved on them the truth of our Spanish proverb that though the treason pleases, we abhor the traitor. For they say that the general ordered the men who brought him the present to be hanged for not bringing him alive.

"Among the Christians captured in the fort was one Don Pedro de Aguilar, who came from somewhere in Andalusia. He had been an ensign in the garrison and was a soldier of great repute and rare intelligence, and he had a remarkable gift for what they call poetry. I mention him because it was his lot to come to my bench in my galley, and to be slave to my own master, and before we left that port this gentleman composed two sonnets by way of epitaphs, one on the Goletta and the other on the fort. And I must really repeat them, for I know them by heart and I think you will probably like them."

The moment the Captive named Don Pedro de Aguilar, Don Ferdinand glanced at his comrades, and all three smiled; then, at the mention of the sonnets, one of them said, "Before you go any further, sir, please tell me what became of this Don Pedro de Aguilar you spoke of."

"All I know," answered the Captive, "is that after he had been two years in Constantinople he escaped, disguised as an Albanian, with a Greek spy. I do not know whether he got his liberty, but I suppose he did, for I saw that Greek a year later in Constantinople, though I could not ask him whether the escape had been successful."

"It was," replied the gentleman. "That Don Pedro is my brother, and he is at our home now, well and rich, and married with three children."

"God be praised," said the Captive, "for all the mercies He did him, for there is no joy on earth in my opinion so good as regaining one's liberty."

"What is more," the gentleman went on, "I know those sonnets my brother wrote."

"Then recite them to us, sir," said the Captive, "for you will be able to do it better than I."

"With pleasure," replied the gentleman, "the one on the Goletta went like this:

⋙ 40 ⋘

The Captive's Story continued

*B*lest souls, discharged of life's oppressive weight,
  Whose virtue proved your passport to the skies,
You there procured a more propitious fate,
  When for your faith you bravely fell to rise.
When pious rage, diffused through every vein,
  On that ungrateful shore inflamed your blood,
Each drop you lost was bought with crowds of slain,
  Whose vital purple swelled the neighbouring flood.
Though crushed by ruins and by odds, you claim
That perfect glory, that immortal fame
  Which, like true heroes, nobly you pursued;
On these you seized, even when of life deprived,
For still your courage even your lives survived;
  And sure 'tis conquest thus to be subdued."

"Yes, those are the words that I know," said the Captive.

"And the one on the fort, if my memory is right," said the gentleman, "goes like this:

"Amidst these barren fields and ruined towers,
  The bed of honour of the falling brave,
Three thousand champions of the Christian powers
  Found a new life and triumph in the grave.
Long did their arms their haughty foes repel,
  Yet strewed the fields with slaughtered hopes in vain;
O'ercome by toils the pious heroes fell,
  Or but survived more nobly to be slain.
This dismal soil, so famed in ills of old,
In every age was fatal to the bold,
  The seat of horror and the warrior's tomb!
Yet hence to Heaven more work was ne'er resigned
Than these displayed; nor has the earth combined
  Resumed more noble bodies in her womb."

The sonnets were much appreciated, and the Captive went on with his tale, delighted with the news they had given him of his comrade.

"Then, when the Goletta and the fort surrendered, the Turks gave orders for the Goletta to be dismantled. But the fortress was in such a state that there was nothing left to demolish. And to save time and labour they mined it in three places. But none of the mines could blow up what appeared its weakest part; which was the old walls, although all that was still standing of the new fortifications, built by El Fratin, came down most easily. Finally the fleet returned to Constantinople, triumphant and victorious, and several months later my master Aluch Ali died. They used to call him *Uchali Fartax*, which means in Turkish 'the scabby renegade,' which he was. For it is a custom among the Turks to name people by any defect, or by any good quality, they may have. That is because they have only four surnames among them, and those belong to families of Ottoman descent. The rest, as I have said, take their names and surnames either from their bodily defects or from their characters. This Scabby was at the oar as a slave of the Great Turk for fourteen years, and when he was over thirty-four turned

473

renegade, in his fury at a Turk who had given him a slap on the face while he was rowing. In fact he renounced his faith to get his revenge. He had such character too that he came to be king of Algiers and, afterwards, Commander of the Sea—which is the third post in their empire—without resorting to the base methods by which most of the Great Turk's favourites rise. He was a Calabrian by birth, a good moral man, and treated his prisoners with great humanity. In the end he had three thousand of them, who were divided after his death, in accordance with his will, between the Grand Turk—who is reckoned a son and heir of all who die and takes his share with the rest of the dead man's sons—and his renegades. I fell to the share of a Venetian renegade, who had been a ship's cabin-boy when Aluch Ali captured him, for whom his master had such a liking that he was one of his most pampered favourites. He proved to be one of the cruelest renegades ever seen. He was called Hassan Aga and became very rich, eventually rising to be King of Algiers. With him I came from Constantinople, rather pleased to be so near to Spain; not because I thought of writing to tell anyone of my unhappy fate, but because I meant to see if Fortune would not be kinder to me in Algiers than in Constantinople, where I had attempted a thousand ways of escape, but had had no luck with any of them. I thought that in Algiers I would find other means of getting what I so much desired. For I never gave up hope of gaining my liberty, and when the result did not shape with my design in such plans as I contrived, worked out and put in practice, I never gave up, but immediately devised some new hope, never mind how slender and weak to keep me going.

"So I passed my life, shut up in a prison-house, called by the Turks a *bagnio,* where they keep their Christian prisoners: those belonging to the King and those belonging to private people, and also those who are called the slaves of the *Almazen*—that is to say, of the township—who are employed in the public works of the city and in other communal employment. Slaves of this last kind have great difficulty in gaining their liberty because, as they belong to the community and have no master of their own, there is no one with whom to bargain for their ransom, even if they have the money. To these *bagnios*, as I have said, some private people of the city take their prisoners, particularly when they are waiting to be redeemed. For they are kept here in idleness and safety until their ransom comes. The King's captives, if they are to be ransomed, do not go out to work with the rest of the gang either, except if their ransom is delayed; in which case, to spur them to write more urgently for it, they make them work and fetch firewood with the others, which is no light job.

"I was one of those put on ransom. For as it was known that I was a captain, nothing could prevent their putting me on the list of gentlemen to be redeemed, although I pleaded that I had small means and no property. They put a chain on me, more as a sign that I was to be ransomed than for my safe keeping; and so I spent my life in that *bagnio* with many more gentlemen and men of quality chosen to be held for ransom. And although hunger and lack of clothes distressed us at times—in fact almost always—nothing disturbed us so much as to hear and witness, wherever we went, the unparalleled and incredible cruelty which my master practised on Christians. Every day he hanged someone, impaled another, and cut off the ears of a third, and this on the slightest excuse or on none at all, so that even the Turks acknowledged that he did it only for the sake of doing it, and because it was in his nature to be the murderer of the entire human race. The only one who held his own with him was a Spanish soldier, called something de Saavedra; for his master never so much as struck him, nor bade anyone else strike him, nor even spoke a rough word to him, though he did things which those people will remember for many years, all in efforts to recover his liberty; and the rest of us were afraid that his least actions would be punished by impaling, as he himself feared they would be more than once. And if it were not for lack of time I would tell you something about that soldier's deeds, which you would find much more entertaining and surprising than this story of mine.

"Now, overlooking the courtyard of our prison were the windows of the house of a rich and important Moor, which, as is usual in

Moorish houses, were more like loopholes than windows, and even so were covered by thick and close lattices. And I happened one day to be on a flat roof in our prison with three companions, trying to wile away the time by seeing how far we could jump in our chains. We were on our own because all the other Christians had gone out to work. It was by the merest chance that I looked up, and when I did I saw a cane with a handkerchief tied to the end of it appear through one of those little closed windows I spoke of. It was being waved and jerked up and down, as though it were summoning us to go and take it. We stared at it, and one of my companions went and placed himself just below it to see if it would be dropped, or what else would happen; but no sooner did he get there than the cane was raised and jerked from side to side, as if someone were shaking his head to say no. The Christian came back, and again the cane was let down, to make the same movements as before. Another of my companions went up, but with the same result as the first. Last of all the third went, and was treated in the same manner as the first and the second. At this I was tempted to try my luck, and as soon as I got there and stood below the cane, it was let fall, and dropped into the prison just at my feet. I ran up at once to untie the handkerchief, in which I found a knot and in it ten *zianies*, which are coins of gold alloy that the Moors use, each worth ten of our *reals*. There is no need to tell you whether I was pleased at this windfall; I was delighted and astonished, but I could not think who could have directed this present, especially to me; since the refusal to drop the cane to anyone else was a clear sign that it was for me the favour was meant. I took my precious money; I broke the cane; I returned to the little roof; I looked up at the window, and saw the whitest of hands emerge to open and shut it very quickly. By this we learnt, or guessed, that it was a woman living in that house who had done us this kindness and, to show our thanks, we made salaams after the Moorish fashion, bowing our heads, bending our bodies, and laying our hands on our breasts. Somewhat later a little cross made of cane was put out of the same window and immediately drawn in again. This signal convinced us that there must be a Christian woman slave in the house and that it was she who had given us the present; but the whiteness of her hand and the bracelets we saw on it contradicted this idea. Then we imagined that she must be a renegade Christian; for often the Moors are glad to marry slaves of this sort, whom they value more highly than women of their own people.

"In all our surmises we were very far from the truth. Our sole occupation from that day on, however, was watching, and the window where our star had appeared was the pole by which we steered. But a good fortnight went by before we saw any further sign. And although in that time we made every effort to find out who lived in the house, and if there was any renegade Christian woman there, no one could tell us anything except that a rich and important Moor called Hadji Murad lived there, and that he had been the governor of Bata, which is one of their most important posts. But when we least expected it to rain more *zianies,* we saw the cane suddenly appear with another handkerchief on the end, tied in another, bigger knot; and this, as before, was at a time when the prison was empty and deserted. We made the customary experiment, each one of the three going before me; but the cane was delivered to none but me, and was dropped as soon as I got there. When I undid the knot I found forty Spanish crowns in gold and a paper written in Arabic, and at the end of the writing there was drawn a large cross. I kissed the cross, took the crowns, and returned to the roof. Then we made our salaams and, the hand appearing again, I promised by signs to read the letter, at which the window was closed. We were all astonished and delighted at events. But, as none of us could understand Arabic, our curiosity to know what was in the paper was great and our difficulty in finding anyone to read it to us even greater. In the end I decided to confide in a Murcian renegade, who professed to be a good friend of mine and had exchanged pledges with me which bound him to keep any secret I might entrust him with. For there is a custom among some renegades, when they have a mind to return to Christian lands, to carry with them certificates from important prisoners, testifying, in such form as they can, that such and such a renegade is an honest man, has always behaved well to Christians, and proposes to escape at the first possible opportunity. Some of them procure these testimonials with honest intentions; others want them for an emergency, meaning to produce them should they happen to be shipwrecked or taken prisoner on a plundering expedition in Christian lands, and to use those certificates as evidence that their purpose in coming is to stay behind on Christian soil, and that this is their only reason for coming on a raid with the Turks. In that way they escape the first violence of their captors, and safely make their peace with the Church; and when they see their chance, they return to Barbary to be what they were before. There are others, though, who make proper use of these papers and get them with the honest intention of remaining in Christian lands. One such renegade was this friend of mine, who had testimonials from all our comrades in which we vouched for him in the highest possible terms; and if the Moors had found these papers on him they would have burnt him alive. I was aware that he knew Arabic very well and could not only speak but write it; but before taking him completely into my confidence, I asked him to read me the paper, saying that I had found it by chance in a hole in my cell. He unfolded it, and spent some time examining it and spelling it over, muttering under his breath. I asked him if he understood it. Perfectly, he said, and if I would give him pen and ink, he would give me an exact translation. We instantly supplied him with what he asked, and he wrote down a literal translation, observing, when he had finished, 'I have translated this Moorish letter into Spanish for you word for word, but you must note that where it says Lela Marien it means Our Lady the Virgin Mary.' We read the paper, and this is how it ran:

When I was a girl my father had a woman slave, who taught me the Christian prayers in my own tongue, and spoke to me often about Lela Marien. This Christian died, and I know that she did not go to the fire but to Allah. For I saw her twice afterwards, and she told me to go to Christian lands and see Lela Marien, who loved me very much. I do not know how to go. I have seen many Christians out of this window, but none of them except you has seemed a gentleman. I am young and very beautiful, and have much money to take with me. See if you cannot find a way for us to go; and you shall be my husband, if you will; and if you will not I do not mind, for Lela Marien will find me someone to marry. I wrote this; be careful to whom you give it to read. Do not trust any Moor; they are all deceitful. That worries me very much. I do not want you to take anyone into your confidence, because if my father finds out he will immediately throw me down a well and cover me with stones. On to the cane I will fasten a thread. Tie your reply to it. But if you have no one who can write Arabic for you, tell me your answer by signs; Lela Marien will help me to understand you. May she and Allah protect you—and this cross, which I often kiss as my slave told me to.

"Consider, sirs, whether we had not reason to be surprised and delighted at the contents of this letter. Indeed, our feelings were so great that the renegade realized we had not found the paper by chance, but that it was really written to one of us. So he implored us, if his suspicions were correct, to take him into our confidence and tell him the truth, for he would risk his life for our liberty. As he spoke, he took a metal crucifix from under his shirt, and swore with tears in his eyes by the God, whose image it was and in whom he, wicked sinner though he was, truly and faithfully believed, and promised to be loyal to us and to keep anything we might reveal to him secret. For he could almost foretell that he and all of us would gain our liberty with the help of the woman who had written that letter, and that he would gain what he so much desired, re-admission to the body of the Holy Mother Church, from whom he had been severed as a rotten limb, cut off by his ignorance and sin. The renegade spoke with such tears of repentance that we all agreed with one accord to tell him the truth of the matter; and so we told him the whole story, concealing nothing. We showed him the little window out of which the cane had appeared, and by that he noted the house, and promised to take great and special care to find out who lived there. We agreed at the same time that it would be as well to reply to the Moorish lady's letter, since we had someone there who could do it; and the renegade at once wrote, straight off, to my dictation. I can give you the exact words, for I have not forgotten a single material detail of that adventure; nor shall I forget one as long as I live. So this is what I replied to the Moorish lady:

'The true Allah keep you, dear lady, and the blessed Marien, who is the true Mother of God and who has put it into your heart to go to a Christian land, for she loves you well. Pray to her to be pleased to teach you how you can put her commands into practice, for she is so kind that she will certainly do so. On behalf of myself and all my Christian companions, I promise that we will do everything we can for you, even unto death. Do not fail to write and inform me of what you intend to do. I shall always reply, for the great Allah has given us a Christian prisoner who can speak and write your language well, as you can judge from this letter. So you need have no fear, and can tell us anything you wish. As to your saying that you would be my wife if you were to reach Christian soil, I promise you as a good Christian that this shall be so. And remember that Christians carry out their promises better than Moors. Allah and Marien His mother protect you, dear lady.'

"When this letter was written and sealed I waited two days till the *bagnio* was deserted as usual, and then I went to the usual place on the little flat roof to see if the cane would appear, which it did not take long in doing. As soon as I saw it, although I could not see who was holding it, I held up the paper as a signal for her to tie on the thread; but I found that it was already on the cane, and attached the letter to it. Then, a little while later, our star appeared once more with the white flag of peace, the knotted handkerchief, tied to it. It

"We stared at it, and one of my companions went and placed himself just below it to see if it would be dropped, or what else would happen; but no sooner did he get there than the cane was raised and jerked from side to side, as if someone were shaking his head to say no." (page 476)

was dropped and, on picking it up, I found inside more than fifty crowns in all kinds of silver and gold coins, which multiplied our joy fifty times more and strengthened our hopes of gaining our liberty. That very night our renegade returned with the news that he had found out that the Moor we had been told of before did live in that house; that he was called Hadji Murad; that he was exceedingly rich, and had an only daughter, the heiress to all his fortune. It was the general opinion, he said, throughout the city that she was the loveliest woman in all Barbary, and many of the Viceroys who came there had asked for her hand; but she would never consent to marry. He had also found out that she had once a Christian slave, who was now dead—all of which agreed with the contents of the letter.

"We then consulted the renegade as to any possible plan for carrying off the Moorish lady and all of us escaping on to Christian soil. But in the end we agreed to wait, for the time being, for a second letter from Zoraida—for that was her name, though she now wishes to be called Maria—since it was quite clear to us that she, and she only, would be able to find a solution of all our difficulties. After we had agreed on that, the renegade told us not to worry, for he would either set us at liberty or lose his life in the attempt. The bagnio was full of people for the next four days, which meant that for four days the cane did not appear; at the end of that time, when the prison was once more empty as usual, it appeared with a big handkerchief which promised a happy delivery. The cane with its burden pointed to me, and I found in it another letter and a hundred crowns all in gold. The renegade was there, and when we had returned to our cell we gave him the paper to read. He translated it like this:

'I do not know, dear sir, how to arrange for our going to Spain. Lela Marien has not told me, although I have asked her. What I can do is to pass you a great deal of money through this window. You can then ransom yourself and your friends; and one of you can go to a Christian country, buy a ship, and come back for the others. I can be found in my father's country house at the Babazoun gate, beside the seashore, where I shall be all this summer with my father and servants. You will be able to carry me off from there by night without risk, and take me to the ship. Remember that you must marry me, or I will pray to Marien to punish you. If there is no one you can trust to go for the ship, ransom yourself and go. For I know that you are more certain to return than anyone else, because you are a gentleman and a Christian. Try to find our country house, and when you come on to the roof I shall know that the *bagnio* is empty and give you large sums of money. Allah preserve you, dear sir.'

"Those were the words of the second letter; and when we had all seen it, each one said he was willing to be the man ransomed, and promised to go and to return with all speed; and I offered myself as well. But the renegade was totally opposed to this plan, and said that he would on no account agree to anyone getting his liberty till we all did so together; because experience had shown him how badly men fulfil the promises which they have made as prisoners once they are free. For very often prisoners of consequence had tried the expedient of ransoming someone to go to Valencia or Majorca with money to equip a boat and return for the men who had ransomed them; but they had never come back, for the fear of losing their new-found liberty had expunged every obligation in the world from their memories. To confirm the truth of this, he briefly told us a case which had happened very recently indeed to some Christian gentlemen, the most extraordinary affair that had ever occurred in those parts, where astonishing and marvellous things happen every day. He concluded by suggesting what should be done with the money intended for the ransom of one of us. We were to give it to him to buy a ship with, there in Algiers, on the pretence that he intended to set up as a merchant to trade with Tetuan and along the coast. Once he was owner of the boat, he would easily contrive a way of getting us out of the *bagnio* and of taking us all on board. Besides, if the

Moorish lady were to give us enough money to ransom us all, as she promised, we should be free; and then it would be extremely easy to get us aboard, even in the middle of the day. Our greatest difficulty was the fact that the Moors do not allow a renegade to buy or own a ship, unless it is a large ship to go on a pirate expedition; for they are afraid that his only reason for buying a small ship, particularly if he is a Spaniard, is to escape on to Christian soil. Our renegade would get over this difficulty, however, by taking a Tagarine Moor as his partner in the purchase of the craft, and in the trading profits. By this subterfuge he would become master of the ship; and once he had got that, he reckoned that the rest would follow. Now, although both my companions and I thought it a better plan to send to Majorca for the ship, as the Moorish lady suggested, we dared not contradict him, for fear that he might betray us if we did not do what he said, and so put us in danger of execution, especially if he were to report the part played by Zoraida, for whose life we would all willingly have sacrificed our own. So we decided to put ourselves in the hands of God and the renegade and, at that juncture, replied to Zoraida that we would follow her suggestions; for she had advised us as well as if Lela Marien had instructed her, and that it rested with her alone whether the plan should be delayed or put into execution at once. I repeated my promise to marry her, and then the bagnio happening to be empty, at various times during the next day she gave us two thousand crowns in gold by means of the cane and handkerchief, together with a letter in which she said that she was going to her father's country house on the next *Juma,*—that is Friday,—and that she would give us some more money before she went. But if that was not enough, we were to let her know; and she would give us as much as we required, for her father had so much that he would not miss it, especially as she had the keys of everything.

"We immediately gave the renegade five hundred crowns to buy the ship, and with eight hundred I redeemed myself, giving the money to a Valencian merchant who was in Algiers at the time. He ransomed me from the King by giving his word that he would pay the money on the arrival of the first ship from Valencia. For if he had paid it down, it would have made the King suspicious that my ransom had been in Algiers for some time, and that the merchant had concealed it for his own profit. In fact, my master was so full of suspicion, he said, that I dared not on any account pay out the money at once. On the Thursday before the Friday on which the fair Zoraida was to go to the country house, she gave us another thousand crowns, and advised us of her departure; asking me, if I ransomed myself, to discover her father's estate at once, and at all costs to find some opportunity of going to see her there. I replied briefly that I would do so, and that she must be sure to commend us to Lela Marien by all the prayers which the slave woman had taught her. After this we set about getting our three companions ransomed, to make it easier for us to leave the bagnio; and in case, seeing me ransomed and themselves not—though we had the money —they might get alarmed, and the Devil might put it into their heads to do something which would endanger Zoraida. For although their characters might have relieved me of that fear, yet I did not wish to put the matter to any risk. So I had them ransomed in the same way as I had ransomed myself, delivering the whole sum into the hands of the merchant, so that he might the more confidently and safely go surety for us. But we never revealed our plan or our secret to him, for that would have been too dangerous.

⫷ 41 ⫸

A Further Continuation of
the Captive's Story

*B*efore a fortnight had gone by
our renegade had bought a very good ship, capable of taking more
than thirty people; and to lend colour to his design and ensure its
success, he proposed to make a trip to a place called Cherchel, which
is seventy-two miles from Algiers in the direction of Oran, where
there is a great trade in dried figs. This he did, and made two or
three trips in the company of the Tagarine I mentioned. In Barbary
they call the Moors of Aragon Tagarines, and those of Granada
Mudejares; and in the Kingdom of Fez they call the Mudajares
Elches—those are the people the King makes most use of in war. To
proceed, each time he passed in his ship she anchored in a cove not
two bow-shots from the country house where Zoraida was waiting;
and there, very deliberately, the renegade would take up his position
with the young Moors who rowed for him, sometimes to say his
prayers and sometimes to rehearse his plan. So he would go to
Zoraida's estate and beg for fruit, which her father would give him
without recognizing him. But although he tried to speak with Zoraida, as he afterwards told me, and tell her she might be happy and

confident, for he was the man who was to carry her away to the Christian country by my instructions, it was never possible; because Moorish ladies never let themselves be seen by any Moor or Turk, unless by the orders of their husbands or fathers, though they let Christian slaves be with them and converse to them, even more than is proper. Indeed, it would have displeased me if he had talked to her, since it might have alarmed her to find her affairs entrusted to the mouth of a renegade. But God decreed otherwise, and did not give this fellow a chance of carrying out his plan. He saw, however, how safely he could go backwards and forwards to Cherchel, that he could anchor when and how and where he chose, and that his Tagarine partner had no will of his own but obeyed him entirely. So seeing that I was ransomed and that all that was left to do was to find some Christians to row, he told me to look out for the men I intended to take with me, in addition to the ransomed men, and to arrange with them for next Friday, which he had fixed on for our start. Thereupon I spoke to a dozen Spaniards, all strong oarsmen and men who could readily leave the city. It was no small matter to find so many at that moment. For there were twenty ships out privateering, and they had taken all the oarsmen with them. These men would not have been available if it had not been that their master had stayed behind that summer to complete a small galley he had on the stocks. I gave them all the same instructions, that the next Friday evening they should creep out one by one, and make their way to Hadji Murad's estate and wait for me there. I gave these directions to each one separately, and told them all that, should they see other Christians there, they were to say nothing except that I had told them to wait for me.

"This part of the business settled, I had still to do one more thing of the greatest importance to me. That was to advise Zoraida how the matter had progressed, so that she might be prepared and on the watch, and not be alarmed if we rushed upon her suddenly before she imagined the Christian's ship would be back. So I decided to go to the garden, and see if I could speak to her; and I went there one day before our departure on the pretence of gathering herbs. The first person I met was her father, who spoke to me in the language that is spoken between slaves and Moors all over Barbary, and even in Constantinople: it is neither Moorish nor Castilian, nor the tongue of any other country, but a mixture of every language, in which we can all understand one another. Well, as I say, he asked me in this tongue what I was looking for in his garden and whose man I was. I answered that I was a slave of Arnaut Mami—this, because I knew for certain that this man was a very great friend of his—and that I was looking for herbs to make a salad. After that he asked me if I was for ransom or not, and how much my master wanted for me. Whilst we were engaged in this conversation the fair Zoraida, who had not seen me now for a long time, came out of the house; and since Moorish women, as I have said, are not at all shy of showing themselves to Christians, and not in the least bashful with them, she made nothing of coming to where her father stood talking to me. Indeed, when he saw her approaching rather slowly, he called to her to come right up.

"It would be too much to describe to you now Zoraida's great beauty and grace, or the rich and gay dress in which she then appeared. I will only say that more pearls hung from her lovely neck, her ears, and her hair than she had hairs on her head. On her ankles which, in the Moorish fashion, were bare, she had two *carcajes*—that is the Moorish word for rings and bracelets for the feet—of purest gold, set with so many diamonds that she told me afterwards her father valued them at ten thousand dollars; and those she wore on her wrists were worth as much. The pearls were in great numbers and very good. For fine and seed pearls are the chief pride and adornment of Moorish women—which is why there are more pearls among the Moors than among all other nations—and Zoraida's father was famous for having some of the best in Algiers, and also for possessing more than two hundred thousand Spanish crowns, of all of which she was mistress, who is now mine. Judge how lovely she must have looked in all her finery from the beauty that still remains after all her troubles.

"Women's beauty, as we know, has its days and times, and varies

489

according to accidents; and it is natural enough for the emotions to increase it or diminish it, though most often they destroy it. But I will be brief, and say that she was then so magnificently attired and so surpassingly lovely that she seemed to me the most perfect creature I had even seen; and more than that, when I remembered my indebtedness to her, she seemed to me a heavenly goddess come down to earth to bring me happiness and relief.

"As soon as she approached, her father told her in their language that I was a slave of his friend Arnaut Mami, and had come to pick a salad. She broke in to ask me in that mixture of languages whether I was a gentleman, and why I did not ransom myself. I replied that I was already ransomed, and the price would show her how highly my master valued me. For I had given fifteen hundred *sultanies* for myself. To which she replied, 'If you belonged to my father I would certainly see that he did not part with you for twice as much, because you Christians always lie and make yourselves out poor to cheat us Moors.'

" 'That may be so, lady,' I answered, 'but I assure you that I have dealt honestly with my master, as I do with everyone in the whole world, and always shall.'

" 'When do you go then?' asked Zoraida.

" 'Tomorrow, I think,' said I, 'for there is a ship here from France which is sailing in the morning, and I intend to go in her.'

" 'Would it not be better,' asked Zoraida, 'to wait until one comes from Spain, and go in that instead of with the French, for they are not your friends?'

" 'No,' I replied, 'although if it is true, as I hear, that there is a ship coming from Spain, I might wait longer for her, but it is more likely that I shall start tomorrow. For I am so eager to be home and with the people I love that I cannot bear to wait even for a better opportunity, should it mean delay.'

" 'Then no doubt you are married in your own country,' asked Zoraida, 'and you want to go and see your wife.'

" 'No, I am not married,' I replied, 'but I have given my word to marry when I get home.'

" 'Is the lady whom you have promised to marry beautiful?' asked Zoraida.

" 'She is so beautiful,' I replied, 'that, to tell you the truth about her beauty, she is much like you.'

"At this her father laughed heartily and cried, 'By Allah, Christian, she must be very beautiful if she is like my daughter, who is the most beautiful woman in the whole kingdom. Look at her well, and you will see I am telling you the truth.'

"Zoraida's father, as the better linguist, acted as interpreter for the greater part of this conversation; for although she spoke the bastard language which, as I have said, is in use there, she expressed her meaning more by gestures than by words. Now whilst we were engaged in this conversation a Moor came running up and shouted out that four Turks had jumped over the fence, or the wall, of the garden and were picking the fruit, although it was not yet ripe. The old man got alarmed, and Zoraida too; for the Moors' fear of the Turks is widespread, and second nature to them, especially their terror of soldiers, who are so overbearing and so tyrannical towards the Moors, their subjects, that they treat them worse than slaves. Therefore it was that Zoraida's father said to her, 'Go back to the house, daughter, and shut yourself in, while I go and speak to these dogs. And you, Christian, pick your herbs and go on your ways in peace. May Allah bear you safely to your own country.'

"I bowed, and he went off to look for the Turks, leaving me alone with Zoraida, who began to make a show of going off as her father had bidden her. But no sooner had she got under the shade of the garden trees, than she turned to me with her eyes full of tears and said:

" '*Tameji*, Christian, *tameji?*' which means, 'Are you going away, Christian, are you going away?'

" 'Yes, lady,' I replied, 'but on no account without you. Expect me next *Juma*, and do not be alarmed when you see us, for we shall most certainly go to Christian lands.'

"I said this in such a way that she now perfectly understood all our previous conversation, and putting her arm round my neck, she began to walk towards the house with trembling steps. As Fortune would have it—and things might have gone very badly with us if Heaven had not decreed otherwise—whilst we two were walking in the manner I have described, with her arm round my neck, her father returned from packing the Turks off, and saw us in this compromising situation; and we saw that he had seen us. But Zoraida was resourceful and self-possessed, and did not take her arm from my neck; but drawing closer to me instead, leant her head on her breast, went limp at the knees, and made as if she were fainting, while I acted as if I were forced to hold her up. Then her father came running to us and, seeing his daughter in this condition, asked her what was the matter. But as she made no answer, he said, 'No doubt she has fainted with fright at those dogs coming into the garden.' And taking her from my breast, he rested her against his. Then she heaved a sigh, and with her eyes not yet dry from their tears, spoke again, "*Ameji,* Christian, *Ameji*' ('Go away, Christian, go away.'). To which her father replied, 'There is no need for the Christian to go. He has done you no harm, and the Turks are gone now. Do not be at all alarmed, for there is nothing to frighten you. The Turks, I tell you, went when I asked them to, by the same way as they came in.'

" 'It was they who alarmed her, sir, as you said,' I observed to her father; 'but seeing that she tells me to go I do not want to annoy her. Peace be with you, and with your permission I will come to this garden again for herbs, if they are needed; for my master says that nobody has better salad herbs than you.'

" 'Come as often as you like,' answered Hadji Murad. 'My daughter did not tell you to go out of annoyance with you or with any other Christian, but probably mistook you for the Turks, or thought it was time for you to pick your herbs.'

"At this I took immediate leave of both of them, and she went off with her father, looking as if her heart were torn. Then I wandered all about the garden at my pleasure, pretending to gather herbs, and took a good look at all the ways in and out, at the defences of the house, and at everything we might make use of for the furtherance of our plan.

"When I had done, I returned and gave the renegade and my companions an account of all that had happened, saying how I longed for the moment when I could enjoy undisturbed the happiness which Fortune offered me in the fair and beautiful Zoraida. Now the time passed; at last the longed-for day arrived; and by following the plan which we had settled on after mature consideration and many long arguments, we achieved the success we had hoped for. On the Friday after the day when I had spoken to Zoraida in the garden, our renegade anchored at nightfall with his boat almost opposite the place where the fair Moor lived. The Christians who were to row were already warned, and hidden in different places in the neighbourhood. They were all anxiously and excitedly waiting for me, and longing to seize the ship, which lay before their eyes. For they did not know the renegade's plan, but thought that they would have to gain their liberty by force of arms and by killing all the Moors aboard. So as soon as my companions and I showed ourselves, all the rest came out of their hiding places. It was already the time when the city gates are shut, and there was no one to be seen over that whole countryside. But once we were all together, we were uncertain whether it would be better first to go for Zoraida or to overpower the Tagarine Moorish oarsmen. While we were in this quandary our renegade came up to us and asked why we were waiting, for it was already time, and his Moors were off their guard and most of them asleep. We told him the reason for our delay, and he said that the most important thing was to get control of the ship first, which could be done most easily and at no risk at all. Then we could go for Zoraida afterwards. We all thought his advice good, and so went to the boat, under his guidance, without further delay. He was the first to jump in and, putting his hand on his cutlass, cried out in Moorish, 'Do not move from where you are, not one of you, unless he wants to be killed.' By this time almost all the Christians were aboard. The Moors were a poor-spirited lot, and terror-

493

stricken at hearing such a threat from their captain. So without a single one of them drawing a weapon—few or hardly any of them had one—they let the Christians handcuff them without a word. This was very quickly done, the captain threatening the Moors that they would all be put to the sword immediately if they raised any sort of alarm.

"When this was done, half of our number stayed on guard, and the rest of us, still under the renegade's leadership, went to Hadji Murad's garden; and, as good luck would have it, when we came to open the door it gave as easily as if it had not been locked; and so, in absolute calm and silence, we reached the house unnoticed. The lovely Zoraida was watching for us at the window, and as soon as she heard people moving, asked in a whisper if we were *Nizarani*, that is to say, Christians. I replied yes, and bade her come down. When she recognized me, she did not delay an instant, but without a word of reply came in a flash and opened the door, revealing herself to us in all her beauty, and so richly dressed that I cannot attempt to describe her. As soon as I saw her I took her hand and began to kiss it; the renegade and my two companions did the same; and the others, who did not understand the situation, imitated us, thinking that we were giving her thanks for our freedom. The renegade then asked her in Moorish if her father was in the house. She replied that he was, and asleep.

" 'Then we shall have to wake him,' said the renegade, 'and take him with us, and everything of value in this lovely place.'

" 'No,' she replied, 'my father must on no account be touched. There is nothing in the house except what I am bringing with me. That will be quite enough to make you all rich and happy. Wait a moment and you shall see.'

"With these words she went back into the house, saying that she would return in a moment, and that we must keep still and make no noise. I asked the renegade what conversation had passed between them; and when he told me I said that Zoraida's wishes must be obeyed in every way. She then came back, bringing a small box full of gold crowns, so heavy that she could hardly carry it. But as ill luck

"Whilst we were engaged in this conversation the fair Zoraida, who had not seen me now for a long time, came out of the house; and since Moorish women, as I have said, are not at all shy of showing themselves to Christians and not in the least bashful with them, she made nothing of coming to where her father stood talking to me." (page 489)

would have it, her father had waked in the meantime, and heard the noise going on in the garden. He had looked out of the window and, seeing that all the men there were Christians, had started to shout loudly and wildly in Arabic, 'Christians, Christians! Thieves, thieves!' These cries threw us all into the greatest confusion and alarm. But, seeing our danger and the importance of getting our plan through before we were detected, the renegade rushed up the steps to Hadji Murad's room, and some of our party with him. As for me, I dared not let go of Zoraida, who had fallen fainting into my arms. To be brief, the men who went into the house managed so well that the next moment they brought Hadji Murad down, with his hands tied and a handkerchief stuffed into his mouth, which prevented his uttering a word—and they threatened him that if he did cry out it would cost him his life. When she saw him, she covered her eyes to avoid the sight; while he was frightened to death, not knowing how very willingly she had put herself into our hands. But at that point all we needed was our legs, and we got aboard ship with all caution and speed. For those on board were already expecting us, and were afraid that we had met with disaster.

"Some two hours of the night must have passed before we were all on the ship, where we untied Zoraida's father's hands and took the gag out of his mouth, though the renegade repeated his threat to kill him if he uttered so much as a word. When he saw his daughter there, however, he began to sigh very deeply; and he groaned when he saw how tightly I was clasping her and that she made no attempt to resist or complain or fight shy, but stayed quiet. Yet, for all that, he remained silent out of fear that the renegade's fierce threats might be put into effect. Then, when Zoraida was on board and saw that we were going to start rowing, looking at her father there and the other Moors, all tied up, she bade the renegade ask me to do her the favour of releasing the Moors and granting her father his liberty. She pleaded that she would rather fling herself into the sea than see her father, who loved her so well, carried off before her eyes, a prisoner on her account. The renegade translated her request and I replied that I would gladly agree, but he objected that

497

it was impossible. For, if we left them there, they would immediately raise the country and give the alarm in the city, which would bring the Unbelievers out after us in light frigates, to cut us off by sea and by land, so that we could not escape. What we could do was to set them free at the first Christian port we touched. We were all agreed on this, and Zoraida also was satisfied when she was told of our decision and of our reasons for not immediately complying with her request. Then, in joyful silence, happily and vigorously, every one of our valiant rowers took his oar and, commending ourselves to God with all our hearts, we began to steer towards the Balearic Islands, which are the nearest point of Christian land. But because a slight north wind began to blow and the sea got rather rough, it was impossible for us to hold our course for Majorca; and we were forced to keep along the shore in the direction of Oran, in considerable fear of being observed from the town of Cherchel, which is about seventy miles along the coast from Algiers. We were also afraid of meeting one of those small galleys which are engaged in bringing goods from Tetuan; though each one for himself, and all of us jointly, felt confident that if we were to meet a merchant galley, so long as it was not armed for piracy, we not only would not be taken, but would capture a ship in which we could finish our voyage in greater safety. And all the while we rowed, Zoraida lay with her head in my arms to avoid seeing her father. I felt that she was calling on Lela Marien to aid us.

"We must have rowed a good thirty miles when dawn found us about three gunshots from the shore, which we saw to be desert without any inhabitants to observe us. But, for all that, we rowed as hard as we could to get farther out to sea. It was now a little smoother; and when we had got about six miles off, the order was given that only every fourth man should row; so that we might have something to eat, for the ship was well provided with stores. But the rowers said that this was no time to rest, and that those who were not rowing could feed them, as they certainly did not mean to let the oars out of their hands. We did feed them. But at that time a stiff breeze began to blow, obliging us to hoist a sail and stop rowing, and to steer for Oran, for it was impossible to make any other course. All this was done with great speed; and so we sailed at more than eight knots, without any other fear than that of meeting some ship which might prove to be a pirate. We gave our Tagarine Moors food, and the renegade comforted them by saying that they were not prisoners, but would be given their freedom at the first opportunity. He gave the same assurance to Zoraida's father, who replied, 'I could expect and believe anything else of your generosity and liberality, Christians, but do not think me so simple as to imagine that you will grant me my liberty. You did not put yourselves to the danger of robbing me of it, only to return it to me so freely, particularly since you know who I am and how much you stand to gain by a bargain. If you would name the sum, I offer you here and now as much as you want for myself and for this unhappy daughter of mine; or failing that, for her alone, who is the greater and better part of my soul.'

"At these words he began to weep so bitterly that we were all moved to pity, and Zoraida was compelled to look in his direction; and she was so melted at the sight of the old man weeping that she got up from my feet and went over to embrace him. Then, as she put her face to his, they both burst into tears of such affection that many of us did the same. But when he saw that she was in her finest clothes and wearing all those jewels, he asked her in their tongue, 'What is this, my daughter? Last night, before our present terrible misfortune overtook us, I saw you in your ordinary houseclothes; and now, though you have not had the time to dress yourself up, nor any good news to celebrate by adorning and beautifying yourself, I find you decked out in the best clothes I was able to give you when Fortune was kindest to us. Answer my question, for this is more surprising and alarming to me even than my present misfortune.'

"The renegade translated to us all that the Moor said to his daughter, but she did not answer a word. However, when he saw on one side of the ship the little box in which she kept her jewels, and which he was certain he had left at Algiers and not taken to their country house, he was even more disturbed, and asked her how the box had come into our hands, and what was inside it. To which the renegade answered, without waiting for Zoraida to reply, 'Do not trouble yourself, sir, to ask your daughter Zoraida so many questions, for I can reply to all of them in one word. Let me tell you that she is a Christian; it is she who has been the file to our chains and the key to our captivity. She is with us of her own free will; as glad, I imagine, to be where she is, as a man coming out of darkness into light, out of death into life, out of pain into glory.'

" 'Is it true, what he says, daughter?' asked the Moor.

" 'It is,' replied Zoraida.

" 'That, in fact, you are a Christain,' asked the old man, 'and it is you who has put your father into his enemies' power?'

"To which Zoraida replied, 'I am a Christian, but it is not I that brought you to this pass, for it was never my wish to leave you or to do you any harm. I only wished to do myself a benefit.'

" 'And what benefit have you done yourself, daughter?'

" 'That,' she replied, 'you must ask Lela Marien, for she will be able to tell you better than I.'

"No sooner did the Moor hear this than he threw himself with incredible agility head foremost into the sea, and no doubt would have drowned if the long and cumbrous clothes he wore had not kept him just above water. Zoraida cried out for us to rescue him, whereat we all instantly went to his aid and, grasping him by his long robes, pulled him out, half drowned and unconscious. And so distressed was Zoraida that she burst into a tender and sorrowful lament over him, as if he were really dead. We turned him face downwards, at which he brought up a great deal of water, and after two hours came to. During this time the wind changed and drove us back towards the land, and we had to row hard to avoid running aground. But by good luck we made a little cove beside a small promontory or cape, which is called by the Moors the Cape of the *Cava Rumia;* which means in our language the wicked Christian woman. For there is a tradition among the Moors that it is the place where that *Cava* lies buried, through whom Spain was lost; for *cava* in their tongue means wicked woman and *rumia* Christian. They even look on it as a bad omen to have to anchor there, if necessity drives them to—and otherwise they never do so. But for us it was no wicked woman's shelter, but a secure haven of refuge, as the sea was running high. We posted our sentries on shore and, without dropping our oars, ate the renegade's provisions, and fervently prayed God and Our Lady to aid and favour us with a happy ending to our adventure which had begun so prosperously. At Zoraida's entreaty I gave orders that her father and the other Moors, who were still bound, should be put ashore; for her courage failed her, and her tender heart grieved at the sight of her father bound and those countrymen of hers prisoners. We promised her to free them at the moment of our departure, since we should incur no danger by leaving them in that uninhabited spot. Our prayers were not in vain, for Heaven answered them. The wind presently changed in our favour, and the sea grew calm, inviting us to resume our voyage with joyful hearts. At this we unbound the Moors and put them ashore one by one, to their great astonishment. But when we came to land Zoraida's father, who had entirely regained consciousness, he said, 'Why do you think, Christians, that this wicked woman is glad you have set me free? Do you think that it is out of pity for me? Not at all. But because my presence would hinder her in the gratification of her wicked desires. Do not imagine that she has been moved to change her faith out of a belief that your religion is better than ours. No, it is because she knows that immorality is more freely practised in your country than in ours.'

"And turning to Zoraida, with myself and another Christian holding him by both arms in case he might do something desperate, he cried, 'Infamous and misguided girl! Where are you going in your blind frenzy, in the power of these dogs, our natural enemies? Accursed be the hour in which I engendered you, and accursed the pleasure and delight in which I brought you up!'

"But when I saw that he was not likely to end quickly, I hurriedly put him ashore; and from there he went on calling out his curses and lamentations, praying to Mahomet to beseech Allah to destroy us, confound us and annihilate us. And when we had hoisted sail and could no longer hear his words, we saw his actions, and watched him plucking his beard, tearing his hair and rolling on the ground. Once indeed he strained his voice so loud that we could hear him cry, 'Come back, beloved daughter—come back to land! I forgive you everything! Give those men the money, for it is theirs; and come and comfort this wretched father of yours, who will lose his life in the sands of this desert if you forsake him.'

"Zoraida listened to all this, and felt it all, and wept, not knowing what else to say in reply but 'May it please Allah, dear father, that Lela Marien, who has been the cause of my becoming a Christian may console you in your grief. Allah well knows that I could have done nothing but what I did, and that these Christians owe me nothing for my goodwill. For even if I had wanted not to come with them, but to stay at home, it would have been impossible. So fast did my soul hurry me towards a deed which I know to be good, beloved father, though it appears wicked to you.'

"This she said at a time when her father could not hear it, and we could no longer see him. I comforted Zoraida, and we all attended to our ship, which was so speeded by a favourable wind that we fervently expected to be on the Spanish coast at dawn next day.

"But as good seldom or never comes pure and unadulterated, accompanied or followed by no alarming evil, our fortune, or perhaps the curses the Moor cast on his daughter—for a father's curses are always to be feared—so willed it, I say, that when we were well out to sea, and almost three hours of the night had gone by, just as we were scudding before the wind under full sail with oars shipped—for the favourable wind relieved us of the labour of using them—we made out, by the light of a clear moon, a square-rigged ship close by us, with her sails spread, steering with the wind on her quarter and standing across our bows. She was so near that we had to lower our sail so as not to collide with her, and they had to put their helm hard up to give us room to pass. They had gathered on the deck to ask us who we were, where we came from, and where we were sailing for. But as they asked us in French, our renegade said, 'Do not reply. They are no doubt some of those French pirates who take everything as a prize.'

"At this warning no one said a word. But when we had got a little ahead and the ship was already on our lee, they suddenly let off two cannon, both loaded, it appeared, with chainshot, for with one shot they cut our mast in half and blew it and our sail overboard. A moment later they fired off another, and the ball hit us amidships, laying the vessel's side entirely open, though it did no other damage at all. But we saw that we were sinking, and all began to shout for help, imploring the men in the ship to take us aboard, for we were drowning. Then they put to, and launched their skiff or ship's boat; and a full dozen well-armed Frenchmen got in, with their arquebuses, and their matches lighted and drew alongside us. Then, seeing how few we were and that our ship was sinking, they picked us up, saying that they had served us in that way for our discourtesy in not replying to them. Meanwhile our renegade took the box with Zoraida's treasures and threw it into the sea, without anyone noticing what he was doing.

"Finally we got aboard among the Frenchmen, who when they had found out all they wanted to about us, robbed us of everything we possessed, as if they were our mortal enemies, stripping Zoraida even of the anklets on her feet. But I was not so much disturbed at Zoraida's distress as at my own fear that, after they had stolen her rich and precious jewels, they would proceed to rob her of the most valuable of all, which she prized the most highly. But these people's desires do not extend beyond money, though of this their lust is insatiable; and on that occasion it was so extreme that they would have stripped us even of our slave's uniforms, if these had been of any use to them. Some of them even wanted to throw us all into the sea, wrapped in a sail, for they meant to pretend to be Bretons and to trade with some Spanish ports; and if they were to take us into harbour, their robbery would be discovered and they would be punished. But the captain—it was he who had robbed my beloved Zoraida—said that he was content with the booty he had, and that he did not want to touch at a

Spanish port; but to slip through the Straits of Gibraltar by night, or in any way he could, and make for La Rochelle, which was the place they had sailed from. So they agreed to let us have their ship's boat and all that was necessary for the short voyage we had still to make. This they did next day, close to the Spanish coast, the sight of which made us forget all our troubles and hardships so completely that they might never have occurred, such is man's joy at regaining lost liberty.

"It must have been about midday when they put us into the boat, giving us two barrels of water and some ship's biscuit. And just as the lovely Zoraida was going, the captain was seized with some sort of pity and gave her some forty crowns; and he refused to let his men rob her of the clothes which she is wearing now. We got into the boat, thanking them for this last kindness and displaying gratitude rather than resentment. They then stood out to sea on a course for the Straits, and we set about rowing most vigorously without looking to any guiding star but the shore, which we could see ahead; and at sunset we were so near that we thought we might make land before the night was far spent. But as there was no moon and the sky looked black, it did not seem safe to us to make for the coast, not knowing just where we were. Yet many of us wished to, even though it were among the rocks and far from any inhabited spot. For, as we said, in that case we need have no fear of the Tetuan pirates, who leave Barbary at night and are on the Spainish coast by dawn, where they generally pick up a prize and have got back home by nightfall. But after a great deal of discussion we decided to approach the land slowly, if the sea was calm enough to allow it, and to put ashore wherever we could. This we did, and it must have been a little before midnight when we arrived at the foot of a great hill, which stood back sufficiently from the sea to leave a little space suitable for our landing. We grounded on the beach, leapt ashore and kissed the earth. With tears of the greatest joy we gave thanks to the Lord God for His incomparable goodness to us. Then, taking out of the boat such

"He went on calling out his curses and lamentations, praying to Mahomet to beseech Allah to destroy us, confound us and annihilate us. And when we had hoisted sail and could no longer hear his words, we saw his actions, and watched him plucking his beard, tearing his hair and rolling on the ground." (page 501)

provisions as were in it, we dragged it ashore and climbed a good way up the hillside. But although we stood on Christian soil, we could not assure ourselves or really believe that it was so.

"Dawn came, I thought, more slowly than we could have wished. We climbed the hill to the top to see if we could make out a village or shepherd's huts. But though we strained our eyes, we could see no house or person, no path or road. So we decided to push on inland, for we could hardly fail to find someone soon who could tell us where we were. What distressed me most was to see Zoraida on foot in this rough country. For though at times I carried her on my shoulders, she was too distressed by my weariness to be refreshed by the rest it gave her. So she made me put her down and walked patiently on with a great show of cheerfulness, holding me by the hand. We must have gone something less than a mile when the tinkle of a little sheep-bell came to our ears, a sure sign that there was a flock somewhere near. We all looked carefully round to find it, and saw a shepherd lad at the foot of a cork-tree, comfortably and idly whittling a stick with his knife. When we called, he looked up and got briskly to his feet. But, as we afterwards learnt, the first of us he caught sight of were the renegade and Zoraida; and at the sight of their Moorish dress he thought that all the hosts of Barbary were upon him and, running at a surprising speed towards the wood ahead of us he began to bawl at the top of his voice, 'Moors! The Moors are ashore! Moors! Moors! To arms! To arms!'

"We were all bewildered by this outcry, and did not know what to do. But realizing that the shepherd's cries would rouse the countryside, and that the mounted coastguards would soon come to see what was the matter, we decided that the renegade should take off his Turkish robes and put on a jacket, or slave's coat, which one of our party gave him at once, though it left him in his shirt. So, commending ourselves to God, we took the path we had seen the shepherd take, expecting every moment that the coastguards would be upon us. And we were not wrong. For two hours had not gone by when, as we left the heath for the plain, we saw about fifty horsemen riding towards us at a very fast half-gallop. At the sight of them we halted and waited. But when they came up and saw a group of wretched Christians instead of the Moors they were expecting, they were puzzled; and one of them asked us if we by chance were the cause of the shepherd's hue and cry. I answered yes. But as I was going to tell him my story and who we were, one of the Christians in our party recognized the horseman who had asked us the question and, without giving me a chance to speak, cried out, 'Thanks be to God, gentlemen, for bringing us to so good a place. For, if I am not deceived, the soil we are treading is close to Velez Malaga. And if my years of captivity have not blotted your image from my mind, you, sir, who are asking us who we are, are my uncle, Pedro de Bustamante.'

"The Christian prisoner had no sooner spoken than the horseman jumped from his mount and ran to embrace the young man, crying, 'My beloved nephew, I do recognize you now. We mourned you for dead, I and my sister—your mother—and all your family, who are still living. For God has been pleased to spare our lives to enjoy the sight of you. We had learnt that you were at Algiers and, to judge by your clothes and the clothes of your whole party, you have had a miraculous deliverance.'

" 'That is so,' replied the young man, 'and we shall have time enough to tell you the whole story.'

"Immediately the horsemen realized that we were Christian captives they dismounted, and each one of them offered us his horse to ride to the city of Velez Malaga, which was about four and a half miles away. We told them where we had left the boat, and some of them turned back to get it and bring it along to the city. Others took us up behind them, and Zoraida rode behind our Christian's uncle. The whole town came out to greet us. For they had already had the news of our arrival from one of the guards, who had ridden ahead. They were not at all surprised at seeing escaped slaves or captured Moors, because all the people of that coast are used to seeing both; but they were astonished at Zoraida's beauty, which was at its height at that moment, by reason of the exertion of the journey and of her joy at finding herself on Christian soil, with no more to fear. This had brought such colour to her cheeks that, unless I was then much deceived by my love, I dare swear that there was no more beautiful creature in the world; at least none that I had ever seen.

"We went straight to the church to thank God for mercies received; and the moment Zoraida went in, she exclaimed that there were faces there which looked like Lela Marien's. We told her that those were her images, and the renegade made her understand, as best he could, what they signified, and that she could worship them as she would the true Lela Marien who had spoken to her. She has a good intelligence and an easy and clear intuition, and so she understood what he said about the images at once. They took us from there, and divided us among several houses in the town, but our companion from that place took the renegade, Zoraida and myself to the house of his parents, who were tolerably well provided with this world's goods, and treated us with as much affection as they did their son.

"We stayed in Velez six days, at the end of which the renegade, having lodged his statement in due form, went off to the city of Granada, to be reconciled to the bosom of Mother Church by means of the Holy Inquisition. The rest of the freed captives went each where he pleased. Only Zoraida and I remained with nothing but the crowns which the Frenchman in his kindness had given her. With these I bought the beast she rides. So I am travelling with her as her father and squire, but not as her husband, with the object of learning whether my father is alive, or if either of my brothers has had better fortune than I; though as Heaven has given me Zoraida as a companion, I do not think that the best lot that can befall me will seem better. Zoraida's patience in bearing the discomforts of poverty, and her desire to become a Christian, fill me with admiration, and bind me to serve her all the days of my life. But my happiness in knowing that I am hers and she is mine is troubled and spoilt by my uncertainty whether I shall find any corner of my country to shelter her. For I fear that time and death may have worked such changes in the fortunes and lives of my father and brothers that, failing them, I shall scarcely find anyone who knows me.

"There is no more of my story to tell you, gentlemen. I leave it to you to judge whether it is strange and entertaining. I can only say that I wish I had told it you more briefly, though fear of boring you has caused me to omit a great number of details."

⊰ *42* ⊱

Of Further Events at the Inn,
and Many Other Noteworthy Matters

*T*he Captive was silent after telling his tale, and Don Ferdinand observed, "I assure you, Captain, that the way in which you have told your strange adventure has been as remarkable as the strangeness and novelty of the events themselves. It is a curious tale and full of astonishing incidents. In fact we have enjoyed listening so much that we should be glad to have it all over again, even if it took till tomorrow morning to tell it."

On his saying this, Cardenio and all the others offered him their utmost services, in such warm and sincere language that the captain was thoroughly convinced of their goodwill. Don Ferdinand, in particular, offered to make his brother the Marquis stand godfather at Zoraida's baptism if he would return with him, and himself to provide him with enough money to appear in his own country with suitable dignity and decency. The Captive thanked him courteously for all this, but would not accept any of his generous offers.

By this time night had fallen, and when it was quite dark a coach came up to the inn with some men on horseback, who asked for accommodation. But the landlady answered that there was not an inch unoccupied in the whole inn.

"However that may be," said one of the horsemen, who had come in, "room must be found for my lord Judge, who is approaching."

At this title the landlady grew confused, and said, "Sir, the trouble is this, I have no beds. If his worship the Judge brings one with him, as I suppose he does, let him come in and welcome. My husband and I will give up our room to accommodate his worship."

"That will do," said the squire.

By this time there had alighted from the coach a man whose dress proclaimed his high office; for his long robe with ruffled sleeves proved that he was a judge, as his servant had said. He led by the hand a young lady of about sixteen in travelling dress, so gay, striking and beautiful that the sight of her impressed them all; and so vividly that, if they had not already seen Dorothea, Lucinda and Zoraida at that inn, they would have doubted whether she had her match for beauty.

Don Quixote was present at the entrance of the judge and the young lady; and as soon as he saw them, he said, "Your worship may certainly enter and take your ease in this castle. For, though it is narrow and uncomfortable, there is no place in the world so narrow and uncomfortable that it does not allow room for arms and learning. Especially if arms and letters bring beauty as their pilot and guide, as your worship's learning does in the person of this fair maiden, before whom not only should castles open and reveal themselves, but rocks split and mountains cleave and bow down to give her entertainment. Come into this paradise, I say, your worship, for here there are stars and suns to attend the heaven your worship brings with you. Here you will find arms at their zenith and beauty in its prime."

The judge was astounded at Don Quixote's speech, and after gazing at him attentively, was no less astounded at his appearance. But finding no words with which to reply, he fell into a fresh amazement at the sight of Lucinda, Dorothea and Zoraida, who had heard of the new guests and of the young lady's beauty from the landlady, and had come out to see her and welcome her. Don Ferdinand, Cardenio and the priest, however, gave the judge a simpler and more courteous greeting. That dignitary was indeed confused, both at what he saw and at what he heard, but the beauties of the inn made the lovely girl welcome. Presently the judge perceived that all the people there were people of quality, though he was bewildered at Don Quixote's figure, face and air. But when they had all exchanged polite greetings and carefully considered the accommodation of the inn, everything was arranged as before. All the women were to share the attic already described, and the men to stay outside, on guard as it were. So the judge was satisfied that his daughter—for such the young lady was—should lodge with the other ladies, which she was delighted to do; and with part of the landlord's narrow bed and half of the one the judge had brought, they managed better that night than they had expected.

Now the first moment he saw the judge the Captive felt his heart leap with the idea that this was his brother. So he asked one of the servants to tell him his master's name, and the district he came from, if he knew it. The squire replied that he was the Licentiate Juan Perez de Viedma, and that he had heard that he came from a little place in the mountains of Leon. This information, together with what he had seen, finally confirmed him in the belief that this was his brother who by their father's advice had followed the profession of learning. The excited and delighted Captive then called Don Ferdinand, Cardenio and the priest aside to tell them, assuring them that the judge really was his brother. What is more, the servant had told him that he was going to take up the post of judge in the Indies, in the High Court of Mexico; also that the young lady was his daughter, whose mother had died at her birth, and that he had become very rich from the dowry left him with the child. The captain asked them to advise him how to reveal himself, or how to find out first whether his brother would be ashamed to discover him poor, or would acknowledge him with open arms, were he to do so.

"Leave it to me to make the experiment," said the priest. "I will gladly do so, for there is no reason to think that you will not be very well received, Captain. Your brother shows every sign of goodness and good sense, and his behaviour does not suggest that he is arrogant or ungrateful, or does not know how to assess the accidents of fortune at their true value."

"All the same," said the captain, "I should like to reveal myself in a roundabout way, and not suddenly."

"I promise you," said the priest, "that I will manage it in such a way that we shall all be satisfied."

By this time supper was ready, and all sat down to table except the captain and the ladies, who were supping on their own in their room. Then in the middle of the meal the priest remarked, "I had a comrade of your name, Sir Judge, at Constantinople, where I was a slave for several years. That man was one of the bravest commanders in all the Spanish infantry; but, brave and enterprising as he was, he was unfortunate."

"What was this captain's name, sir?" asked the judge.

"His name," replied the priest, "was Ruiz Perez de Viedma, and he came from a place in the mountains of Leon. He told me of an incident that had happened to him and his brothers, which I should have taken for an old wives' tale told over a winter fire, if it had not been related by so truthful a man. What he told me was that his father had divided his property among his three sons, and had given them some advice which was better than Cato's. By his father's advice, anyhow, he went into the army; and in a few years, by his courage and application, he rose to be an infantry captain, by his own merits alone, and was on the way to be a colonel very soon. But fortune went against him. For when he might have expected things to be good his luck broke, and he lost his liberty as well, on that most happy day when many recovered theirs, at the battle of Lepanto. I lost mine at the Goletta, and afterwards, by various accidents, we found ourselves comrades in Constantinople. From there he went to Algiers, where, as I learnt, one of the strangest accidents in the world happened to him."

From there the priest went on, and briefly told him the story of

Zoraida and his brother, which the judge heard with greater attention than he had ever given to a case before. The priest stopped at the point when the French robbed the Christians in the boat, and ended with a description of the poverty in which they had left his comrade and the fair Moorish lady. He said that he had not heard what had become of them since, whether they had reached Spain or if the Frenchmen had carried them off to France.

The captain listened to all that the priest said, standing some way off and noting all his brother's movements. And when he saw that the priest had come to the end of his tale, the judge gave a deep sigh and exclaimed, with his eyes filling with tears, "Oh, sir, if you knew what news you had given me, and how nearly it touches me! But I cannot help showing it by the tears which spring to my eyes in spite of all my fortitude and self-control! This brave captain you speak of is my eldest brother. He was stronger and more courageous than my other brother or I, and chose the honourable and worthy profession of arms—one of the three courses our father proposed to us, as your comrade told you in that tale of his which you thought was a fiction. I followed the career of learning, in which God and my own hard work have raised me to the rank you see. My younger brother is in Peru, and so rich that, with what he has sent to my father and me, he has more than made up for the capital he took away. He has even given my father enough to satisfy his natural prodigality; and thanks to him, I have been able to follow my studies in a very fitting and creditable fashion, and to reach my present position. My father is still alive, though dying with desire for news of his eldest son, and praying God night and day not to let death close his eyes before he has seen him alive. I am astonished that such a sensible fellow could have failed to send my father news in his great troubles and afflictions, or in his times of prosperity. Had our father or either of us been informed, he would not have had to wait for that miraculous cane to get his ransom. But it troubles me now not to know whether those Frenchmen set him free or killed him to cover up their robbery; and for that reason I shall not continue my journey joyfully as I began it, but in sadness and melancholy. Oh, my dear brother, who can tell where you are now? How gladly I would seek you and relieve you of your hardships, even at the cost of hardships to myself! Who will bear the news to our father that you are still alive, though perhaps in the deepest dungeons of Barbary? But even from there his riches, my brother's, and mine will rescue you. Oh lovely, generous Zoraida, who could ever repay you the good you have done my brother? Who will be present at your soul's rebirth, and at that wedding which would give us all such happiness?"

These were the judge's words, and he said more to the same effect, full of emotion at this news of his brother; and all the rest of the party too showed their compassion for his anxiety. The priest, however, seeing that he had succeeded by his trick in carrying out the captain's wishes, did not want to keep them any longer in sadness. So, getting up from the table and going into the room where Zoraida was, he led her out by the hand, followed by Lucinda, Dorothea and the judge's daughter. The captain stood waiting to see what the priest would do; and what he did was to take him by the other hand, and lead them both up to the place where the judge and the rest of the gentlemen were sitting.

"Cease your tears, Sir Judge," said he, "and your wish shall be crowned with all happiness. For here you have your dear brother and your dear sister-in-law before you. Here is Captain Viedma, and this is the lovely Moorish lady, his benefactress. The Frenchmen, as I told you, reduced them to their present plight only so that you might show them the generosity of your noble heart."

The captain started forward to embrace his brother, but the judge held him off awhile, with his arms on his shoulders, to look at him from a little farther off. Once he had recognized him, however, he embraced him so warmly and shed such tender tears of happiness, that most of the company had to weep as well. The words the two brothers uttered and the feelings they displayed can hardly be conceived, still less written down. First they exchanged brief accounts of their adventures; then they displayed the warmth of brotherly love; next the judge embraced Zoraida; then he offered her

516

Don Quixote was present at the entrance of the judge and the young lady; and as soon as he saw them, he said, "Your worship may certainly enter and take your ease in this castle. For, though it is narrow and uncomfortable, there is no place in the world so narrow and uncomfortable that it does not allow room for arms and learning." (page 512) all his possessions; then he made her embrace his daughter; then the lovely Christian girl and the most lovely Moor moved everyone to fresh tears. And there stood Don Quixote, listening and speechless, pondering on these extraordinary events and attributing them all to the chimaeras of knight errantry.

Soon they arranged that the captain and Zoraida should return with his brother to Seville and advise their father of his finding and deliverance, so that the old man might be able to come and be present at Zoraida's marriage and baptism. For it was not possible for the judge to abandon his present voyage, as he had news that the fleet was leaving Seville in a month's time for New Spain, and it would be most inconvenient for him to lose his passage.

The whole company was more than delighted at the captain's good fortune; and as by now almost two-thirds of the night was gone, they agreed to retire and spend the rest of it in sleep. Don Quixote took it on himself to mount guard over the castle, in case they might be attacked by some giant or unscrupulous villain, greedy for the great treasure of beauty which lay therein. Those who knew him thanked him, and gave the judge an account of the knight's strange humour, which delighted him more than a little. Only Sancho Panza was annoyed at the delay in going to bed; and he made himself more comfortable than any of them, throwing himself down on his ass's harness—which cost him very dear, as shall be told by and by. The ladies then having retired to their apartment, and the others accommodating themselves with the least discomfort possible, Don Quixote went out of the inn to be sentinel of the castle, as he had promised.

Now a little before dawn there reached the ears of the ladies a voice so sweet and musical that it compelled them all to listen, especially Dorothea, who was awake, though Doña Clara de Viedma—for this was the name of the judge's daughter—was asleep at her side. No one could imagine who it could be that sang so well; it was a single voice without instrumental accompaniment. At times it sounded as if the singing came from the yard, at times from the

519

stable; and, while they were listening thus undecided, Cardenio came to the door of the room and said, "If anyone is awake, listen and you will hear a mule-lad singing. As he chants, he enchants."

"We can hear him, sir," replied Dorothea. At which Cardenio departed, and Dorothea, listening with great attention, heard the words that he was singing. They were these:

❧ 43 ☙

The Charming Story of the Mule-Lad,
with Other Strange Happenings at the Inn

I am a mariner of love,
And in his depths profound
Sail on, although without a hope
Ever to come to ground.

My eyes are on a distant star,
Which serves me for a guide
More beautiful and bright than all
That Palinurus spied.

I know not where it's leading me;
And so, confused, I steer,
My heart intent on watching it,
Careless, yet full of care.

And her unkindly shyness,
And too much modesty
Are clouds that shroud her from my eyes,
Whom most I long to see.

My Clara, clear and shining star,
I fade beneath thy light,
And when you hide your beams from me
For me it's darkest night.

When the singer had reached this point in his song, Dorothea thought it would be a pity if Clara did not hear such a lovely voice, and so she shook her until she woke her up, saying, "Forgive my waking you, child. But I want you to enjoy the finest voice you will ever hear in all your life."

Clara woke up very drowsy, and did not understand at first what Dorothea was saying, but asked her to tell her again. She then repeated her words, upon which Clara began to listen. But scarcely had she heard two verses of the song than she was seized with a violent trembling, as if she had been taken with a serious attack of the quartan ague, and hugged Dorothea tightly, crying, "Oh, my dear, dear lady, why did you wake me up? For the greatest good that Fortune could do me now would be to keep my eyes and ears shut, so that I should neither see nor hear that unhappy musician."

"What is that you say, girl? They tell me that the singer is a mule-lad."

"No, he is not," replied Clara, "but a lord of many estates, and one he holds in my heart so firmly that, unless he wishes to quit his tenure, it will be his for ever."

Surprised at the girl's passionate words, which seemed to her much in advance of her apparent youth, Dorothea then said, "You speak so obscurely that I cannot understand you. Explain yourself more clearly. Tell me what you mean by heart and estates, and about this singer whose song disturbs you so. But do not tell me anything now. I do not want your transports to rob me of the pleasure of hearing the singer, for I think he is going to sing again, with new words and to a new tune."

"Let him by all means," replied Clara. But she put her hands over both her ears to avoid hearing him, which surprised Dorothea once more. But she listened to the song, which ran like this:

Sweet hope of mine,
That break'st impossibilities and briars,
And down that path dost run
Which thou thyself didst make for thy desires,
Be not dismayed to see
At every step thyself nigh death to be.

Sluggards do not deserve
The glory of triumphs or of victory;
Good luck will never serve
Those who resist not fortune manfully,
But weakly fall to ground,
And in soft sloth their senses all confound.

That love his glories holds
At a high rate is reasonable and best;
No precious stones nor gold
Excel those pledges by love's hand impressed;
And 'tis a thing most clear,
Nothing is worth esteem that costs not dear.

An amorous persistence
Will often win things most impossible;
So though I find resistance
To my soul's deep desires, in her stern will,
There's not a fear denies
That I shall climb from earth to her fair skies.

Here the voice ceased, and Clara broke into fresh sobs, all of which excited Dorothea's desire to know the cause of the sweet singing and the mournful tears. So once more she asked Clara what it was she had meant to say before. Then, out of fear that Lucinda might hear her, Clara hugged Dorothea tightly and put her mouth so close to her ear that she could safely speak without being overheard.

"The singer, my lady," she said, "is the son of a gentleman of the Kingdom of Aragon, the lord of two villages, who used to live opposite my father's house in Madrid. And although my father has the windows of his house covered with canvas in the winter and with blinds in the summer, I do not know how it was, but this young student saw me, either in church or somewhere else. He fell in love with me, in fact, and gave me to understand so from the windows of his house, so emphatically and with such tears that I had to believe him and love him too, though I did not know what it was he wanted of me. One of the gestures he made me was to clasp his two hands together as a sign that he wanted to marry me; and although I should have been very glad for that to be, as I was alone and motherless I did not know whom to tell about it. So I let things be, and showed him no favour; though, when my father was out of the house and his father too, I did lift the curtain or the blind a little and let him see all of me; and he was so enraptured that he seemed almost beside himself. Then the time came for my father's departure; and he learnt of it, though not from me, for I could never tell him. He fell ill of grief, I understand, and so on the day we left I could not see him to say good-bye, not even by a glance. But when we had been two days on the road, as we were riding into an inn in a village a day's journey from here, I saw him at the door of the house, dressed as a mule-lad; and so much like one that if I had not borne his portrait in my heart, I should have found it impossible to recognize him. I knew him; I was amazed; I was delighted. He stole a look at me, undetected by my father, from whom he always hides his face when he passes in front of us on the roads, and as we come to the inns. But knowing who he is, and reflecting that it is for love of me that he travels on foot and endures all these hardships, I am dying of grief, and I follow his every step with my eyes. I do not know his purpose in coming, nor how he managed to escape his father, who loves him extremely, both because he has no other heir and because he deserves it, as you will find when you see him. What is more, let me tell you that all that he sings comes out of his own head, for I have heard that he is a very great scholar and poet. And there is another thing, each time I see him or hear him sing, I tremble all over, for fear my father will recognize him and come to know of our feelings. I have never spoken a word to him in my life, but, all the same, I love him so much that I cannot live without him. That is all that I can tell you, dear lady, about the musician whose voice has pleased you so; but from that alone you can clearly tell that he is no mule-lad, as you say, but a lord of hearts and lands, as I have told you."

"Say no more, dear Doña Clara," said Dorothea at this point, kissing her countless times. "Say no more, I tell you, but wait till the day dawns. For I hope, with God's help, to set your affairs on the way towards the happy ending such a good beginning deserves."

"But what ending can we expect, dear lady," asked Doña Clara, "seeing that his father is so rich and important that he will not think me fit to be his son's servant, much less his wife? Then, I would not marry without my father's knowledge for anything in the world. I only want the young man to go back and leave me. Perhaps with not seeing him, and with the great distance we are going to travel, the pain I feel now might grow less; though I must say that I do not think this remedy I am imagining can be of much use to me. I do not know what witchcraft there has been, nor how this love I feel for him has entered into me, since we are both so young—for I really believe we are of the same age, and I am not quite sixteen yet, nor shall be, my father says, till Michaelmas day."

Dorothea could not prevent herself from laughing at Doña Clara's childish way of talking, and said, "Let us sleep, dear lady, for a little of the night is still left, I think. God will send us morning, and things will go well if my skill does not fail me."

With this they fell asleep, and the whole inn lay in deep silence. Only the innkeeper's daughter and her maid Maritornes were not asleep. For, knowing the ideas that possessed Don Quixote, and that he was outside the inn, mounted on guard, the pair of them decided to play him a trick, or at least to get some amusement by listening to his nonsense.

Now there was not a single window in the whole inn that opened on to the fields, but only a hole in a loft, used for throwing out the straw. At this hole the two demi-virgins placed themselves, and espied Don Quixote on his horse, leaning on his lance and, at intervals, heaving such mournful and deep sighs that each one of them seemed to tear out his soul. At the same time they heard him speak in soft, delicate and amorous tones, "O my lady Dulcinea del Toboso, sum of all beauty, summit and crown of discretion, treasury of grace, store of virtue and, lastly, pattern of all that is beneficent, modest and delightful in the world! What is your grace doing at this moment? Can it be that you are mindful of your captive knight, who has submitted himself freely to so many perils, only to serve you? Let me have news of her, O three-faced luminary, Diana! Perhaps you are gazing on her now in envy of her looks, and see her pacing some gallery of her sumptuous palaces, or leaning with her breast upon some balcony rail, considering how, without danger to her modesty or greatness, she may alleviate the torment my aching heart suffers for her sake, with what glory she may crown my labours, what assuagement she may give to my anxiety, and lastly, what life to my death, and what reward to my services. And you, sun, who must even now be saddling your steeds in haste to rise and see my lady, I pray you, when you see her, salute her from me! But beware, when you gaze on her and salute her, not to kiss her on the face, or I shall be more jealous of her than you were of that wanton and fickle maid who made you sweat and run across the plains of Thessaly, or by the banks of Peneus—for I do not well remember where you ran then in your jealous passion."

When Don Quixote had reached this point in his mournful harangue the innkeeper's daughter began to call to him softly, "Dear sir, come this way, if you please."

At this sound Don Quixote turned his head, and saw by the light of the moon, which was then at its brightest, that someone was beckoning him from the hole, which seemed to him to be a window, and even to have gilded bars, which are proper to such rich castles as he imagined that inn to be. Instantly he conceived in his wild imagination that once again, as before, that beauteous damsel, the daughter of the warden of that castle, had come, overwhelmed by love of him, to ask for his favours. With this thought, not wishing to show himself discourteous or ungrateful, he turned Rocinante's head and went up to the window. Then, when he saw the two wenches there, he said, "I pity you, beauteous lady, for fixing your amorous desires where it is impossible for you to find a response befitting your great merit and breeding, for which you must not blame this wretched knight errant, whom love makes incapable of engaging his heart to any but that maiden whom, from the first moment his eyes lighted on her, he made absolute lady of his soul. Pardon me, kind lady, and retire to your room. Please do not reveal your desires to me further, that I may not appear yet more thankless. Though if, of the love you bear me, you can discover in me anything other than love itself by which I may satisfy you, demand it of me; and I swear to you, by that sweet and absent enemy of mine, to bestow it upon you out of hand, even if you should demand of me a lock of Medusa's hair, which was all snakes, or even the very rays of the sun enclosed in a flask."

"My lady needs none of that, Sir Knight," put in Maritornes at this juncture.

"What then does she need, discreet lady?" asked Don Quixote.

"Only one of your beautiful hands," replied Maritornes, "with which to appease the great desire which has brought her to this window, at such risk to her honour that if my lord, her father, came to know of it, the least slice he would cut off her would be her ear."

"I should like to see him do that!" answered Don Quixote. "But he will take good care not to, if he does not wish to come to the most disastrous end that ever a father met in all the world, for laying his hands on the delicate limbs of his enamoured daughter."

Maritornes had now no doubt that Don Quixote would give her the hand she had asked him for and, turning her plan over in her mind, got down from the hole and went to the stable, from which she fetched the halter of Sancho Panza's ass. Then she hastily returned to the hole, just as Don Quixote was standing up on Rocinante's saddle to reach the barred window at which he imagined the love-lorn lady was standing. And, as he gave her his hand, he said, "Take this hand, lady, or rather this scourge of the world's malefactors. Take this hand, I say, which no other woman's has touched, not even hers who has complete possession of my whole body. I do not give it to you to kiss, but that you may gaze on the structure of its sinews, the interlacement of its muscles, the width and capacity of its veins, from all of which you may judge what strength must be in the arm to which such a hand belongs."

"We shall see that presently," said Maritornes, and making a running knot in the halter, she threw it over his wrist. Then, as she came down from the hole, she tied the other end very firmly to the bolt of the hay-loft door. At which Don Quixote exclaimed, feeling the roughness of the cord on his wrist, "Your ladyship seems to be grating my hand rather than fondling it. Do not ill-treat it so. It is not to blame for the ill my heart does you, nor is it right that you should avenge your whole displeasure on so small a part of me. Consider, one who loves so well should not take such ill vengeance."

But no one was listening to this speech of Don Quixote's. For as soon as Maritornes had tied him up the two of them went off, dying of laughter, and left him so secured that it was impossible for him to free himself. He was, as we have said, standing upon Rocinante, with his arm thrust through the hole and attached by the wrist to the bolt of the door, in the greatest fear and anxiety that he would be left hanging by the arm, if Rocinante were to stir to one side or the other. So he dared not make any movement; though, to judge from Rocinante's patience and quietness, he might well have expected him to stand there motionless for a whole century. In the end, finding that he was tied up and that the ladies had vanished, Don Quixote began to imagine that all this was a matter of enchantment, as on the previous occasion when the enchanted Moor of a carrier had mauled him in that same castle. And in his heart he cursed his lack of sense and judgement in venturing to enter it a second time after coming off so badly the first. For it is a rule among knights errant that their having once attempted an adventure and failed in it is a sign that it is not reserved for them but for others, and that they are therefore under no necessity of making a second attempt. However, he pulled his arm to see if he could get free, but he was so

Then she hastily returned to the hole, just as Don Quixote was standing up on Rocinante's saddle to reach the barred window at which he imagined the love-lorn lady was standing. And, as he gave her his hand, he said, "Take this hand, lady, or rather this scourge of the world's malefactors." (page 527) fast tied that all his endeavours were in vain. It is true that he pulled cautiously, for fear that Rocinante might move; but though he longed to sit down on the saddle, he could do nothing but remain standing or tug off his hand.

At times he longed for Amadis' sword, which was proof against any kind of enchantment; at others he cursed his fortune; then he dwelt upon the loss the world suffered through lack of him all the while he remained there enchanted, as he had no doubt at all he was. Then once more he remembered his beloved Dulcinea del Toboso; then he started calling for his good squire Sancho Panza, who lay drowned in sleep, stretched on his ass's pack-saddle, and oblivious at that moment even of the mother who bore him; then he called on the sages Lirgandeo and Alquife to help him; then he invoked his good friend Urganda to come to his rescue; and in the end morning found him there, despairing, bewildered and bellowing like a bull. For he had no hope that day would relieve his plight, which he believed to be eternal, since he imagined he was bewitched. This belief was strengthened when he found that Rocinante did not move or stir, from which he concluded that he and his horse would have to remain like that, without eating, drinking or sleeping, until that malign influence of the stars should pass, or until another more learned enchanter should break the spell.

But in these beliefs he was much mistaken. For it was no sooner dawn than four well-dressed and equipped horsemen rode up to the inn with their firelocks on their saddle-bows. They called and thundered at the inn doors, which were still shut; and when Don Quixote saw them from the position in which he was still on guard, he cried out to them in loud and commanding tones, "Knights, or squires, or whoever you may be, you have no right to knock on the doors of this castle; for it is abundantly clear that at such an hour those within are either asleep or, at least, unaccustomed to opening their fortress until the sun has covered the whole land. Retire without, and wait till day grows bright, and then we shall see whether it be right or not to open to you."

"What the devil's this fortress or castle," cried one of them, "to keep us standing on these ceremonies? If you're the landlord, have the doors opened for us. We are travellers, and all we want is to bait our horses and ride on, for we are in a hurry."

"Do I seem to you, knights, to have the air of an innkeeper?" asked Don Quixote.

"I don't know what you look like," replied the traveller, "but I know you're talking nonsense when you call this inn a castle."

"A castle it is," replied Don Quixote, "one of the finest in the whole province, and there are people within who have carried a sceptre in their hands and a crown on their heads."

"It would be better the other way round," said the traveller; "a sceptre on their heads and a crown branded on their hands. Though perhaps what you mean is that there's some company of actors inside; they often wear these crowns and sceptres you talk of. For I can't think that people good enough to have crowns and sceptres are lodging in a little inn like this one, and where it's so quiet too."

"You know little of the world," replied Don Quixote, "since you are ignorant of the events which occur in knight errantry."

The questioner's companions, growing impatient at his conversation with Don Quixote, began to knock furiously again, and so hard that the innkeeper and everyone else in the inn woke up. The host then got up to enquire who was knocking.

In the meanwhile one of the four travellers' horses happened to smell Rocinante, who was standing motionless, melancholy and sad, with drooping ears, bearing up his outstretched master; and being, after all, of flesh and blood, though he seemed of wood, he could not resist showing some feeling and smelling back at the creature who was making these endearing advances. But no sooner did he make the slightest movement than Don Quixote's feet, which were close together, slipped and, sliding from the saddle, would have landed him on the ground, had he not been hanging by his arm, which caused him so much pain that he felt as though his wrist were being cut off or his arm torn from its socket. For he was hanging so near the ground that he could touch it with the tips of his toes; which made his plight worse because, when he felt what a little way the soles of his feet were from the earth, he struggled and stretched his utmost to get them down. In fact, he was very like someone put to the torture of the "strappado," in which the victim's feet neither quite touch nor quite fail to touch the earth, and so he increases his own agony in his anxiety to stretch himself, in the delusory hope that with a little more stretching he will reach the ground.

⊰ *44* ⊱

Of More Extraordinary
Adventures at the Inn

*F*inally Don Quixote raised such a clamour that the inn doors were suddenly opened, and the inn-keeper came out in a fright to see who it was shouting so loud. Maritornes too was awakened by his cries and, guessing what it was, went to the hay-loft where, unobserved, she untied the halter which held Don Quixote up. The knight then fell to the ground in front of the innkeeper and the travellers, and they went up to him to ask him what it was that made him shout so loud. He did not reply, but slipped the cord from his wrist and rose to his feet. Then, mounting Rocinante, he braced his shield, couched his lance and, making a wide sweep round the field, came back at a canter, exclaiming, "Should anyone affirm that I have been rightfully enchanted, if I have the leave of my lady, the princess Micomicona, I will give him the lie, and challenge and defy him to single combat."

The new arrivals were astounded at Don Quixote's speech; but the landlord relieved their surprise by telling them who he was, and that they need pay no attention to him, for he was out of his mind.

They then asked the innkeeper whether a lad of about fifteen, dressed as a mule-lad, had by any chance come to his inn, and gave a description of him which tallied with the appearance of Doña Clara's lover. The landlord answered that there were so many people in the inn that he had not noticed the person they were asking for. But when one of them saw the coach in which the judge had come, he exclaimed, "He must be here. There can be no doubt of it, for this is the coach they say he was following. Let one of us stay at the door, and the rest go in and look for him. No, it might be as well if one of us were to ride round the inn, in case he should get away over the yard walls."

"Let's do as you say," replied another of them. Then two of them went in, one stayed at the door and the fourth started riding round the inn. The landlord watched all this, and could not conceive what they were taking these precautions for, though he knew quite well that they were looking for the lad whom they had described to him.

By now it was broad daylight; and for that reason, and because of the noise Don Quixote had made, everyone was awake and getting up, particularly Doña Clara and Dorothea, who had been able to sleep very little that night, one of them from excitement because her lover was so near, the other from eagerness to see this lad. Now Don Quixote felt near to bursting with rage, anger and fury when he found all four travellers ignoring him, and not one of them replying to his challenge; and could he have found it in his code of chivalry that a knight may lawfully undertake another enterprise despite his plighted word first to complete the one he is pledged to, he would have attacked them all and forced an answer out of them. But as it did not seem to him right or proper to begin a new undertaking till he had established Micomicona on her throne, he had to hold his tongue, keep quiet and wait to see the result of the travellers' searching. It ended by one of them finding the young gentleman he was looking for sleeping beside a mule-lad, and little dreaming that anyone was looking for him or still less that he was found. The man, however, pulled him by the arm, and said, "Really, Don Louis, the clothes you are wearing are *most* suitable to your rank, and the bed I find you on accords *in every way* with the luxury your mother brought you up in!"

The lad rubbed his sleepy eyes and, staring for a while at his captor, finally recognized him as a servant of his father's. This gave him such a surprise that for some time he could not manage to speak a word. And so the servant went on, "There is nothing else for it now, Don Louis, but to be patient, and give in, and come back home, if you don't want your father, my master, to take a journey to the other world. For it's very much to be feared he will, he's so upset at your absence."

"Why, how did my father know," asked Don Louis, "that I had come this way and in this disguise?"

"There was a student you told your plan to, and he was so upset at your father's grief when he missed you that he gave you away. So our master sent off four of us servants to look for you; and here we all are at your service, more delighted than you can think that we can go back so quickly and restore you to the sight of your very loving father."

"That shall be as I wish, or as Heaven decrees," replied Don Louis.

"What can you wish or Heaven decree, except that you agree to come back with us? There is no other course possible."

All these arguments were overheard by the mule-lad lying next to Don Louis, who got up to tell Don Ferdinand, Cardenio and the rest, who were now dressed, what was happening. He reported that the man was calling the lad "Don," and repeated their conversation, saying that the man wanted the boy to go back to his father's house, but that he would not. This and so much as they already knew of him—the fine voice Heaven had blessed him with—made them all most anxious to learn more about him, and even to help him, should the men try to do him any violence. So they went to the spot where he was, and found him still protesting to his servant. At the same moment Dorothea came out of her room, and Doña Clara after her in great alarm. Dorothea called Cardenio aside and told him very briefly the story of the singer and of Doña Clara; and he told her what had happened when his father's servants had come to look for him. But he did not speak quite quietly enough, for Doña Clara overheard him, and got into such a state that she would have fallen down if Dorothea had not managed to catch her. Then Cardenio told Dorothea to take the girl back to their room, and promised to try and set everything to rights. So back they went.

Now all four of Don Louis' pursuers had entered the inn, and were standing round him, urging him to come back instantly, without losing a moment, and console his father. He replied that on no account could he do so until he had completed a matter on which depended his life, his honour and his heart. The servants then insisted, saying that under no circumstances would they return without him, and that they would take him whether he agreed or not.

"That you will not do," replied Don Louis, "unless you take me dead; although whatever way you take me, I shall be lifeless."

Now by this time everyone else in the inn had come up to hear the argument, in particular Cardenio, Don Ferdinand, his companions, the judge, the priest, the barber and Don Quixote, who now thought that there was no more need to guard the castle. Cardenio, who knew the boy's story already, asked the servants what motive they had for wishing to take the lad against his will.

"Our reason," replied one of the four, "is to save his father's life, for he's in danger of losing it through this gentleman's absence."

To which Don Louis replied, "There is no reason why I should give an account of my business here. I am free. I shall go back if I please, and if I do not, none of you shall compel me."

"Reason will compel you to," replied the man, "and if that's not enough for your worship, it's enough to make us do our duty, which is what we came for."

"Let us know what is at the bottom of this," put in the judge at this point.

But the man, who recognized him as a neighbour, replied, "Do you not know this gentleman, my Lord Judge? He is your neighbour's son, and he has run away from his father's house in a disguise most unbecoming to his quality, as your worship can see."

The judge then looked at the lad more closely, recognized him and embraced him, saying, "What childishness is this, Don Louis? What mighty reason can you have had for coming out in this fashion, and in a dress so unfitting to your rank?"

Tears came into the lad's eyes, and he could not answer a single word. But the judge told the four servants to rest assured that everything would be all right. Then, taking Don Louis by the hand, he drew him aside and demanded his reasons for coming.

While the judge was asking him various questions, a great uproar was heard at the inn door. The cause of it was that two guests who had stayed the night there had seen that everyone was busy enquiring about these four men, and had tried to get away without paying their reckoning. But the innkeeper was more attentive to his own business than to other people's and, laying hold of them as they were going out of the door, demanded his money. He called them such names, too, for their dirty trick that they were moved to reply with their fists, and had begun to do so with such vigour that the poor innkeeper had to shout for help. The landlady and her daughter could see no one who was not too busy to help him except Don Quixote, and it was to him the daughter shouted, "Help, Sir Knight, by the power God gave you, help my poor father, for here are two wicked men thrashing him like corn."

To which Don Quixote replied slowly and with great composure, "Beauteous damsel, your petition is ill-timed, for I am prevented from embarking on any other adventure until I have brought the one to which I have pledged myself to a successful conclusion. But what I can do to serve you I will inform you now. Run and tell your father that he must hold his own in the battle as best he can, and on no account let himself be conquered, whilst I beg Princess Micomicona's permission to help him in his distress; and if she gives it to me, you may be assured that I shall rescue him."

"Sure as I'm a sinner," said Maritornes, who was standing near, "before your worship gets this permission of yours, my master will be in the other world."

"Allow me, lady, only to get this permission," replied Don Quixote. "For once I have got it, it will matter very little if he is in the other world. I will fetch him out of it, if the whole of that world oppose me. Or, at least, I will wreak such vengeance for you on those who sent him there that you will be more than moderately satisfied."

Then without another word he went down on his knees in front of Dorothea, begging her in knightly and errant-like words that her Highness would be pleased to give him permission to help and succour the warden of that castle, who was in a grievous pass. The Princess gave it him most readily, and he instantly buckled his shield, grasped his sword and ran to the inn door, where the two guests were still pounding the landlord. But no sooner did he get there than he wavered and stood still, although Maritornes and the landlady demanded what it was that prevented him from helping their master and husband.

"I delay," said Don Quixote, "because it is not lawful for me to draw my sword against squires and the like. Call my squire Sancho here, for this defence and vengeance properly concerns him."

In the meantime the fight at the inn door was reaching a climax, and the landlord was getting the worst of it, which infuriated the landlady, her daughter and Maritornes, who were beside themselves at the sight of Don Quixote's cowardice and the damage their husband, father and master was sustaining.

But let us leave him there, for someone is bound to help him; or, if no one does, let him suffer in silence for his rashness in taking on more than his strength warrants; and let us go back fifty paces and see how Don Louis answered the judge, whom we left asking him privately the reason for his travelling on foot in such poor clothes. The boy then clasped him tightly with both hands, in sign that his heart was oppressed by some great sorrow and, shedding copious tears, answered, "My dear sir, the only thing that I can tell you is that from the moment when Heaven fated us to be neighbours and I

539

saw Doña Clara, your daughter and my lady, I made her mistress of my heart; and if your wishes, my true lord and father, do not hinder me, she shall be my wife this very day. For her I left my father's house; for her I put on these clothes, to follow her wherever she went, as the arrow does the mark, or the sailor the pole-star. She knows no more of my passion than she has been able to learn on the few occasions when she has seen from a distance the tears in my eyes. Now you, sir, know that my family is rich and noble, and that I am their only heir. If these seem to you sufficient advantages, venture to make me completely happy and accept me now as your son. For though my father may be intent on other plans of his own, and may not approve the blessing I have found for myself, yet time has more power to undo and alter things than has human will."

With this the enamoured youth fell silent. The judge was astonished, perturbed and perplexed, as much by Don Louis' sensible way of revealing his feelings as at finding himself in such a predicament. In fact he did not know what line to take in this sudden and unexpected situation. His only reply, therefore, was to ask Don Louis to keep calm for the time being and arrange with his servants not to go back that day. Then he would have time to consider what was best for everybody. At this Don Louis seized and kissed his hands, bathing them with tears, which would have melted a heart of stone, let alone the judge's. As a man of the world, he had already realized how good a match this would be for his daughter; though he hoped it would be possible for it to be concluded with the consent of Don Louis' father who, he knew, was aspiring to get a title for his son.

By this time the guests and the innkeeper had made their peace, for, through Don Quixote's persuasion and fair words rather than by threats, they had paid their full reckoning. Don Louis' servants, too, were waiting quietly for the judge to conclude his speech and for their master to make his decision, when the Devil, who never sleeps, ordained the sudden arrival at the inn of that barber from whom Don Quixote had taken Mambrino's helmet, and Sancho Panza the ass's harness which he had exchanged for his own. As this barber

Maritornes too was awakened by his cries and, guessing what it was, went to the hay-loft where, unobserved, she untied the halter which held Don Quixote up. The knight then fell to the ground in front of the innkeeper and the travellers, and they went up to him to ask him what it was that made him shout so loud. (page 534) was taking his ass to the stable, he saw Sancho Panza mending some part of the pack-saddle; and as soon as he recognized him, he attacked him boldly, crying, "I've got you now, master thief! Give me back my basin and my saddle with all the harness you robbed me of."

Finding himself suddenly attacked, and hearing this abuse poured on him, Sancho grasped the saddle in one hand and gave the barber a punch with the other, which bathed his jaws in blood. But this did not make him leave go of the saddle; instead, he gave such a shout that everyone in the inn hurried towards the noise of this scuffle.

"Help, in the name of the King and of justice!" cried he. "For I am taking back my property. This thief, this highwayman wants to kill me."

"You're lying," answered Sancho. "I'm no highwayman, for my master Don Quixote won these spoils in fair fight."

Don Quixote, who had now come up, was delighted to see his squire attacking and defending himself so well, and from then on he thought of him as a man of courage. He decided at that moment in his heart to knight him at the first available opportunity, confident that he was a fitting recipient of the order of chivalry. Now one of the things which the barber said in the course of the fight was, "Sirs, this saddle is as much mine as the death I owe God. I recognize it as positively as if I had brought it into the world, and there is my ass in the stable who will not let me lie. Try it on him and see; if it doesn't fit just right, call me a liar. What is more, the same day they took it from me they took a new brass basin as well. It had never been used and was worth a good crown."

Here Don Quixote could not refrain from answering him, and pushing himself between the pair to part them—the pack-saddle being laid on the ground for public inspection until the truth should be cleared up. "Gentlemen," he cried, "you may clearly and man-ifestly see this good squire's error in calling that a basin which was, is and shall be Mambrino's helmet, that I won from him in fair fight, thus becoming its legitimate and lawful owner! In the matter of the pack-saddle I will not interfere. All that I can say is that my squire

Sancho asked my permission to strip the trappings from the horse of this vanquished coward and to adorn his own with them. I gave it him, and he took them. As for their being changed from horse's harness to pack-saddle, I can give no other explanation than the common one, that these transformations occur in affairs of chivalry. To confirm which, run Sancho my son, and bring the helmet which this good fellow says is a basin."

"Good Lord, sir," said Sancho, "if we've no better proof of our case than what your worship's saying, Mambrino's helmet is as much a basin as this good fellow's harness is a pack-saddle."

"Do what I bid you," replied Don Quixote, "for it cannot be that everything in this castle is governed by enchantment."

Sancho went and fetched the basin and, as soon as Don Quixote saw it, he took it in his hands and said, "Look, your worships, how can this squire have the face to say that this is a basin and not the said helmet? I swear by the order of chivalry, which I profess, that this was the same helmet I took from him, without addition or subtraction."

"There is no doubt of that," put in Sancho, "for from the time my master won it till now he has not fought more than one battle in it, when he freed that unlucky chain-gang. And if it hadn't been for this basin-helmet, things would have gone badly with him that time, for there was a lot of stone-throwing in that engagement."

⊰ *45* ⊱

In which the Question of
Mambrino's Helmet and the Pack-Saddle
is finally cleared up,
with Other Adventures which
most certainly occurred

*W*hat do you think about it,
sirs," asked the barber, "when you hear these gentlemen swearing
and insisting that this isn't a basin but a helmet?"

"Whoever says anything to the contrary," said Don Quixote, "if
he is a knight, I will teach him that he lies, and if he is a squire, that he
lies a thousand times."

Our barber, who was looking on all the while and knew Don
Quixote's idiosyncrasies so well, decided to encourage his craziness
and to give them all a laugh by carrying the joke further. So,
addressing the other barber, he said, "Sir barber, or whoever you
are, learn that I am also of your profession, and have held a cer-
tificate for more than twenty years. I know all the instruments of the
barber's art very well, without exception; and, what is more, I
was a soldier for a while in my youth, and I know what is a helmet,
and what is a morion, and what is a closed casque and other things
concerning soldiering—I mean the different military arms. And I
say, under correction, always submitting myself to better judgment, that this piece before us, which the good gentleman is holding,

not only is not a barber's basin, but is as far from being one as black is from white, or the truth from a lie. But I do say that, though this is a helmet, it is not a complete helmet."

"Certainly not," said Don Quixote, "because half of it—that is the beaver—is missing."

"That is true," said the priest, who had now grasped his friend the barber's purpose. Then Cardenio, Don Ferdinand and his comrades backed him up, and even the judge would have taken a hand in the joke if he had not been so concerned with the business of Don Louis; but the serious subject of his thoughts held him so engrossed that he paid little or no attention to these pleasantries.

"Good Heavens alive!" exclaimed the poor butt of a barber at this. "Can so many honourable gentlemen possibly say that this is not a basin but a helmet? That's enough to surprise a whole university, be it ever so wise. Well, if this basin is a helmet, then, this pack-saddle must be a horse's harness as well, as this gentleman said."

"It looks like a pack-saddle to me," said Don Quixote, "but, as I have already said, I am not interfering in that."

"Whether it is a pack-saddle or a harness," said the priest, "Don Quixote has only to say; for in these matters of chivalry all these gentlemen and myself defer to him."

"By God, sirs," said Don Quixote, "so many strange things have befallen me in this castle on the two occasions I have lodged here that I dare not give any positive answer to any question asked me concerning anything in it; for I imagine that whatever goes on here is by way of enchantment. The first time I was much annoyed by a Moorish enchanter who dwells here, and Sancho fared rather badly at the hands of some henchmen of his; and last night I was suspended by this arm for almost two hours, without knowing either the means or the cause of my misfortunes. So to interfere now in so perplexed a matter and to give my opinion would be to make a rash judgment. Concerning their statement that this is a basin and not a helmet, I have already answered; but as to declaring whether that is a pack-saddle or a harness, I am not so bold as to give a definitive decision, but leave the matter to your worship's better judgment. Perhaps, since none of you are knights, as I am, the spells in this place will have no effect on you, your understanding will be free, and you will be able to judge of the affairs of this castle as they really and truly are, and not as they appear to me."

"There is no doubt," Don Ferdinand replied to this, "that Don Quixote has spoken very wisely today in saying that the decision in this case lies with us; and so that it may rest on sounder foundations I will take the votes of these gentlemen in secret, and give you a clear and full account of the result."

All this caused the greatest amusement to those who knew Don Quixote's idiosyncrasies; but it seemed the greatest nonsense in the world to those who did not, particularly to Don Louis' four servants, and to Don Louis himself, and to three more travellers who had happened to arrive at the inn and appeared to be troopers of the Holy Brotherhood, which indeed they were. But the most perplexed of all was the barber, whose basin had been turned into Mambrino's helmet before his eyes, and whose pack-saddle he fully expected to be transformed into a fine horse-harness. All of them, however, laughed to see Don Ferdinand go from one to another, taking their votes and whispering in their ears that they must declare in secret whether this pretty thing, which had been the subject of such fighting, was a pack-saddle or a harness. Then, after taking the votes of all those who knew Don Quixote, he loudly proclaimed, "The fact is, my good fellow, that I am tired of taking so many opinions. For I find that everyone I ask declares that it is ridiculous to affirm that this is an ass's pack-saddle, for it is the harness of a horse, and of a thoroughbred horse at that. So you will have to be patient, for in spite of you and your ass, this is a harness and no pack-saddle, and you have stated and proved your case very badly."

"May I never have a place in Heaven," cried the poor barber, "if your worships aren't all wrong; and may my soul as surely appear before God as this appears to me a pack-saddle and no harness. But might is right—I say no more. But I promise you I'm not drunk, for I haven't broken my fast today, unless it be to sin."

The barber's simple language caused no less laughter than the craziness of Don Quixote's, who remarked at this juncture, "There is nothing more for it now but for each one to take his belongings, and what God gives may St. Peter bless."

But one of the four servants observed, "If this isn't a concerted joke, I can't understand how intelligent men can swear that these things aren't a basin and a pack-saddle. But you all seem intelligent enough, and yet you insist that you're right. So I suppose there must be some mystery about it all, for what you're saying goes clean against obvious truth and good sense, and I swear by"—and here he let out a round oath—"that this is a barber's basin, and that's an ass's pack-saddle—and the whole world won't convince me to the contrary."

"It might be a she-ass's," observed the priest.

"It's all the same," cried the servant, "and that isn't the point. Either it's a pack-saddle or, as your worships say, it isn't."

When he heard this one of the troopers, who had come in and listened to the argument, cried out angrily, "It's as much a pack-saddle as my father's my father, and any one who says anything else must be drunk."

"You lie like a base villain," answered Don Quixote. And, raising his lance, which he had never let out of his hand, he aimed such a blow at the trooper's head that, unless he had dodged it, it would have left him stretched on the ground. The lance broke to pieces on the earth, and when the rest of the troopers saw their comrade assaulted they raised a shout for help for the Holy Brotherhood. The innkeeper, who was one of the fraternity, ran in an instant for his staff and his sword, and took his place beside his fellows. Don Louis' servants gathered round their young master, so that he should not escape in the scuffle. The barber, seeing the house in a turmoil, grasped his pack-saddle once more, and Sancho did the same. Don Quixote drew his sword and fell upon the troopers. Don Louis called to his

servants to leave him and help Don Quixote—and Cardenio and
Don Ferdinand, who were on Don Quixote's side. The priest was
shouting; the landlady screaming; her daughter wailing; Maritornes
weeping; Dorothea was distracted; Lucinda in a flurry; and Doña
Clara in a faint. The barber was mauling Sancho; Sancho pounding
the barber; and Don Louis, whom one of his servants had been so
bold as to seize by the arm to prevent his running away, had dealt
the fellow a blow which bathed his jaws in blood; the judge was
defending him; Don Ferdinand had one of the officers under his
feet, and was trampling his carcass most heartily; and the innkeeper
was straining his voice once more, shouting for help for the Holy
Brotherhood. So the whole inn was full of tears, shouts, screams,
amazement, fear, alarm, dismay, slashings, punches, blows, kicks
and effusion of blood.

In the middle of this confused and chaotic tangle, the idea came
into Don Quixote's head that he had been plunged head over heels
into the discord in Agramante's camp, and so he cried in a voice
which thundered through the inn, "Hold, all! Sheathe your swords,
all! Be calm, all! And listen to me, all of you, if all wish to remain alive!"

At this mighty voice they all stopped, and he continued, saying,
"Did I not tell you, gentlemen, that this castle is enchanted, and
must be inhabited by some legion of demons? Behold the confirmation of my words, and gaze upon the discord in Agramante's
camp transferred here and performed in our midst. See here they
are fighting for the sword, yonder for the horse, here for the eagle,
there for the helmet; we are all fighting and all at odds. Come then,
Sir Judge, and you, Sir Priest; let one of you stand for King
Agramante, the other for King Sobrino, and make peace amongst
us. For, by God Almighty, it is a great villainy that people of
such quality as we are here should slay one another for such
trivial causes."

The troopers, who did not understand Don Quixote's phrase-
ology and found themselves roughly handled by Don Ferdinand,
Cardenio and their companions, were unwilling to be pacified; but

the barber was willing, for both his beard and the pack-saddle had been torn in the fight. Sancho, like a good servant, obeyed his master's slightest word. Don Louis' four servants grew calm, seeing how little they stood to gain by being otherwise. Only the inn-keeper insisted that this madman's insolences must be punished, for he was always upsetting the inn. At last the uproar was quelled for a time, the pack-saddle remained a harness till Judgment Day, and in Don Quixote's imagination the basin remained a helmet and the inn a castle.

When, at the persuasion of the judge and the priest, everyone was pacified and had made friends, Don Louis' servants once more insisted that he must come with them at once; and whilst he was settling with them, the judge consulted Don Ferdinand, Cardenio and the priest as to what he should do in the matter. He told them what Don Louis had said to him. It was finally agreed that Don Ferdinand should reveal himself to Don Louis' servants and say that it was his wish that Don Louis should come with him to Andalusia, where he would be received by his brother the Marquis in a manner suitable to his quality; for he knew that Don Louis was determined not to return to his father's presence even if they tore him to pieces. When the four of them were aware of Don Ferdinand's rank and Don Louis' obstinacy, they decided amongst themselves that three of them should return and give his father an account of events, and that the fourth should stay and wait on their young master, and not leave him till the others should return for him, or until he should learn what his father's orders were. Thus this tangle of quarrels was resolved by the authority of Agramante and the wisdom of King Sobrino.

However, the enemy of concord and adversary of peace, finding himself slighted and mocked, and seeing how little fruit he had reaped from plunging them all into this labyrinth of confusion, decided to try his hand again and bring some new quarrels and disturbances to life. It arose thus: the troopers calmed down when they overheard the rank of the men they had been fighting, and retired from the combat, it seeming to them that they would get the worst of the battle, whatever happened. But one of them—the one who had been pounded and trampled by Don Ferdinand—remembered suddenly that, among some warrants he was carrying for the arrest of various delinquents, was one for Don Quixote, whose seizure the Holy Brotherhood had ordered for his freeing the galley-slaves, as Sancho had had good reason to fear they would. When this occurred to him he decided to make certain that the description in the warrants tallied with the knight. So, taking a parchment from his breast, he lighted on what he wanted. Then he set himself to read it slowly—for he was no great reader—and at each word he read he clapped his eyes on Don Quixote, comparing the details in his warrant, one by one, with the knight's features, and found that beyond a doubt it was he that the warrant described. As soon as he had made certain of this, he folded up the parchment and, taking the warrant in his left hand, seized Don Quixote so firmly by the collar with his right that he could not breathe. Then he shouted, "Help for the Holy Brotherhood! And to prove that I'm serious, read this warrant where it's written that this highway robber must be arrested."

The priest took the warrant, and saw that all that the trooper said was true and that the description tallied with Don Quixote. But the knight was infuriated at finding himself roughly handled by this base scoundrel, and every bone in his body creaked as he clasped the trooper with all his might, with both hands round his throat. And if the fellow had not been rescued by his companions he would have breathed his last there and then, before Don Quixote would have let go his hold. The innkeeper, who was bound to help his fellow troopers, immediately ran to his aid. The landlady, seeing her husband in a fight once more, screamed again, and was instantly joined by Maritornes and her daughter, all three calling on Heaven and the company for help. And Sancho, seeing what was going on, remarked, "By the Lord, all that my master says about the enchantments in this castle is true, for it's impossible to stay quiet an hour here."

Don Ferdinand parted the trooper and Don Quixote and, to the relief of both, unlocked their hands which were clenched fast, the trooper's on the knight's collar, and the knight's round his adversary's throat. But, nevertheless, the troopers persisted in claiming their prisoner and the company's help in delivering him bound at their disposal, for such help it was their duty to the King and the Holy Brotherhood to give. So they once more demanded aid and assistance in the arrest of this robber, brigand and highwayman. But Don Quixote laughed at this description and said very calmly, "Come here, filthy and low-born rabble! Is it highway robbery you call it, freeing the enchained, releasing prisoners, succouring the unfortunate, raising the fallen, relieving the needy? You infamous brood whose low and vile intelligence deserves no revelation from Heaven of that virtue which lies in knight errantry, nor any knowledge of your sin and ignorance in not reverencing the shadow—how much more the actual presence—of a knight errant! Come here, you pack of thieves, for you are no troopers, but highwaymen licensed by the Holy Brotherhood! Tell me, who was the dolt who signed a warrant of arrest against such a knight as I am? Who was it who did not know that knights errant are exempt from all jurisdiction, that their law is their sword, their charters their courage and their statutes their own will? Who was the idiot, I repeat, who does not know that there is no patent of nobility with so many privileges and immunities as a knight errant receives on the day when he is knighted and undertakes the stern practice of chivalry? What knight errant has ever paid tax, duty, queen's patten money, statute money, customs or toll? What tailor was ever paid by him for a suit of clothes? What warden who received him in his castle ever made him pay his score? What maiden was not in love with him, and did not give herself up to his will and pleasure? And, lastly, what knight errant has there been, is there, or will there ever be in the world, who has not courage enough, on his own, to deal four hundred beatings to four hundred troopers, should they dare confront him?"

⊰ 46 ⊱

Of the Notable Adventure with
the Troopers and the Great Ferocity of
Our Good Knight Don Quixote*

While Don Quixote was making
this proclamation the priest was persuading the troopers that the
knight was out of his mind, as they could see by his deeds and his
words, and that, therefore, they need carry the matter no farther.
For even if they were to arrest him and take him away, they would
have to release him as a madman. But the man with the warrant
replied that it was not for him to judge of Don Quixote's madness,
but to carry out his superior's orders; and that once he was arrested
they could let him out three hundred times if they chose.

"For all that," said the priest, "you must not take him this time;
nor, so far as I can see, will he let you."

In the end the priest thought of so much to say and Don Quixote
of so many crazy things to do that the troopers would have to have
been madder than he if they had not recognized Don Quixote's
infirmity. So they judged it best to be quiet, and even to make the
peace between the barber and Sancho Panza, who were still quar-

* This heading is misplaced, for the adventure is over. The oversight is the author's.

relling with great bitterness. As officers of justice, therefore, they intervened in the case and arbitrated to such purpose that both parties remained, if not entirely content, at least partially satisfied, it being settled that they should exchange pack-saddles but not girths or headstalls. In the matter of Mambrino's helmet, too, the priest, unknown to Don Quixote, paid eight *reals* for the basin, and the barber wrote him out a receipt, promising not to take action for fraud thenceforth and for ever more, amen.

These two disputes being settled—and they were the most serious and urgent—nothing remained but for Don Louis' servants to agree that three of them should go back, and one stay to accompany their master wherever Don Ferdinand might take him. And as by now good luck had begun to shift obstacles and smooth difficulties in favour of the lovers and the brave folk in the inn, so Fortune was pleased to complete the task and bring everything to a happy ending. For the servants fell in with Don Louis' request, which so delighted Doña Clara that no one who looked into her face at that time could fail to recognize the rejoicing in her heart. As for Zoraida, although she did not very clearly understand everything she had seen, she was sad or gay by turns, according to the expressions she saw on everyone's face; but it was on her Spaniard's that her eyes were always fixed, in absolute dependence. The innkeeper, who had not failed to note the gift in compensation which the priest had given the barber, demanded payment of Don Quixote's account, and for the damage to the wine-skins and his loss of wine, swearing that neither Rocinante nor Sancho's ass should leave the inn until he had been paid to the last farthing. All this the priest peacefully settled, and Don Ferdinand paid although the judge had also very generously offered to do so. And so they all remained in peace and quietness, so that the inn no longer recalled the discord in Agramante's camp, as Don Quixote had said, but the peace and quiet of the times of Octavian. And it was the general opinion that they owed thanks for all this to the priest's good sense and great eloquence and to Don Ferdinand's incomparable generosity.

The issue was that they dragged him to the cage and shut him in, nailing the bars so fast that they could not be knocked down in a hurry. They then took him on their shoulders. But as they left the room they heard a fearful voice, as awful as the barber could make it . . . "O Knight of the Sad Countenance!" he cried, "be not grieved at your confinement. It is needful for the speedier conclusion of the adventure to which your great courage has committed you."
(page 561)

Don Quixote, then, seeing himself free and quit of all quarrels, both his squire's and his own, thought it would be well to continue the journey he had begun, and complete the great adventure for which he had been called and chosen; and so, firm in his resolution, he went to kneel down before Dorothea, who refused to let him utter a word until he arose. So he obediently got upon his feet and said, "It is a common proverb, beauteous lady, that diligence is the mother of good fortune; and in many grave matters experience has shown that the solicitude of the suitor brings a doubtful matter to a happy ending. But in no affairs is this truth more evident than in those of war, in which promptness and speed forestall the enemy's designs, and gain the victory before the adversary has established his defences. All this I say, exalted and precious lady, because it seems to me that our sojourn in this castle is now profitless, and may do us very great harm, too, as we may one day discover. For who knows if your enemy the giant has not learnt, by means of secret and diligent spies, that I am on my way to destroy him, and, taking advantage of this delay, may not be fortifying himself in some impregnable castle or fortress against which my endeavours and the might of my untiring arm may avail me little? So, my lady, let us forestall his designs, as I have said, by our diligence, and depart immediately while our fortune is good; for to keep it on our side, as your Highness will desire, you must wait no longer than I delay in facing your adversary."

Don Quixote fell silent and said no more, but most calmly awaited the beautiful Princess's reply; and she, with a lordly air, adapted to the style of Don Quixote, answered him as follows, "I thank you, Sir Knight, for the desire you display to aid me in my great distress, like a true knight whose function and concern it is to succour the orphan and the needy. Pray Heaven that your desire and mine may be fulfilled, and that you may learn that there are grateful women in the world. As for my departure, let it be immediate, for I have no other wish than yours. Dispose of me wholly at your will and pleasure, for she who has once entrusted the defence of her person to you, and put into your hands the restoration of her domains, must not dare to go contrary to what your wisdom shall ordain."

"By God's hand," cried Don Quixote, "seeing a lady humble herself before me, I cannot forbear the opportunity of raising her and placing her on her hereditary throne. Let our departure be immediate, for the saying that there is danger in delay puts spurs to my desire to be on the way. And since Heaven has never created, nor Hell seen, anyone to daunt or intimidate me, saddle Rocinante, Sancho, and harness your ass and the Queen's palfrey. Let us take our leave of the warden and these gentlemen and be away from here immediately."

But Sancho, who was standing by all the while, shook his head and answered, "Oh, sir, sir, there are more tricks done in the village than make a noise—saving her ladyship's presence."

"What nastiness can there be in any village, or in all the towns in the world, which can be noised to my discredit, peasant?"

"If you're getting annoyed, your worship, I'll hold my tongue and not say what it's a good squire's duty to say, and what a good servant ought to say to his master."

"Say what you like," replied Don Quixote, "so long as your words are not intended to strike fear into me; for if you are afraid, you are acting true to your character, and if I am fearless, I am acting true to mine."

"It's not that, I swear to God as I am a sinner," replied Sancho, "but I'm positively certain that this lady, who calls herself Queen of the great Kingdom of Micomicon, is no more a queen than my mother; for if she was what she says she is, she wouldn't go kissing with somebody in this company every time anyone turns his head, and round every corner."

Dorothea blushed at Sancho's remarks, because it was true that her husband, Don Ferdinand, had sometimes, when no one was looking, gathered from her lips some of the rewards his love had earned. This Sancho had seen; and such immodesty had seemed to him more fitting in a courtesan than in the queen of a great kingdom. But as she could not contradict Sancho, she had to let him go on with his observations, "I'm saying this, sir, because if the gentleman who is enjoying himself in this inn is going to gather the fruit of our labours, when we've travelled the highways and by-ways and passed bad nights and worse days, I've got no reason to be in a hurry myself about saddling Rocinante, or harnessing my ass, or getting the palfrey ready. It will be better for us to stay quiet —and let every whore spin and us eat."

Goodness, what a fury Don Quixote flew into when he heard his squire speak with such disrespect! So tremendous was it that, with a trembling voice and stammering tongue, his eyes darting fire, he exclaimed, "Villainous peasant, unmannerly, disrespectful, igno-rant, blasphemous, foul-mouthed, presumptuous, backbiting slanderer! Dare you utter such words in my presence, and in the presence of these illustrious ladies? How have you presumed to breed such infamies and effronteries in your muddled imagination? Begone from my sight, unnatural monster, storehouse of lies, ar-moury of deceit, sink of knavery, inventor of iniquities, publisher of ravings, foe to the respect due to royal persons! Go, never appear before me again, on pain of my wrath!"

As he spoke, he frowned severely, puffed out his cheeks, glared in all directions, and stamped loudly on the ground with his right foot in sign of the rage pent up in his heart.

His words and his furious gestures so terrified Sancho that he would have been glad if the earth had opened at that instant before his feet and swallowed him, and he could think of no other course but to turn his back and quit his master's furious presence. But the wise Dorothea, who was now so well schooled in Don Quixote's idiosyncrasies, sought to mitigate his wrath by addressing him thus, "Do not be vexed, Sir Knight of the Sad Countenance, at the idle words which your good squire has spoken, for perhaps he did not speak them without good reason; nor can we suspect his good understanding and Christian conscience of making false accusa-tions against anyone. So we must positively believe that, as every-thing in this castle happens by way of enchantment, as you yourself say, Sir Knight—it may be, I say, that Sancho may have seen, by diabolical illusion, what he says he beheld, so much to the prejudice of my honour."

"By the Almighty God," cried Don Quixote at this point, "I swear your Highness has hit the mark. Some wicked vision has risen before that sinner Sancho's eyes, and shown him what he could not possibly have seen by any other means than by sorcery. For I know the poor man's goodness and innocence too well to believe that he would make false accusations against anyone."

"That is the truth, and so let it rest," said Don Ferdinand. "Therefore your worship must pardon him and receive him once more into the bosom of your favour 'as it was in the beginning,' before these visions distracted his senses."

Don Quixote replied that he would pardon him, and the priest went for Sancho, who came in very humbly and, falling on his knees, begged for his master's hand. The knight gave it him, and let him kiss it, and then after bestowing a blessing on him, he said, "Now you will be convinced, Sancho, my son, that what I have so often told you is true, and that all events in this castle are performed by way of enchantment."

"Indeed, I believe it," said Sancho, "except for the matter of that blanket-tossing. That really happened in the ordinary way."

"Do not you believe that," replied Don Quixote, "for if that had been the case I should have avenged you then, or would do so even now. But neither then nor now have I been able to take vengeance for your injury, nor to see anyone on whom I could take it."

Everyone wanted to know what this business about a blanket was, and so the innkeeper gave them a circumstantial account of Sancho Panza's flight through the air, at which they all laughed not a little; and Sancho would have been not a little ashamed if his master had not assured him once more that it was enchantment. But for all that, Sancho's folly never reached such a pitch that he did not believe it was absolute and certain truth, without any shadow of illusion, that he had been tossed by creatures of flesh and blood, and not by any unreal or imaginary phantoms, as his master believed and affirmed.

Two days had now passed since that illustrious company had

come to the inn; and thinking that the time for departure had come, they devised a plan which would spare Dorothea and Don Ferdinand the trouble of going back with Don Quixote to his village under pretence of restoring Queen Micomicona, and allow the priest and the barber to bear him off, as they wished, and try to get him cured of his madness at home. And this was the scheme they contrived. They made a bargain with a waggoner, who happened to be passing that way with a team of oxen, to take him in this way: they made a sort of cage of criss-crossed poles, sufficiently large to hold Don Quixote comfortably; then Don Ferdinand and his companions, with Don Louis' servants, the troopers and the innkeeper, all under the orders and directions of the priest, covered their faces and disguised themselves in various ways, so that Don Quixote should take them for different people from those he had seen at the castle. This done, in absolute silence they entered the room where he was asleep, taking his rest after the late conflicts. They went up to where he was sleeping peacefully, with no suspicion of any plot and, grasping him firmly, securely tied his hands and feet, so that when he woke up with a start he could not stir or do anything but gaze in wonder at the strange faces he saw before him. And at once he fell into the illusion his wild imagination was continually suggesting to him, and assumed that those figures were the phantoms of that enchanted castle, and that he was now positively under a spell, since he could neither stir nor defend himself. All this was precisely what the priest, the inventor of the scheme, had expected. Of all those present only Sancho was in his right mind and undisguised; and although he was not far from sharing his master's disease, he did not fail to recognize those disguised figures. But he did not dare to open his mouth until he saw what this assault and seizure of his master would lead to, and the knight did not speak a word either, waiting also to see the issue of this disaster.

The issue was that they dragged him to the cage and shut him in, nailing the bars so fast that they could not be knocked down in a hurry. They then took him on their shoulders. But as they left the room they heard a fearful voice, as awful as the barber could make it—not the barber of the pack-saddle but the other one, "O Knight of the Sad Countenance!" he cried, "be not grieved at your confinement. It is needful for the speedier conclusion of the adventure to which your great courage has committed you. The which shall be concluded when the furious Manchegan lion shall be united with the white Tobosan dove, and after they have humbled their lofty crests to the soft matrimonial yoke, from which miraculous mating shall issue to the light of the sun brave whelps, who will emulate the ravaging talons of their valorous father. This shall come to pass ere the pursuer of the fugitive nymph shall twice in his swift and natural course have visited the bright constellations. And you, most noble and obedient squire that ever bore sword in belt, beard on chin, or smell in nose, be not dismayed or displeased to see the flower of knight errantry thus borne away before your eyes. For very speedily, if it please the Artificer of the world, you will find yourself so exalted and ennobled that you will not know yourself, nor shall you be defrauded of the reward your good master has promised you. I assure you, on behalf of the sage Mentironiana, that your wages shall be paid you, as the proof will show. Follow then in the footsteps of your valorous and enchanted lord, for it is fitting that you should go to that place where you both will stay. And now, as it is not lawful for me to say more, God be with you, for I return, I well know whither."

Towards the end of this prophecy the barber raised his voice to such a pitch, and then lowered it to so quiet a tone, that even those in the joke almost believed in the truth of what they heard. Don Quixote was much consoled by this prophecy. For he immediately grasped its whole meaning, and saw that it promised him union in holy and lawful wedlock with his beloved Dulcinea del Toboso, from whose happy womb would issue the whelps, his sons, to the everlasting glory of La Mancha. So, believing all this sincerely and firmly, he raised his voice and said with a deep sigh, "You, whoever you may be, who have prognosticated such happiness for me, I pray you, beg in my name that sage enchanter who has my affairs in his charge not to let me perish in this captivity in which I am borne off, until I see the fulfilment of the joyful and incomparable promises that have just been made to me. But, however that may be, I shall account the pains of my prison glory, these chains which bind me comfort, and this litter upon which I am laid no hard field of battle, but a soft couch and happy marriage-bed. And regarding the consolation of my squire Sancho Panza, I trust in his honesty and good conduct that he will not leave me in good or evil fortune. For though it should not happen, from his ill luck or mine, that I shall be able to bestow on him the isle or other equivalent gift which I have promised him, at least he cannot lose his wages, since in the will which I have made I have provided for his payment, not in proportion to his many good services, but to my means."

Sancho bowed his head in deep respect and kissed both his hands, for he could not kiss one alone, since they were tied together. Then the phantoms lifted the cage on to their shoulders and placed it on the ox-cart.

⊰ *47* ⊱

Of the Strange Way
in which Don Quixote was enchanted,
and Other Matters

*W*hen Don Quixote himself was
thus caged and placed on the cart, he said, "I have read many serious
histories of knights errant; but I have never read, or seen, or heard of
enchanted knights being carried in this fashion and at the pace
which these slothful and lazy animals promise. For they are generally borne through the air with extraordinary speed, enclosed in
some thick and dusky cloud, or on some chariot of fire, or on some
hippogriff or other such beast. But to be carried as I now am on an
ox-cart, God help me, it puts me to confusion. But perhaps chivalry
and magic in our day must follow a different course from that
pursued by the men of old; and it may be, too, that as I am a new
knight in the world, and the first to resuscitate the long-forgotten
profession of knight errantry, they have invented fresh kinds of
enchantment and other methods of carrying the enchanted as well.
What do you think about it, Sancho, my son?"

"I don't know what to think," replied Sancho, "not being so well
read as your worship in the errant writings. But, all the same, I'd be
prepared to swear that these apparitions here around us are not
altogether Catholic."

"Catholic? Holy father!" replied Don Quixote. "How should they be Catholic, if they are all demons who have taken fantastic bodies to come and throw me into this state? If you want to convince yourself of that, touch them and feel them, and you will see that their bodies are only air, and are nothing but an out-ward semblance."

"By God, sir," replied Sancho, "I've touched them already, and this devil bustling about here is plump and tender. He has another property, too, very different from anything that devils are said to have. They all stink of brimstone and other foul odours, but this one smells of ambergris from a mile off."

This remark of Sancho's referred to Don Ferdinand who, being a gentleman, must have smelt as Sancho said.

"Do not be surprised at that, Sancho my friend," replied Don Quixote, "for I would have you know that devils are very crafty. But although they carry smells about them, they do not smell, because they are spirits; and if they do smell, they cannot smell of good things, but only of evil and stinking ones. The reason is that they carry hell with them wherever they are, and can receive no kind of relief from their torments. Now, a good smell is something to delight and please; so it is not possible for them ever to smell sweet; and if this demon of yours seems to you to smell of ambergris, either you are mistaken or he seeks to deceive you and make you think that he is not a devil."

All this conversation passed between master and servant; and as Don Ferdinand and Cardenio were afraid that Sancho would tumble to the whole of their plot, which he had already come very near to doing, they decided to cut the parting short. So they called the innkeeper aside and ordered him to saddle Rocinante and har-ness Sancho's ass, which he very quickly did. In the meantime the priest had come to an arrangement with the troopers to escort him to his village for so much a day. Cardenio hung the knight's shield on one side of Rocinante's saddle and the basin on the other. Then in dumb show he bade Sancho mount his ass and take Rocinante by the reins, and posted the troopers with their firelocks on either side of the cart. But before it moved off, the landlady, her daughter and Maritornes came out to say good-bye to Don Quixote, pretending to weep with sorrow at his misfortune; and he said to them, "Do not weep, good ladies, for all these mischances are incidental to the calling I profess; and if these calamities did not befall me I should not consider myself a famous knight errant. For such things never happen to knights of small name and fame, since there is no one in the world to cast them a thought. But to the brave they do, for many princes and other knights envy them for their virtue and their valour, and seek by evil ways to destroy these good men. But, for all that, virtue is so powerful that of itself alone it will emerge victorious from any trial, despite all the necromancy ever known to Zoroaster, its first inventor, and will shed its light on the world as the sun does in heaven. Pardon me, fair ladies, if I have inadvertently done you any displeasure, for wilfully and consciously I have never done so to anyone. And pray God to deliver me from these chains, into which some ill-intentioned magician has cast me, for if ever I am free from them I will never forget the favours you have done me in this castle, but shall acknowledge them, requite them, and repay them as they deserve."

Whilst this passage was taking place between the ladies and Don Quixote, the priest and the barber took leave of Don Ferdinand and his comrades, of the captain and his brother, and of all those happy ladies, of Dorothea and Lucinda in particular. They all embraced, and agreed to send one another their news. Don Ferdinand made a point of telling the priest where to write and let him know Don Quixote's fate. He insisted that nothing would give him more pleasure than to hear, and promised to let the priest have any news that might please him, about his own marriage and Zoraida's baptism, or Don Louis' affairs and Lucinda's homecoming. The priest promised to comply most punctually with his request. Once more they embraced, and once more exchanged compliments. Then the innkeeper went up to the priest and gave him some papers, saying that he had found them in the lining of the trunk in which he had discovered *The Tale of Foolish Curiosity*, and told him that he might

The landlady, her daughter and Maritornes came out to say good-bye to Don Quixote, pretending to weep with sorrow at his misfortune; and he said to them, "Do not weep, good ladies, for all these mischances are incidental to the calling I profess; and if these calamities did not befall me I should not consider myself a famous knight errant." (page 566) take them all with him as its owner had never come that way again. For, as he could not read, he did not want them himself. The priest thanked him and, on opening the manuscript, saw written at the head: *The Tale of Rinconete and Cortadillo,* from which he assumed that this was another story; and he expected that it would be a good one, since *The Tale of Foolish Curiosity* had been, and it was probably by the same author. So he kept it, intending to read it when he had an opportunity.

Then he and his friend the barber, both wearing their masks so that Don Quixote should not recognize them, mounted and set out after the cart. The order of the procession was the following: first went the cart, driven by its owner; on either side, as we have said, went the troopers with their firelocks; then followed Sancho Panza on his ass, leading Rocinante by the rein; last of all came the priest and the barber on their heavy mules, their faces covered as before mentioned, riding with a grave and sober air as fast as the slow pace of the oxen permitted. Don Quixote travelled seated in his cage, with his hands tied and his feet stretched out, leaning against the bars, as silently and patiently as if he had been no flesh-and-blood man, but a stone statue. And so they rode slowly and silently for about six miles, until they came to a valley which the carter thought would be a convenient place for resting and feeding his oxen. He told his thought to the priest, but the barber was of the opinion that they should go on a little farther; for he knew that behind a hill which showed up not far away there was a valley with more and much better grass than there was there, where they wanted to stop. So the barber's advice was taken, and they resumed their way.

At this moment the priest looked round and saw six or seven horsemen behind them, well dressed and mounted, who soon overtook them. For they were not riding at the slow and leisurely pace of oxen, but as people mounted on canons' mules, and anxious to press on and take their siesta at the inn, which could be seen less than three miles ahead. The swift travellers overtook the slow and greeted them courteously. Now, when one of the newcomers, who proved to be a canon of Toledo and the master of the rest, saw the orderly procession with the cart, the troopers, Sancho, Rocinante, the priest and the barber and Don Quixote, in particular, imprisoned in his cage, he could not help asking the reason for their carrying a man in that manner; though he had already concluded from seeing the troopers' badges that he must be some habitual highwayman or other malefactor whose punishment was a matter for the Holy Brotherhood. But one of the troopers, to whom he had put the question, replied, "Sir, we don't know what it all means. The gentleman must tell you himself why he is carried like this."

Don Quixote heard this question and answer, and replied, "Are you gentlemen, perhaps, versed and skilled in matters of knight errantry? For, if you are, I will communicate my misfortunes to you. But if you are not, there is no reason for my tiring myself by telling you."

By this time the priest and the barber had seen that the travellers were in conversation with Don Quixote de la Mancha, and had come up to answer for him, in case their plot might be discovered. But the canon, whom Don Quixote had addressed, replied, "Truly, brother, I know more about books of chivalry than about Villalpando's Logic. So, if that is all, you can safely tell me whatever you please."

"Then, in God's name I will," replied Don Quixote. "I would have you know, sir, that I am travelling in this cage under a spell, because of the envy and fraud of evil enchanters, for virtue is persecuted by the wicked more than it is loved by the good. I am a knight errant—not one of those whose names Fame has never thought to record in her memory, but one who, in despite and defiance of envy itself, and of all the Magi ever born in Persia, all the Brahmans of India, all the Gymnosophists of Ethiopia, shall write his name in the temple of immortality, to serve as a pattern and example to future ages, wherein knights errant may see what steps they should follow if they would climb to the honourable summit and pinnacle of arms."

"The knight Don Quixote de la Mancha is speaking the truth," put in the priest at this juncture, "for he is travelling in this cart beneath a spell, not for his own faults and sins, but through the malignity of those to whom virtue is loathsome and valour odious. This, sir, is the Knight of the Sad Countenance—if you have ever heard speak of him at any time—whose valorous achievements and mighty deeds will be written on stubborn brass and eternal marble, however tirelessly envy and malice may work to obscure and conceal them."

When the canon heard both prisoner and free men talk in this style he almost crossed himself with astonishment, unable to imagine what had happened, while the same amazement struck all his companions. At this Sancho Panza, who had drawn near to hear the conversation, sought to make everything plain by remarking, "Now, gentlemen, whether you like it or not, the fact of the matter is that Don Quixote is no more enchanted than my mother. He is in possession of all his faculties; he eats and drinks and does his business like other men, and just as he did yesterday before they put him in the cage. As that's the case, how can they expect me to believe that he's under a spell? For I've often heard it said that people who've been bewitched don't eat, or sleep, or speak, while my master will out-talk thirty lawyers, if they'll only let him alone." Then, turning to face the priest, he went on, "Oh, Master Priest, Master Priest! Do you think I don't recognize you? Do you imagine I don't see what you're up to? Do you think that I don't see through these new enchantments? Of course I know you, even though you've a mask on your face, and understand you, however much you disguise your tricks. In fact, where envy reigns virtue can't exist, and generosity doesn't go with meanness. Damn it all! If it wasn't for your reverence my master would be married to the Princess Micomicona at this very moment, and I should be a count at least, for I could have expected no less, considering the generosity of my master, the Knight of the Sad Countenance, and the greatness of my services. But I see now that it's true, as they say in these parts, that Fortune's wheel goes swifter than a mill wheel, and the man who was at the very top yesterday is on the ground today. It's my wife and my children I'm sorry for. For just when they might have expected to

see their father come in at the door a governor or viceroy of some
isle or kingdom, they'll see him enter as a stable-boy. I'm saying all
this, Master Priest, to urge you to have some conscience about
ill-treating my master like this. You take care that God doesn't call
you to account in the other life for imprisoning him like this. He'll
make you answer for all these succours and benefits my master, Don
Quixote, leaves undone all this time he's a prisoner."

"Tell that to your grandmother!" put in the barber at this point.
"What, Sancho, are you of your master's fraternity, too? I swear to
God I'm beginning to think you'll have to keep him company in his
cage, and labour under the same spell as he does, for you've caught
something of his humour and chivalry. It was an ill moment when
you fell with child by his promises, and worse still when you got that
isle you're so set on into your brain."

"I'm not with child by anyone," replied Sancho; "and I'm not a
man to let anyone get me with child, not the King himself. For
though I'm poor, I'm an old Christian, and I owe nothing to any
man. If I'm set on isles, other people are set on worse. Every man's
the son of his own deeds; and since I'm a man, I can become pope, let
alone governor of an isle, especially since my master's capable of
winning so many that he may have no one to give them to. Mind
how you talk, Master Barber, for shaving beards isn't everything,
and there's some difference between Peter and Peter. I say this
because we all know one another, and there's no passing false dice
on me. As to this enchanting of my master, God knows the truth, so
let it rest there, for it won't improve for stirring."

The barber did not care to answer him, in case Sancho should let
out in his simplicity what the priest and he were trying so hard to
keep hidden. With the same fear in his mind the priest invited
the canon to ride with him a little ahead, promising to reveal the
mystery of the cage and other things which would amuse him. The
canon agreed and, going ahead with his servants, listened attentively
to all that the priest told him about Don Quixote's character, life,
madness and habits, to a brief account of the beginnings and cause
of his distraction, to the whole course of his history up to his

confinement in the cage, and finally, to their plan for getting him back to his own village to see whether they might find any sort of cure for his madness. The canon and his servants were amazed anew at hearing Don Quixote's strange history, and when it was finished he said, "Truly, Sir Priest, my own experience tells me that so-called books of chivalry are very prejudicial to the commonwealth; and although, out of idleness and bad taste, I have read the beginnings of almost all that have been printed, I have never managed to read one right through. For they all seem to me more or less the same, and there is no more in one than in another. Besides, in my opinion this sort of composition falls under the heading of Milesian Fables, which are extravagant tales, whose purpose is to amaze, and not to instruct, quite the opposite of Moral Fables, which delight and instruct at the same time. And even though the principal aim of such books is to delight, I do not know how they can succeed, seeing the monstrous absurdities they are filled with. For the delight that the mind conceives must arise from the beauty and harmony it sees, or contemplates, in things presented to it by the eyes or the imagination; and nothing ugly or ill proportioned can cause us any pleasure. What beauty can there be, or what harmony between the parts and the whole, or between the whole and its parts, in a book or story in which a sixteen-year-old lad deals a giant as tall as a steeple one blow with his sword, and cuts him in two as if he were made of marzipan? And when they want to describe a battle, first they tell us that there are a million fighting men on the enemy's side. But if the hero of the book is against them, inevitably, whether we like it or not, we have to believe that such and such a knight gained the victory by the valour of his strong arm alone. Then what are we to say of the ease with which a hereditary Queen or Empress throws herself into the arms of an unknown and wandering knight? What mind not totally barbarous and uncultured can get pleasure from reading that a great tower, full of knights, sails out over the sea like a ship before a favourable wind, and that one night it is in Lombardy and by dawn next morning in the land of Prester John of the Indies, or in some other country that Ptolemy never knew nor Marco Polo visited? If you reply that the men who compose such books write them as fiction, and so are not obliged to look into fine points or truths, I should reply that the more it resembles the truth the better the fiction, and the more probable and possible it is, the better it pleases. Fictions have to match the minds of their readers, and to be written in such a way that, by tempering the impossibilities, moderating excesses and keeping judgment in the balance, they may so astonish, hold, excite and entertain, that wonder and pleasure go hand in hand. None of this can be achieved by anyone departing from verisimilitude or from that imitation of nature in which lies the perfection of all that is written. I have never seen a book of chivalry with a whole body for a plot, with all its limbs complete, so that the middle corresponds to the beginning, and the end to the beginning and middle; for they are generally made up of so many limbs that they seem intended rather to form a chimaera or a monster than a well-proportioned figure. What is more, their style is hard, their adventures are incredible, their love-affairs lewd, their compliments absurd, their battles long-winded, their speeches stupid, their travels preposterous and, lastly, they are devoid of all art and sense, and therefore deserve to be banished from a Christian commonwealth, as a useless tribe."

The priest listened to him with great attention, for he found him a man of good sense, and approved all that he said. And so he told him that, being of the same opinion himself, and bearing a grudge against books of chivalry, he had burnt all Don Quixote's large library of them. Then he went on to tell the story of the inquisition he had held over them, and to say which he had condemned to the flames and which he had spared, at which the canon laughed a great deal. Yet he continued that, for all that he had said against such books, he found one good thing in them, the fact that they offered a good intellect a chance to display itself. For they presented a broad and spacious field through which the pen could run without let or hindrance, describing shipwrecks, tempests, encounters and battles; painting a brave captain with all the features necessary for the part; showing his wisdom in forestalling his enemies' cunning, his eloquence in persuading or dissuading his soldiers, his ripeness in counsel, his prompt resolution, his courage in awaiting or in making an attack; now depicting a tragic and lamentable incident, now a joyful and unexpected event; here a most beautiful lady, chaste, intelligent, and modest; there a Christian knight, valiant and gentle; in one place a monstrous, barbarous braggart; in another a courteous prince, brave and wise; representing the goodness and loyalty of vassals, and the greatness and generosity of lords. Sometimes the writer might show his knowledge of astrology, or his excellence at cosmography or as a musician, or his wisdom in affairs of state, and he might even have an opportunity of showing his skill in necromancy. He could portray the subtlety of Ulysses, the piety of Aeneas, the valour of Achilles, the misfortunes of Hector, the treachery of Sinon, the friendship of Euryalus, the generosity of Alexander, the courage of Caesar, the clemency and truthfulness of Trajan, the fidelity of Zopyrus, the prudence of Cato and, in fact, all those attributes which constitute the perfect hero, sometimes placing them in one single man, at other times dividing them amongst many. "Now," he concluded, "if all this is done in a pleasant style and with an ingenious plot, as close as possible to the truth, there is no doubt at all that the author will weave a beautiful and variegated fabric which, when finished, will be perfect enough to achieve the excellent purpose of such works, which is, as I have said, to instruct and delight at the same time. For the loose plan of these books gives the author an opportunity of showing his talent for the epic, the lyric, the tragic and the comic, and all the qualities contained in the most sweet and pleasing sciences of poetry and rhetoric; for the epic may be written in prose as well as in verse."

⊰ *48* ⊱

In which the Canon pursues
the Subject of Books of Chivalry
and Other Matters worthy of His Genius

*W*hat you say is true, Sir Canon,"
said the priest, "and for that reason the writers of such books are
most blameworthy, since up to now they have paid no attention to
good sense or to the art and rules. For if they had been guided by
them, they might have become as famous in prose as the two princes
of poetry, Greek and Latin, are in verse."

"For my part," replied the canon, "I have been somewhat
tempted to write a book of chivalry, observing all the points I have
mentioned. To tell you the truth, I have written more than a
hundred pages, and to find out whether they came up to my opinion
of them, I have shown them to learned and judicious men given to
that kind of reading, and to other ignorant men who merely want
the pleasure of listening to nonsense, and I gained flattering approval from them all. But, for all that, I have not continued, because
it seemed to me a task unfitting to my profession, and because I
found the ignorant were more numerous than the wise; and though
it is better to be praised by the few wise and mocked by the many
fools, I do not want to subject myself to the muddle of judgment of

the opinionated crowd, who are generally the most given to reading such books. But most instrumental in making me drop the task of finishing it, even from my thoughts, was an argument which I drew from the comedies that are being played nowadays. For I reflected, if those now in fashion, the fictitious ones and the historical as well, are all, or most of them, notorious nonsense, monsters without feet or head; and if, despite that, the crowd enjoy seeing them, and approve of them and reckon them good, when they are so far from being so; and if the authors who write them and the managers who put them on say that they must be good, because the crowd likes them like that and not otherwise, and that the authors who observe a plan and follow the story as the rules of drama require only serve to please the three or four men of sense who understand them, while all the rest are left unsatisfied and cannot fathom their subtlety; and since these managers add that it suits them better to earn their bread from the many than approval from the few—such would have been the fate of my book after I had scorched my eyebrows studying to keep the rules I spoke of; it would have been love's labour lost. Sometimes I have tried to persuade the managers that their judgments are false, and that they would draw a bigger audience and get better reputations by playing comedies that follow the rules, instead of these extravagant pieces; but they are so bound and wedded to their opinion that there is no argument or proof that can move them from it. I remember saying to one of these obstinate fellows one day, 'Tell me, do you remember how a few years ago they were playing three tragedies in Spain by a famous native poet? They were so good that they delighted, surprised and amazed everyone who saw them, learned and simple, the best people and the crowd, and those three alone earned the players more money than thirty of the best produced since?'

"The manager I am speaking of replied, 'Of course, your worship means *Isabella, Phyllis* and *Alexandra.*' 'Those it was I meant,' I replied. 'Now, did not they keep carefully to the rules of drama, and did that prevent their being the successes they were and pleasing everybody? So the fault is not in the public for demanding absurdities, but in people who cannot put anything else on the stage. For there is no absurdity in *Ingratitude Avenged* or in *Numancia.** You will not find any in *The Merchant Lover*, not yet in *The Friendly Enemy*, nor in quite a few others written by various good poets, to their own fame and glory, and to the profit of the players.' I said a good deal else as well, and I think I left him in some confusion, but not so satisfied or convinced as to retract his mistaken opinions."

"You have touched on a subject, Sir Canon," said the priest at this, "which wakes in me an old grudge I bear against the plays they act today. It is as great as my grudge against books of chivalry. For though Drama, according to Tully, should be a mirror to human life, a pattern of manners, and an image of truth, the plays that are performed nowadays are mirrors of absurdity, patterns of foolishness and images of lewdness. For what greater absurdity can there be in our present subject than for a child to come on in the first scene of the first act in swaddling clothes, and in the second as a grown man with a beard? What could be more ridiculous than to paint us a valiant old man and a young coward, an eloquent servant, a statesmanlike page, a king as a porter, and a princess a scullery-maid? And they pay no more regard to the place or the time in which their action is supposed to occur. I have seen a play whose first act opened in Europe, its second in Asia and its third ended in Africa. And if there had been four acts, the fourth no doubt would have finished up in America, and so it would have been played in all four quarters of the globe. If imitation is the chief aim of a play, how is it possible to satisfy any average intelligence, when an action pretends to take place in the time of King Pepin and Charlemagne, and yet they make the principal character in it the Emperor Heraclius, who enters Jerusalem bearing the Cross and wins the Holy Sepulchre, like Godfrey de Bouillon, though there was a whole age between the one event and the other? And when the comedy is based on a fictitious story, how can they introduce historical events into it, and mix in incidents that happened to different people at different times;

* By Cervantes himself.

They scoured the roads, searched the woods and everywhere they could, and at the end of three days found the fickle Leandra in a mountain cave, clad only in her shift and without the store of money and the precious jewels which she had brought away with her. (page 608) and, even then, with no attempt at verisimilitude, but with obvious errors inexcusable on every count? The worst of it is that there are idiots who say that this stuff is perfect and to look for anything else is to fish for dainties.

"And when we come to sacred drama? What a multitude of false miracles they invent! What apocryphal and unintelligible plots —the miracles of one saint attributed to another! Even in their profane plays they make bold to introduce miracles without any more reason or consideration than because they think that some miracle—or effect, as they call it—will go well, and that the ignorant public will enjoy it and come to the play. But all this is prejudicial to truth, and to the detriment of history. It shames our Spanish wits before foreigners, who observe the rules of drama with great strictness and consider us ignorant barbarians when they see the absurdities and extravagances of the plays we write. It is not sufficient excuse to say that the principal purpose for which well-ordered states allow public plays to be acted is to give the common people a respectable entertainment, and to divert the ill-humours which idleness at times engenders; and that since any play can do that, whether it is good or bad, there is no reason to impose laws or compel writers and actors to compose their plays in the proper way, because, as I have said, they can achieve their purpose with any play at all. To this I should reply that their purpose could be incomparably better achieved by good plays than by bad ones, because the audience would come out from a well-written and well-constructed play entertained by the comic part, instructed by the serious, surprised by the action, enlivened by the speeches, warned by the tricks, wiser for the moral, incensed against vice and enamoured of virtue. All these effects a good play can work in the mind of an audience, however rough and sluggish; and it is absolutely impossible for a play with all these qualities not to amuse and entertain, satisfy and please, much better than one that lacks them, as most of the pieces generally played nowadays do. It is not the fault of the poets who write them, for some of them know very well where they are wrong and are thoroughly conscious of what they ought to do.

But as plays have become a marketable commodity they say, and say truly, that the players would not buy them if they were not of the usual kind. And so the poet tries to adapt himself to the requirements of the manager who pays him for his work. The truth of that can be seen by the infinite number of plays written by one most fertile genius of these kingdoms with so much splendour and so much grace, with such well-turned verses, such choice language, such serious thought and lastly, with so much eloquence and in so lofty a style, that the world is full of his fame, and yet, because he wishes to suit the taste of the actors, not all his pieces have achieved, as some have, the perfection which art requires. Other authors pay so little attention to their task that when the play is over the actors have to run away and hide, for fear of being punished, as they have often been, for acting scenes offensive to some prince or libelling some family.

"Now, all these evils, and many more of which I will not speak, would cease, if there were some intelligent and judicious person at court to examine all plays before they are performed, not only those that are acted in the capital, but all that are to be played anywhere in Spain. Then no magistrate in any town would allow any play to be performed without this man's approbation, under his hand and seal; and so the comedians would take good care to send their plays to Madrid, and could then act them in safety. The writers, too, would take more pains with their work, out of fear of the rigorous examination they would have to pass at the hands of someone knowing the business. In this way good plays would be produced, and the purpose of such entertainment successfully achieved, which is not only popular amusement, but also the good reputation of Spanish genius, the profit and security of the actors and the avoidance of the need to punish them. Now, if the same person or some other were entrusted with the task of examining newly written books of chivalry, no doubt some would be produced of the perfection your worship requires, thus enriching our tongue with the charming and precious treasure of eloquence, and causing the old books to be eclipsed in the bright presence of the new. They would provide honest amusement not only for the idle but for the busiest of men; for it is impossible for the brow to be always bent, nor can our frail human nature sustain itself without some lawful recreation."

When the canon and the priest had reached this point in their conversation the barber rode forward, caught them up, and said to the priest, "Here, Master Priest, is the place I told you of. We can take our siesta here, and the oxen will find plenty of fresh pasture."

"It looks good to me," replied the priest, and told their intentions to the canon, who was attracted by the sight of the lovely valley before them and decided to stay with them. And so as to enjoy the scene and the conversation of the priest, for whom he had taken a liking, and to hear Don Quixote's adventures in greater detail, he ordered some of his servants to go to the inn, which was not far away, and bring enough for them all to eat, as he had decided to rest there that afternoon. One of his servants replied, however, that the baggage-mule, which must be at the inn already, carried sufficient provisions, and that they would need nothing from there but barley.

"If that is so," said the canon, "take all our mounts there and bring the baggage-mule back."

While this was going on Sancho saw an opportunity of talking to his master without the continual presence of the priest and the barber, whom he regarded with suspicion. So he went up to the cage, and said, "Sir, I want to relieve my conscience, and tell you something about your enchantment, and that is, that those two with their faces covered are our village priest and the barber. I think they've played this trick of carrying you off like this because they're envious of your worship for beating them in doing famous deeds. Supposing, then, that I'm right. It follows that you're not under a spell, but humbugged and fooled. Now, to prove it to you, I want to ask you one question, and if you answer me as I think you will, you'll put your finger on this trick and see that you're not enchanted, but have had your wits turned upside down."

"Ask what you like, Sancho my son," replied Don Quixote, "and I will satisfy you and answer you to your heart's content. But as to your saying that the men accompanying us are the priest and the barber, our friends and fellow-villagers, it may well be that they look the same, but you must not believe for a minute that they really and truly are so. What you must believe and understand is that if they are like them, as you say, it must be because my enchanters have taken on their likeness and semblance, for it is easy for magicians to take on any appearance they please. And they will have assumed the likeness of our friends to give you cause to think as you do, and to put you into a maze of conjectures, from which not even the clue of Theseus could extricate you. Their intention will also be to confuse my brain and make me incapable of guessing the cause of this disaster. For if you tell me, on the one hand, that our village priest and barber are travelling here beside me, and if, on the other, I find myself caged and know that only superhuman power could encage me—for no human strength would be sufficient—what would you have me say or think, except that the manner of my enchantment is stranger than any I have read of in any history that treats of the enchantment of knights errant? So do not be disturbed by supposing that they are whom you say, but rest assured that they are no more the priest and the barber than I am a Turk. But as for these questions you wish to ask me, speak, for I will answer you, even though you go on asking till tomorrow."

"Holy Mother!" replied Sancho, raising his voice. "Can you possibly be so thick-skulled and brain-sick, your worship, that you can't see it's the sober truth I'm telling you, and that there's more roguery than enchantment about this unfortunate confinement of yours? Anyhow, I'll clearly prove it to you that you're not enchanted. Now, tell me, as God shall deliver you out of this trouble, and as you would find yourself in the arms of my lady Dulcinea when least you expect it—"

"Stop your hocus-pocus," cried Don Quixote, "and ask what you will. I have promised already to reply faithfully."

"That's what I want," said Sancho; "for you to tell me the *whole* truth, without additions or subtractions, as those, like your worship, who make a profession of arms under the title of knights errant are expected to do."

"I tell you that I will not lie on any matter," replied Don Quixote. "Get on with your questions; for really, Sancho, you weary me with all your oaths, your supplications and preambles."

"Well," said Sancho, "I'm confident that my master's a good man and truthful. And so, I'll ask you one question that's very much to the point. Speaking with all respect, your worship, since you've been cooped up and enchanted, as you think, in this cage, have you been taken with any desire or inclination to make either big or little waters, as the saying is?"

"I do not understand what you mean by making waters, Sancho. Be more explicit, if you want me to answer you fully."

"Is it possible that your worship doesn't understand what making big or little waters is? Why, boys learn that when they go to school. But what I mean is, have you had no mind to do what nobody can do for you?"

"Oh, I understand you now, Sancho. Yes, very often. In fact I want to at this moment. Get me out of my plight, for things are none too clean."

❧ 49 ❧

Of the Shrewd Conversation between
Sancho Panza and His Master Don Quixote

*A*h," said Sancho, "now I've
caught you. I was longing to know that with all my heart and soul.
Come now, sir, can you dispute the saying that's in everyone's
mouth when some one's in a bad way, 'I don't know what's the
matter with so and so. He doesn't eat or drink or sleep, or answer
straight when you ask him a question; it really looks as if he's
bewitched.' From which you may gather that people who don't eat
or drink or sleep or perform the natural functions I mentioned are
enchanted; but if they have the desire your worship has, and drink
when it's given them, and eat when they have something to eat, and
answer all the questions they are asked, then they are certainly
not bewitched."

"You are right, Sancho," replied Don Quixote; "but I have told
you already that there are many kinds of enchantments; and time
may have changed the fashion from one kind to another. It may be
usual now for people under a spell to do all that I do, although they
did not before; so that there is no arguing or drawing conclusions
against the customs of the times. I most certainly know that I am

586

enchanted, and that is sufficient to ease my conscience, which would
be greatly burdened if I thought that I was not under a spell, and yet
remained in this cage like an idler and a coward, defrauding the
many distressed and needy of the succour I could give them. For
there must be many at this hour in positive and urgent need of my
help and protection."

"But for all that," replied Sancho, "for your greater security and
satisfaction, it would be well, I think, if your worship were to try to
get out of your prison. I promise to help you with all my power, and
even to release you. Then you could try to mount once again on
your good Rocinante, who seems to be enchanted as well, he's so
melancholy and sad. And when you've done that, we can try our
luck and look for more adventures. If we don't succeed there'll still
be time to come back to the cage. And I promise you, on the faith of
a true and loyal squire, I'll shut myself up alongside your worship, if
you should chance to prove so unlucky or I so stupid as not to bring
off this plan of mine."

"I am content to do as you say, brother Sancho," replied Don
Quixote, "and when you see an opportunity of managing my
deliverance, I will obey you absolutely. But you will see, Sancho,
how mistaken you are in your opinion about my misfortune."

Our errant knight and ill-errant squire entertained themselves
with this conversation until they reached the place where the priest,
the canon and the barber had dismounted and were awaiting them.
The carter then unyoked his oxen from the cart and turned them
loose in that green and pleasant place, whose freshness invited not
only enchanted persons like Don Quixote, but also such a rational
and sensible creature as his squire. Sancho begged the priest to let his
master out of his cage for a while, for otherwise his prison would not
be as clean as decency required the accommodation of such a knight
as his master to be. The priest understood him, and said that he
would gladly oblige him, if it were not for his fear that once Don
Quixote found himself at liberty he would play them one of his
tricks, and go off and never be seen again.

"I'll go bail for his not running away," replied Sancho.

"And I, for any sum," said the canon, "particularly if he gives me his word as a knight not to leave us without our consent."

"I give it," answered Don Quixote, who was listening all the time, "the more so because anyone enchanted, as I am, is not at liberty to dispose of his person as he will. For his enchanter can make him powerless to stir from one spot for three centuries; and if he were to escape he would be brought back flying through the air." Since this was the case, he said, they could certainly release him, especially as it would be to everyone's advantage; in fact, if they did not let him out, he protested, he could not refrain from offending their noses, unless they were to retire to some distance.

The canon took him by one of his hands, although they were tied, and on his pledged word, they let him out of his cage, at which he was vastly delighted. The first thing he did was to stretch his whole body, and then he went over to Rocinante and gave him two slaps on the haunches, saying, "I still trust in God and his blessed Mother, flower and mirror of steeds, that we two shall soon find ourselves in the state our hearts desire, you with your master on your back, and I on top of you, exercising the function for which God sent me into the world."

After saying this Don Quixote went aside with Sancho Panza to a distant spot, from which he returned much relieved, and still more eager to put his squire's plan into execution.

The canon gazed at him, and wondered at the strangeness of his crazy humour and at the excellent sense he displayed in his conversation and in his answers, only losing his stirrups, as we have said before, on the subject of chivalry. And so, once they were all seated on the green grass waiting for the provisions, the canon was moved by compassion to ask him, "Can the idle and unsavoury reading of books of chivalry, my good sir, possibly have had such an effect on you so as to turn your brain that you have come to believe that you are under a spell, and other things of that kind, which are as far from being so as falsehood itself is from the truth? How is it possible for human reason to persuade itself of the existence of all those countless Amadises, of that multitude of famous knights, and of so many

\

But the goatherd did not see the joke and, finding himself thus damaged in good earnest, took no account of the carpet or the tablecloth or the diners round it, but jumped upon Don Quixote and, grasping him round the neck with both hands, would no doubt have choked him if Sancho Panza had not come up at this point. (page 612)

Emperors of Trebizond? Who could really believe in Felixmarte of
Hyrcania, and all those palfreys, all those wandering damsels, all
those serpents, all those dragons, all those giants, all those extraordinary adventures, all those varieties of spells, all those battles, all
those desperate encounters, all that fine raiment, all those love-lorn
princesses, all those squires who became counts, all those facetious
dwarfs, all those love letters, all that wooing, all those courageous
ladies and, in fact, all those monstrous absurdities contained in books
of chivalry? For myself I can say that they give me a certain pleasure
when I read them—so long as I do not deliberately reflect that they
are all triviality and lies. But when I consider what they are I throw
the very best of them against the wall, and I would pitch them into
the fire if I had one near at hand. For such a punishment they
certainly deserve for being liars and impostors, beyond the realms of
common sense, as founders of new sects and new ways of life, and
for causing the ignorant crowd to accept all the nonsense they
contain as gospel truth. They have even the audacity to confuse the
minds of intelligent and well-born gentlemen, as is clear from their
effect on your worship, whom they have reduced to the state of
being shut in a cage and carried on an ox-cart, as they transport a
lion or a tiger from town to town to exhibit it for money. Come,
Don Quixote, take pity on yourself; return into the bosom of
discretion, and learn to use the generous talents that Heaven has
blessed you with, by applying your mind to some other course of
study which may redound to the profit of your soul and to the
increasing of your honour. But if your natural inclination is so
strong that you must read books of adventures and chivalry, read the
Book of Judges in Holy Scripture, where you will find grand and
authentic exploits, which are both heroic and true. Portugal had its
Viriatus, Rome had its Caesar, Carthage its Hannibal, Greece its
Alexander, Castile its Count Ferdinand Gonzalez, Valencia its Cid,
Andalusia its Gonzalo Fernandez, Estremadura its Diego Garcia de
Paredes, Jerez its Garci Perez de Vargas, Toledo its Garcilaso,
Seville its Don Manuel de Leon; and their valorous exploits will
entertain, instruct, delight and surprise the highest intelligence that

reads them. They are certainly a study worthy of your excellent mind, my dear Don Quixote, and you will rise from reading of them learned in history, enamoured of virtue, instructed in goodness, improved in manners, valiant but not rash, bold and no coward; and all this to the honour of God, your own profit and the glory of La Mancha, whence, as I have learnt, you derive your birth and origin."

Don Quixote listened most attentively to the canon's arguments, gazed at him for some time when he saw that he had finished, and said, "Sir, your discourse was intended, I think, to persuade me that there have never been knights errant in the world, that all books of chivalry are false, lying, hurtful and unprofitable to the commonwealth, and that I have done wrong to read them, and worse to believe in them, and worst of all to imitate them in setting myself to follow the very hard profession of knight errantry they teach. And, what is more, you deny the existence of either Amadis of Gaul or of Greece, and of all those other knights of whom the writings are full."

"I meant precisely what you say," answered the canon at this. To which Don Quixote replied, "You were pleased to add also that such books have done me much harm, that they have turned my brain, and caused my present imprisonment, and that it would be better for me to make some amendment, and change my reading to other books more truthful, enjoyable and instructive."

"Just so," answered the canon.

"Why then, in my opinion it is you," replied Don Quixote, "that are deranged and enchanted, for daring to blaspheme against an institution so universally acknowledged and so authenticated, that anyone denying it, as you do, deserves the very punishment you say that you inflict on certain books when you have read them and they displease you. For to attempt to convince anyone that there were no such persons as Amadis and the other knights errant of whom so many records remain, would be like trying to persuade him that the sun does not shine, nor the frost chill, nor earth yield sustenance. For what intellect could there be in the world capable of persuading another that the story of Princess Floripes and Guy of Burgundy was not true? Or the adventure of Fierabras at the Bridge of Mantible, which took place in the time of Charlemagne, and which, I swear, is as true as that it is now daylight? And if that is a lie, then it must follow that there existed no Hector, nor Achilles, nor Trojan War, nor Twelve Peers of France, nor King Arthur of England, who is still wandering about the world to this day transformed into a raven, and is hourly awaited in his kingdom. Yes, they will even say, no doubt, that the history of Guarino Mezquino is false, and the Quest of the Holy Grail as well, and that the loves of Sir Tristan and Queen Iseult, and of Guinevere and Lancelot are apocryphal, although there are persons who almost remember having seen the Lady Quintañona. She was the best wine-server Great Britain ever had, and her existence is so authentic that I remember my grandmother on my father's side saying, when she saw an old lady with a stately head-dress, 'My boy, that woman is very like the Lady Quintañona.' From which I conclude that she must herself have known her, or must have seen some portrait of her, at least. Then who can deny the truth of the story of Peter and the fair Magalona, since even to this day you can see in the King's armoury the peg with which the brave Peter guided the wooden horse on which he used to ride through the air, and which is a little bigger than the pole of a coach? And near this peg is Babieca's saddle, and at Roncesvalles is Roland's horn, which is the size of a great beam; from which it can be inferred that the Twelve Peers existed, and the Peters, and the Cids and other such knights, of the sort commonly termed adventurers. If that is denied I shall be told it is not true that the brave Lusitanian Juan de Merlo was a knight errant, who went to Burgundy and fought in the city of Arras with the famous Lord of Charny, called Monseigneur Pierre, and after that with Monseigneur Henri de Remestan in the city of Basle, coming off from both exploits victorious and crowned with honour and glory. They will also deny the adventures and challenges also performed in Burgundy by the valiant Spaniards, Pedro Barba and Gutierre Quixada—from whose stock I am descended in the direct male line—when they beat the sons of the Count St. Pol. Nor will they agree that Don Ferdinand de Guevara went to Germany in quest of adventure, and fought there with Messire George, a knight of the Duke of Austria's house. They will say, too, that the jousts of Suero de Quiñones of the Honourable Pass were a fable, and the exploits of Sir Luis de Falces against the Castillian knight Don Gonzalo de Guzman, and all the many deeds performed by Christian knights of these and foreign realms, so authentic and true, I repeat, that anyone denying them must be devoid of all reason and right understanding."

The canon was amazed to hear Don Quixote so mingling truth and fiction, and at the knowledge he displayed of everything in any way concerning the exploits of his knight errantry. And so he replied, "I cannot deny, sir, that some of what you say is true, especially what you say of the Spanish knights errant; and I would admit also the existence of the Twelve Peers of France, though I cannot believe that they performed all those deeds that Archbishop Turpin attributes to them. For the truth of it is that they were knights chosen by the Kings of France, and were called peers as being all equal in worth, in rank and in valour; or at least, if they were not, they should have been. They were an order like the present-day order of Santiago, or of Calatrava, whose professing knights are presumed to be, or should be, worthy, valiant and well born; and as we now speak of a Knight of St. John or of Alcantara, so they used to speak in those days of a Knight of the Twelve Peers, because they were twelve equals, chosen to be members of that military order. As for the Cid, there is no doubt about him, and even less about Bernardo del Carpio; but that they performed the deeds attributed to them is a very doubtful matter. As for that other matter you speak of, Count Pierre's peg and its standing near Babieca's saddle in the King's armoury, I must confess that I am so ignorant or so short-sighted that, although I have seen the saddle, I have never noticed the peg, big as you say it is."

"Yet it is there without a doubt," replied Don Quixote, "and what is more, they say that it is kept in an ox-hide sheath, to save it from rusting."

"That may well be so," replied the canon, "but I swear by my holy orders I do not remember having seen it. Though, supposing I grant that it is there, that is no reason for my having to believe the stories of all these Amadises, or of all that multitude of knights we are told about. Nor is it reasonable for a man like yourself, possessed of your understanding, your reputation and your talents, to accept all the extravagant absurdities in these ridiculous books of chivalry as really true."

⊰ 50 ⊱

Of the Learned Arguments
between Don Quixote and the Canon,
and Other Matters

*T*hat is a good joke!" replied
Don Quixote. "Books which are printed by royal licence and with
the approval of those to whom they are submitted, and which are
read with universal delight and applause by great and small, poor
and rich, learned and ignorant, plebeians and gentlefolk—in short,
by all kinds of persons of every quality and condition—could they be
lies and at the same time appear so much like the truth? For do they
not specify the father, the mother, the family, the time, the place
and the actions, detail by detail and day by day, of this or that
knight? Be silent, sir, do not speak such blasphemies; and, believe
me, if you take my advice you will be acting like a man of sense.
Only read these books, and you will see what pleasure you get from
them. For, tell me, could there by anything more delightful than to
see displayed here and now before our eyes, as we might say, a great
lake of pitch, boiling hot, and swimming and writhing about in it a
great number of serpents, snakes and lizards, and many other sorts
of savage and frightful creatures; and then to hear issuing from the
middle of that lake a most dismal voice crying, 'You, Knight,

whoever you may be, that gaze on this dreadful lake, if you would reach the treasure hidden beneath these black waters, show the valour of your dauntless heart and plunge into the middle of its dark, burning liquor; for if you do not do so, you will not be worthy to see the mighty marvels hidden within the seven castles of the seven witches who dwell beneath this gloomy water.' No sooner has the knight heard this dreadful voice than he abandons all thought for himself, and without reflecting on the peril to which he is exposing himself, or even easing himself of the weight of his ponderous armour, he commends himself to God and his lady, dives into the middle of the boiling lake; and then unexpectedly, and when he least knows where he is going, he finds himself amidst flowery meadows, incomparably finer even than the Elysian fields. There the sky seems to him more transparent and the sun to shine with a new brightness. Before his eyes opens a pleasant grove of green and leafy trees whose verdure charms his vision, while his ears are ravished by the sweet, untaught song of innumerable little bright-coloured birds which flit about the interlacing branches. Here he discovers a small stream, whose fresh waters glide like liquid crystal over delicate sand and little white stones, which resemble sifted gold and purest pearl. There he spies a fountain made of mottled jasper and smooth marble; here another, roughly fashioned, where tiny mussel shells, mingled with the twisted yellow and white houses of the snails, lying in disordered order among pieces of glittering crystal and counterfeit emeralds, form so gracefully varied a composition that art, the imitator of nature, seems here to surpass herself. Then suddenly there appears in the distance a strong castle or handsome palace with walls of solid gold, with turrets of diamonds, and gates of jacinth; so admirably built, in fact, that though the materials of which it is constructed are nothing less than diamonds, carbuncles, rubies, pearls, gold and emeralds, the workmanship is still more precious. And after this, could there be a finer sight than a lovely troop of maidens coming out of the castle in such gay and gorgeous attire that, if I were to set out now to describe them as the stories do, I should never end? And then for the one who seems the chief of them all to take the bold knight who plunged into the burning lake by the hand, and silently lead him into the rich palace or castle, and strip him as naked as his mother bore him, and bathe him in warm water, and then anoint him all over with sweet-smelling ointments, and put on him a shirt of finest samite, all fragrant and perfumed? Then for another maiden to come and throw over his shoulder a mantle, reputed to be worth a city, at the very least, or perhaps more? What finer sight, then, than after all that, to see them take him to another room where the tables are laid so magnificently that he is speechless with amazement? And to watch him sprinkle on his hands water all distilled of ambergris and sweet-smelling flowers? And to see him seated on an ivory chair? And to see all the maidens serve him, still preserving their miraculous silence? And bring him such variety of dishes, so deliciously cooked that the appetite is at a loss to know where to direct the hand? How pleasant it must be to hear the music which sounds all the while, without his knowing who is singing or whence it comes? And when the feast is over and the tables are cleared, for the knight to stay reclining on his chair, perhaps picking his teeth as his custom is, when suddenly there enters through the door of the hall another maiden more lovely than any of the first, who sits down beside him and begins to tell him what manner of castle it is, and how she lives there under a spell, and other things which surprise the knight and astonish the readers of his story.

"I will enlarge on this no further, for you can gather from what I have said that any passage from any story of knight errantry is bound to delight and amaze a reader. Believe me, sir, I repeat, and read these books. You will see how they drive away the melancholy, and improve your temper if it happens to be bad. I can say of myself that since I became a knight errant I have been valiant, courteous, liberal, well-bred, generous, polite, bold, gentle and patient, and an endurer of toils, imprisonments and enchantments. And although for the last little while I have been imprisoned in a cage like a madman, I expect by the valour of my arm, if Heaven favours me and fate is not against me, to find myself in a few days king of some kingdom, in which I can display the gratitude and liberality enclosed in this bosom of mine. For, by my faith, sir, a poor man is incapacitated from showing the virtue of liberality towards anyone, even though he may possess it in the highest degree; and gratitude which consists only of desire is a dead thing, as faith is dead without works. For that reason I could wish that fortune would speedily offer me an opportunity of making myself Emperor, so that I might show my will to do good to my friends, especially to this poor Sancho Panza, my squire, who is the best man in the world; and I should like to give him the countship which I promised him a long while ago, were it not that I am afraid he will not have the capacity to govern his estate."

At this Sancho, who had overheard these last words of his master's, exclaimed, "Set to work, Don Quixote. Get me that countship you've promised me so often and I've waited for so long. I've no lack of capacity to govern, I assure you; and if I had, I've heard of men who take noblemen's estates in farm, giving them so much a year and looking after the management. Then the lord lies with his feet up, enjoying the rent they pay him without a care in the world; and that's what I'll do. I won't haggle over a few pence more or less. I'll give it all up at once, and enjoy my income like a duke. Then let the world go hang."

"That, brother Sancho," said the canon, "applies to the enjoyment of the revenues. But there is the administration of justice, which the lord of the estate must attend to. That is where capacity and a sound judgment come in and, above all, an honest intention to do right; for if that is lacking in the beginning, everything will go wrong in the middle and the end, and Heaven usually assists the good intentions of the simple, and confounds the evil designs of the crafty."

"I don't understand these philosophies," replied Sancho Panza. "I only wish I were as sure of the countship as of my ability to govern. For I've as large a soul as the next man, and as stout a body as the best of them, and I'd be as good a king of my estate as any other King; and being so, I should do as I liked; and doing as I liked, I should take my pleasure; and taking my pleasure, I should be contented; and when one's content, there's nothing more to desire; and when there's nothing more to desire, there's an end of it. So for Heaven's sake let me have the estate, and then we'll see, as one blind man said to the other."

"These are not bad philosophies, as you say, Sancho," put in the canon; "but all the same there is a great deal to be said on this subject of countships."

But Don Quixote answered his squire, "I do not know what more there is to say. I am guided solely by the example of the great Amadis of Gaul, who made his squire Count of the Firm Isle. So I need have no scruple of conscience in making Sancho Panza a count, for he is one of the best squires that ever served knight errant."

The canon was astonished at this well-reasoned nonsense of Don Quixote's, at his description of the adventure of the Knight of the Lake, and at the impression made on him by the deliberate lies in the books he had read. And he marvelled, too, at Sancho's foolishness in so ardently desiring the countship his master had promised him.

By this time the canon's servants, who had gone to the inn for the baggage-mule, had returned. So, making a carpet and the green meadow-grass their table, they sat down in the shade of some trees and took their meal there, so that the carter could profit from the pasture there, as has already been said. Now, whilst they were eating they suddenly heard a considerable noise and the sound of a little bell from some brambles and thick bushes which grew close by; and at the same moment they saw a fine she-goat speckled with black, white and grey, run out of the thicket. After her came a goatherd calling to her in the language they use when they want their beasts to stop and come back to the fold. But the truant goat ran up to the company, scared and trembling, as if for their protection, and there stayed still till the goatherd arrived and, catching her by the horns, addressed her, as if she were capable of speech and reason, "Oh, wild one, wild one! Speckle, Speckle, how you've gone

*Coming up, then, to the procession, he halted Rocinante,
who already wanted a little rest, and cried out in a hoarse
and angry voice, "You who, perhaps because you are evil,
keep your faces covered, stop and listen to what I am going
to say to you." (page 614)*

limping about these days! What wolves have scared you, little one? Won't you tell me what it is, pretty one? But it can only be that you're a woman and can't stay still! The Devil take your moods, and the moods of all like you. Come back, come back, friend! You'll be safer in your fold, or with your companions, even if you're not so happy. For if you, who should guide them and lead them, go unguided and astray, what will become of them?"

The goatherd's words amused his hearers, especially the canon, who said to him, "Come, come, do not be angry, brother, I beg you, and do not be in such a hurry to drive this goat back to her fold. For since she is a female, as you say, she must follow her natural instinct, despite all your pains to stop her. Take a snack and drink a drop with us; it will soothe you and the goat can rest a while."

As he said this he handed him the hindquarter of a cold rabbit on the point of a knife. The goatherd took it and thanked him. Then when he had drunk and rested, he said, "I shouldn't like your worships to take me for a simpleton for talking to this animal so sensibly, for in truth my words are not without some meaning. I'm a peasant, but not so much of one that I don't understand how to converse with men and beasts."

"I can very well believe that," answered the priest, "for I already know by experience that the mountains breed scholars, and sheep-cotes contain philosophers."

"At least, sir," said the goatherd, "they house men who have learnt by experience. And to convince you of that, and to give you an example, too—though, being uninvited, I may seem to be obtruding myself—if it doesn't bore you, gentlemen, and you will lend me your attention for a little, I'll tell you a true tale which will confirm that gentleman's words"—pointing to the priest—"and mine."

To which Don Quixote answered, "Seeing that this matter has a slight tinge of knightly adventure about it, I will listen to you, for my part, brother; and so will all these gentlemen, who are men of good sense and fond of the curious, the entertaining and the marvellous, all of which, I have no doubt, your story contains. Begin, then, friend, and we will all listen."

"Count me out," said Sancho. "I am off to the stream with this pie, and I'm going to fill myself with enough for three days. For I have heard my master, Don Quixote, say that a knight errant's squire must eat his fill when he gets the chance, since they may lose their way for six days together in some wood that's so thick they can't find a way out; and if a man doesn't go in with a full belly or a well-stored haversack, he may very well stay there, as very often he does, till he is turned into mummy flesh."

"You are quite right, Sancho," said Don Quixote. "Go where you like and eat what you can, but I am satisfied already. All I need is refreshment for my mind, which I will now give it by listening to this good man's story."

"And so will we all," said the canon.

But before beginning the promised tale, the goatherd gave the goat, which he was holding by the horns, a couple of slaps on the back, and said, "Lie down beside me, Speckle, for we shall have time enough to return to our fold." The creature seemed to understand him, for when her master sat down, she stretched herself calmly beside him, and looking up into his face, signified that she was listening, as he began the following story.

⊰ *51* ⊱

What the Goatherd told
Don Quixote's Escort

$\mathcal{N}$ine miles from this valley is a
town which, although small, is one of the richest in all this district. In
it there lived a farmer greatly honoured, both for his native virtue
and for the wealth he had acquired, though honour always goes with
riches. But his greatest fortune in his own eyes was the possession of
a daughter of such consummate beauty, rare good sense, charm and
virtue, that everyone who knew her, or even set eyes on her, was
amazed at the surpassing qualities with which Heaven and nature
had endowed her. As a child she was pretty, and she went on
increasing in loveliness until at the age of sixteen she was exceedingly beautiful. The fame of her loveliness began to spread
among all the near-by villages—but why do I say near-by villages? It
reached to distant cities, and even entered the royal palace and came
to the ears of many sorts of people, who would come to see her from
all parts, as if she were a rare sight or a wonder-working image. Her
father guarded her carefully, and she guarded herself, for there are
no locks, bolts or bars which keep a maiden better guarded than
does her own modesty. The father's wealth and the daughter's

beauty led many, both of their own town and strangers, to ask for her hand. But, having so rich a jewel to dispose of, he was much perplexed and unable to decide upon which of her infinite number of wooers to bestow her. Now, among the multitude who desired her I was one, and I derived very great hopes of success from her father's knowing me and because I was a native of their town, of pure blood, in the flower of my youth, rich in goods, and no less well endowed in mind. But a fellow-townsman with all the same qualifications was also her suitor; and this caused the father to put off his decision and keep things in the balance, for it seemed to him that either of us would be a good match for his daughter. To solve his difficulty, he decided to refer it to Leandra—for that is the name of the rich maid who has plunged me into such misery—thinking that, as we two were equal, it was best to leave it to his beloved daughter to choose according to her own liking, a course that should be imitated by all fathers with children to marry. I do not mean that they should leave them to make a choice among bad or evil persons, but that they should put the good before them, and let them choose among them according to their taste. I do not know what choice Leandra made; I only know that her father put us both off on the score of his daughter's youth, in general terms which neither bound him nor dismissed us. My rival's name is Anselmo, and mine Eugenio—for I would have you know the names of the persons involved in this tragedy, the end of which is still unresolved, though it is clear enough that it is bound to be disastrous.

"At this time there came to our town one Vicente de la Roca, the son of a poor local farmer, which Vicente had returned from Italy and other places where he had been soldiering. He had been carried off from our town as a lad of about twelve by a captain who happened to be passing through with his troop; and now, about twelve years later, returned as a youth in a soldier's uniform, pranked out in countless bright colours, and hung with innumerable glass trinkets and fine steel chains. One day he would put on one bit of finery, the next another, but all of them flimsy, gaudy, weighing little and worth less. The country people, who are malicious by

nature—and when idleness gives them an occasion are malice itself—
—noted and reckoned up each one of his bits of finery and trinkets,
and found that he had only three suits of different colours, with
stockings and garters to match. But he made so many transformations and variations with them that, if no one had counted them, one
would have sworn that he had shown off more than ten suits of
clothes and more than twenty plumes of feathers. Now, do not
presume that what I am telling you about his clothes is a digression
or superfluous, for they play a principal part in my story.

"Now, he used to sit on a bench under a great poplar in our
market-place, and there he would keep us all open-mouthed,
hanging on the exploits he described to us. There was no country in
the whole world he had not visited, and no battle he had not taken
part in. He had killed more Turks than there are in Morocco and
Tunis, and engaged in more single combats, according to his own
story, than Gante and Luna, Diego Garcia de Paredes, and a thousand others whom he named, and from every one of them he had
come off victorious, without losing so much as a drop of blood.
Then, again, he would show us scars of wounds, and although we
could not make them out, he would persuade us that they came from
musket-shots received in various actions and skirmishes. What is
more, he would have the unparalleled effrontery to patronize his
equals, even those who knew him, and say that his right arm was his
father, his deeds his lineage, and that, as a soldier, he owed nothing
even to the King himself. In addition to these pretensions he was
something of a musician and plucked the guitar to such effect that
some people said he could make it speak. But his accomplishments
did not stop here, for he had also a talent for poetry, and used to
make up a ballad a mile and a half long on every trifling thing that
happened in the town.

"This soldier, then, whom I have just described, this Vicente de la
Roca, this braggart, this swaggerer, this musician, this poet, was
often seen and admired by Leandra from a window of her house
which looked on to the market-place. She was captivated by the
bright tinsel of his clothes, enchanted by his ballads—for he would

give away twenty copies of every one he composed—the exploits which he attributed to himself came to her ears and, in the end—for so the Devil must have decreed—she fell in love with him before the presumptuous idea of wooing her had come into his head. And as no love affair is more easily brought to fruition than one which is backed by the lady's desire, Leandra and Vicente came to an agreement without any difficulty; and before any one of her many suitors had realized her infatuation she had already satisfied it by running off from her dearly beloved father's house—she has no mother—and eloping from the village with the soldier, who came off from this enterprise more triumphantly than from all the many others he had laid claim to. This event filled the whole place with astonishment, and everyone else who heard of it, too. I was confounded, Anselmo thunderstruck, her father distressed, her relations ashamed, Justice aroused and the troopers on the watch. They scoured the roads, searched the woods and everywhere they could, and at the end of three days found the fickle Leandra in a mountain cave, clad only in her shift and without the store of money and the precious jewels which she had brought away with her. They took her back before her unhappy father and questioned her about her plight. And she confessed quite freely that Vicente de la Roca had deceived her, persuading her, under promise of marriage, to leave her father's house, and offering to take her to the richest and most delightful city in all the world—he meant Naples —and that she had been sufficiently ill-advised and deceived to believe him. For after robbing her father she had entrusted herself to him on the same night she had been missed, when he had taken her to a wild mountain and shut her in the cave where they had found her. She also affirmed that the soldier had not robbed her of her honour, though he had taken everything she had before going off and leaving her in the cave, a fact which astonished everyone afresh.

"It was difficult, sir, to believe in the youth's self-restraint, but she vouched for it with such persistence as partly to console her disconsolate father, who set no store by the valuables they had taken so long as his daughter was left in possession of that jewel which, once lost, is beyond all hope of recovery. The very same day that Leandra appeared her father removed her again from our sight, taking her and shutting her up in a nunnery at a town not far from here, in the hope that time would work off some part of the disgrace she had brought upon herself. Leandra's youth served as some excuse for her wickedness, at least for such as had nothing to gain from proving her good or bad; but those who knew her intelligence and considerable shrewdness attributed her fault not to ignorance, but to frivolity and the failings natural to woman-kind, who are generally ill-balanced and unsteady.

"With Leandra put away, Anselmo's eyes became blind, or at least there was no sight that gave him any pleasure, and my own were in darkness, without a light to guide them towards joy. In Leandra's absence our sorrow increased, our patience diminished, and we cursed the soldier's finery and railed at her father's lack of precaution. In the end he and I agreed to leave the village and come to this valley, where we spend our lives among the trees, he grazing a large flock of his own sheep, and I a large herd of goats, also my own. Here we give vent to our passion, either singing together in praise or dispraise of the lovely Leandra, or sighing separately and alone, and confiding our complaints to Heaven. Many others of Leandra's suitors have followed our example, and come to these wild mountains to follow the same employment; so many that this place seems to have become the pastoral Arcadia, for it is so crammed with shepherds and sheep-folds that there is not a corner in it where you will not hear the fair Leandra's name. One man curses her and calls her fickle, inconstant and immodest; another denounces her as forward and light; yet another absolves and pardons her; one more tries her and condemns her; one celebrates her beauty; another execrates her character; in fact, all disparage her and all adore her; and the madness extends so far that some complain of her disdain without ever having spoken to her, and some bewail their fate and suffer the maddening disease of jealousy, for which she never gave anyone any cause. For, as I have said, her fault was discovered before her infatuation was known. There is not a hollow rock, nor river bank, nor shade of a tree, that is not occupied by some shepherd or other recounting his misfortunes to the winds; and echo repeats Leandra's name wherever it can sound; the hills ring with Leandra, the streams murmur Leandra and Leandra keeps us all distracted and enchanted, hoping against hope and fearing without knowing what we fear.

"Among all these distracted men, the one who shows the least but has the most sense is my rival Anselmo who, having so many other things he might complain of, complains only of her absence, and sings his lament in verses which show his excellent talents, to the sound of a fiddle, which he plays admirably. I follow an easier and, in my opinion, a wiser path, which is to curse the fickleness of women, their inconstancy, their double-dealing, their unkept promises, their broken faith and, last of all, the lack of judgment they show in their choice of objects for their desires and affections.

"And that was the reason, gentlemen, for the words I addressed to this goat on my arrival here; for as a female I despise her, although she is the best of all my flock. This is the story I promised to tell you. If I have been tedious in my tale I will make amends. Near here is my cottage, where I have fresh milk and most delicious cheese, and various fruits now in season, no less pleasant to the sight than to the taste."

❧ *52* ☙

Of the Quarrel between
Don Quixote and the Goatherd,
with the Rare Adventure of the Penitents,
which he successfully achieved by
the Sweat of His Brow

*T*he goatherd's tale much de-
lighted all who heard it, especially the canon, who was particularly interested in the manner of its telling, which made the
narrator appear more like a polished courtier than a rustic goatherd.
In fact he remarked that the priest was right when he said that the
mountains bred scholars. The whole company complimented Eugenio, but Don Quixote showed himself the most liberal of all in this
respect, and said, "I promise you, brother goatherd, that were I
in the position to be able to embark on any adventure, I would
immediately set about bringing yours to a happy conclusion. I
would deliver Leandra from the nunnery, where there can be no
doubt she is kept against her will, in despite of the abbess and all
who might oppose me. Then I should place her in your hands, to be
dealt with according to your will and pleasure—observing, however, the laws of chivalry, which command that no violence be done
to a damsel. Yet I trust in our Lord God that one malicious enchanter may not be so powerful that another better-intentioned
enchanter may not prevail over him. And when that time comes I

promise you my favour and aid, as I am bound to do by my profession, which is none other than to succour the weak and the distressed."

The goatherd stared at him and, seeing Don Quixote so ragged and ill-favoured, asked the barber in astonishment who his neighbour was, "Sir, who is that man who looks so strange and talks so oddly?"

"Why, who should it be," answered the barber, "but the famous Don Quixote de la Mancha, the redresser of injuries, the righter of wrongs, the protector of damsels, the terror of giants and the victor of battles?"

"That sounds to me like the stuff in books about knights errant," observed the goatherd. "They did all these things you say this fellow does, though I take it that either your worship is joking, or the gentlemen must have some of the rooms in his brain vacant."

"You are a very great rascal," cried Don Quixote at this point, "and it is you that is vacant and deficient. For I am a good deal fuller than ever that whore's daughter, the whore that bore you, was."

As he spoke, he took up a loaf which lay beside him and hit the goatherd full in the face with it, with such force that he flattened his nose. But the goatherd did not see the joke and, finding himself thus damaged in good earnest, took no account of the carpet or the tablecloth or the diners round it, but jumped upon Don Quixote and, grasping him round the neck with both hands, would no doubt have choked him if Sancho Panza had not come up at this point. Seizing him by the shoulders, the squire threw him on to the tablecloth, breaking the plates, smashing the cups, and upsetting and scattering everything on it. Then Don Quixote, finding himself free, rushed to get on top of the goatherd who, with his face covered in blood from Sancho's kicks, was feeling about on all fours for a knife off the cloth to take some bloody vengeance. But this the canon and the priest prevented. However, with some help from the barber, the goatherd managed to get Don Quixote down, and rained such a shower of blows on him that the knight's face poured blood as freely as his. The canon and the priest were bursting with laughter; the troopers danced for joy, and everyone cheered them on, as men do at a dog-fight. Only Sancho Panza was in despair, because he could not get himself loose from one of the canon's servants, who was preventing him from helping his master. In the end when everyone was enjoying the sport except the two combatants, who were worrying one another, they heard the call of a trumpet, so mournful that they turned their faces in the direction from which it seemed to come. But the person who was most excited at the sound was Don Quixote who, although much against his will, lay underneath the goatherd, pretty well bruised and battered.

"Brother Demon," he cried to his enemy; "for it is impossible that you can be anything else, since you have the valour and strength to subdue mine—I pray you, let us call a truce, for just one hour. For the dolorous sound of that trumpet which reaches our ears seems to call me to some new adventure."

The goatherd, who was now tired of pummelling and being pummelled, let him go at once; and Don Quixote stood up, turning his face too in the direction of the sound, and suddenly saw a number of men dressed in white after the fashion of penitents, descending a little hill.

The fact was that in that year the clouds had denied the earth their moisture, and in all the villages of that district they were making processions, rogations and penances, to pray to God to vouchsafe His mercy and send them rain. And to this end the people of a village close by were coming in procession to a holy shrine which stood on a hill beside this valley. At the sight of the strange dress of these penitents Don Quixote failed to call to mind the many times he must have seen the like before, but imagined that this was material of adventure, and that it concerned him alone, as a knight errant, to engage in it. And he was confirmed in this idea by mistaking an image they were carrying, swathed in mourning, for some noble lady whom these villainous and unmannerly scoundrels were forcibly abducting. Now, scarcely had this thought come into his head, than he ran very quickly up to Rocinante, who was grazing nearby and, taking off the bridle and shield which hung by the pommel, he had him bitted in a second. Then, calling to Sancho for his sword, he mounted and, bracing on his shield, cried in a loud voice to everyone present, "Now, valiant company, you will see how important it is to have knights in the world, who profess the order of knight errantry. Now, I say, you will see, by the freeing of this good lady who is being borne off captive, what value should be set on knights errant."

As he spoke, he dug his heels into Rocinante, for he had no spurs, and at a canter—for we do not hear in all this authentic history that Rocinante ever went at a full gallop—rode to meet the penitents, although the priest, the canon and the barber tried to stop him. But they could not do so, nor could even Sancho keep him back by calling, "Where are you going, Don Quixote? What demons have you in your heart that incite you to assault our Catholic faith? Devil take me! Look, it's a procession of penitents, and that lady they're carrying upon the bier is the most blessed image of the spotless Virgin. Look out, sir, what you're doing, for this time you've made a real mistake."

Sancho laboured in vain, for his master was so set on reaching the sheeted figures and freeing the lady in black, that he did not hear a word; and, if he had heard, he would not have turned back, even at the King's command. Coming up, then, to the procession, he halted Rocinante, who already wanted a little rest, and cried out in a hoarse and angry voice, "You who, perhaps because you are evil, keep your faces covered, stop and listen to what I am going to say to you."

The first to stop were the men carrying the image, and one of the four priests who were chanting the litanies, observing Don Quixote's strange appearance, Rocinante's leanness and other ludicrous details which he noted in our knight, answered him by saying, "Worthy brother, if you wish to say anything to us, say it quickly, for these brethren of ours are lashing their flesh, and we cannot possibly stop to hear anything, unless it is so brief that you can say it in two words."

"I will say it in one," replied Don Quixote, "and it is this, now, this very moment, you must set this beautiful lady free, for her mournful appearance and tears clearly show that you are carrying her off against her will, and that you have done her some notable wrong. I, who was born into the world to redress such injuries, will not consent to your advancing one step farther unless you give her the liberty she desires and deserves."

At this speech all his hearers concluded that Don Quixote must be some madman, and began to laugh most heartily. Their laughter was like gunpowder thrown on to Don Quixote's anger. For, without another word, he drew his sword and attacked the litter. Then one of the bearers left the burden to his companions, and came out to meet the knight, brandishing a forked stick or pole, which they used to prop the litter up while they rested. And though Don Quixote dealt it a heavy sword stroke, which cut it in three, with the remaining third which remained in his hand he dealt the poor knight such a blow on the shoulder of his sword arm that his shield was powerless to protect him against the peasant's attack, and down he came to the ground in a sad state. Now when Sancho Panza, who came panting at his heels, saw him down, he called out to his assailant not to strike another blow, for his master was a knight under a spell and had done no harm to anyone in all the days of his life. But what stopped the countryman, however, was not Sancho's shouts, but his seeing that Don Quixote stirred neither hand nor foot; and so, in the belief that he had killed him, he hastily tucked up his robe into his belt and started to run across the country like a deer.

By this time all Don Quixote's company had reached the place where he lay; but when the men in the procession saw them come running up, and with them the troopers with their cross-bows, they were afraid of some mischief and made a ring round the image. Then raising their hoods and grasping their scourges, while the priests wielded their candlesticks, they awaited the assault, determined to defend themselves and even, if they could, to attack their assailants. But by good luck things turned out better than they expected, for all that Sancho did was to throw himself upon his master's body and break into the most doleful and ridiculous lament in all the world, in the belief that he was dead. Our priest was recognized by another in the procession, and this recognition calmed the apprehensions of both parties. The first priest gave the second a brief account of Don Quixote. Then he and the whole crowd of penitents went to see if the poor knight was dead, and heard Sancho Panza proclaim with tears in his eyes, "O flower of chivalry, whose well-spent life one single blow of a stick has cut short! O glory of your race, honour and credit to all La Mancha, and to the whole world besides, which, now that you are here no longer, will be overrun by malefactors who will no longer fear chastisement for their iniquities! O liberal beyond all Alexanders, since for only eight months' service you have given me the best isle surrounded and encircled by the sea! O humble to the proud and arrogant to the humble, undertaker of perils, sufferer of affronts, enamoured without reason, imitator of the virtuous, scourge of the wicked, enemy of evildoers, in a word, knight errant, which is the highest that man can desire!"

Sancho's groans and lamentations brought Don Quixote back to consciousness, and the first words he uttered were, "He who lives absent from you, sweetest Dulcinea, is subject to greater calamities than these. Help me, Sancho my friend, to get up upon the enchanted car, since I am not fit to burden Rocinante's saddle, for all this shoulder of mine is shattered."

"I will, sir, with the greatest of pleasure," replied Sancho. "Let us return to our village with these gentlemen who wish you well, and there we'll plan another expedition, which may bring us more profit and fame."

"You are right, Sancho," replied Don Quixote. "It will be highly prudent to wait till the malign influence of the stars, which now reigns, has passed over us."

The canon, the priest and the barber commended him for this resolution, and when they had enjoyed Sancho Panza's simplicities to the full, they placed Don Quixote on the cart, as before. Then the procession formed up once more, and went on its way. The

There they arrived at midday, and as it happened to be a Sunday all the people were in the market-place when Don Quixote's cart passed through. They all rushed to see what was in it and, when they recognized their fellow-townsmen, they stood in amazement. (page 619) goatherd took his leave of the company, and when the troopers declined to go any farther, the priest paid them what he owed them. The canon then begged the priest to let him know what might happen to Don Quixote—whether he was cured of his madness or remained in it—and with this took his leave. Here in fact they all divided and went their several ways, there remaining only the priest and the barber, Don Quixote, Panza and the good Rocinante, who bore himself throughout all this experience as patiently as his master.

The waggoner yoked his oxen and settled Don Quixote on a truss of hay. Then he followed the priest's directions and took the road, travelling at his usual deliberate pace, till at the end of six days they reached Don Quixote's village. There they arrived at mid-day, and as it happened to be a Sunday all the people were in the market-place when Don Quixote's cart passed through. They all rushed to see what was in it and, when they recognized their fellow-townsman, they stood in amazement. Then a boy ran off to tell the knight's housekeeper and niece the news that their master and uncle had come back, lean and sallow, and lying on a pile of hay on an ox-wagon. It was pitiful to hear the cries that these two good ladies raised, the slaps they gave themselves, and the curses which they launched afresh against his accursed books of knight errantry, all of which were renewed when they saw the knight enter the house.

At the news of Don Quixote's arrival Sancho Panza's wife ran up, for she knew by this time that her husband had gone with him to serve as his squire. And as soon as she saw Sancho her first inquiry was after his ass, to which Sancho replied that he was in a better state of health than his master.

"Thanks be to God," she replied, "for His goodness. But tell me now, my friend, what profit have you got out of your squire-ships? Have you brought me a skirt? Or some pretty shoes for the children?"

"I haven't brought any of that, wife," said Sancho, "although I bring other things of greater value and importance."

"I'm very glad of that," replied his wife. "Show me these things of greater value and importance, my friend. The sight of them would be a joy to this heart of mine, for I have been most sad and sorrowful all the ages you have been away."

"I'll show you them at home, wife," said Panza. "Be satisfied for the present. But if God permits us to go on our travels again, in search of adventures, you will soon see me a count or governor of an isle—and not of one of these local isles, but the best that can be found."

"Heaven grant you may, husband, for we're in great need of it. But tell me, what is this about isles? I don't understand you."

"Honey is not for the ass's mouth," replied Sancho. "You will see in due course, wife, and you'll be surprised when you hear all your vassals calling you 'Your Ladyship.' "

"What's that you're saying, Sancho, about Ladyships, isles and vassals?" asked Juana Panza, for that was the name of Sancho's wife—not that they were related by blood but because it is usual in La Mancha for wives to take their husband's surnames.

"Don't fret yourself, Juana, and be in such a hurry to know everything. It's enough that I'm telling you the truth, so shut your mouth. But there's one thing I can say to you in passing, that there's nothing so pleasant in the world for an honest man as to be squire to a knight errant, that seeks adventures. It's true that most of them one finds don't turn out as much to one's liking as a man could wish, for out of every hundred you meet ninety-nine generally turn out cross and unlucky. I know it by experience, for I've come off blanket-tossed from some and bruised from others. But, for all that, it's a nice thing to be looking out for incidents, crossing mountains, searching woods, climbing rocks, visiting castles and lodging in inns at your pleasure, with the devil a farthing to pay."

While this conversation was taking place between Sancho Panza and Juana Panza his wife, Don Quixote's housekeeper and niece received him, undressed him and laid him in his ancient bed, where he stared at them with eyes askance and could not understand where he was. The priest charged the niece to look after her uncle very carefully and to keep good watch that he did not escape again, telling her all the trouble they had had in bringing him home. At this, the two women set up their cries anew. Once more they burst out in abuse of his books of knight errantry and implored Heaven to plunge the authors of so many lies and absurdities into the bottomless pit. In fact they were distracted and frightened that as soon as their master and uncle felt a little better they would find him missing once more. And events fell out as they feared.

But though the author of this history has anxiously and diligently inquired after Don Quixote's exploits on his third expedition, he has been able to discover no account of them, at least from any authentic documents. Though fame has preserved a tradition in La Mancha that the third time Don Quixote left his home he went to Saragossa, and took part in some famous jousts in that city, and that adventures there befell him worthy of his valour and of his sound intelligence. Our author, in fact, would have been able to learn nothing of his mortal end, nor would he even have learnt of it, if good fortune had not thrown an aged doctor in his path. This man had in his possession a leaden box which, so he said, he had found among the ruined foundations of an ancient hermitage, that was being rebuilt. In this box he had found some parchments written in the Gothic script but in Castilian verse, which contained many of the knight's exploits and dwelt upon the beauty of Dulcinea del Toboso, the shape of Rocinante, the fidelity of Sancho Panza, and the burial of this same Don Quixote, together with various epitaphs and eulogies on his life and habits. Such of these as could be read and understood the trustworthy author of this original and matchless history has set down here, and he asks no recompense from his readers for the immense labours it has cost him to search and ransack all the archives of La Mancha in order to drag it into the light. All that he asks is that they shall accord it such credit as intelligent men usually give to those books of chivalry which are so highly valued in the world. With this he will feel both rewarded, and satisfied, and

621

will be encouraged to seek and discover other histories, perhaps less authentic than this one, but at least as ingenious and entertaining.

The first words written on the parchment found in the leaden box were these:

THE ACADEMICIANS OF ARGAMASILLA,
A TOWN OF LA MANCHA, ON THE LIFE AND DEATH OF
THE VALOROUS DON QUIXOTE DE LA MANCHA,
HOC SCRIPSERUNT.

MUMBO JUMBO, ACADEMICIAN OF ARGAMASILLA,
UPON THE TOMB OF DON QUIXOTE

Epitaph
The dunderhead who for La Mancha won
More trophies than did Jason for his Creta,
The wit whose weathercock was over-fine,
When something broad and blunter were far meeter;
The arm which from Cathay to far Gaeta
Broadened the boundaries of his mighty reign;
The Muse, none dreadfuller and none discreeter,
That carved on brazen plate the poet's line;
He that the Amadises far outstripped
And made the gallant Galaor look a fool,
Leaving them both in love and war well whipped,
And made the Belianises to quail,
He who on Rocinante erring went
Lies now beneath this cold stone monument.

Sonnet

She that you see here, stout and heavy featured,
High-bosomed, with a rather martial mien,
Is Dulcinea, El Toboso's queen,
Of whom the great Don Quixote was enraptured.

For her it was he travelled far and wide
Over the great Brown Hills to the renowned
Montiel plain, and down to the grass-crowned
Aranjuez gardens, wearily he trod.

The fault was Rocinante's! O hard doom
Of this Manchegan dame and errant knight
Unconquered! Dying in her beauty's bloom,

Of tender years, quenched is her beauty's light,
And he whose fame the inscribed marble proves
Could not escape the wrath and wiles of love.

WHIMSICAL WILL, A VERY WITTY ACADEMICIAN OF
ARGAMASILLA, IN PRAISE OF ROCINANTE,
DON QUIXOTE DE LA MANCHA'S STEED

Sonnet

Upon the lofty throne of adamant
Trodden by mighty Mars's bloody heel,
The mad Manchegan did his standard plant,
Hanging his arms and that sharp blade of steel,

With which he hacked, wasted and cleft in twain.
New feats of arms, for which art must devise
A style to suit the newest paladin.

And if Gaul prides herself on Amadis,
   Whose brave descendants have ennobled Greece,
And filled it full of triumphs and of fame,
Today Bellona crowns Don Quixote's brows.
   Let high La Mancha ne'er forget his name,
Who rode on Rocinante, braver far
Than gallant Bayard or steel Brillador.

Sonnet

Here Sancho Panza lies, in body small,
But yet, strange miracle, in valour great,
As guileless squire and simple, truth to tell,
As in this world, I swear, lived ever yet.
   Of being a count he came within an ace,
Had not this wicked century conspired
Malignantly to harm him; for an ass
Insults and injuries are never spared.
   An ass he rode—it shames me to record—
This meek squire meekly following behind
The mild steed Rocinante and his lord.
   How vain are all the hopes of humankind!
How sweet their promises of quiet seem,
And yet they end in shadows, smoke and dream.

Epitaph
Here lies the knight in death.
Well bruised and ill errant, he
Was borne by Rocinante
O'er road and track and path.
Beside him Sancho's laid,
The foolish Sancho Panza,
As faithful as e'er man saw
One of the squirish trade.

Epitaph
Here Dulcinea's laid,
Once of flesh so lusty.
Ashes now cold and dusty
By ugly death she's made.
Of godly parentage
And fairish stock she came.
She was great Quixote's flame,
And glory of her village.

These were such verses as could be deciphered. The rest, as the characters were worm-eaten, were entrusted to a university scholar to guess out their meaning. We are informed that he has done so, at the cost of many nights of study and much labour, and that he intends to publish them, which gives us hope of a third expedition of Don Quixote.

Forse altri canterà con miglior plettro.